DARK
TORT

ALSO BY DIANE MOTT DAVIDSON

CATERING TO NOBODY

DYING FOR CHOCOLATE

THE CEREAL MURDERS

THE LAST SUPPERS

KILLER PANCAKE

THE MAIN CORPSE

THE GRILLING SEASON

PRIME CUT

TOUGH COOKIE

STICKS & SCONES

CHOPPING SPREE

DOUBLE SHOT

DARK TORT

• Diane Mott Davidson •

HarperLargePrint

An Imprint of HarperCollins*Publishers*

HarperCollins books may be purchased for educational, business, or sales promotional use. For information please write: Special Markets Department, HarperCollins Publishers, 10 East 53rd Street, New York, NY 10022.

FIRST HARPER LARGE PRINT EDITION

Printed on acid-free paper

3 3113 02456 0924

Library of Congress Cataloging-in-Publication Data

Davidson, Diane Mott.
    Dark tort / Diane Mott Davidson.—1st ed.
        p.   cm.
    ISBN-13: 978-0-06-052731-0 (Hardcover)
    ISBN-10: 0-06-052731-5
    1. Bear, Goldy (Fictitious character)—Fiction.   2. Women in the food industry—Fiction.   3. Lawyers—Crimes against—Fiction.
    4. Caterers and catering—Fiction.   5. Colorado—Fiction.
    6. Cookery—Fiction.   I. Title.

    PS3554.A925D37   2006
    813'.54—dc22   2005044912

ISBN-13: 978-0-06-111992-7 (Large Print)
ISBN-10: 0-06-111992-X

06 07 08 09 10 WBG/RRD 10 9 8 7 6 5 4 3 2 1

This Large Print Book carries the Seal of Approval of N.A.V.H.

To Sandra Dijkstra
and her marvelous team
Thank you for your decades of
work to support Goldy and me

But jealous souls will not
be answered so.
They are not ever jealous for the
cause but jealous for they're jealous.
'Tis a monster begot on itself,
borne on itself.

—**OTHELLO,** ACT III, SCENE IV

Chapter 1

I tripped over the body of my friend Dusty Routt at half past ten on the night of October 19.

At first I thought it was a joke. Loaded down with bread-making supplies, I had just pushed through the heavy wooden door of Hanrahan & Jule, the boutique law firm in Aspen Meadow where I'd been catering breakfasts for several months. My foot caught and I stumbled forward. I thought, **Those H&J clowns are up to something. Again**.

The bag of flour I was carrying slid from my hands and exploded on the carpet. Two jars of yeast plummeted onto the coffee table, where they burst into shards and powder. My last bottle of molasses sailed in a wide arc and cracked open on the receptionist's cherrywood desk. A thick wave of sweet, dark liquid began a gluey descent across the phone console. My steel bowl of bread sponge catapulted out of my arms and hit the wall.

I wasn't sure I'd be able to change my own trajectory toward an end table. It was one of two rough-hewn, cabin-style monstrosities that the decorator had thought necessary to make Hanrahan & Jule look like what it claimed to be: "your Rocky Mountain neighborhood law firm!"

I hit the end table, ricocheted over to the desk, cried out, and finally landed on my stomach. I had tripped over I-knew-not-what in a spectacular manner, and now I was prone on an imitation Native American rug. I shrieked, "Very funny, fellas!" But the lawyers who pulled these pranks didn't appear.

I wiped flour out of my eyes and waited for the guys to reveal themselves. When they didn't, I tried to focus on what I could see of the small lobby space. Lamps made of elk horns sat on the clunky tables. The bentwood couches, which were placed beneath homey paintings of food, were empty. I was lying on a sponge-soaked picture of a tepee. The pain assaulting my tailbone was excruciating.

Gritting my teeth, I figured I was about as upset as any caterer could be, when the bread for the following morning's breakfast has been wrecked the night before. I still hadn't seen what had caused my fall. Nor was there any telltale noise. In fact, the law firm of Hanrahan & Jule was completely quiet.

I'd ended up on the far side of the massive coffee table, a thick column of wood carved, I'd been told, from the trunk of an ancient blue spruce tree. I rubbed my behind and stared at the dark lacquered bark. Had I just stumbled over my own feet? No, I was sure the small cadre of lawyers who were not in Maui this week, ostensibly engaging in continuing education, was responsible for this mishap.

I heaved myself onto my back, wondering if the guys—and that's what all ten H&J lawyers were, guys—would think this was more funny than when they'd put green food coloring into the cheddar omelettes. Or how about the live moths that had fluttered out of one of my folded tablecloths? And then, oh Lord, then—there was the gin-switched-for-water in my espresso machine. Soon after that trick, I'd seen one of the partners pouring vodka into the very same machine's water well. I'd used my tray to whack him from behind—accidentally, of course—and spewed forty dollars' worth of Stolichnaya across the firm's huge kitchen.

Staring at the ceiling, I sighed. Now that my flour, yeast, molasses, and sponge were kaput, was the partner who'd ordered the breakfast going to run out and buy freshly baked loaves for his Friday-morning meeting with clients? I doubted it very much. I wrenched my body around to survey the damage.

And there, sprawled on the far side of the coffee table, was Dusty Routt.

In addition to being a friend, Dusty was our neighbor. She was also in training to become the firm's second paralegal, and she often got drafted into playing a part in these high jinks. At the very least, she was sometimes pressed into trying to cover them up, as I'd discovered after the spiked-coffee affair, when I'd caught her disposing of a plastic bag holding two empty gin bottles. "Orders from King Richard," Dusty had whispered conspiratorially. "He says I have to get rid of the evidence. Without you catching me, that is," she'd added with a characteristic giggle as she slammed the Dumpster lid shut. Since King Richard was Dusty's uncle, Richard Chenault, the same partner whose Stoly I later disposed of, I knew a confrontation was out of the question. Just this past August, Richard's secretary had been summarily fired when she'd had the audacity—or stupidity—to send a locket engraved for Richard's mistress to his, uh, wife. Richard's wife, a doctor named K.D., had promptly filed for divorce.

I stared at Dusty's back, waiting. I couldn't see her face. Still, I knew it was Dusty. There was her highlighted-at-home hair; there was the like-new beige Calvin Klein suit she was wearing. I'd actually found the suit for her at Aspen Meadow's secondhand store. Now I wanted to hear her high, joyful voice as she jumped up to cry, "Surprise!" I anticipated a trio of attorneys leaping out from behind the receptionist's desk and squealing, "Gotcha!"

But I still couldn't hear anything at all.

"Dusty!" I whispered hoarsely. "Get up. Gag's over."

She didn't move. I did finally hear something, but it was only the steady **plink plop** of beaten egg dripping onto one of the end tables. My gaze shifted from Dusty to where the sponge liquid had first landed, on Charlie Baker's painting of ·peach pie, one of three of his famous pictures of food that adorned the lobby walls. The frame was broken. Had **I** done that to dear, departed Charlie Baker's artwork?

Charlie Baker. I swallowed. **Don't go there,** I ordered myself. But then I squinted at some splotches and drips that had stained the painted pie, with its list of ingredients meticulously penned underneath . . .

Fear scurried down my back. I hauled myself up onto my hands and knees. Dusty Routt, the pretty, ambitious twenty-year-old whose family had lived across the street from us for the last three years, lay a foot away. She still wasn't moving.

"Oh God, Dusty!" I yelled. "Get **up!**"

Dusty's body was twisted, I saw now, and that was why her face was turned toward the carpet. Her twenty-first birthday was the next day, she'd excitedly informed me. The carrot cake I'd made for her still sat wrapped in my caterer's van. But she hadn't even twitched since I'd tripped over her.

"Dammit!" I hollered as I scooted forward and grabbed her wrist. I couldn't feel a pulse.

Maybe it's just weak. Maybe I'm not feeling in the right spot. I struggled to a half-standing position. Dusty looked as if she'd fallen sideways. Her pretty face was obscured by her tumble of blond-brown hair. I gently shook her shoulders, but nothing happened.

I pushed my fingers into a new place on Dusty's wrist, then noticed that the beige skirt had somehow gotten caught up around her hips, hips she had ruthlessly slimmed by riding an exercise bike at Aspen Meadow's new rec center every morning before showing up for work. When King Richard had hired Dusty, as ambitious a niece as any tightfisted uncle could ever hope to have, she'd been determined to look as mature as possible. She'd just finished her associate's degree and was starting paralegal school, and was set on acquiring—and fitting into—a professional wardrobe. Remembering her happy gratitude when I'd presented her with the suit, I gently shook her again with my free hand.

"Dusty, it's me, Goldy," I murmured as I let go of her wrist and reached under her shoulders with both hands. "I'm going to turn you over."

Her body was limp, but warm. There was redness around her neck. I saw now that blood was seeping out of a small gash at the top of her forehead, and her pretty face was flushed on one side. Her blue eyes were half open. Her slack mouth contrasted with her bright, curly hair. She didn't moan or blink, and I cursed silently. When I shook her again, her legs sprawled like a scarecrow's; her hands flopped open, palm up. The thoughts **I should get out of here** and **Don't touch anything** competed ferociously with **If she's still alive, I could help her**.

I felt in my apron pocket for my cell phone. Not there. I patted my pants pockets. Again, nothing. I'd been in a hurry to get over here after my van wouldn't start, and I must have left the phone in the front seat. I gently let go of Dusty and jumped over to the reception desk. But when I picked up the molasses-covered receiver to call for help, there was no dial tone. I raced to the first office on the hall, felt for a light, and found another phone. I jabbed buttons, to no effect. Did the H&J folks shut down all telecommunications at night? I hadn't a clue.

I returned to Dusty and frantically started CPR. I noticed that the redness around her neck was quite dark, not just pink. My heart faltered. I wanted to talk to Dusty, to ask if someone had hurt her, and why. But I couldn't do any of those things, because I was trying to breathe life into her lungs.

As I worked feverishly on my young neighbor, I kept thinking, **This isn't happening**. There was fake blood. There were weak pulses. I still half expected her to jump up, erupt into giggles, and shout for everybody to leap out from assorted hiding places. I felt the other wrist for a pulse. **Even if it's weak,** I remembered from my days in Med Wives 101, **keep going**. I momentarily stopped CPR and waited for Dusty to breathe on her own. She didn't.

Leave, that same inner voice commanded me. **Get out. Call for help from somewhere else**. But I couldn't. Not yet. I was bent on bringing about the resuscitation part of cardiopulmonary resuscitation.

After—What was it? Five minutes? Ten? A half hour?—I gave up. Later, the cops wanted to know when I'd left the H&J office. And every time they asked, I told them I didn't know, that time had turned fluid once I'd discovered Dusty. And why did that matter so much? I wondered. I could not pinpoint the actual moment when I exhaled, got to my feet, and again glanced in vain around the office for something that might explain what was going on. Feeling foolish, I peeked around the firm's massive front door to make sure no one was waiting in the hall. Then I dashed out.

The door closed with a firm **k-chook**. I pulled the red metal ring with my two office keys out of my pocket. I always kept the H&J keys on a separate ring, because I had been warned that losing them meant a five-hundred-dollar fine. I secured the bolt with the second key and raced down the half-lit hallway.

If only, if only, if only I'd been here on time, I repeated to myself, **Dusty would still be alive.** But I wasn't going to think that way. It was possible she could still be revived. Possible, but not probable. Feeling like a failure, I pushed through the metal service door.

Outside, the chilly-sweet autumn air smacked my face and made me cough. A sharp mountain breeze was lashing the trees that circled the rear parking lot. Nearby, a neon light illuminated pines, spruce, and a stand of aspens. The golden leaves cloaking the aspens' white-barked branches quaked and shuddered. Another whip of air sprayed dust and ice into my eyes. I needed my cell phone. Had I locked my van after parking back here in the service lot? I could not remember.

My breath came out in frosted white tatters as I

trotted, half blind, toward my normally trustworthy vehicle, which had delayed me tonight with its drained battery. I could imagine the voice of my husband, Tom, a sheriff's department investigator, urging me to **get cracking. Get out of there**. But I didn't know what had happened, and I desperately wanted to help Dusty. Tom's voice drilled my inner ear: **Never stay alone at a crime scene that hasn't been secured**. Right, right. This was a rule every cop learned at the academy. But I wasn't sure I'd actually been at a crime scene, because of course, I wasn't a cop. But being married to a cop, I'd learned the rules—sometimes the hard way. And I often didn't exactly follow them, as Tom frequently was at pains to point out.

Hugging my sides, I hurtled awkwardly across the gravel. Dizziness assaulted me, and I slowed to a walk and tried to breathe normally. What was the swooshing noise in my ears? I tried to ignore it, tried to tell myself it was the hum of traffic from Interstate 70. My white shirt gleamed in the neon haze drifting down from the crown of a nearby light pole. Where was my jacket? Inside the van, probably. I rummaged in the pockets of my pants, and realized I had dropped my car keys in the law firm office. With just the smallest amount of hope, I pulled on the van door. Locked, of course.

I turned around and tried to think. Was it close

to eleven? What place would be open? Where would there be a pay phone? Did anyone actually use pay phones anymore? I shook my head to rid myself of the drumming in my ears and tried to force myself to think clearly.

As I trotted around the building I scolded my-self again for not getting here right at ten, when I was scheduled to show Dusty how to make the high-protein bread King Richard had asked I serve his clients the next morning. I cursed as I surveyed the front lot, where a freezing nighttime mist hugged the grid of streetlights in front of the long, two-story office building. This was where the lawyers, clients, and staff parked . . . but the space held only Dusty's Civic.

My breath puffed as I ran, panting, toward the shopping center across the street. I thought of Dusty again, sprawled out on the reception-area carpeting. Back in my pre-Tom days, I'd been un-happily married to John Richard Korman, a phys-ically abusive doctor who was the father of my fifteen-year-old son, Arch. It was during my years with the Jerk, as his other ex-wife and I had called him, that I'd learned the lessons of Med Wives 101, our own version of medical authority. **Some-times you can't feel a pulse,** I stubbornly re-minded myself for at least the tenth time.

After glancing around for traffic—there was

none—I hopped onto the road beside the parking lot. A combination of dropping temperature and frigid humidity had sheeted the pavement with ice. I shivered. Why hadn't I worn my jacket into H&J? Because I'd been in a hurry to meet Dusty for our sixth and final cooking lesson. She'd said she had something to tell me.

I scooted across the street to the access road that led up to the three-sided strip mall. Ahead, a few lights twinkled in the chilly fog. The main tenant of the shopping center was a supermarket. There were also a liquor store and two bars, a reminder of our saloon heritage here in the West. Other occupants included a store called Art, Music, and Copies, various and sundry clothing, shoe, and westernwear stores, and Aspen Meadow Café. These all appeared abandoned and wreathed in darkness.

Please, God, I prayed, as I jumped carefully onto the access road's slippery pavement. **Please let Dusty be okay.** The thin, vulnerable face of Sally Routt, Dusty's mother, loomed before me. She'd already lost a son, Dusty's older brother, whom I hadn't known. I couldn't even contemplate talking to Sally about Dusty being hurt. Or worse.

The cord to one of the pay phones outside Aspen Meadow Café was torn off. The other phone had no dial tone. Another sudden, glacial breeze stung my skin as I tried to make out shapes in the near distance. The shopping center was not abandoned, after all. About ten folks, their bodies padded with puffy down jackets, huddled outside the grocery store. But the store was closed. What was going on? I wondered. Then I remembered a special on ski-lift tickets beginning at midnight. The first two dozen people to buy a hundred bucks' worth of food got a season pass at Vail. The would-be bargain hunters stomped and stamped, but they were tough—again, this was the West—and had no intention of wimping out in heated cars.

It would take me at least five minutes to jog up there, and several more to find someone with a cell phone who could call an ambulance. Plus, I was freezing. I needed to find someplace closer.

I peered along the line of nearby storefronts. Next to the unopened café was Art, Music, and Copies. Inside, a gray fluorescent bulb blinked, as if someone had forgotten to turn it off. Still, I thought I remembered that the copy place, as we called it, was supposed to be open late. I trotted up the sidewalk and banged on the large plate-glass window, which boasted hot pink lettering that screamed "You Own It, We'll Clone It!" I tried the door, which rattled reassuringly: it was locked, but loose. Someone had to be in there, I reasoned. Still, as I knocked harder, I wondered if I should be running up to the grocery store.

When there was no response, I hammered mercilessly on the glass door. And it broke.

Finally someone appeared. I even recognized him: a young fellow, twentyish, Dusty's boyfriend. Vic Something. I'd seen him over at the Routts' house from time to time.

He yelled, "Why did you do that?"

"I need help!" I called, surveying the shards now littering the inside of the store. "It's an emergency!"

"I **guess so**." Vic was tall and very slender, his peaked face set off by an explosion of curls the color of straw. As he moved toward me, his young, high forehead wrinkled like folded tissue.

"Could you just hurry up?" I implored.

Vic's long legs finally brought him to the door. "You didn't have to break the **door**. Oh, it's you, Goldy," he said breathlessly. "Well, I can only let you do a couple of copies, and you're going to have to pay cash because—"

"I need a phone!"

His hand was unexpectedly warm and moist as he grabbed mine. "Take it easy, take it easy. Okay, step over the glass." His last name swum up into consciousness: Vic Zaruski. Yes, definitely Dusty's boyfriend, but did I recall that they'd broken up? I wasn't sure what kind of connection Vic had with Dusty now, if any, because my mind wasn't working properly.

"I simply have to call help." I stumbled forward over the pile of glass and into the store's warm interior. "Show me the phone. **Please**. Someone's hurt."

Vic, his wide, dark brown eyes blinking in disbelief, his hair glowing like a ragged halo in the flickering neon, seemed at a loss for words. But he moved to the counter, picked up the phone, and handed it to me.

As I punched in the three digits, Vic's worried glance took me in. He reached underneath the counter and pulled out a sweatshirt. "Put this on," he whispered. I clutched it and nodded thanks. When the emergency operator answered, I told her what I'd found, and where. I said we needed medical help right away.

Vic drew back, his face drained of color. He said, **"What?"** But I had to ignore him, as I was telling the operator that in addition to an ambulance, she needed to send the sheriff's department.

I pulled the sweatshirt over my head as the operator continued to talk, telling me to be calm, that help was on the way.

"What's going on?" Vic demanded. Wind blew

through the hole where the door had been, and a couple of curious ticket seekers from the grocery store peeked in. How much had they heard? What if they decided to go across the street to poke around and try to see what I was so upset about? Abruptly, I hung up the phone and bolted for the smashed door.

"Was there a break-in?" Vic persisted from behind me. "You said you needed an ambulance for Dusty? Why? Why do the cops need to come?"

When we reached the glass, I suddenly turned back. Vic collided with me and I caught a whiff of his scent, some musky boy-cologne.

"Vic," I said, my voice low. "You need to herd these people back up to the grocery store. It's important that they not go across the street. Please."

"I can't—" he began to protest. But I ignored him, as well as the people staring at me as I stepped over the glass and onto the sidewalk.

"Hey, Goldy—" came one voice, but I didn't look back.

"I'll get my cell," a female voice announced, but I didn't pay any attention to that either. My skin needled under the huge sweatshirt as I walked quickly down the slick sidewalk. I knew I shouldn't be talking to anyone now except medical and law enforcement people. No sense making more of a mess of this than I already had.

Behind me, Vic's excited voice told the curiosity seekers to get back up to the grocery store. He ordered them not to follow us. **Us?** Dammit. Vic's footsteps echoed down the pavement behind me.

"Vic, you cannot follow me," I shouted. He didn't answer, and soon he was right at my side. As we walked, he begged me to talk to him, but I just shook my head. Finally we arrived at the grass-covered hill that overlooked the road. We stood, waiting, for what felt like an eternity, but which in actuality was probably not more than fifteen minutes. Vic's frustration and fear radiated like a negatively charged aura.

In the time since I'd raced across the street, the darkness had deepened and the cold intensified. On the far side of the street, the parking lot still held Dusty's forlorn Civic. Vic began to cough in a vain attempt to disguise the fact that he was crying. When I told him again to stay put, he moved away from me.

Across the street, a long black car moved into the parking lot. Then another dark vehicle, this one coming from the I-70 side, pulled into the lot. Not even a moment later, a third car followed them. **Oh, Lord,** I thought as I recognized all three cars. Maybe the woman with the cell, or perhaps someone else outside the grocery store, had seen me bolting from the building occupied by Hanrahan & Jule. I had to have looked suspicious, frantic and coatless, as I leaped across the street, ran up the shopping-center sidewalk, and banged on the copy-place door. When I'd broken the glass and shouted for a phone, then called for an ambulance and the sheriff's department, anyone within fifty yards would have heard me.

I stopped at the bottom of the hill and glanced back at the crowd of folks outside the grocery store. They were moving en masse, making their way down to where Vic and I were standing. Welcome to living in a small town. Someone had thought, **What's up at this time of night, with the caterer running away from the office building occupied by H&J?** That same someone had put two and two together and made a call. And now, across the street in the H&J lot, we were faced with the result.

The lawyers are coming! The lawyers are coming!

Great.

Chapter 2

As I slipped down the embankment on my way to the road, I tried to think. I could not, **could not** allow anyone to go into the firm without telling them what they'd find. Shivering, I rushed across the street.

"Wait!" I called to the figures emerging from the pair of precisely parked black BMWs. Heeding me, two tall people stood outside their respective car doors, their arms crossed. As they gazed in my direction, they neither talked nor acknowledged each other's presence. My breath wheezed in the cold, thick fog. Still, I recognized the commanding presence of lean, silver-haired Richard Chenault, the well-built, late-fifties partner who was Dusty's uncle—the attorney we had dubbed King Richard. This week, King Richard was the only one of the three partners not doing continuing education on Maui.

Standing nearby was his soon-to-be-divorced doctor wife, the statuesque K. D. Chenault, formerly K. D. van Ruisdael. K.D., whom I liked and admired immensely, was an emergency-room doc who had known the Jerk—and hated him. During my divorce, she'd been one of my few supporters. K.D.'s black coat hung open; underneath it, she was wearing a surgical suit. Her long, light chestnut hair, held back in an ineffective ponytail, was slightly disheveled. I wondered if she had just arrived at the big Flicker Ridge house she and Richard still shared—while they fought over property—when the call from who knows whom had summoned Richard. As tired as I was sure K.D. was bound to be, if she was indeed coming after a shift, I could still imagine her insisting on driving out this late. Yes, the weather was inhospitably cold. But she would have wanted to see if she was needed.

"K.D.," I gasped as I rummaged in my pants pockets for my set of office keys. "Dusty's upstairs. It looks as if . . . as if her heart's stopped. Maybe you could try to help her?"

In one swift movement, K.D. nodded, nabbed the keys, and turned to race up the steps to the firm.

"Dusty?" Richard Chenault asked me, his voice incredulous. "**Our** Dusty? What happened? Was there a break-in?"

"I don't know." I faltered.

A pair of H&J attorneys approached us from the

other car. Donald Ellis, an associate at the firm who was in his midthirties, was short and very thin, with a pale face that bore the ghost of teen freckles. His shock of rust-colored hair glowed in the shrouded streetlight. Donald was a quiet fellow who holed up for hours in his office, which was more messy than Arch's room had ever been at any stage of his childhood. While five of the seven associates had opted to join the partners in Hawaii, Donald had said he desperately needed to catch up on his paperwork. Which begged the question: How was he going to **find** his paperwork?

The other lawyer was the final associate who'd stayed home from Maui: Alonzo Claggett, or "Claggs," as the other attorneys called him. I'd learned that fifteen years ago, he and his wife had moved from Baltimore to Vail, where they'd decided to slum it for a couple of years until their wedding-gift money ran out. When it had, Alonzo had continued to be a ski bum while his athletic wife, Elizabeth, whom everyone had always called by her nickname, Ookie, taught squash during the day and worked as a waitress at night. When Ookie's parents had heard their country-club-raised daughter was spending her evenings waiting on tables, they had flown out to Colorado and created a family storm that rivaled any hurricane ever to hit the Chesapeake Bay. So much for slumming.

Claggs, humbled, had finally figured the only way to feed his skiing habit was to do a law degree at the University of Colorado **and** live and work within an hour's driving time from the resorts. Ookie had gleefully begun work as a squash instructor only, and the two of them had embarked on their happily-ever-after life. Or so it always seemed to me.

Alonzo had dark curly hair and blue eyes, the startling product of mixing an Italian mother with a WASP father. He was slightly taller than yours truly, and as slim and fit as a short basketball player or tall gymnast. He frequently came into the law firm with Dusty, since he worked out at the new Aspen Meadow rec center, called the Butterfield, where Dusty rode the exercise bike. I'd always thought it made Dusty feel appreciated, one of the gang, to come into the office at Alonzo's side, although Louise Upton, the ultrasevere office manager, clearly disapproved. One didn't mix the lower and higher totems on the pole, after all.

And of course, I realized belatedly, with only three lawyers working in the firm this week, I probably shouldn't have expected a bevy of joke-playing attorneys to come jumping out of nowhere to yell, "Surprise!" when I tripped over Dusty.

The final car that had pulled into the lot made

me shudder, but not from the cold. It was Louise Upton, in the dark green Lexus she'd bought used at a great price, as she always told anyone who would listen. She banged out of her car and began to stride toward Richard. She was wearing a long gray coat that emphasized her broad shoulders and broad backside. Her step was military stiff, but as she marched, her steel-wool pad of hair did not budge.

I recalled the time I'd pointed out two errors of grammar in my contract, a contract that had been drawn up by one of the partners, to Louise, or Miss Upton, as I'd been told I should call her. She was a sixtyish, formidable guard dog of a woman, and she had told me if I wanted to be the firm's caterer, I needed to learn my place. She'd actually said that: I needed to learn **my place**.

When I'd quietly asked her what my place was, she'd told me she didn't think I was cute. Not one bit. And if I wanted to **act** cute, and make grammatical corrections to my contract, I could tear up said contract, and they would simply find somebody else to cater their meetings.

While I'd frowned and pretended to contemplate a saddle nailed to the wall in the cowboy-themed conference room, I'd tried to think of a cute joke, or at least how I could make a cute-acting exit. But we'd been spared a confrontation by the sudden appearance of Donald Ellis. When Donald had summoned Louise and told her she was needed in a partner's office, I'd quickly penned in the needed corrections, initialed them, and signed on the dotted line. Acting distracted, Donald had taken over the negotiation and said how much they appreciated the fact that such a well-known local caterer would be working for them. In fact, he was going to recommend that his wife, Nora, hire me for their next party. Then he'd told me to go make him some coffee, and bring it to him. When Louise Upton had reappeared, Donald, the contract, and yours truly had all disappeared. The office manager was **not** a happy camper.

So. Ever since then, I had not been Louise Upton's favorite person. I'd figured I could do without her friendship, but the upcoming confrontation was bound to be particularly terrible. Lucky for me, the chilly nighttime fog prevented me from reading her facial expression, which was sure to be negative.

"Goldy!" Louise exclaimed. "I would like to know—"

"Louise!" Richard Chenault barked. "Please be quiet!" He turned to me. "Goldy, I'm worried about you." His suddenly caring tone penetrated the soup of frigid mist. "Are you all right? Do you have any idea what happened to Dusty?" Richard's silver hair was swept up and back in a way most folks, present company included, found intimidating. But his tanned, handsome-featured face was quite young-looking. It was a disconcerting combination, the gleaming, neatly combed hair and the gorgeous, unwrinkled face with its startlingly pale gray eyes. I dreaded telling him that his niece Dusty Routt—daughter of the ne'er-do-well brother who'd abandoned his family—might be dead.

"It's bad," I said, trying to keep my voice steady. "I found Dusty . . ."

"You found Dusty?" Donald Ellis echoed. He glanced up to where K.D. had gone. "In the office?"

"Yes." I inhaled. "She was here to help me cook for the Friday breakfast meeting. When I arrived, she was on the floor, not moving. I don't know what was wrong with her. She . . . she wasn't breathing."

"Omigod," said Alonzo Claggett. "You called for an ambulance?"

I assured him that I had, and it should be along any minute. Meanwhile, I added grimly, maybe K.D. would have some luck reviving her. I hugged my sides. I was chilled to the bone, and the sweatshirt Vic had given me still wasn't helping.

"Everybody looks cold," Richard said, his voice gentle but firm. "Let's go inside and check on Dusty and K.D." He lifted his chin at Donald, Alonzo, and Louise, to indicate that everyone should follow him.

"We probably ought to avoid the office," I managed to say. My breath came out in a ghostlike puff. "I mean, we should wait for the cops." I wasn't quite ready to say, **Because it might be a crime scene**.

"I have a key to the second conference room," Richard said, his voice softer than I had ever heard it. "It's down the hall from our office. We hardly ever use it because it hasn't been redecorated yet." He said, "Let's go, everybody," then walked purposefully toward the sidewalk.

"I feel a little dizzy," Alonzo said, his voice low.

"Sit down on the ground," I commanded, quickly putting an arm around him. "Let me lower you."

"I'll help," Donald offered. His voice cracked, too, but he had enough composure to take on half of Alonzo's weight and get him down to the curb. "Try to breathe, Claggs."

"I'm okay," Alonzo replied weakly, when he clearly was not. He bit his upper lip and took several deep breaths. "We need to get inside—I mean, to the conference room, where Richard

wants us. I just feel so . . . cold, all of a sudden."
He inhaled several lungfuls of air and then announced that he was getting up.

"Lean on me," Donald directed, as he grunted
and groaned, and finally hauled Alonzo up from
the pavement.

We followed the others. Our footsteps made
gritty sounds as we headed up the main steps to
the office. I scanned the parking lot, but there was
still no sign of emergency vehicles. I prayed K.D.
was having more luck with Dusty than I'd had.

Once we were inside the building, our little
brigade marched past the closed door to the office. There was no sign of K.D. At the far end of
the dark hall, Richard ushered us into a dusty,
scruffy-looking Queen Anne–style conference
room. Dimly lit with filthy crystal chandeliers,
the space had an oak floor covered with a navy-
and-burgundy Oriental rug, an oval cherry conference table, a hidden sink, and a grit-covered
glassed-in cabinet that housed wine and
double–old-fashioned glasses, along with cups
and saucers. Hanging on the walls between brass-
and-crystal wall sconces were Charlie Baker
drawings, these presumably less valuable than
the actual paintings in the H&J lobby. Despite the
grime, I liked this space much better than the
cowboy-style insanity of the main office. But

maybe clients wanted to be reminded they were in the West.

Richard began: "This woman I know called me and said she saw someone hurrying over from the law office. She thought maybe you were a burglar. Donald and Alonzo happened to be at my house, discussing a case, and came with me, as did K.D. We called Louise on our way over. Were you hurt? Was there an assailant outside our office? Had he gotten inside?" His gray eyes bore into me, at once concerned and wanting to get at what exactly was going on. "She said you were hysterical."

"Well—" I began.

"This same woman said you banged on the door of that art-and-music store until it broke. Then you demanded that somebody call an ambulance and the police." Again, his sharp eyes questioned me.

"I don't know what happened, Richard," I began, whereupon Louise Upton loudly cleared her throat. Well, tough tacks. I wasn't going to call him "Mr. Chenault" when he had repeatedly told me not to. "Richard," I went on, "I'm just telling you what I saw when I came in to start the bread for your meeting with clients tomorrow. Dusty was lying on the floor of the lobby." I pressed my lips together and took in all their faces. "I think . . . I don't think . . . I need to say that I very much doubt K.D. will be able to revive her."

There was a collective intake of breath. Alonzo Claggett and Donald Ellis exchanged a glance.

"You don't?" Richard's unfailingly polite facade slipped for a moment. "You think she died in this office? **Our** office? You think our Dusty died **here**?"

"No," Donald Ellis said. His face turned scarlet to the roots of his red hair. "This is our . . . we've been here since . . . I don't believe it. Dusty?" Tears welled in his eyes. Stupefied, he turned to glare at Alonzo Claggett. Alonzo covered his face with his hands.

Richard was having trouble staying composed. He licked his lips and stared at me. "Do you—you said maybe she had a heart attack? We could help K.D. with CPR . . . Dusty was too young—"

"I did CPR on Dusty for a long time," I said. "It felt like half an hour but might have been less. It looked as if she . . . she had been . . . attacked."

The conference room fell completely silent.

"She must have been associating with the wrong element," announced Louise Upton, her voice steely. "Someone had to have followed her into our office. She must not have closed the **door** completely. Maybe it was a teenager, looking for someone to rob. He ran into Dusty and killed her."

I tried not to think of how many times Arch had complained to me that when something went wrong, the first person suspected was always a teenager.

"Well! When Richard called, **I** was just leaving the Aspen Meadow Chorale's performance of **The Pirates of Penzance,**" Louise went on blithely. "I guess I should have stayed home. Then I could have done something about this. Although I don't know how I could have possibly envisioned such a thing happening to one of our . . ." She left the sentence unanswered.

"Has anyone called her family?" Richard asked, his voice barely audible.

"No," I told him. "I just dialed 911."

"What in **the hell** is this going to mean?" Alonzo looked up. His expression was wild; his voice high and querulous. "That is"—he struggled to put together his question—"what will it mean for the firm?"

"Alonzo," said Richard, "you need to . . ." He left the sentence unfinished.

"Goldy?" Donald Ellis, distraught, was fidgeting in his chair. His flushed face still bore the marks of tears. "Goldy?" Donald said again, placing his restless hands palm down on the rosewood table. "What do you think happened?"

"I don't know."

My answer hung in the air until finally, **finally,** sirens screamed in the distance.

I stood and took in the men's grim faces. I said, "I have to talk to the cops. Please, don't anyone go into the office."

"Take my keys, Goldy," Richard said. He handed me a gold key ring. When I looked at him, uncomprehending, he added, "You gave yours to K.D., remember?"

Louise Upton had left the table and was clanking around underneath the sink in the corner bar. She brought up a bottle of Johnnie Walker Black and clapped it down on the dusty bar, then squeaked open the cabinet and started pulling out glasses.

"Goldy," Louise inquired, "do you suppose you could go get us some ice?"

I didn't look at her as I opened the door. Before the door shut, I heard Louise say, "Richard, that girl never does a thing I tell her."

I walked down the hall, out the main second-story entrance to the building, and down the steps.

In the parking lot, red, blue, and white lights flashed in the fog, which had become thicker and more frigid as the night wore on. I hopped onto the grass, and then hugged my sides as the icy blades fingered their way through my shoes, stockings, and pants. Vic had crossed over to this side of the street. He now stood alone next to

Dusty's Civic in the middle of the parking lot. He looked dazed. I walked up beside him and began waving in the emergency vehicles.

Cops and med techs spilled onto the pavement. When the first pair of policemen trotted up to us, I gave them Richard's gold key ring and told them to take the medics upstairs, to the office of Hanrahan & Jule. There was a doctor on-site, I added. I asked the cops if they wanted me to come; they said no. As the paramedics traipsed up the stairs behind the law enforcement team, Vic made his way to the sidewalk. I thought he might try to follow the medics into the office, so I went after him. But instead of going anywhere, he stopped at the foot of the outside steps, then flopped onto the cold, wet grass. I sat down beside him.

"Vic? Talk to me."

"I—I can't. Is it really bad? Tell me it isn't."

"I'm not sure." I hesitated. Finally I said, "Can I get you a drink? They've got some scotch upstairs."

"No, no." He sighed.

His voice was shaking. "What happened, will you tell me?"

I'd told the lawyers, hadn't I? "I found Dusty upstairs. She . . . she wasn't breathing."

"You found Dusty?" Vic echoed. "What do you mean? What was the matter with her?"

"I don't know, except that she just wasn't taking any breaths. But a doctor went right up to the office when I came over here. Now they've got a whole team of medics in the office."

Vic uttered a stream of profanities and ran his large hands through his head of sandy curls. He didn't seem to want to talk anymore, but I was still worried about him, and scooted over closer to where he was sitting. He abruptly stood and marched over to Dusty's Civic, where he let out a moan. When I walked to his side, my feet crunched over glass. Great. The cops would say I destroyed one crime scene and mindlessly tampered with another. Gently, I put my arm around Vic. His body shook under my touch.

"Vic," I said, feeling dreadful, "we need to move back over to the sidewalk."

"Tell me the worst isn't true. What did you find?"

"It looked as if she'd been attacked."

He began to sob. I murmured comforting words and guided him back to the staircase.

The moon had risen and lightened the darkness. I finally thought to look at my watch, which said it was half past twelve. Had it really been two hours since I'd showed up at the law firm? It felt like nothing; it felt like forever. A solitary cop approached us.

"Which one of you called the department?" he asked, his voice matter-of-fact.

"I did," I replied. For the first time, my own voice cracked. "I found her."

The cop eyed me, his gaze impenetrable. He was short and stockily built, and he wore a sheriff's department leather jacket that made him look even wider than he was. He had dark, close-set eyes and equally dark eyebrows. His frown was formidable.

"I'm Officer Nelson," he began. "You went into that office first?"

"Yes," I said. Nearby, Vic tried to stifle his weeping.

"I'm going to need to see some ID from you."

"I'm Investigator Tom Schulz's wife," I said. Officer Nelson flinched. Why? I wondered. Was he intimidated by Tom's reputation? "In terms of ID, my purse and driver's license are locked in my van, which is in back of this office building. My cell phone's in there, too. I dropped my van keys when I . . . when I made the discovery."

"I remember you. The caterer, right?" When I nodded, he went on: "Where did you go after you left here?"

I paused as Vic shuffled up. The cop regarded him without curiosity. "She came to our place. Art, Music, and Copies. It's right over there." Vic pointed across the street.

"Sir," the cop said to Vic, "would you please move back across the street, back to your place of business? Someone will be over shortly to take your statement." Nelson turned his attention back to me. "Was anyone else around? People who could have seen someone leave this office?"

"Not that I know of."

"We had another call to the department from someone who said she was outside the grocery store."

I wormed my frigid hands up inside the sleeves of Vic's sweatshirt. "Officer Nelson, as far as I know, I was the only one over on this side of the street when I . . . made the discovery."

"Let's go back to my car, okay?"

Feeling queasy, I followed Officer Nelson to his car. Furman County is one of the biggest counties in Colorado, and their sheriff's department is impressively large. This cop knew me, but I didn't know him. That made me even more nervous as I tried to formulate the words to describe what I'd done, and why.

When we slid into the black-and-white, the cop handed me a sheriff's department blanket. "So you're Schulz's wife. How 'bout that." I nodded, feeling only slightly less ill at ease. It wasn't as if Nelson was offering to shake my hand. Instead, he pulled out a clipboard. "When and how did you find this woman?"

"Is she—?" I demanded. "Did she—"

The cop shook his head, then continued with his questions. What was the woman's full name, where did she live? Why did she happen to be here, and why did I? He wrote everything down, then told me not to go anywhere. He stepped out of the patrol car, shut the door, and motioned for Vic Zaruski, who hadn't moved, to come over. I turned in the seat to watch them. Vic seemed to be explaining that his place of employment was not where he should be headed. After dispersing the waiting-to-see-what-was-going-on crowd, Nelson led Vic to another police car.

The sheriff's department's white criminalistics van pulled into the lot and parked beside the Beemers. Armed with cameras, the crime-scene technicians descended on the office building. I focused my eyes far away.

Almost four miles distant, the portion of Aspen Meadow Lake that hadn't yet frozen shimmered in the moonlight. What was the cop asking Vic? I shivered, even though the motor was running and metallic-smelling heat blasted out of the dashboard fans. Actually, I did know what Officer Nelson was demanding of Vic Zaruski. How do you know this woman, Goldy Schulz? When this Mrs.

Schulz came into your store to report the crime, how did she act? Did she seem upset? What did she say, exactly? He was asking those questions because I was the one who'd found Dusty, and therefore was automatically the first person whom law enforcement would suspect. This was another thing I wasn't quite ready to face.

Sudden shouting startled me. A moment later, a very upset Richard Chenault, his face set in frustration, his cashmere coat billowing around behind him, loped ungracefully down the steps from the building's upper level. Alonzo Claggett and Donald Ellis, unsure of anything except that they probably were supposed to follow, hurried fast on Richard's heels. Louise Upton maneuvered down after them, then immediately marched purposefully over to the nearest policeman, who happened to be standing on the sidewalk directing the crime-scene techs. Louise raised her voice so high I caught every word, unfortunately.

"Mr. Chenault is a very well-respected member of this community," Louise cried, shaking her finger in the unsuspecting cop's face. "It's **his** office, and he deserves to know what is going on in there! Now, did someone break in? Is his niece dead? We need to know these things! Also, we have many valuable items and irreplaceable files inside—"

The cop interrupted her, speaking words I

couldn't make out. Louise Upton promptly stopped talking, pressed her lips together, and stepped back a pace. The cop leaned in toward her and raised **his** forefinger, talking all the while. Louise ducked her chin, pressed her lips together, and listened, looking humbled, for once. I thought, **Oh, man, if only I had a camera.**

Donald Ellis and Alonzo Claggett, meanwhile, shook their heads as they spoke to two other policemen. Richard Chenault, his voice subdued and his face stricken, talked to a third cop.

Two more cops were leaning in to stare at the area in front of Dusty's old Honda. I squinted at the Civic. Dusty had been fond of telling me that she left her car, a donation from a St. Luke's parishioner, as far from the office building as possible, to get a bit of extra exercise walking to the law firm. Once summer was over, she'd started working out at the rec center with Alonzo. Then they'd drive separately over to H&J. At the office, she changed into whatever suit she was wearing at the office that day. I sighed.

So, what was going on with Dusty's Civic? It was parked right under a streetlight. Dusty had been as meticulous about the appearance of that little car as she was of her own person. But the paint job was a wreck, and the rear lights had been . . . what? Smashed? I got out of the patrol car, motioned to a nearby cop, and pointed to the car. In a garbled voice, I informed him it was Dusty's, and that it had been vandalized.

He nodded, then looked at me sympathetically. "She was a friend of yours, this girl?" I nodded. "For long?"

"A few years."

The cop closed his eyes and raised his eyebrows, as in, **Too bad.** He told me the detectives would want to talk to me after a bit, and I shouldn't go anywhere. Then he walked away.

I swallowed and watched him. Why hadn't he asked more about Dusty? I knew what questions I'd face once the detectives arrived. The same ones I'd gotten from Officer Nelson. And then there were the questions that were important to **me,** questions the cops were very unlikely to ask.

Why was Dusty so special to you? Because I still thought of her as a high-school kid. Because she and her low-income family lived in a Habitat for Humanity house, just down the street from us, and people in town still made fun of them. Because until her uncle Richard, who didn't believe in handouts, had agreed to pay off her student loans for community college, foot the bill for her paralegal training, and hire her, she'd never seemed to have a bit of luck.

She'd been a scholarship student at Elk Park

Prep. Julian Teller, my part-time assistant and our occasional boarder, had been a classmate of Dusty's at EPP. He, too, had been a scholarship student, and he and Dusty had been boyfriend-girlfriend for a while. He said Dusty had been smart . . . not just bright, but brilliant. And then she'd been expelled from Elk Park Prep because she'd become pregnant . . . not by Julian.

That spring, I'd been dealing full-time with the Jerk, who, even though we were divorced, managed to make my life miserable. I had taken meals over when Dusty had miscarried, but the Routts hadn't offered any details of the misbegotten pregnancy. Nor had I asked any. I did know that Dusty had managed to get her GED after the Elk Park Prep meltdown. The next time I'd come in close contact with her, she'd been working at a cosmetics counter at a department store.

"Those bastard Routt children," the mean-spirited had snorted. "We wonder if Dusty is selling those free samples she gets."

Dusty had taken everything in stride. She'd worked her way up to being a highly compensated cosmetics associate before being lured away to a full-service spa. When the spa had gone belly-up, she'd enrolled in community college. Sometime later, she'd told me about her uncle, previously unknown to the family, getting altitude sickness on his way back from an attorneys' conference in Vail. Dusty's mother, Sally Routt, may not have known about Richard, but he had known about her, and he'd called his sister-in-law and begged for help, having just vomited all over his rental car. Not sure of the cause of Richard's distress, Sally and Dusty had rushed him down to the Southwest Hospital ER, where he'd ended up mewling and puking in his doctor's arms, and that doctor had been K.D.

Richard's recovery had been near miraculous, and he had proceeded to sweep K.D. off her feet. He'd sold his partnership in a Los Angeles firm and opened his own office in Aspen Meadow. A year ago, he and K.D. had bought their big place in Flicker Ridge, and Richard had offered to pay off Dusty's loans, give her a job, and pay for her training.

Maybe Richard had seen it as an investment in having his very own paralegal, with on-the-job training in estate law, to boot. Perhaps his guilt at having so much in the material-goods department had finally begun gnawing at him. I had no way of knowing, because between a polite, solicitous manner with clients and staff, occasional bursts of regal temper, and showing a nutty tendency to pull practical jokes, King Richard was pretty hard to read. Dusty hadn't complained about him to me, in any event. Nor had she lauded him. She'd only laughed her wonderful tinkling giggle and called her uncle "the King."

In any event, Dusty had confided to me that now she was working to build a career, a real **life,** as she put it. She was going to push to quit her humble surroundings. She was **moving, moving, moving,** as she put it, **moving up in the world**!

I stared at the bustling parking lot. Cops were turning away bystanders. Other law enforcement folks began to unroll yellow crime-scene tape around the imposing stone-and-wood entry to Hanrahan & Jule. Donald and Alonzo appeared to be pestering the cops with questions, but their curiosity was met with a grim silence. Was I imagining it, or was the officer in charge wearing a happy smirk as he asserted his authority over the attorneys? I did not have time to contemplate this question, because a detective ordered a sergeant to whisk me down to the department for questioning.

Chapter 3

The detective, who identified himself as Britt, handed me my car keys. I'd actually dropped them between two of the steps going up to the law firm. He also gave me my office keys, which K.D. had apparently asked to be returned to me.

As the coroner's van pulled up, Britt drove me around the back of the law office, where I jumped out and grabbed my coat and purse from my own van. We took off just as another pair of cars from the Furman County Sheriff's Department showed up. The H&J crew were scattered along the sidewalk outside where the cops were now finishing unrolling the crime-scene tape. Donald and Alonzo still stood together, their heads bowed in conversation. Richard Chenault, looking stricken, sat alone on the curb. There was no sign of K.D. or Louise Upton.

The glaze of frost that had whitened the streets was beginning to melt, and a breeze moved through the stiff brown grass that bordered the road to the interstate. I asked the detective if I could please call my husband. He seemed to know who Tom was, and nodded. After fishing my cell phone from the bottom of my purse, I punched in Tom's cell number.

"Thank God you called," Tom's gruff voice announced, before the first ring had finished. "Where are you? Did your van die again? I'm dressed and ready to go."

"Oh, Tom. I'm at, well, I was at H&J. Dusty Routt . . . well, it looks as if Dusty is dead," I blurted out. My voice cracked.

There was shuffling in the background. "I'm writing Arch a note." A moment later, I could hear a door closing. "Wait. I'm on my way to my car." I imagined Tom's tall, muscular body, of which I knew every groove, even the old scar from a bullet wound. I saw his handsome face drawn into a frown as he folded himself into his car, turned on the engine, and pulled out his trusty spiral notebook that went everywhere with him. "Okay, start over," he said in that commanding voice that made subordinates smile and suspects cower.

"I was supposed to give Dusty her last cooking lesson tonight, the way we've been doing for the last five weeks. We were working on bread baking and she said she wanted to talk to me about something, too. But I fell over her in the reception area . . ." A sob erupted from my throat. "I'm on my way to the department now with a fellow named Britt."

"I'll meet you down there."

"But I want to tell you how I tried to do CPR—"

"Stop talking," Tom commanded. "All cop cars are wired for sound. Don't tell me any more about what you found, because they'll compare it with what you say at the department." In the background, his engine growled. "You were supposed to be there at ten, but you didn't make it because I had to give you a jump, right? Just answer yes or no."

"Yes. I think I got there about—"

"Stop." He considered. "Arch is all set, so don't worry. If he wakes up early, he'll know where we are. He can get his own breakfast, and the car pool will pick him up at the usual time. Listen. I don't know if you want to think about this right now. But Gus's grandmother called right after you left tonight. Wants to know if Gus can come over after school to sell candy in the neighborhood."

My mind reeled. Gus Vikarios was Arch's recently discovered half brother. I truly **did** want Gus and Arch to spend time together, get to know each other, and all that. But trying to make those plans now, after what I'd seen tonight, felt too trivial to contemplate.

"Tell you what," Tom said. "I'll take care of it. You want me to call Marla?"

Marla Korman, the Jerk's other ex and my best friend, wouldn't want yes or no answers to any of **her** questions. Marla craved gossip more than a crack addict needed a daily hit. As the patrol car sped down the mountain to the department, I could just imagine the details she'd demand. **Who else knew you were there at night? Was Dusty involved with someone? Someone I might know?** My mind erupted with worry: Arch. Marla. Sally Routt. Dusty. "I can't think about this stuff now, Tom, I can't—"

"I'm telling you, let me take care of Arch being with Gus. Okay, the catering. You're done for today, 'cause now that it's after midnight, it's officially Friday. The cops will close the firm office probably for the weekend. But what about tomorrow, Saturday?"

"Uh, birthday party," I stammered. "Ellises. It's for Donald Ellis, a lawyer in the firm." But that was tomorrow. And as Tom had pointed out, this was today, Friday, just after midnight. And I had all I could handle.

"Okay, Mrs. Schulz," said Britt. "Wrap it up."

"I . . . don't have a way to get home," I told Tom.

"That's why I'm coming down, among other reasons."

"Listen, Tom. Somebody needs to go be with Sally Routt." Pain cramped my throat as I pictured Dusty's diminutive, wan, single mother. In her late thirties and taking care of a toddler son and blind father in addition to Dusty, Sally Routt never seemed to be able to do more than keep body, soul, and family together. Sally had been right to be overprotective of her only daughter. Not that it had done much good.

He let out a long breath. "She's going to be in bad shape, you know."

"Tom, don't."

"Her father was blinded in prison. Her older son died while he was in custody for a DWI. You think she's going to trust the cops to find out what happened to her daughter?"

The patrol car swung into the sheriff's department's mammoth parking lot.

"I can't deal with this right now," I whispered.

"Okay. I'll see you later. Just think, I could have let Arch drive me down to the department. For practice."

I took a deep breath. Arch was officially fifteen and a half, with a fresh learner's permit. So far, he had **not** proved himself adept at driving. But this was cop humor. It was how Tom and his cronies dealt with the dark side, the misery and death, the evil. And they won't let up. They will spin something for laughs until your hair turns gray and you've forgotten what you were thinking about in the first place.

"Whatever." The patrol car stopped. Britt, his eyes facing forward, turned off the engine and waited for me.

I closed my cell phone. Dizziness gripped my brain. Without warning, jokes, humor, laughter, hysteria—all these bubbled simultaneously inside my brain. **Stop it,** I ordered myself as I got out of the car. But my inner ear registered the Hanrahan & Jule attorneys cackling over the gin-laced espresso. I blinked and heard Tom and his department buddies howling when the coroner poked fun at the uninitiated who thought **autopsy** was a kind of car, **artery** the study of pictures.

I walked slowly across the paved lot, trying to keep my balance as Britt led the way to the massive steel double door. A blast of warm, metallic air rushed out of the department entrance. I felt like hell.

After I was seated in one of the department's interrogation rooms, my head began to throb, and I belatedly realized that even though it was the middle of the night, I was probably going through caffeine withdrawal. Britt reluctantly agreed to get me some java.

I assessed Britt when he came back through the

door holding a thin cardboard tray with two foam cups. He was thirty, I guessed, since most cops didn't make detective until then. Still, with his baby face, dark hair, and perpetually puzzled expression, he looked younger.

"Okay, Mrs. Schulz. How did you come to work in that law office? Don't leave out any details, okay?"

I sipped some life-giving caffeine. Then I began to talk.

From the beginning of July until tonight, I told Britt, I'd been making and serving breakfasts to the early arrivals at Hanrahan & Jule, one of the three law offices in Aspen Meadow. As catering jobs went, I continued, this was a relatively high-stress assignment, not least because I'd never catered to so many talkative, joking, obsessed-with-work folks before. Ordinarily, I'd get there at five every morning, and within an hour, the place would be buzzing. But not on Thursdays. Thursdays I came in at night, since Richard scheduled breakfast meetings with clients on Friday mornings.

There was a knock on the door. A uniformed officer poked his head through and told Britt he was needed elsewhere, but not for long.

"Keep that thought," Britt ordered, before whisking away.

But I was temporarily incapable of holding **any** thought. I sipped more coffee and allowed the memories to surface.

By the beginning of October, I'd become worn out from the H&J job, although I'd been trying to convince myself that I wasn't. Every morning, after moving through my yoga routine and getting dressed, I'd give myself a pep talk in our bathroom mirror. A slightly plump, slightly weathered early-thirties face, with brown eyes and unfashionable Shirley Temple–blond curls, would stare back. **Admit it,** I'd say to myself, **you're not quite ready for the lawyers today**. But I'd button up my white caterer's shirt anyway. I'd bustle containers of eggs whisked with cream and fresh herbs, applewood-smoked bacon, breakfast sausage, fresh-squeezed orange juice, fragrant homemade bread, and sliced fruit out to my van. And I'd tell myself to buck up, drink a latte, and pull myself together.

Besides that, I'd reassure myself, I wasn't alone. The lawyers of H&J also catered. Unlike yours truly, though, these guys were paid **extremely** well to work at coddling **extremely** wealthy clients. Here we shared another trait, as I'd often experienced the crankiness of well-moneyed people. Rich folks' quirks and caprices often cost caterers time, money, and endless aggravation.

But unlike the attorneys, I wasn't paid by the hour. And every whim an enraged H&J client wanted dealt with in the next twenty-four hours meant **Billables, baby!** Billables, aka hours billable to the client, were what the guys lived for, what they assured one another they were generating tons of as they scarfed down Cuban sandwiches I sometimes brought in at supper-time, long after a CEO with a trophy wife or a silk-suited octogenarian had huffed out of the office.

"I want to cut my children out of my will" was a frequent threat.

"I'm bequeathing everything to the new Anglican mission" was another one. "I don't ever want to be hugged in church again."

"My niece hasn't written to me in two years, Goldy. Who do **you** think I should give my pearls to?"

Aw, give 'em to your niece anyway, I wanted to say as I pressed focaccia loaded with garlic-infused pork between the metal plates of my indoor grill. But as the attorneys were so very fond of saying, "What you pay for the advice is what it's worth." Unfortunately, any counsel doled out by yours truly wasn't worth a grain of my favorite hand-harvested sea salt.

I'd been referred to H&J in June by a criminal attorney named Brewster Motley. Unlike his not-a-hair-out-of-place colleagues, Brewster was well tanned and laid back. He'd warned me, though. "Listen up, Goldy," he'd said as he ran his hands through his mop of blond hair. "H&J lawyers do mostly estate law, but they're still uptight as hell. Watch your kitchen equipment, okay? Ditto the food. I don't need to act nuts to relieve stress, but they do. You don't want to be serving cheesecake flavored with soy sauce. Okay? Be cool." He'd pointed his thumbs heavenward, which in Brew-sterese meant anything from "Stay calm" to "Surf's up." Anyway, Brewster had helped me out of a jam recently, when I'd desperately needed help. When he'd referred me to H&J, I'd felt obligated—but also grateful—to take on the firm as a client. How hard could it be to make early breakfasts, cater occasional meetings, and be on call to deliver a tray of sandwiches at six in the evening, every now and then? Wouldn't the hungry attorneys and assorted staff be supergrateful for my proffered goodies?

Sometimes I'm amazed I have any naïveté left.

In any event, I'd become their caterer. At the beginning of September, Dusty Routt, our pretty, enthusiastic neighbor, had asked me to teach her to cook. Because of her class and work schedule, we met every Thursday night at ten in H&J's beautifully outfitted kitchen, to plan and prep

Richard's Friday-morning meetings. We would chat, roast rashers of bacon so that they would just need a quick heating in the microwave, mix up bread to rise overnight, cut creamy chèvre into dot-sized bites, check for jams and preserves, count croissants and slices of prosciutto . . . I'd enjoyed Dusty's company, and I'd taught her to flip omelettes with the best of them.

So.

I put my head down on the steel table in the interrogation room. **Earlier, earlier, I should have been there earlier,** I repeated silently to myself. Birthday or no, Dusty had wanted to discuss "something important" with me. Something to do with the stunning bracelet I'd seen her wearing last week? She'd giggled and promised to tell me about the opal-and-diamond bracelet "soon." I remembered telling **her** to practice taking deep breaths, because twenty-one candles on a carrot cake was a conflagration! She had smiled quickly, before her face had turned uncharacteristically grim.

But then there was that issue of my son driving, which Tom had found so humorous. For the past few weeks, I'd been trying to teach Arch to drive in various parking lots . . . with zero success. Our last session had been the previous afternoon, at our local Safeway. Okay, I admit it, I'd given Arch conflicting directions on reversing, and he'd ended up crushing a line of grocery carts. When we'd finally arrived home, I'd apologized and offered my son another driving lesson on Saturday. But since I'd already lost my temper in the grocery-store lot, then lost it again when I wrote the grocery-store manager a check for the destroyed carts, Arch had refused either to forgive me or to get out of the van.

I'd stomped away, and Arch had left the van lights and radio on—inadvertently, I was sure. So before driving to the firm tonight, I'd had to take Tom away from polishing his beloved antique highboy, which was what he did for relaxation. Once he had located the jumper cables, he'd eased his sedan out into the street and started working on my vehicle. The van engine had ground and groaned, wheezed and coughed, and finally turned over. I'd shown up at the law office with my caterer's load . . . half an hour late.

So I'd failed Dusty. I'd failed her **monumentally**.

Britt reappeared with his clipboard and apologized for the delay.

"We were talking about your meeting with Dusty on Thursday nights, Mrs. Schulz. Was this every Thursday night?"

"Yes, for just over a month."

"Who else knew that was when you met?"

"I have no idea. Everyone could have known, because we didn't make a secret of it. She helped me prepare and set out the food for the Friday-morning meeting, and folks sometimes complimented her on it."

"Who complimented her on the food, specifically?"

I closed my eyes. Well, King Richard always thanked Dusty, proudly and loudly. I told Britt about Richard Chenault, how he was Dusty's uncle and enjoyed taking pride in her accomplishments.

"Which were by extension compliments for him?" I nodded. Britt went on: "Anyone who **wouldn't** compliment her on the food?" Britt asked slyly.

"Well, there's Louise Upton. She's the office manager, and she never compliments anyone, except for **guys** who are higher up the totem pole than she is."

Britt's baby face broke into a smile. "Not your favorite person, then."

I shrugged. "She's okay, I suppose. She runs a tight ship, and she loves Hanrahan and Jule."

"A tight ship with a totem pole."

"Detective, it's the wee hours of the morning, and I don't know if you're making a joke or what. I also don't know how much longer I can last."

"Would you say Dusty Routt and Louise Upton were enemies?"

"Not enemies, really. Louise just uses no social skills with people she believes are beneath her."

"Okay. So you were set to meet Dusty tonight?"

"Yes, at ten, our usual time. But then my car wouldn't start because my son drained the battery." I explained about my not looking properly into the rearview mirror and directing my son into a line of grocery carts, and how that had precipitated a furious argument between the two of us, which in turn had led to Arch staying in the car with the lights on and the radio running . . .

"You were parked in a garage," Britt asked, "or on the street?"

"On the street," I said, "because I knew I was going out later, and I didn't want Tom to block me in when he got home."

"After this argument with your son, do you know whether he locked the van when he got out of it?"

"No," I admitted. "I don't. Gee, do you think . . . maybe one of my neighbors saw someone messing around with my car."

Britt took a deep breath. "We'll canvass your neighborhood. Now, Investigator Schulz gives you a jump, you take off for H&J, and you get there at what time?"

"The **exact** time?" I sipped more coffee, which tasted as metallic as the building smelled. "I'm pretty sure it was right around ten-thirty. Yeah, pretty sure. I didn't check my watch, though." Britt gave me a narrow-eyed look, and my mind conjured up the image of him informing his pals that Tom Schulz's wife . . . you know, the caterer? . . . was as flaky as one of her renowned piecrusts. "I came into the office, and tripped. I didn't know what was going on. I certainly didn't think I'd stumbled over a body." I sighed. "At first I thought it was a joke. The lawyers in the firm like to pull pranks. But then I saw something wrong with one of the paintings in the lobby . . ."

"Something wrong?"

"You know, it's one of Charlie Baker's paintings of food. The firm has several."

"I'm familiar with his work. Like it, too. But it's out of a detective salary's reach. So what was wrong with it?"

"The bread dough I was carrying slopped onto the painting when I fell, which is why I noticed anything. The frame on the painting looked broken and there was a darker stain. I think it may have been blood." My weak voice indicated a brain thicker than cold oatmeal. "Then when I tried to get up, I saw Dusty lying there. I went to her and realized she wasn't moving or breathing."

"So you thought . . . what?"

I looked him square in his puzzled dark eyes. "I

didn't think. I used to be married to a doctor, and I learned a lot. Not anything good about him, mind you. But I do know about medical procedure, so I did CPR." I shook my head. "But nothing happened. She had a gash on her forehead, so that might explain the blood on the painting."

"Was she warm when you started CPR?"

"Yes."

"How long did you try to revive her?"

"I'm not sure. It seemed like a long time, maybe half an hour, but it might have been less. I couldn't think about anything except trying to get a pulse . . . but the CPR wasn't working. My cell phone was back in the van, and the office phone lines weren't operating, so then I just left the lobby to try to find help."

"So you did CPR and then you left. Please, please tell me what time you think it was."

"I don't know," I said through clenched teeth. "I didn't think to check my watch or a clock. I peeked both ways down the hall, then ran out back to my car, but—"

"Wait. Think back to that parking lot in front of the H&J office building. Before you went around back. Did you see anything there? I need to know precisely, especially if it was something suspicious."

I frowned. "Well, no. That I can recall, anyway.

You see, I went out the service entrance. It leads out back."

"Did you see Ms. Routt's car?"

"Not until I went around to the front. I saw her Honda Civic, parked alone in the lot."

"Did you see anything else around the building? Other cars, trucks, anybody coming in or going out?"

"Not that I noticed."

"What about when you were on your way up the stairs to the law firm, when you were coming in, or in the office itself? Anything unusual?"

"Not that I haven't told you. Look, I'm really beginning to feel tired and stressed out. My husband said he'd be waiting for me—"

"Yeah, yeah, we know." The dark eyebrows knit into a sympathetic expression. "Just a couple more things. Why did you agree to give Ms. Routt cooking lessons at the firm?"

I explained to him about how Dusty and I were friends and neighbors. "We talked a lot. It was fun for both of us. And in the firm's kitchen, we could cook and visit without the interruption of phones and whatnot."

"But you're a thirtyish married woman and she was a twentyish single female. What was so much fun to talk about?"

"Her studies, her work, my work, my clients,

the law firm, the people there. Dusty wanted to . . . get ahead. She was ambitious, and I was flattered that she wanted my advice about this or that."

"This or that?"

"What she should wear to a lunch meeting with big clients. Whether she should take golf lessons. That kind of thing."

"Did Ms. Routt have any problems with anyone in the law firm? Was she scared of someone on staff there?"

Of course, this was what I'd been wondering ever since I'd raced across the street. Who, who, who? And yet I was still unprepared for this question.

"Mrs. Schulz? I'm asking you again. You said Louise Upton was hard on her?"

"No, no, not really. Louise Upton just enjoyed savoring her power, that's all." I thought for a minute. "Dusty did have to be careful about protocol at the firm. One time, at a staff meeting I was catering? Dusty's uncle, Richard Chenault, asked a question about how a particular kind of will could avoid probate. Nobody seemed to know. Finally Richard said, 'Come on, Claggs, for God's sake! This is your area!' "

"Claggs?"

"Alonzo Claggett, one of the associates. He's really a great guy, and he cared about Dusty. He came tonight, after I found her—"

"We're getting ahead of ourselves. Back to this meeting."

I blew out air. "Well, as all the lawyers were filing out, Dusty motioned her uncle aside. She whispered to him that you could avoid probate with the kind of estate they were discussing by setting up a particular kind of irrevocable trust. I didn't really understand the details, but I gather she had them correct."

"Then what happened?"

"What happened? Richard wouldn't let Alonzo Claggett forget it. In other meetings, he'd joke that maybe instead of asking Alonzo a question, he'd just consult with Dusty. It was funny to everybody but Alonzo, and Dusty hated it."

"How do you know that?"

"Because she told me. At a lunch I catered for the lawyers and their wives, Nora Ellis, Donald Ellis's wife, scolded Dusty. Nora said that Dusty shouldn't give legal opinions, since she wasn't a lawyer. In fact, she wasn't even a paralegal yet. And Ookie Claggett, Alonzo's wife? She went out of her way to ignore Dusty through that whole lunch. All over **one** intelligent remark from Dusty, who was just trying to please her uncle."

"You're sure it was only one?"

"Well, it was the only one I witnessed. Maybe there were others."

"Maybe Mr. Chenault began asking for help from Dusty when he should have been consulting his associates."

I shook my head. "I think Dusty would have told me, if that had been true."

"Who did Dusty hang out with at the law firm?"

"Only one other person besides me. She was good buddies with Wink Calhoun, the firm's receptionist."

"Wink? Ookie? Claggs? Where do these people get their names?"

I was so tired, I laughed. "I don't know."

"Spell Wink's full name for me, would you?" This I did. Then Britt said, "Did they go for lunch together? Hang out on the weekends?"

"Yes, Dusty and Wink were friends. I saw Wink over at the Routts' house sometimes, and I know Dusty went to see her."

"And at the firm, were they friendly?"

"Sure."

"With each other and the lawyers, or just with each other?"

It was all I could do not to start laughing again. "When I serve breakfast, from Monday through Thursday? There's a dining room, with two big dining tables. The staff—Wink, Dusty, and

Georgina, their paralegal who's now in Hawaii with the other attorneys—would always sit at the second table. They didn't really mix with the bigwigs."

"The bigwigs?"

"You know. The lawyers. I mean, the lawyers were okay, but—"

Britt poised his pen over his notebook. "Describe them to me. How'd you get hired by H&J in the first place?"

"I was referred by Brewster Motley. He's a friend of Richard Chenault, who's the head honcho. Brewster is a criminal attorney who—"

"Yeah, I know him," Britt interrupted. "Looks like a beach bum, talks like Perry Mason. Did he get along with Ms. Routt?"

I frowned. "I don't even think they knew each other."

"Can you name the rest of the staff that's in Hawaii?" Britt tilted his baby face as I recited the names. In the fluorescent light of the interrogation room, his skin looked pale and clammy. "Describe Richard Chenault to me."

"Late fifties, combs his silver hair straight back, so he always looks like he just got out of a swimming pool. A strong guy, and proud of it. Does a lot of bodybuilding, I think."

"And the kind of work he was doing with Dusty?"

"I don't know **exactly**. Wills, estates, that kind of thing. That's what they do at H&J."

"Chenault easy to get along with?"

I smiled. "I wouldn't go that far. He is imperious. And he loves to play jokes on me." I told him about the gin in the coffee, the moths in the tablecloth, the green food coloring in the eggs.

"He just sounds like a ton of fun."

"He sort of is, really. He fell in love with a friend of mine, a doctor." I told him about K.D. and the altitude sickness. "They moved to a big house in Aspen Meadow and Richard bought a partnership in Hanrahan & Jule. But he had a little something on the side, and it wasn't asparagus. K.D. found out, and now they're getting divorced."

"Did Richard Chenault get along with his niece?"

"I'm telling you, **everybody** seemed to get along with Dusty. And really, because she was working so hard for Richard, it had gotten to be that I didn't see her a whole lot outside of the firm, except for our cooking lessons together."

Britt asked, "You live across the street from her family, right?"

"Yes."

"They get along? Any problems?"

"They all get along. No problems. Really, they're great. Sally, Dusty's mother, adores her, as do both her grandfather, who lives with them, and Dusty's little brother, Colin."

"Go on." When I gave him a quizzical look, he said, "Tell me more about her family."

"Dusty's father, Richard's brother, took a hike while Sally Routt was pregnant with Colin, Dusty's very little brother. He left her with nothing but debts, and hasn't been heard from since. Sally was forced out on the street, literally. One of the first things she did was to take back her maiden name, Routt. Sally's father, John, lives with them, because he was blinded in prison."

Britt's forehead furrowed. "Blinded in prison?"

"Back before rabbits were the guinea pigs for cosmetics companies, those companies tested their products on prisoners." Britt closed his eyes and shook his head. "John Routt was a guinea pig for a cosmetics company testing mascara, and the stuff blinded him. Dusty loves . . . loved her grandfather. He's one of the reasons she went to work for a cosmetics company after high school . . . she said she didn't want that to happen to anybody else. Naive, but sweet, which is the way Dusty was."

"So she went from a cosmetics company to a law firm? Just like that? Seems like an odd leap, for a young woman, anyway."

"No, she went to community college in between. It was her uncle who hired her to work for H&J."

"But why would she want to work in a law firm?"

I pressed my lips together and tried to remember exactly what Dusty had said about that particular leap. We'd been working on a breakfast pie at the time, a light-tasting but hearty concoction of blue cheese, eggs, and cream cheese, mellowed with sautéed shallot and chopped scallion. We'd just decided to call the dish Blue Cheesecake, when Dusty launched into a story about a family on our street suing a Colorado electric company. When a March blizzard dumped five feet of snow on our little burg, we'd lost power for a couple of days. But west of Aspen Meadow, the outage had lasted for five days, because some dummy at the power company had sent every one of their tractors over to the western slope. This family on our street had been particularly distraught, as their very independent eighty-year-old grandmother lived out in the area that didn't have power. Cell-phone service in the mountains is iffy at best, and the family hadn't been able to raise the grandmother or any of her neighbors. By the time the power company managed to bring a tractor over from Grand Junction and replace the fuse that had blown in the neighborhood, the grandmother had run out of firewood. She had frozen to death.

The family on our street had been unable to get the county attorney to charge the power company with negligent homicide. But they'd been determined to sue the power company in civil court for wrongful death. This had gotten Dusty interested in torts, and the law. She hadn't had the wherewithal to go to college, but she received a partial scholarship to a community college. After that, she was determined to become a paralegal, and maybe even eventually a lawyer. If the family whose grandmother had died was going to sue the power company, then maybe, Dusty reasoned, she could eventually help people like her grandfather, who had been treated so abominably by that cosmetics company, all those years ago. And then her uncle had shown up, and been willing to foot the bill and hire her, so Dusty had seen it as divine intervention.

All this I explained to Britt. He whistled.

"Sounds like a pretty extraordinary young woman."

"She was."

He asked, "What about Dusty's love life?"

I thought back, trying to remember what had been just out of reach when I'd first seen Vic a few hours ago. "A couple of months ago, Dusty told me about some problems she was having with her boyfriend. He's Vic Zaruski, the fellow who helped me tonight. I just happened to run into him when I was looking for a phone."

"Stop and tell me about that."

This I did, as Britt wrote. "Vic was very nice and helpful, and he seemed extremely broken up when he heard something had happened to Dusty." I went on to explain that I knew little of Vic, beyond a short but friendly chat I'd had with him one time when I'd brought a meal over to the Routts, and he'd been waiting for Dusty. He was going to a technical and vocational school somewhere outside of Denver, and he loved to play the piano. I did remember that he was particularly proud of his car, a vintage white Chrysler Sebring convertible that he kept in immaculate condition. This summer, I'd admired the way Vic glided that ultracool car into the Routts' driveway, when he came to pick up Dusty. I didn't know the details of the breakup, I only was aware that I hadn't seen the Sebring for a while. Still, what twenty-year-old woman didn't have romantic ups and downs?

"So, did Dusty have a current boyfriend?"

"I'm not sure. Maybe."

"Dusty told you all this stuff while you cooked together, but you don't know whether she had a boyfriend?"

"Wait a minute." She'd said she had something to tell me. And she'd promised to explain the new bracelet. My brain finally recalled what had been bothering me. "There might have been somebody, though she didn't exactly tell me about it."

"What do you mean?"

I bit my lip. I was so tired. And was it warm in this room, or was that my imagination? "I'm not sure," I said finally.

"Tell me anyway."

"When Dusty came last week for her cooking lesson, she was wearing a bracelet. It wasn't the kind of jewelry she could possibly afford."

"What do you mean?"

I shook my head. "It was a complex arrangement of opals and diamonds. I asked her about it, almost, you know, playfully. Anyway, she . . . glanced down at it and kind of frowned. Then she said she'd go take it off, she really shouldn't cook while she was wearing it. Then I said, 'Aren't you going to tell me about it?' And she said, 'How 'bout this? I'll wear it next week and explain it to you.'"

"Meaning what?"

"I don't know. Did you find a bracelet on her?"

"Did **you**, Mrs. Schulz?"

"No, I did not."

"Was she wearing it when you discovered her?"

"I don't remember."

Detective Britt closed his eyes and shook his

head. Then he opened his eyes and half grinned. "What do you think was going on with this bracelet?"

"I thought I wasn't supposed to speculate."

"Exactly. So, in all your cooking lessons, Dusty Routt never mentioned a boyfriend. But once, you caught sight of a bracelet? And she said she had something important to tell you? Something important to tell you last night, to be exact, when she was going to explain the bracelet."

"That's correct."

Since I wasn't supposed to speculate, what I didn't tell Britt was that I had thought Dusty was kidding around one time when she had told me that her **real** motivation in learning to sauté vegetables, steam fish, bake bread, and roast lamb was to attract a wealthy husband. This dream fellow would fall in love with her cooking, she reasoned, with a laugh and a shake of her newly highlighted hair. But it had felt so much like a joke that I'd never taken it seriously. And in all our time together, she'd never talked again about this inspiration for learning to cook. Maybe I'd inform Britt of this particular conversation at some point.

"Look," I said, "I have a ton of kitchen work to do for a big party tomorrow, if the party actually takes place. And I mean what I keep telling you, I really am exhausted. Do you have any idea when I could get back the kitchen equipment that I dropped in the H&J office?"

"We'll have your husband bring it to you."

"Thanks. Sorry about the mess I left in the reception area."

"Not your fault. A cleaning team will come in when we're done with the crime-scene analysis."

"Good." I rubbed my eyes. If there had been a bed there in that toasty-warm interrogation room, I think I would have lain down on it.

"Okay, Mrs. Schulz. Where will you be for the next couple of days? In case we need to talk to you some more."

I gave him our address, the Ellises' address, where I was supposed to be doing Donald Ellis's birthday party the next day, and the location of St. Luke's Episcopal Church in Aspen Meadow, where I was catering Gus's christening on Sunday. Almost as an afterthought, I said, "I sure don't feel like going back to work after a friend of mine has died. I don't want to think about having to act happy when I see people."

"Oh, Mrs. Schulz," said Britt. "Tell me about it."

Chapter 4

Tom was waiting for me in the department snack room. I blinked in the bright light of the pop and candy machines that lined the walls. In one, glassed-in shelves offered limp, plastic-wrapped sandwiches that looked like one of Arch's lab experiments. Several patrol officers, appearing even more exhausted than the sandwiches, sat talking at one of the small tables. Upon our entrance, they put down their foam coffee cups and surveyed us with hooded, curious eyes. Tom nodded to me and tilted his head, indicating the door. The less said in the department, he seemed to be saying, the better.

Fine by me.

"I was just bringing in the bread ingredients," I explained to him ten minutes later, once we were headed up the interstate, back toward Aspen Meadow. A blanket of clouds now obscured the moon, and the night was once again impenetrably dark. A chilly wind slapped the dark sedan and swirled up flakes of ice from the roadway. I went on: "When I went in, I tripped over her. It took me a few minutes to realize Dusty was just lying there . . . and that she wasn't moving."

Tom drew his mouth into a frown and concentrated on keeping the car from swerving out of the lane. "First tell me how you're doing. Then we'll get to Dusty." He flicked me a quick glance, which seemed to tell him I wasn't doing very well, as a matter of fact. He turned his eyes back to the road and held out his right arm. "Come here."

I leaned in to his embrace. My seat belt cinched my torso and I unbuckled it. What was he going to do, arrest me? I was numb, cold, unable to feel anything. The reassuring way Tom tugged me into his warmth, the way his strong hand held on to my right shoulder . . . these were what I needed, and he knew it.

"Did you get somebody to go over there, to be with Sally?"

"I called Father Pete. I know he's recovering from that coronary, but I also knew he'd probably have another one if I didn't call him about this."

"Will I be able to see Sally when we get home?"

"Nope. You're a witness, and they're going to try to keep you apart."

"But she's my friend," I pleaded. "A neighbor, Tom. Please. I just feel responsible, dammit. I keep thinking, if I'd only arrived on time—"

"Stop. Look, let me see what I can do. Father

Pete should be there, and our team is probably finishing up at the Routts' house. Then the victim-assistance people will go in, try to be helpful, that kind of thing."

I shuddered. I didn't want to picture the victim-assistance team, with their quilts and their counseling. **Your daughter's just been killed, Mrs. Routt, you need anything from the grocery store?** But I knew they would do better than that.

"I want to be there for Sally. Her family has been through too much."

Tom's hand tightened on my shoulder. "I'll talk to my people. Don't worry. Knowing you, you'll be there, Miss G."

I snuggled into Tom's side, closed my eyes, and thought about the Routts. I liked them. And I felt empathy for Sally, since I'd spent quite a few years as a single mom myself. But life had been much more challenging for her than it had been for me. When Colin's father had skipped, Sally had told me she'd been forced to patch together funds for food, clothing, and shelter from a variety of government agencies. Our parish, Saint Luke's Episcopal, had coordinated with Habitat for Humanity to chip in with materials, muscle, and weeks' worth of meals, coordinated by yours truly, to help build Sally, her father, Dusty, and little Colin a modest, two-story house across the street from us.

But there had been other disasters, like Dusty's pregnancy and loss of her scholarship. Dusty had told me she wanted the baby. She'd been excited. And then she'd miscarried. On and on it seemed to go for the Routts. Now gossip in town would center on how "the welfare people" were clearly unwilling or unable to break out of the pattern of screwing up their lives. Unfortunately, Dusty's murder would appear to be confirmation of this cruel judgment.

I opened my eyes. Had I slept? I thought so. What time was it? The dashboard clock said it was half past three. The road was now cloaked in a frigid fog that promised snow. Despite the icy slick that was glazing the roads, I wanted Tom to drive faster. I wanted to get home, take a shower, and get into bed. I wanted my dear warm husband to lie down beside me, wrap his arms around me, and tell me everything was going to be all right. Which, of course, it wasn't.

The sedan crested the hill and I pulled away from Tom. The dark cloud surrounding us obscured the mountains of the Continental Divide. There, the peaks had been iced with snow since the beginning of September, and I suspected they were now getting a fresh dumping.

"So," I asked Tom, "what are the cops doing at the Routts' house now? I mean, right this minute?"

Tom exhaled. "The usual. If the mother's not a suspect—"

I snorted and checked the rearview mirror. Pinpricks of snow were tapping on the windshield. "Of course she's not a suspect."

"They'll ask if anyone else has rights to the house."

"What are you talking about?"

"Miss G. Let me finish. Our guys don't want anyone to be able to go into the Routts' house and plant things."

"Plant things?"

Tom's voice turned weary. "Put things in there that would tend to implicate someone else. Or indicate suicide."

"Tom, for God's sake. There was redness around her neck and on one of her cheeks. Her face had been bashed into a glass-covered picture."

"Okay then, look at it from another angle. The department doesn't want anyone entering and removing incriminating evidence. Once our guys have those two things established—that is, nobody strange can come in, and nothing can be taken out—they'll talk to the mother, see if she knew anything suspicious going on with her daughter. Threatening phone calls, that kind of thing. Then they'll ask permission to go through Dusty's stuff. Drawers, pockets, correspondence, you name it.

They'll be seeing if they can come up with some clues as to what happened to her, and why."

We headed past the closed shops on Main Street, where the fog softened the smiles from the merchants' electrified jack-o'-lanterns. When Tom pulled into our driveway, I glanced at the two police cars parked outside the Routts' house. When we finally stepped carefully across our ice-crusted deck, I began to shiver.

Coming into the chilly house did not help. With fall temperatures fluctuating from thirties in the mornings to the eighties in the afternoons, we kept the heat off in most of the rooms. And despite the absence of the Jerk, all the windows remained closed and security wired, unless we were home. The reason for this was simple.

Roger Mannis, our arrogant, creepy county health inspector, was the prime suspect in a head bashing I'd received before a June catered event at the Roundhouse, a catering-events center by Aspen Meadow Lake that I'd opened last spring. The center, too, was finally fully wired for security. Now, unfortunately, the Roundhouse was having a whole set of pipes replaced, and the trenches dug around the former restaurant made it look like a giant prairie-dog village.

I'd expected that Roger was still plotting against Goldilocks' Catering, Where Everything Is Just

Right! until Tom explained to me that he and Roger had had a **talk**. Tom could intimidate anybody, all the while keeping his voice easygoing and his hand resting gently on his gun. Roger's manner had been stiff, but comprehending, Tom said. But when we weren't at home, Tom added, the windows were to remain closed and armed.

So here we were, unfortunately, with the October chill permeating the shut-up house. Arch, who had his own thermostat, had kept his room positively balmy when he was younger. But now that he was involved in sports, he liked his own cold. If he became chilled, which was rare, he tucked himself inside a sleeping bag on his floor.

The clock indicated it was four o'clock. Arch would be getting up in three hours. With Tom always involved trying to solve murders, how would I tell Arch that our lovely friend from across the street had met such a fate? I did not know. I couldn't even remember whose turn it was to drive carpool.

Tom turned off the security system, then announced he was bringing in firewood from the pile he'd stacked next to our deck. I moved, zombielike, through the house to the living-room windows. Several neighbors had leashed their dogs and were trailing behind them up the sidewalk, ever curious about what new crisis was overtaking "the welfare people." Anger prickled my skin, but there was nothing I could do. Maybe I was wrong, anyway; maybe they wanted to help. The police cars were still parked outside the Routts' house, and Father Pete's car was behind them. There was no movement from within.

"Goldy, go get in bed." Tom's voice was tender. Down on one knee, he was carefully laying pine logs on top of kindling he'd meticulously stacked. The sound of the match igniting startled me.

"Miss G. Please."

"All right, all right." I moved up the stairs, dropped my clothes spattered with bread sponge into the hamper, and eventually found my way into the shower. I let steaming water run over my aching face and body and tried not to think. Moments later, I was in bed. Oddly, I slept a profound, dreamless sleep until twenty after six. I dressed quickly, came downstairs, and found Tom lying, eyes half open, on the living-room couch.

"Is Arch up?" I asked as I sat down next to him.

"Not yet. Friend of mine brought back your van with your supplies. I unloaded everything."

"You're the best." I stared at the fire.

"Did you get any sleep?"

"Couple of hours. Enough."

I hesitated. "I should be doing something. For the Routts, I mean."

Tom sat up and ran his large hands through his wavy brown hair. The doorbell startled both of us. Tom sighed, then got up to answer it.

"Who could that be?" I wondered aloud. "If it's a reporter, get out your gun and use it."

But it was not a reporter, and the commingled voices in our hallway indicated the new arrival was Julian, my assistant. Of course, Julian would have wanted to be here. So despite the wee hour, Tom had undoubtedly called Julian's apartment in Boulder and asked him to make the drive to Aspen Meadow to be with us. As they exchanged murmured greetings, I wondered if it would be good for Julian to come with me when I finally did go over to check on Sally. Julian had been close to Dusty for a time. **Oh God,** I thought as I laid my head on the couch cushion. This was all too much.

Julian's voice asked: "Goldy? Where are you?"

I heaved myself up on my elbow and turned around. Julian, compact and muscled, stood not quite six feet. His dark hair was tousled; his jeans, wrinkled oxford-cloth shirt, and secondhand leather jacket clearly had been donned in haste. His handsome face was splotched from crying. He shifted from one foot to the other, waiting for me to answer him. With his awkward stance and clenched fists, he looked more shook up than I'd seen him in a long time.

I mumbled, "Thanks for coming."

"Dusty?" His voice was incredulous. "Who would want to hurt Dusty?" He moved into the living room and sat heavily on one of our chairs. He uttered an expletive and stared at the floor. The three of us were quiet for what seemed like a very long time.

At length, Julian asked, "Are you going over there?"

"Tom says we can't while the cops are still inside the house. Then he's going to call the department to see if we're allowed to go over."

"You found her?" When I nodded, he said, "Was it bad?"

"I tried to revive her." I shook my head. "Yeah, it was bad."

"Do they have any idea who . . ." But he let the question dangle.

"Not yet," Tom said. "But we will."

Silence filled the living room again. Julian stared at the fire. "When we go over, will we be able to take them some food?"

"Sure," I said.

"I guess . . . I guess we'd both feel better if we hit the kitchen."

He was right. I needed to clear my brain, and the way I did that was by cooking. At the moment, that was also the only thing I could do for Sally Routt.

"Okay," Tom said, "I'm going to go check on Arch and wake him up in twenty. I'll make sure he's got his backpack and, uh, learner's permit."

"Tom," I said, "don't even think about—"

"Just kidding!"

"Have you got anything going today?" Julian asked as he walked slowly down the hallway toward the kitchen. Once there, he flipped on the espresso machine and began hunting through our cupboards for the sugar. Julian never took fewer than four teaspoons of the sweet stuff in his caffeine jolts. The memory of accidentally sipping a titanically sweet, Julian-fixed demitasse popped me out of my stupor. I didn't want **that** to happen again. Opening my eyes wide, I clattered two cups under the machine's spout.

"In the catering department, I haven't got anything until tomorrow," I told him. "That's when I cater Donald Ellis's thirty-fifth birthday party. I can't imagine Nora will go forward with it, after what happened to Dusty." I sighed. "Then on Sunday, Nora's father is baptizing Gus. Nora's father is a bishop named Sutherland."

Julian sat in one of our kitchen chairs, his expression confused. "Sutherland? That name's familiar."

"You remember Father Pete had a mild coronary in July?" When Julian nodded, I went on:

"Sutherland's been taking over his liturgical and administrative duties, even some pastoral ones, since then. He was the bishop of the diocese of southern Utah until the end of last year, when he developed heart problems. He took early retirement and moved in with Nora and Donald. Your hometown's in southern Utah, even though it's in a different diocese. Think that might be why you recognize the name?"

"Yeah," he said after a moment. "That's it. He came around to do confirmations in Bluff one year, when the bishop of Navajoland was sick. Bishop Sutherland's not a very good preacher."

"Then let's hope for a brief sermon on Sunday. Why don't you see what you can find in the walk-in? Pick out ingredients that look good to you. We'll pull together something nice for the Routts."

Julian's sneakers squeaked as he moved across our wooden floor to the walk-in. After what seemed like an age, he emerged loaded down with unsalted butter, several bags of vegetables, fruit, fresh herbs, and huge wrapped packages of Brie, Fontina, Gruyère, and Parmigiano-Reggiano cheese. Once Julian had arranged his load on the counter, I pressed the button on the espresso machine and watched the dark, syrupy liquid twine into our cups. Overhead, I could hear Tom walking around in that authoritative way he had. I felt strangely comforted. Julian sat down, ladled sugar into his cup, took a sip, then stared at the calendar on the computer screen. "You're doing a party for Nora Ellis? I've encountered her, too. She wasn't the easiest person I've ever had to work for. Typical very wealthy lady, wants the best-quality stuff, but only at a steep discount."

I smiled at him. "So you don't like Bishop Sutherland, and you don't like his daughter, Nora Ellis. One is a bad preacher and one isn't easy to work for, is that it?" I sipped my coffee. "Have to tell you, big J., Nora's been perfectly nice to me."

Julian set his coffee aside and slowly unwrapped the cheeses. "Okay, let me think. I did a dinner party over in Boulder, a charity thing? It was when I was working for Doc's Bistro, and Doc really believed in this organization that Nora was involved with to help underprivileged kids. It was called Up and Coming. Anyway, Doc couldn't do the dinner, so I filled in. Nora Ellis kept sending people into the kitchen to see how I was doing. I had the feeling she was having them check that I was using real cream, real butter, and Parmesan that didn't come out of a tube with holes in the top."

I finished my coffee, rinsed my cup, and began grating my own **real** Parmesan, unsure even what we were going to do with it. But still, I was focusing on Julian's story, because it was getting my mind off the vision of Dusty lying on the H&J floor. I said, "It would drive me nuts if a client kept bugging me like that. What was her problem?"

"Oh, everything," Julian said as he disappeared into the walk-in, then reappeared with a jar of homemade pesto. "You know how clients can be."

Golden strands of cheese fell in front of the grater as I worked. "She was probably just freaking out over the event going well."

"Charity events are the worst," Julian said bitterly.

I suddenly felt queasy about working with Nora Ellis. Then again, maybe I was just feeling queasy, period. As I was rewrapping the cheese, Tom walked into the kitchen.

"Arch is getting ready," he announced. "I told him about Dusty, so he wouldn't be upset by the police cars. But I just said she was in an accident." He moved toward the phone. "Anyway, I'm calling Marla. Asking her to come over, too."

"You'll wake her up," I warned him.

"She'll live."

Julian slowly moved his cutting board piled with perfect slices of Brie to the far end of the marble counter. "You're calling Marla?" he said, his voice quavering. "Could you ask her to bring a dozen more eggs?" Julian looked at me as if he was going to say something, then shook his head. I fixed us both second cups of espresso while Tom dialed Marla.

"Is Arch going to attend the baptism?" Julian asked as he spooned sugar into his cup. He glanced warily at Tom, who had reached Marla and appeared to be arguing with her. In a very low voice, Julian said, "I thought you told me Arch had stopped going to church."

"He insists he's going." I slugged my coffee decisively, again rinsed the cup, and made my own foray into the walk-in. Staring at the shelves, I couldn't remember why I'd come into the cooled space, or what I was seeking. Without thinking, I pulled a large bag of Granny Smith apples off the shelf. **Apple Betty,** I thought. Apple Betty with ice cream was the ultimate comfort food and it was easy to prepare. I slammed the door too hard behind me, and it shuddered. "Arch wants to support Gus. He wants to be a part of the significant events in his half brother's life. Can you blame him? Arch figures if he lies low, no one will mention the fact that he's taken a sabbatical from the ecclesiastical experience."

For the first time since he'd arrived, Julian smiled. "Is Meg Blatchford going to be there?" he asked.

"You bet." At seventy-nine, Meg Blatchford

was the oldest Episcopalian in Aspen Meadow. After a person was baptized at St. Luke's, Meg was the one who took the baby or stood beside the child or adult and said, "You may welcome the newly baptized." Liturgically speaking, it wasn't strictly kosher for Meg to ask this question, as the celebrant was supposed to do it. Still, it had been such a long-standing tradition in our parish that no one objected. It added a nice touch, the oldest Christian in the place welcoming the newest.

Julian shrugged. "I hope I can be as strong as she is when I'm in my seventies. I've been taking her pastries every week for over a year. Last time I was there, she was pitching a softball so hard into that little basket she uses for practice, you know what I'm talking about? Anyway, I thought she was going to break the basket."

I nodded. "She's pretty amazing."

Julian slurped down the last of his coffee. After clattering our cups into our big commercial dishwasher, he methodically began to rinse a bunch of scallions.

"You got some blue cheese? I've changed my mind on what I'm going to make. I'm going to wrap up this Brie and use it for something else, and instead, I want to make that pie you and Dusty . . . Oh, Christ." At the mention of Dusty's name, tears unexpectedly spilled out of

Julian's eyes. He walked quickly into the ground-floor bathroom, where he started running the faucet. A wave of sadness engulfed me. I turned on my computer, told myself to buck up, and printed out the Blue Cheesecake recipe.

When Julian returned to the kitchen, he didn't mention the incident. Instead, he said, "Um, I need some tomatoes to make a salad. I didn't see any in the walk-in."

"I'll go downstairs to look for some."

"Downstairs?"

"Just trust me, okay?" I said as I traipsed down the steps to the basement. Our brief mountain growing season had not deterred Tom from planting a dozen cherry-tomato plants in June. When a September frost had threatened to ruin his crop—then only masses of chartreuse nuggets—he'd grumbled and pulled the plants up by the roots. After stringing a dozen meat hooks across our laundry-room ceiling, he'd hung entire plants—including roots with dirt still clinging to them—upside down, and declared the fruit would ripen by Halloween. **Great,** I'd replied, as I surveyed the grit covering the concrete floor. Tom, abashed, had swept up the mess. But we were still treated to a fresh shower of dirt every time someone picked some of his crop.

To my surprise, I was able to find a couple dozen

good-looking cherry tomatoes from Tom's batlike plants. I placed them on the washing machine, swept up the dirt, and brought my haul upstairs. My sauté pan held chopped shallots that were sizzling in a golden puddle of melted butter. Julian was busy beating cream cheese, so I turned my attention to the apples. They were just ripe, and I'd planned to take a pie into the firm . . . **Oh, Dusty, I thought suddenly, I'm so sorry**. A blade of sorrow stabbed my chest.

Just cook, my inner voice commanded. **Get on with things**.

So I did, with Julian at my side. While we were working, Arch came in with Tom. Arch looked spiffy in his new wire-rim glasses and de rigueur Abercrombie clothing: rumpled white shirt and baggy gray trousers. His toast-colored hair was dark and wet after his shower.

"Dusty?" Arch began, pushing his glasses up his nose. He looked from me to Tom to Julian. "Dusty from across the street? Tom said you tried to help her?"

I faced him and held my arms out. Too old for a hug, Arch stayed in place. "Yes, hon," I said, "I did try to help her."

"There're a bunch of police cars parked in front of the Routts'. Why? Why not just the coroner's van?"

Sometimes I wished my son did not know quite so much about police procedure.

"Our guys are helping Mrs. Routt," Tom supplied.

"Dusty was killed, wasn't she?" Arch blurted out, his voice accusing. His narrowed eyes took in Tom, Julian, and me. Then he dropped his backpack and stalked out of the kitchen.

"Don't worry, I'll get him," Tom offered.

Julian slumped in a kitchen chair, the savory blue cheesecake and tomato salad momentarily forgotten. "What's Tom going to say?"

"He'll tell him the truth. You want more coffee?"

"What the hell, why not."

Within five minutes Julian had finished his third espresso and we were again working side by side at the counter. Unspoken but understood between us was the knowledge that our energy came from the fact that we were making food for Dusty's family.

Not much later, Arch shuffled back into the kitchen. He stared at the floor as he asked, "Julian, are you coming to pick Gus and me up from school today?"

"Can't, bud. Sorry. I promised Marla I'd go to her place tonight. But," he said suddenly, "I'll be back to help your mom tomorrow. Want me to spend the night after we do that party?"

"Sure," Arch said, his voice low. That would be great, thanks." I felt bad that Arch was feeling sad about Dusty. But clearly, he didn't want to discuss it at the moment. He heaved up his backpack and turned to me. "Tom canceled my car-pool ride. He's taking me out for breakfast on the way to the Vikarioses' house. After that, the Vikarioses are going to drive Gus and me down to school." I lifted my eyebrows at Tom, who shrugged. Arch went on: "And Gus is coming over today after school. Is that okay? And for dinner, too. Tom just talked to them. Then they want me to go over there to spend the night." He looked at Julian, his brow furrowed. "Wait a sec. Want me to stay home, Julian?"

"I'm going to be coming back here anyway after I see Marla," Julian said, as if he hadn't doubted it for a moment. "So whether you decide to go to Gus's or not, I'll be around."

Cheered that he could stay home with Julian if he needed to, Arch smiled. "Thanks."

In addition to phoning the car pool and the Vikarioses, Tom had called one of his friends in the department, to see if it would be okay for us to go over to the Routts' house. We'd been given the go-ahead. Tom had also phoned the Routts themselves, to ask if we could come over sometime in the next couple of hours. When he got the green light on that one, too, he gave me the news, a promise that he'd be back as soon as he dropped Arch off, and a kiss. Then he and Arch were gone.

Julian and I got back to work. Within ninety minutes, Julian had pulled puffed cheesecake out of the oven and arranged sourdough rolls and butter in a covered basket. Tom, meanwhile, had returned and shaken up a fresh garlic vinaigrette for the tomatoes, which he arranged on a bed of romaine and Bibb lettuce and sprinkled with scallions. I carefully pulled the Apple Betty out of the oven. It oozed spicy, lusciously scented juices out from under its crumb crust. At five past nine, Marla rang the doorbell. I went to greet her.

My best friend had swathed her wide figure in a black silk pantsuit. Her curly brown hair, usually held marginally in place by jeweled barrettes, was pulled back from her pretty face by a black velvet headband. Her large brown eyes were puffed and bloodshot.

"I can't believe this," she said, handing me a plastic grocery bag with a pack of eggs inside.

"Thanks," I said. "And no, we can't believe it either."

I stowed the eggs, and the four of us packed up the food. Finally, we began our slow trek across the street to the Routts' house. The sheriff's department cars had pulled away. Tom had told us that it had been Sally's father, Dusty's grandfather John, who had choked and said yes, he'd be happy to have us come over, since Father Pete hadn't been able to stay long. Tom also said Dusty's little brother, three-year-old Colin, had been screaming inconsolably in the background.

I surveyed our offerings: Julian's steaming, golden-crusted savory pie, Tom's precisely arranged tomato salad, the breadbasket with its pats of butter, my spicy apple Betty with its crumbly crust. Without realizing it, we'd all created concoctions that demanded the precise cutting of vegetables and fruit, as if organizing food could somehow order experience and make life neat. Like most folks, we believed that performing that small ritual of comfort, bringing nourishing gifts, could make life after a sudden death more bearable.

Which, of course, was doubtful.

I pressed my lips together and led the way as we walked toward the door of the Routts' small house.

Chapter 5

When we arrived, Marla marched up the cement steps and rang the bell. Tom, Julian, and I followed her to the small red-painted landing. When no one came to the door, Marla pressed the buzzer again. Still there was no answer. She turned around and frowned at us, then tried again.

"Go away!" a voice shrieked: Sally Routt. She couldn't have been more than six feet from what I knew was a thin door. Yet we had heard no movement from within. "I don't want to talk to you anymore! I haven't got a lawyer, so you're just going to have to deal with it."

Marla raised her hands: Now what? Tom lifted his eyebrows at Julian.

I walked up next to the door. "Sally, it's us," I said in a low voice. "Goldy and Tom from across the street. And our friends Marla, from the church, and Julian Teller. We've brought some food for you. You can just take it, or you could let us in, if you like." After a beat I said, "Your father said it was okay for us to come over."

The stained, hollow door opened a crack. "Your husband, Tom, is a cop," Sally, still unseen, announced in a high, frightened voice. "I don't want any more cops in here. Suggesting my baby deserved to die." She erupted in a sob.

Suggesting **what**?

"Mrs. Routt, it's Julian Teller." Julian nodded confidently at me. "You know we loved Dusty." He hesitated respectfully. "But if you don't want us just yet, we can leave our trays here, then come back later for them. Or you could, you know, come over to Goldy's place—"

The door creaked open and Sally appeared. Short and slender, she was dressed in a graying sweatshirt and faded blue jeans. Her thin, frizzy light brown hair looked like a frayed broom. Her slender face, usually quite pale, was pink from crying. Her eyes were so swollen I didn't know how she could see out of them.

Without looking at our little party, she said, "I'm never leaving this house again. There's nothing out there for me."

With that, she departed, but she swung the door all the way open, which I took as an invitation. She could always tell us to leave, I reasoned, as we pushed our way into the small living room, with its bedspread-covered couch, flimsy coffee table, and mismatched chairs. I'd only been inside the

Routts' place a few times, but it invariably depressed me. The church might have helped build and pay for the house, but they hadn't provided much in the furniture department.

Sally slumped on the couch and gazed at the floor. Julian placed his tray on the battered coffee table. I followed suit.

"Kitchen must be back here somewhere," Tom muttered. He swung past us around a short corner. There was a clattering of wood hitting counter—presumably Tom's suddenly putting the tray down—and then a guttural sobbing emanated from the same direction. But I knew this voice, too: it was John Routt.

Tom's comforting voice interspersed the deep groans and sobs. I felt confident Tom could handle Mr. Routt; it just would take a while. Meanwhile, Sally began to rock back and forth and wail. Before I could turn my attention to her, though, someone started banging on the front door. Sally rolled sideways on the couch and buried her face in a folded, incongruously cheery red-and-white-patterned quilt, no doubt brought by the deputies. After rubbing her cheeks and eyes with the quilt, she stopped crying momentarily. The pounding on the front door started up again, more loudly and insistently than before.

"I can't . . . take any more," Sally whispered to

me. As she lay on the couch, her puffy eyes sought out mine. "Get rid of whoever that is, would you please, Goldy?"

I nodded. Marla and Julian, eager to be helpful, had been building blocks with Colin on the far side of the room. But the knocking had scared him, and he began to cry. He toddled over to his mother's side and threw himself on top of her legs. Sally reached out a limp arm and patted Colin's head.

What were neighbors supposed to do to be helpful in times like this? **Just work on getting your friends through the next hour,** an inner voice said. **Failing that, attend to the next fifteen minutes**.

I shouldn't have been surprised to see Vic Zaruski at the door. His face, like Sally's, was blotched, his expression stricken.

"What's going on?" he asked me. The humidity from the previous night's fog had made his head of straw-colored curls wild. "Why are **you** here?"

"Vic, you know we live across the street," I said gently. Behind me, Colin raised his crying a notch. "Look, it would help if you didn't **bang on the door**."

He looked in over my shoulder. "Where is everybody? Mrs. Routt? Her father? Colin?"

Get rid of them, Sally had said to me. But

surely she would want to see her daughter's ex-boyfriend? Would it help to have him here? I hesitated. Julian appeared from behind me.

"The little guy hasn't had any breakfast," he announced. "I checked their refrigerator, and they don't have any eggs, juice, bread, butter, stuff like that. Mind if I get some goodies from your place? I'm not sure the kid would like that quiche, so I thought I'd make him French toast. I've got my own keys."

"Sure," I said, then turned my attention back to Vic. He had been so kind and helpful to me after I'd found Dusty. Still, I was uncertain about how to proceed. What if Sally, in the way of mothers of teenage daughters from the beginning of time, had not actually **liked** her daughter's boyfriend?

Stepping agilely around Vic, Julian trotted down the stairs. "Oh yeah, Goldy," he tossed over his shoulder. "You'd better check on Sally, see what she wants to do about . . . visitors."

"Stay here," I ordered Vic. I walked quickly back to Sally, who still lay on the couch, with a steadily weeping Colin leaning against her knees. "Vic's here," I said softly. "Do you want to see him, or should I tell him to come back later?"

Sally closed her eyes and shook her head. "He's a nice boy, but I'm not ready to see him."

Great. I leaned in to Colin. "Will you come into

my arms, Colin?" I crooned. Colin shook his head steadfastly and gripped his mother's legs.

"Seems to me," Marla called from the opposite side of the room, "that Colin's auntie Marla has some chocolate candy deep in her purse!" She picked up her voluminous Louis Vuitton bag and began to rummage through it. Then she stopped and stared into it. "I know that candy bar is in here somewhere. If only I had Colin to help me look for it!"

Colin, suddenly alert, but still wary from not quite comprehending the source of the chaos around him, nevertheless unclasped his mother's legs. He ran toward Marla as fast as his short legs would take him. So much for a nutritious breakfast.

I turned and wiggled through the barely open front door, which I shut behind me. "Vic, look, you were **so** great and helpful last night. Could you come back later? They're all a mess in there—"

"**I'm** a mess." His voice was fierce. He turned away, stuffed his hands in his pockets, and stared at his white Sebring convertible, its top still down in defiance of the gathering clouds and the cooling days. "I just . . . I can't . . ." He twisted his head and lifted his pointed chin. "So do the cops have any idea who did this?"

I exhaled. "I don't know, Vic. They just left here a short while ago. I had to go down to the department to answer their questions, just as you did. Did you see Dusty last night?"

He sank down on the red concrete landing and put his head in his hands. "No, no. I . . . hadn't seen her for a couple of weeks." He paused. Then his words came out in a sudden rush. "We were supposed to have lunch together today. She said she had something important to tell me. It's her birthday, too. But she told me not to get her anything." He ran his fingers through his wild hair. "Oh, God. If she just would have talked to me."

I ran my right sneaker across the Routts' dusty gray doormat, with its inscribed "Welcome" worn down to nubs. "Talked to you about what?"

He shook his head, despairing. "Everything. Nothing. I don't know."

"Did she get along with the people at the law firm?" I asked mildly, my voice low.

Vic jerked his head around and stared up at me. "Now what do you think, Goldy? I mean, look what's happened. It's just like at that stupid school. Elk Park Prep. Everybody **else** screws up, and Dusty gets blamed."

Everybody else screws up? I knew Dusty had become pregnant; I knew she'd been expelled. But who had **screwed up**? I asked calmly, "What are you talking about? Someone made a mistake and Dusty got blamed for what?"

Vic jumped up, dusted off the seat of his jeans, and pulled his keys out of one of his pockets. "I'm out of here. You want to know the details of Dusty's history, maybe Julian will tell you." He jumped down the stairs two at a time. "Nobody wants me here, right? 'Could you come back later?'" He mimicked my voice so cannily that chills scurried down my back.

"Wait, Vic," I pleaded. "Why don't you go across the street to our house and wait for us? We'll be over in a little while. Julian just needs to get some supplies, and after he does some cooking, he can stay with you—"

"Forget it!" He jumped over the Sebring's driver-side door and landed in his seat with a **whack**. He shoved on a pair of dark glasses and revved the engine. **"Could you come back later?"** he aped again. He hooked a long arm over the passenger seat, twisted his head, and backed too fast out of the Routts' steep dirt driveway. The Sebring rocked and bumped until it reached the street. Vic braked hard in the street and stared at me, all the goodwill from the previous night evaporated. Then he drove away.

Shaking my head, I watched Julian cross from our house. He was carrying two brown paper grocery bags.

"What was **he** yelling about?" Julian demanded. "He's just going to upset Mrs. Routt even more."

"I don't know." I frowned. "He wanted to come in, and she didn't want to see him yet. Vic helped me last night, when I ran away from the law firm and was desperate for a phone. He was very upset when he learned the news about Dusty. Maybe talking to the cops pushed him over the edge—"

Julian shifted the bags and started up the porch steps. In a low voice, he announced, "Word I heard was that he and Dusty had broken up recently."

"Yes, Dusty told me. She didn't tell me the reason, though."

"You know how ambitious she was. She must have been thinking, How far can a guy working his way through vocational school go? Can you open the door for me?"

"Sure." Was that really what Dusty had been thinking? I wondered.

Twenty minutes later, Colin was shoveling Julian-made, syrup-soaked squares of French toast into his mouth so fast I was afraid he would choke. Julian rolled his eyes at me as he stood guard over Colin's little table and waited to be told "More!" The dull yellow chair-within-a-table where Colin sat was a thick plastic square with a small seat cut out of the middle. It may have been the modern version of a high chair, but it was so scuffed and worn that I was willing to bet it had served at least four toddlers before it was given to the Routts.

Everything else in the kitchen, and in the house, looked second-, third-, or fourth-hand. In the living room, Sally still lay on the spread-covered couch. John Routt, whose elderly face always reminded me of an enormous piecrust that had spilled over the edges of its dish, tapped his way in with his cane, with Tom by his side. As usual, John Routt had his very thin white hair neatly combed back from his large forehead. He was wearing clean but extremely wrinkled clothing, including a large, formerly white shirt that hugged his copious belly. His much-washed black chinos had shrunk above his ankles.

He had composed himself somewhat, although his skin was still mottled and the area around his blue, sightless eyes was very red.

"Thank you for coming," John said. "You all have always been very kind."

"Oh, you're certainly welcome," I mumbled.

When I lowered myself onto one of the chairs, Sally sat up. She pressed her hands between her knees and stared down at them. Marla, murmuring reassurances, sat next to her and put her arm around Sally's shoulders. It wasn't at all clear if Sally was listening to her. I looked around the living room. The low walls held no pictures. Ranged across the space were an old portable TV on a dented pressed-wood console, a set of TV tables from the fifties, and a dinosaur-era computer on a seen-better-days card table.

After Colin had eaten, Julian and Marla and I all looked at one another: Now what? John Routt stood shakily, and seemed to be asking himself the same question as he swayed, sightless, chin held high, his right ear cocked, waiting for a cue.

"Sarah?" his low, brittle voice inquired. "Where are you, dear?"

"Here, Dad." Sally rose and gently led him to the couch. Marla hastily stood as the old man felt his way into a sitting position. He set his cane onto the floor. When Sally sat down beside him, he put his right arm around his daughter's shoulders.

I looked up at Marla, who shrugged. Tom said, "The food is all in the refrigerator, and I wrote out directions on how it should be heated up."

"That's very kind of you, Tom," John said, his voice rusty.

Julian tipped his head toward the door, as in **We should split**. But I couldn't just yet. I had to say something to the Routts, offer to help, to ask if I could do something practical besides just saying, "If there's anything I can do . . ." I'd heard that sorry phrase enough at funerals, when it was offered to the bereaved as an exit line. To me it always meant "Don't bug me."

"I'd like to bring in your meals this week," I announced to Sally. "I can call St. Luke's, too, if you want, to ask, uh, Bishop Sutherland to come over, help you with the arrangements . . ." I stopped talking when Sally raised her head and gave me a sour look.

Sally snorted. "Please don't insult me, Goldy. After Father Pete had his heart attack and that guy came in, I went to see him. Just to say hi, introduce myself. He asked if I was there for money. Before I could reply, he asked if I'd availed myself of the job-search services available through the county. I said no, because I had a three-year-old and a blind father to care for. I was so embarrassed, and I so wished I'd never stopped by. But it got worse. He sat there wearing his expensive, hand-tailored clothes—believe me, I can recognize fancy garments, even if I don't wear them—and said our house had been paid for by the church, and he didn't have the authority to give us any more funds. Goldy, I wasn't **there** for money. But I was so taken aback, I just shook my head. My voice wouldn't work, so I turned around and left his office. Later, of course, I thought I should have said, 'Nice to meet you, too!' "

My brain muttered, **God help us**. "I, uh, I'm sorry—"

"You see, Goldy," Sally said, her voice suddenly fierce, "that's what you don't understand." She lifted her chin, and her thin face quivered. "I know you're married to a cop, and Tom, I know you're a good man. Julian, thanks also for your help." She took a deep breath. "But as far as the rest of the world goes? We're trash. I learned that when my dear—" Her voice cracked. "When my sweet son Edgar died in custody, who cared? Nobody, except us. I learned it again when Dusty was going to Elk Park Prep. One of her teachers gets her pregnant, and whose fault is that? Who gets kicked out? Not the teacher! He claimed she was lying, but she wasn't."

One of her **teachers** got her pregnant? Now this was a part of the Elk Park saga that I had not heard. "I—I'm sorry." I faltered. "I didn't know—"

Sally's voice didn't drip with sarcasm, it was a veritable **waterfall** of sarcasm. "Oh yes, the cops are going to find Dusty's killer. Just like they found Edgar's. The cops will find out what happened!" She rubbed her forehead with stiffened fingers. "Like hell."

I said firmly, "You know our phone number—"

Sally shook her head. She stood up, as if to usher us out. Tom, Marla, and Julian responded with alacrity, hustling to the front door. Colin, sensing that another dramatic change was taking place, began to whine to be let out of his chair.

But my feet were glued to the living room's thin, faded rug.

"We'll wait for you outside," Julian announced as he held the door open for Marla and Tom.

"Sally," I repeated, my voice hopeless, "I just feel so awful—"

Sally kept rubbing her forehead, her face down. "How did my baby look?" she whispered. "Did she look as if she suffered?"

I thought of Dusty's bloodied forehead, of her darkened cheek, of the broken glass of the picture frames. Her neck had been very red, too red, when I was doing CPR. Had she been strangled? I remembered from Med Wives 101 that it took four minutes for the brain to be deprived of enough oxygen to die. Four minutes of having someone's hands grasping your throat so tightly that you can't breathe. Four minutes of struggling with a choker's deadly grip. Four minutes of being swung around an office, getting your face smashed into glass and your legs and torso whacked mercilessly into desks and furniture. Four minutes.

"No," Sally interjected. "Don't tell me, I don't want to hear about it. I want to imagine her the way she was. Trying to grow up. Trying to get ahead in the world." Sally's bloated eyes sought mine. "But you know what? The world didn't want her. When she was down, that's what she'd say. 'The world's against me, Mom,' she'd say. And then she'd start over on some new project. Some new job. Some new boyfriend." Sally exhaled again in disgust. "And for what? For nothing."

"Oh, Sally."

Sally put her hand on her hip. "I don't need meals, Goldy. What I need is for you to find out what happened to my baby."

"What?"

"I read the paper. I know you help Tom sometimes."

"Well, I . . . the police are—"

"You really think they're going to help the **welfare people**? The way Bishop Sutherland did, for example? Please. That law firm was a nest of vermin. Vermin, all of them. Dusty knew it. Something was going on, I'm sure of it. I know my . . . I knew my daughter. The past month, she'd been acting really secretive. Something was going on, and that's what got her killed."

"Did you tell the detectives this?"

Sally's laugh was shrill. "No, Goldy, I didn't **tell the detectives this,** because then the next thing you know, they'll start spreading rumors about Dusty, and who she was going out with, and what she was up to, and then **oops!** All of a sudden some dark facts will come out. They tried to say my son Edgar was a violent drunk. Goldy"—her eyes implored me—"he was a kid. And I don't want to be hearing that my daughter did this or that, she was involved with so-and-so. And by the way, wasn't she expelled from Elk Park Prep, and oh yeah, didn't she use her wiles to try to break up the marriage of one of her teachers? And on and on, until in the minds of the public, she deserved to die."

I sighed, unable to think of anything to say. She was right. I'd seen it again and again. A low-income person without power is blamed for a crime and goes to jail on scanty evidence. A wealthy person who's guilty as hell impugns the job the police are doing, impugns the victim, impugns whoever's around, and gets away with rape . . . or murder.

"You want to help us?" Sally asked, her voice both defiant and pleading. "Then help. I'm not saying you're a bad cook. We think you're a **great** cook. But if you really want to help me? Find out what was—what **is** going on in that scumbag law firm. Then you'll be able to tell us who killed my baby girl."

I looked her in the eye and licked my lips.

"Please," she begged me. "Please find out what happened to my baby."

I nodded. I thought, **What the hell am I doing?** But I said, "Okay, Sally."

As I walked carefully back across the street, I again saw Dusty's lifeless body. I remembered her eager expression as she learned to cook. I recalled how disappointed she'd been when one of her own cakes had fallen. I remembered how her face had lit up when I found her the vintage Calvin Klein suit.

I thought of the birthday cake I'd made her.

And then I remembered a joke Marla had told me when I'd started working at Hanrahan & Jule.

Q: Who's the only kind, courteous person at a law-association breakfast?
A: The caterer.

Well, I thought as I entered our house. Not anymore.

Chapter 6

Our kitchen clock said it was just eleven, aka back-to-reality time. Or at least, that's what I tried to tell myself. I stared at the phone. What did I need to do? Oh yes, call Nora Ellis to see if she still wanted to throw a birthday party for hubbie Donald the next day.

She wasn't there, so I left a message. **Even if the sky falls in, never assume a client will cancel a party,** André, my mentor had told me. Feeling numb, I moved mechanically over to my computer to check the prep schedule for my three upcoming events: the party, the christening, and the ribbon cutting for the new Mountain Pastoral Center. That last was supposedly going to be held at my catering and conference center, the Roundhouse. The plumbers had assured me they would be done by then. I had too much on my mind to call them for the fifteenth time and bug them.

In the hallway, Tom, Julian, and Marla were talking in low tones about Dusty's friends, who should be called, who else in the church could bring in meals and run errands for the Routts. I should have been helping them. But somehow talking about the Routts, after all I'd been through during the last eighteen hours, was more than I could handle at the moment. I walked into the kitchen.

Nora had handed me the recipe for the birthday cake she wanted for her husband. It was from one of Charlie Baker's last paintings, she said, **The Cake Series II**. She'd bought the painting for Donald and was giving it to him for his present. Charlie's recipe, Nora claimed, was an historically accurate version of Journey Cake, a confection the pioneers had baked on a board and eaten as they journeyed across America in their covered wagons. Actually, what Nora had given me was just a list of ingredients, which was all that my good old pal Charlie Baker, for whom I'd catered and with whom I'd cooked for the St. Luke's bazaar, had ever put at the bottom of his paintings. I made myself a latte and remembered Nora's happy expression when I said I was an old hand at Journey Cake, also known as Johnny Cake.

I pulled out flour and spices and thought about tall, cheerful Nora Ellis, whose straight blond hair fell in a perfect curtain around her head. When we first met, she told me she'd had good and bad luck with caterers. She'd already been burned, figura-

tively speaking, by both a Denver and a Boulder
caterer. Worrying about these mishaps must have
been why she was so stressed out when she was
running the charity event Julian had catered, I reasoned now. Anyway, my talks with her had always
been very amicable. To avoid a repeat of her two
unfortunate events, she wanted tastes of the
dishes I proposed to serve. I'd acquiesced. In point
of fact, most party givers wanted a taste test these
days. Problem was, you couldn't measure efficiency of service, politeness of wait staff, heat of
the food, and myriad factors that were just as important as how things tasted. Nora had told me
she'd heard that unscrupulous caterers often made
blatantly dishonest substitutions. At the Boulder
party, her guests were supposed to be served
poached salmon. Instead, they'd gotten chouli-
biac, an infinitely cheaper dish made from leftover
bits of salmon. The Denver caterer had un-
abashedly offered up pork loin instead of the
promised roast suckling pig.

"Oops," I said.

"Yeah, oops," Nora replied, her pretty face
alight with an equal mixture of anger and humor.
"Oops, guess what caterers got reported to their
respective Better Business Bureaus?"

In the end, Nora had decided on stuffed Portobello mushrooms and empanadas with guacamole

for appetizers. For the main course, she'd opted for beef tenderloin, that long, luscious piece of meat from which filets mignons were sliced. Hot beef in the middle of a cold October day was appropriately festive, I assured her. Served with feathery mashed potato puffs, a light salad, and steamed vegetables, the lunch would not be too heavy. And, I added with a smile, beef tenderloin was something a caterer simply **could not** fake.

As Nora and I had drunk cup after cup of spiced apple cider in her mammoth kitchen, I'd assured her that things would go well. I had a long list of references, which I handed to her. She'd been very jovial, waving her hand and saying she was easy to please. I'd smiled. But now I was more wary, as I wanted to keep Julian's experience in the back of my mind.

I didn't have time to ponder this issue, but I **did** need to make the Journey Cake. If the party did not go forward, I could serve it at Gus's christening the following day. I drained my espresso cup and put it into the sink. Unfortunately, the first time I'd done a dry run of Nora's, or rather, Charlie Baker's Journey Cake recipe, it had flopped. It had fallen, sunk, collapsed. If you wanted a historic angle, you'd have to think of San Francisco after the 1906 earthquake.

Once again, I edged over to the espresso maker.

Too much caffeine, you drink too much caffeine, I heard my doctor saying. Tough tacks, I'd replied. And anyway, the machine felt like my anchor. "Or warm teddy bear," Tom had joked.

Well, I needed a hug from my teddy bear, not only because of worry over how Arch and Julian were dealing with Dusty's death, but also because I had something infinitely more banal to ponder: the plumbers and their work, or lack thereof, at the Roundhouse. I remembered an old joke we used to tell back in New Jersey. I'd always thought it came from **The Tonight Show,** but I wasn't sure:

A doctor calls a plumber in the middle of the night because his toilet is running and keeping him awake. The plumber drives out and fixes the problem in about fifteen minutes. A week later, the doctor receives a bill for four hundred dollars. Enraged, he calls the plumber to complain. "I'm a doctor and I don't even charge sixteen hundred bucks an hour!" And the plumber calmly replies, "I didn't either when I was a doctor."

I fixed myself a one-shot espresso, drank it down, and put in a call to Front Range Plumbing. As usual, I got their machine. I told them who I was and reminded them this Monday evening, that is, in three days, I had an event to cater at the Roundhouse. I needed the plumbing fixed. Please, I added, before hanging up.

Well, I consoled myself as I again rinsed a cup, if the guys laying the pipe were not done, we would have to hold the post-ribbon-cutting event for the new Mountain Pastoral Center in a small room at the Aspen Meadow Country Club. Luckily, a very foresighted Marla had booked it "just in case."

"Hello, Goldy, are you in there?" Marla's voice seemed to be coming from far away. "I'm dropping my Mercedes off for some work in a few minutes, and a repairman is driving me out to Creekside Spa. I'm supposed to be at the spa in half an hour. Do you want me to stay with you for a while longer, or not?"

"Yes, please stay."

"Let me make us all some more coffee." Tom was suddenly at my side. "Sit down, Goldy."

"I don't want any more caffeine, thanks."

Tom lowered his voice. "Are you all right?"

I shrugged and didn't mention the Journey Cake, the food for the christening and the ribbon-cutting receptions, the plumbing problems, or Dusty. Instead, I sat down at our kitchen table next to Julian, who looked disconsolate. Was he remembering a time he'd been with Dusty, to the movies, for a hike? Was he recalling what it was like to kiss her? I didn't want to think about it.

Tom, all assurance, placed a pair of cups under the nozzles and pressed buttons. Rich ropes of espresso hissed out. Marla placed plump, bejeweled hands on Julian's and my arms.

"You two should take some time off," she advised.

I snorted; Julian looked out the window. Tom placed the cups in front of Marla and Julian, then raised an eyebrow in my direction.

"Miss G., Julian, Marla's right." He unhooked his cell phone from his belt. "Let me call Victim Assistance."

I squealed, "Forget it!" with such ferocity that Tom put down his phone and patted my shoulder.

"Okay, Miss G.," he murmured. "Whatever you want."

"Goldy. Julian." Marla's voice was full of alarm. "Don't cook today, please. Don't even stay at home. Come with me to the spa. We can leave now and I'll call them on the cell, book the two of you with the same package I'm getting. They take guys, Julian, no worries. You could each get a ninety-minute massage, oil and water treatment, full-body wrap—"

I cleared my throat. Did neither Tom nor Marla understand that they **just weren't helping**? Julian gave me a knowing glance. Finally he stood up and clicked buttons on my kitchen computer. I squinted. He'd brought up my catering schedule and was pushing more buttons. My printer spat out recipes.

Oh yes, Julian, also in the food business, knew that cooking healed. The two of us could try the Journey Cake again. Creaming butter and sugar, sifting flour, and mixing, mixing, mixing: all these would help. Listening to Tom and Marla, on the other hand, was driving me nuts.

"All right, all right, I give up. My body will be done at half past two," Marla said, her voice suddenly plaintive. "But my car won't be done until five. I hate to bring this up, Goldy, but you promised to pick me up at the spa. Want me to get the repairman to come get me?"

"No, no, I'll do it. It'll help me get my mind off the fact that I promised Sally Routt I'd look into her daughter's death."

I was escorting her to the front door, but she stopped in the hallway so she could point a crimson-painted nail at my face. "You're nuts. You also look like hell. Don't go anywhere without me. I mean, after you pick me up."

I smiled. "So does that mean you're willing to come down to Christian Brothers High School with me to pick up Arch?"

An unexpected cloud passed over Marla's features. She mumbled, "You're not taking him for another driving lesson, are you?"

"C'mon, girlfriend. I am, after all, a very good teacher."

"That's what I'm worried about," she said. "That and the fact that Arch asked if he could try out my Mercedes."

"Oh yes? Let's see, your new car's at least five months old. I mean, it already needs work. If you let Arch drive it sometime, well, who knows—"

The bejeweled fingers flashed in front of my eyes. "I know you're kidding, so don't even finish that thought." With a mumbled farewell, she flounced out.

When I came back into the kitchen, Tom was arranging slices of goat cheese and cooked beets on salads of mixed field greens. Julian was concentrating on measuring out ingredients for a vinaigrette.

"C'mere, Miss G." Tom motioned me forward, and I walked into his arms. "I'm in this crime-fighting business. I know you never get used to . . . what you saw last night."

"Yeah. You're right." My voice next to his shoulder was muffled. I shuddered, and he pulled me in tighter. "She was just so . . . so—"

"I know. Young. Unfinished. Hopeful."

"Right." I pulled away from Tom. "I need to make a call."

"Goldy," Tom said, "take it easy for a while, will you?"

"Just one call," I replied, thinking of Sally's plea that I help her find out what had happened to her daughter. I snagged the phone and my purse and slipped into the living room. There, I took out my little handheld and looked up the home number of Wink Calhoun, receptionist at H&J. I tapped in the numbers, without knowing what I was going to say. Wink was, had been, Dusty's closest friend at the firm. But Wink and I were also chums of a kind, since she had adopted Latte, a basset hound we had inherited from a friend.

Wink answered on the first ring. I could hear Latte howling in the background. "Hello?" As usual, Wink's Southern drawl was more pronounced when she was upset. "Goldy? I have caller ID," she explained, her voice cracking. "What happened to Dusty? The police have been here, and Richard is on his way over . . . Latte! Stop howling, please!"

The dog ignored her.

"Oh, Wink," I said, "I'm so sorry. I know how close you and Dusty were—"

"I'm in **hail**." Hell. Yeah; me, too. Her voice turned pleading. "Why would someone do this?"

"I don't know. Do you want to come over to our place? I have to go out for a while, but my husband, Tom, and our family friend Julian Teller are here. I . . . just thought you might not want to be alone."

"I can't." **Caint**. "King Richard is bringing over some work for me to do here at my house. The

cops won't let us back into . . . back into . . ."
She started crying again, then clearly made a huge
effort to stop. "I'd like to see you."

"You want to come to our house later?" I asked.
"Say for dinner?"

Another sob. "I don't know. I'm not feeling so
good. I want to know why someone did this. Can't
you help the cops? Haven't you done that before?
What if somebody gets away with this crime?"

"I'm trying, Wink. Look, come over to our
house when you finish your work, okay? Julian
Teller will be here and can let you in."

"Well, maybe."

"You know how you were talking about my
helping with the case, Wink?" When she **mmm-
hmmed,** I made my voice firm. "I was hoping
you could write down everything Dusty was
working on."

"**I** don't know that stuff. That's why they had
her doing it."

My stomach was growling, I was exhausted, and
Wink was being Wink.

"Well, if you can think of anything, anything at
all, we could go over it later." That was about as
far as I was going to get in one phone call, I reasoned. People want you to figure something out,
but when you ask them to do some work in helping
with the figuring, they get schizzy. We signed off.

"Hey," I said, surveying the kitchen table, which Tom had carefully set with three place settings. "I just realized I'm starving."

Tom beamed. Soon he and Julian and I were tucking into beds of crunchy greens, whose accents of sweet, crunchy fall beets and creamy, tart cheese were perfectly complemented by Tom's sharp balsamic vinaigrette and the soft rolls he'd heated—with a pat of butter melting inside each one.

"So who were you on the phone with?" Julian asked, once we were washing the dishes.

"Wink Calhoun. Remember she took Latte off our hands when Scout kept attacking him?" Julian and Tom nodded, their faces grim. Our adopted cat had not taken well to the new, ultrafriendly basset hound, and had used his claws to show it. "She's the receptionist at Hanrahan and Jule. Anyway, I invited her over here for dinner, hope that's okay. She might be willing to talk to us about her best friend at that law firm, Dusty Routt."

Tom's cell rang and he moved into the hallway. When he came back, he asked if Julian would be staying at the house to cook. When Julian replied that he was, Tom said he was going down to the department. Before leaving, he gave me another hug and told me to call him if anything, anything at all, came up. I promised I would, and he took off.

Julian placed the printed-out recipes for Donald

Ellis's birthday party in a neat pile on the counter. "Where do you want to start?"

"Worst first," I replied.

So. With the index card that Nora Ellis had given me for her husband's birthday cake laid on the counter, Julian and I began placing the ingredients on our workspace: unsalted butter, apple cider, flour, spices.

"What, no eggs? Why isn't there a real recipe?" Julian wondered aloud. "Are you just supposed to add things in order without a thought as to how they're incorporated?" He stopped measuring sugar and stared at the list of ingredients. "This recipe doesn't look right."

I sighed, placed the butter in the mixer, and flipped the switch. "I know. The folks coming across the country in covered wagons didn't have all our ingredients, and I know most recipes for Journey Cake don't have eggs. But I've tasted Journey Cake, and it's good. So you're right. Something is wrong with Nora's recipe, or rather, Charlie Baker's recipe—"

"But Charlie Baker was a **great** cook," Julian interjected. "I know he just listed ingredients on his paintings, but everything I've made from them has been great."

"Ditto. Maybe I messed this thing up when I made it the first time. Plus, the recipe needs to be doubled to make enough for the party. My proportions could have been off."

Julian stared at the mixer blades cutting swathes through the butter. "Are you sure this was one of Charlie's recipes? **Nora Ellis** sure doesn't cook, and she proudly informed me that **her** mother grew up with a cast of thousands. Thousands of servants, that is."

"The cake is related to her present for Donald." I picked up the wax paper cradling the sugar and allowed it to snow into the butter. "She's giving him a painting by Charlie Baker. It was one of the last ones he did before he died. He gave it the name **Cake Series II**."

Julian whistled. "That must have set her back a bit. Last I heard, Charlie's paintings of food, with the ingredients lettered underneath, were worth fifty thousand each. And up. That's a lot of cakes."

"I know, I know. But I was happy for Charlie to make all that money, even if he had an awful short time to spend it. Once he got that diagnosis of pancreatic cancer, all the money in the country couldn't help him."

"**Such** a bummer," Julian agreed.

"So I want to get his recipe right. This time, anyway."

Julian nodded. I added half the dry ingredients

to the sugar and butter, stirred carefully, poured in the cider, then tipped in the rest of the dry ingredients.

"Looks awful thick," Julian mused.

"Like cement." The biceps and triceps in my arms were nowhere near equal to the task, so Julian took over while I buttered the pan. "Sometimes coffee-cake batter is really thick," I said hopefully. "Cookie batter, too, and both of them turn out moist and great."

Julian scraped the batter into the pan and slid it into the oven. Then he sat down at the kitchen table and put his head in his hands.

"Oh God, Julian, I'm sorry. You want to go up and rest?"

"No, boss, it's not that. It's . . . It's Dusty. I mean, I hadn't seen her too much over the past couple of years—almost three years, I guess, since I started college. We broke up when she was . . . well, seventeen, I guess. But we always got along after that. I mean, we were **friends**. I just . . . imagined she'd always be there, you know?" He exhaled. "You really don't think that kids you went to school with are going to be murdered."

"I know." I sat down beside him. "I'm sorry. Wink's going to be a wreck, too." Julian rubbed his face. "She and Dusty were such great buds. I can't imagine what **she's** feeling right now."

"This is **so** bad."

I murmured comfort while Julian ran his hands through his short, dark brown hair. Julian had first come into our lives with a bleached-blond Mohawk haircut, and an over-the-top hostile attitude. He'd gradually become an indispensable part of our family, inspiring Arch with his dedication to swimming and studying, inspiring **me** by being a genius in the kitchen, and gradually dropping his chip-on-the-shoulder to wrap all of us in a stubborn, bearlike affection. Yet like Arch, he now felt desolate and guilty.

I peeked in at the cake, which looked as if it was shrinking into a hard sponge. I muttered a curse under my breath. Julian looked in the oven and shook his head.

"Just make a regular butter cake," Julian said. "Trust me, Goldy. Nora Ellis will **never** know the difference."

"Yeah. But what if, one day, she decides she **wants** to cook? And if she tries to make Journey Cake and it flops, she'll ask me why I didn't use her recipe, and demand her money back."

"She might ask for her money back, yeah, but she is **much** too tied up with shopping, manicures, and talking on the phone with her girlfriends ever to want to cook, or ever to bake a cake. Why is this recipe so important, anyway?"

"Because it's on the painting. Have to say, now I'm really curious to know if Charlie screwed up this recipe, or if Nora did when she copied it down. But I don't know where I'd get another recipe from Charlie Baker to test."

Julian bit his lip, deep in thought. "Wait a sec. Don't you remember when we did that fund-raising spaghetti party for the football uniforms at Arch's new school? Turns out, Charlie Baker was an orphan who went to the Christian Brothers High School, back when it was an orphanage. He gave them a bunch of his paintings, and they're hanging in one of the halls. Didn't you see them? I just glanced at a couple on the way to the men's room. What caught my eye was the one for Asparagus Quiche."

"Oh, man, now I'm **really** curious. Let me phone the school."

I put in a call to CBHS, where an obliging secretary said they were asked for Charlie's recipes all the time. They'd put together a leaflet that they sold for five bucks—payable to the Football Boosters—to anyone who wanted one. I asked the secretary about the quiche, and if she'd heard of Charlie's **Cake Series.** Maybe **I** or **II**? She had no idea what I was talking about.

"But we'd be very happy to sell you a booklet," she sang out. "We keep them in with his paintings, so people can see the real thing if they want. We had to move them out of the hallway," she said, her voice suddenly morose. "They got too valuable to keep them hanging between the lockers."

I thanked her, hung up, and stared at Nora's card again. "I **still** think Nora could have copied it down wrong. Perhaps Charlie was getting addled toward the end of his life."

Julian shrugged. "It's more likely Nora screwed it up. If the CBHS secretary doesn't know about Charlie's cake recipes, then let's just make 'Old Reliable.'"

"That's a possibility. What would I do without you, Julian?"

"Fall apart," Julian muttered, but then he smiled as he removed the hard disk of fallen cake from the oven.

I was taking out more butter and eggs when the doorbell rang. When I looked through the security peephole, I saw Nora Ellis, tall, blond, and blue-eyed, looking perfect in a herringbone blazer and black pants, standing next to Ookie Claggett, wife of Alonzo Claggett, aka Claggs. Ookie, a muscled, short-haired brunette, was always dressed for squash. Today, despite the fact that it was now October, she wore white shorts and a white T-shirt with the logo of Aspen Meadow Country Club.

She was even carrying a squash racket, which she lofted and waved at the peephole.

My heart vibrated in my chest as I opened the door.

"You need help?" Julian yelped from the kitchen.

"No, thanks."

"Hi there," I said as I slid out onto the front porch. I certainly did not want to precipitate another conflict between Julian and Nora Ellis. "We're working inside," I stammered, "so things are a mess and I can't . . . well, you two probably heard about the . . . death at H&J this morning."

"Oh, heavens," said Ookie, tapping her racket on her thigh. "We did. That **poor** girl."

I couldn't interpret her tone. According to Marla, who kept track of such things, Nora Ellis and Ookie Claggett had a love-hate, gossip-dependent, ultracompetitive friendship. I addressed Nora. "Under the circumstances, Mrs. Ellis, Nora, I . . . didn't think you'd want to go ahead with—"

"My husband's birthday party?" Her voice was querulous as she brushed the curtain of platinum hair back from her fine-featured face. "Well, I don't know what to do, actually. He's a mess. Everyone at the firm is."

"Well, um, you might want to ask him about the

party. It's possible he'll think it . . . wouldn't work."

"I know," she said. "Maybe we shouldn't go ahead with it. Still, I think everyone desperately needs cheering up." She hesitated. "Were you able to make the cake?" she asked.

"I'm working on it right now. Actually, just double-checking here, but do you still happen to have that list of ingredients?"

"Why, yes," said Nora, surprised. While Ookie sighed and rolled her eyes and indicated this was a huge waste of her time, Nora dug around in her Prada bag until she found an index card. "Do you want to just take this?" she asked.

"No, I'll copy it, thanks." I excused myself, wiggled back through the front door, and returned with my own index card and a pen. Nora proceeded to read me the exact list of ingredients we'd already used. "Are you set now?"

"Absolutely," I said, trying to sound more confident than I felt.

"All right, then, I **will** check with Donald," she said as she and Ookie turned to go. After a moment, she added, "Everyone is going to be so upset, if we do go forward. Maybe you need some help."

"No, thanks, I'm fine—" I began.

She lifted her chin and shook her blond hair in a

gesture of impatience. "Tell you what. If Donald is okay with us having the party, then we'll do it."

"Uh, when you make a decision, I just need to know as soon as—"

But Nora and Ookie were already walking toward a black Hummer.

When I returned to the kitchen, I slapped my index card on the counter and told Julian the content of my conversation with the two associates' wives. He raised his eyebrows, as in **I told you so**.

I eyed the shrunken Frisbee of cake, then checked my new index card with its list. The ingredients were the same. "To hell with Nora's cake. Let's whip up Old Reliable."

"That's the spirit." Julian began creaming the butter while I assembled the dry ingredients. During my years at boarding school, Old Reliable had been a staple of our bake sales. To buy new sticks for the field-hockey team or fund a field trip to Chancellorsville, the day students would bring in platters of cookies and cakes that we boarding students would then slice and sell after lunch. I had a vivid memory of girls carrying paper napkins topped with huge slices of tender yellow cake that had been slathered with chocolate buttercream icing. Those Southerners knew how to cook, I'd give them that. Maybe our school bake sales weren't on the level of some of the fancy fund-raisers we did at St. Luke's Episcopal, but the principle of "You Can Eat Blamelessly if You're Raising Money" was identical.

If we did indeed cater Donald Ellis's birthday party, I would need to double the ingredients, I realized, as I printed out my old recipe. I worked the math and wrote up the proportions, then handed the paper to Julian to make sure I'd done it right. He recalculated the ingredients and found I'd only failed to double the baking powder. **Agh!**

"You're distracted," Julian said encouragingly. "I can't believe you're trying to . . . well, I can believe it, given everything you've told me about that law firm. Let's boogie on this cake so you can pick up Arch and Gus on time."

I sifted the dry ingredients, then creamed the sugar into the butter while Julian separated eight eggs. Julian rarely complained, and he took to his tasks with determination, eyeing each yolk and white carefully to make sure none of one mixed in with the other. Working with him in the kitchen was like skiing with someone you've known forever. He goes one way, you go the other, and no one skis over anyone's toes.

We put the cake pans into the oven and observed the batter's progress through the glass, as anxious as parents watching their **own** kid ski down a slope for the first time. But the cake rose beautifully, and emerged puffed and golden.

After we'd placed the pans on racks to cool, Julian frowned at Charlie's cake recipe, or rather his recipe for cake **failure**.

"It really **was not** like Charlie to do this incorrectly," Julian said, his voice stubborn.

"Well, let it go for now. Julian? Sally Routt has asked me to look into Dusty's death. Just tell me, how did Dusty seem to you, when you were going to school together? I mean, was she friendly, standoffish, smart, not so smart, what?"

Julian turned, leaned against the counter, and folded his arms. After a moment, he said, "She was smart, yeah. I mean, Elk Park Prep gave her a full ride, until everything fell apart."

"We're talking about before the Routts moved in across the street."

"Yeah."

Julian pointed to the espresso machine and raised his eyebrows, as in **How many shots?** I thought, **To hell with my doctor,** and said, "A couple. With some cream, if you don't mind. Thanks. Whenever I do get to bed, I'm going to sleep no matter what."

Julian's sneakers squeaked as he moved quickly around the kitchen to fetch demitasse cups, whipping cream, and to refill our bowl of sugar, which he had emptied. He pulled the shots, doused mine with cream, and placed the cups on the kitchen table. I sat down and, as usual, averted my eyes as he proceeded to ladle obscene amounts of sugar into his coffee. Why did he have such perfect teeth? I wondered.

"What do you mean," I prompted him, "until everything fell apart?"

"Okay," he began, after taking a preliminary slurp, frowning, and dumping in another dose of the sweet stuff. "You have to remember, this was before teachers started being held accountable if they had sex with students. It's hard to think of a time when the student got blamed, but that's exactly what used to happen. Anyway, that's certainly what went down at Elk Park Prep when Dusty had an affair with the drama teacher, Mr. Ogden. Ogden was totally pathetic. He kept moaning about how his acting career was being foiled because his wife was so jealous of the time he spent on his work. Everybody felt sorry for him. Or at least, the girls did."

My stomach churned, and it wasn't from the espresso, which was actually excellent. Men could be just as manipulative as women, thank you very much.

"Nobody felt sorrier for him than Dusty," Julian went on. "And then she got pregnant, even though Ogden told her he'd had a vasectomy! Dusty told me later that she really had thought Mr. Ogden would leave Mrs. Ogden and be with her, but forget that. Next thing anyone knew, Ogden was going to the headmaster, claiming Dusty was a slut who was falsely accusing him of fathering her child, which he could not have done, because he'd had that vasectomy. And also, Ogden insisted, Dusty needed to be expelled because she was with child, and that had violated the terms of her scholarship." Julian finished his coffee and made a face. "Anyway, that lily-livered son of a bitch headmaster did expel her. Ogden's version of the story came out in the papers. You didn't see it? Dusty had falsely accused a teacher of impregnating her, blah, blah, blah."

"No, I never saw that. Poor Dusty. Couldn't she have insisted on a paternity test?"

Julian held up a stubby finger. "While Dusty was studying for her GED, she had an early-term miscarriage. This was while the Habitat house was being built. Then Dusty's family moved in across the street from you, and she started to work for Mignon Cosmetics. She was determined to put Ogden behind her, and she became really focused on getting ahead, being ambitious. Remember?" I nodded. "After another cosmetics company hired her, she thought she was on her way up, but **that** cosmetics company went belly-up. So then Dusty got her associate's degree down at Red Rocks. It just took her eighteen months, if you can believe it. And then Dusty's uncle, Richard Chenault, joined the law firm in Aspen Meadow, and felt sorry for his niece. Supposedly. Anyway, he hired her and is paying for her tuition bills at the Mile-High Paralegal Institute."

I sipped my coffee. "Do you know anything about this brother, Edgar?"

"Just that he died in custody after being picked up on a DUI. He got beaten along the way, but nobody seems to know exactly what happened. Yeah, **right**. When I was going out with Dusty, Mrs. Routt could not stop talking about Edgar's death. She was, like, obsessed. Then one day, she said she wasn't going to talk about it anymore, because it was making her totally nuts, and she needed to pay attention to the present. She didn't tell you about that either, did she?"

"No, she didn't." I stared out the window at aspen leaves being blown off the trees at the side of our house. "Still, no wonder Sally Routt hates the police and the press."

Julian said, "Yeah, no wonder."

Chapter 7

Julian offered to clean up. He said it would help him deal with how ticked off the story about Dusty always made him feel. When I thanked him, he nodded, his face still flushed from his outburst detailing Dusty's problems. Even though the lovely scent of baked cake was a tempting reason to stay and try to chat some more, I thought it better to make a quick exit. When I stood up to help Julian gather dirty bowls, beaters, and pans, he stopped me.

"C'mon, let me do this by myself. You remember I'm cooking dinner for Marla and spending the night over there, right?"

Right, right, he had told us this. Marla was, in fact, Julian's aunt by blood, and I was always happy to see them getting together. Julian promised to be back in the morning to help me finish the prep for Donald Ellis's birthday party.

That was the thing about Julian, I reflected, as I bounded up the stairs to wash my hair. He was reliable and he was kind. And there was something else. There's a stereotype embedded in people's mind, and it runs through literature, movies, and TV. And that is that men are unemotional, logical, and analytical. Living with Arch, Julian, and Tom, I'd concluded that nothing could be further from the truth. Okay, so none of them was prone to teary outbursts. But they felt injustices, cruelties, and loss just as severely as any female I'd ever met.

I thought about poor Dusty as the warm water poured over my scalp. Everything she'd tried to have—a career, money, a relationship, a good education—all these had come to naught. And then she'd been killed.

A rock formed in my throat as I blew my hair dry. After I pulled on a sweater and denim skirt, I felt dizzy, and sat on Tom's and my bed. I was severely sleep-deprived. But I was also suffering from finding a corpse the previous night.

Work, business, activity, forward movement— all these were needed to help me get going again. I had to pick up Marla at the Creekside Spa, then dash down to Denver to collect Arch and Gus. And I was determined to grab a recipe booklet and look at the collection of Charlie Baker's paintings at CBHS. Were all of his recipes screwed up, or just Nora's? I wanted to know, doggone it.

I headed up Main Street, now festooned with crepe-paper ghosts, skeletons, and pumpkins. Ordinarily, I loved Halloween, chiefly because it marked the beginning of the big party season. Most caterers—and I was no exception—made the bulk of their profit during the two months between Halloween and New Year's. I already had a slew of events scheduled to take place at the Roundhouse, which was situated beside Cottonwood Creek several miles before the spa. If I could ever get the **doggone** plumbing completed . . . but I veered away from that thought.

I had already booked a designer to come in and decorate the Roundhouse for Christmas. My throat again closed up, thinking of the five thousand dollars it was going to cost me to transform the place into a garlanded indoor forest twinkling with "millions"—so said the decorator blithely— of tiny colored lights. But that was what well-heeled clients expected these days for a Christmas party, and I'd transferred the cost of the decorations into the contracts for office parties, wedding receptions, family-and-friends dinners, and ladies'-clubs holiday luncheons. So far, the only one who had blinked was yours truly, and that was because the plumbing was running me another ten thousand bucks.

When I passed the conference center, I steeled myself to have a look, since the head contractor had told me firmly not to come by anymore, as all my questions slowed down his workers. Happily, despite the cold weather, I saw half a dozen men in heavy work outfits plodding across the ground outside the hexagonal building. Several trucks in the lot were parked at odd angles, and one of them boasted a winch. Did that mean pipe was being laid? I certainly hoped so. I hadn't had an event for the last couple of weeks, as people didn't seem to want to get married or be otherwise festive in the latter part of September and early part of October. Up until today, I'd been thankful for my breakfast-meeting contract at Hanrahan & Jule.

Yes, I thought as my hands gripped the steering wheel. **Up until today**.

At twenty past two I pulled into the parking lot of the Creekside Spa and eased my van with its painted logo "Goldilocks' Catering, Where Everything Is Just Right!" between a gold Mercedes and a black BMW. I waited in fear for a slender, imperious receptionist to come out and tell me to move my vehicle to the service entrance! Now! This had happened more often than I cared to remember. But I still wasn't quite used to it.

I turned off the van's engine. It grumbled and shook, then sighed to silence. Across the street, Cottonwood Creek, swollen with snowmelt from the first mountain storms, surged over a clump of rocks, then flowed placidly farther on. On this side of the road, I could just make out the grumble of earthmoving machines and the **beep-beep-beep** of tractors in reverse. Peering to the edge of the parking lot, I saw tractors and dump trucks moving and smoothing dirt, one more example of the relentless construction that always seemed to envelop Aspen Meadow.

My skin prickled with gooseflesh. This was the first time I had been alone, really alone and able to **think,** since I'd tripped over Dusty's body. I swallowed. Then again, maybe I didn't want to **think.** Maybe I didn't want to get myself all depressed. After all, I still had to pick up Arch and Gus.

Gus. The story of Gus, Arch's half brother, was what made the memories of death come up anyway. It seemed that when he'd been married to me, Dr. John Richard Korman's endless list of sexual conquests had included Talitha Vikarios, daughter of Ted and Ginger Vikarios, who now lived in Aspen Meadow. Talitha had become pregnant by the Jerk, and, in a supreme act of putting others before self, had left home rather than risk destroying our family. When Talitha died in a freak car accident in Utah, her son Gus came to Aspen Meadow to live with his grandparents. With him, he brought a letter to me from his dead mother, telling the truth of Gus's paternity and begging me to forgive her and to be compassionate toward her son. Which, of course, I'd been happy—more than happy—to be.

Arch, taken aback at first with the prospect of having a living, breathing half brother, had slowly come to welcome Gus. The two boys looked so similar, they could have been twins. Following the advice of a counselor, the Vikarioses had sent Gus to the Christian Brothers High School, where Arch was a sophomore. We had Gus to dinner at least once a week, and to sleep over as much as he wanted. At fourteen and a half, Gus, confident and outgoing in a way that Arch was not, had adjusted quickly to his new environment. He laughed and joked with Arch's friends and worked hard at his school assignments. Despite the hippie atmosphere of the Moab commune where he'd grown up, Gus was fiercely competitive for grades. Gus also excelled at soccer, where he had quickly become a much-valued member of the CBHS junior varsity.

As far as my predator-bird mom eyes could tell, Arch was not jealous of ninth-grader Gus's popularity at CBHS. Instead, my son was in awe. It even seemed that Gus truly cherished Arch. He regaled us with tales of life on the commune, and was always eager to invite Arch to his grandparents' house to play games or watch movies. An unexpected by-product of all this affection was that Gus was being baptized at our parish, St. Luke's Episcopal Church, this Sunday. "Because it's important to Arch," Gus had solemnly told me. But how could it be important to Arch, who had stopped going to church? Another question for the ages.

The only problem with all this as far as I could see was that the christening was being done by Bishop Sutherland. Yes, Father Pete was still recovering from his coronary, and yes, we'd all agreed that the bishop should do the honors. But hearing Julian's stories had suddenly made me wary.

The biblical adage "Speak of the devil, and he doth appear" stunned me out of reverie. Tall, slender, white-haired Bishop Uriah Sutherland himself, wearing (yes!) a purple polo shirt that said "Bish! Bish! Bish!" along with stylish white shorts and expensive running shoes, was standing next to my van, panting. His coarse-featured face was flushed and matched the purple shirt. Had he been jogging? Hadn't he moved here from Utah because he had heart trouble? Was running up Cottonwood Creek Road, which rose from eight thousand to nine thousand feet above sea level, really a good idea? I didn't have time to contemplate these issues, because Bishop Sutherland was using his big bishop's ring to rap on my window.

I pressed the button to lower the window and

gave him what I hoped was a cheerful, inquisitive expression.

"Hi there!" he said, placing an icy hand on my forearm.

"Hi!"

"Could you move your van, please?" he said. "I can't back out." He continued to grip my arm. Did he need help? Was he having a heart attack?

"Uh, sure, I'll move it. No problem. Sure. Sorry!" But I couldn't drive the car if he didn't let go of my left arm. I cleared my throat. "Uh, do you remember me? I'm . . . a relative of Gus Vikarios, whom you're baptizing on Sunday."

"Yes, yes, of course." He let go of my arm to wipe his brow. Then he walked around to the driver side of the black BMW. As I put the van in reverse and eased out of the space and up into the lot, I wondered if he had on one of those medical-alert bracelets, and if he had a cell phone in his car, or what was probably actually his daughter's car.

What is he, your kid? I could hear Tom's voice admonishing me. I sighed as the BMW shot out of its space.

"Was he running?" Marla demanded as she slid into the van's passenger seat. "Don't you think that's dangerous if you have a weak heart? And do you think St. Luke's is paying him enough to buy all his fancy duds, or did Donald and Nora foot his bills?"

"Yes, running is not a good idea if you've had cardiovascular problems, and I don't know who finances his lifestyle. Let's just go get the boys." I drove out of the lot and onto Upper Cottonwood Creek Drive. I had barely noticed the trees on the way up to the spa. But a breeze had picked up, and a sudden shower of golden leaves dappled the windshield. Marla and I squealed with delight as my windshield wipers smacked off the aspens' detritus. We commented on how thick the clusters of lemon-slice leaves were this year, how they quivered and quaked above the trees' thin white trunks. Why does the beauty of nature hurt after the loss of someone you care about? Dusty would never see these forests, would never feel the sweet-scented breeze of fall in Colorado again.

"Have you heard anything about Dusty?" Marla wanted to know.

"Not a word. Tom's down at the department now, so he should find out something. But it looks as if Nora Ellis might go ahead with the party for Donald. She's going to call me back after she talks to him."

Marla shook her head. "I made some inquiries at the spa, after my facial and before my massage. Everyone wanted to know what had happened, so

I told them. I also said you were looking into it, because Sally Routt was so broken up, she asked for your help."

We rounded a curve where stands of blue spruce hugged the road. I tried to think of how to tell Marla that I really **didn't** want people to think of me when someone was killed, just because I was married to a homicide investigator and helped him out from time to time. When I finally told her as much, she shook her head.

"More than time to time, girlfriend. Anyway, some of the gals did give me wary looks, like they wanted to tell me something, or at least they wanted to know dark things about Dusty or the law firm. So I wrote my phone number on little pieces of paper, and handed them all around, and said if anyone had some hot gossip, I was the one who could relay it to you. Hope that's okay."

I exhaled. Was it okay? Sure it was, I reasoned. If a bit of useful information did come in from one of the society ladies, I could just pass it along to Tom, who would forward it to the department. The grateful investigators would be happy to follow up on any leads I provided, wouldn't they?

Don't answer that question.

We passed the Roundhouse, where workers were continuing to hop over the trenches they'd made for the pipe. I tried not to think how much they were charging by the hour.

When we were almost to the interstate, we slowed to enter the parking lot that abutted the garage for Aspen Meadow Imports. The Mercedes was ready. Marla paid and said she wanted us to go down to Denver in it, as it was more comfortable for her than my van. I assented, and left the van at the edge of the lot, which happened to face the office building housing Hanrahan & Jule. Inside the barrier of yellow ribbons, a team of investigators had broken up into small groups to talk among themselves or peer solemnly at the pavement of the parking lot. I shuddered.

"What do you suppose happened to Dusty?" Marla asked, her husky voice lowered a notch.

"She either surprised somebody or somebody was waiting for her. Anyway, she was attacked and fought back enough to break a picture frame." I hesitated. "It looked to me as if she'd been strangled."

"Good God."

"I feel so sorry for Sally. Oh, and by the way, remember how she said she didn't trust the police? Do you want to know why?" I mentioned the stories of Edgar dying in custody, of the drama teacher and Dusty supposedly having an affair, which the drama teacher had vociferously denied.

"Do you remember this story about Ogden, the drama teacher?"

"Where were you, Mars?" Marla said.

"When the Jerk used to bother me, or when I get busy with catering, I don't even glance at the papers."

"Well. That was back when 'blame the woman' was the first thing everyone did." Marla's tone turned bitter. "He claimed Dusty was a slut, and that he'd had a vasectomy anyway, and people believed him. That man has a lot to answer for, but I doubt he ever will. Poor Dusty."

Marla piloted the Mercedes down the mountain toward Denver. We didn't talk, which was unusual for us. I tried just to focus on what I had to do next, which was to check out Charlie Baker's artworks, to pick up Arch and Gus, and to bring them home. And then, hopefully, to visit with Wink Calhoun over dinner.

The Christian Brothers High School lies on twenty acres snuggled at the base of the foothills, just on the westernmost edge of Denver. Set up in the twenties as an orphanage for boys, the institution had evolved into a boys' boarding and day school in the forties, then a boys' day school in the sixties. With the population of Denver and environs burgeoning in the eighties and nineties, the demand for parochial high schools had shot up.

Under pressure from hordes of Catholic parents, CBHS had gone coed and soon doubled its student body to a thousand kids.

But the thing I liked best about CBHS, I thought as I turned off of the interstate and headed south, was the energetic, can-do attitude of the place. Unlike Elk Park Prep, the status-conscious, materialistically driven school where Arch had spent three miserable years, the main money emphasis at CBHS was: "We Need to Raise the Money for More Needy Kids' Tuition!" To my astonishment, different parent groups and committees enthusiastically ran all manner of fund-raisers throughout the year, and ended up bringing in half a million dollars annually, earmarked entirely for need-based scholarships. And what competition there was to raise more money than the other groups! And what medals and buttons and ribbons did they all vie for at the end of the year, given to folks who had shown the most devotion to fund-raising! The place never ceased to amaze me.

I turned into the parking lot in front of the long, squat brick school building with its mansard roof composed entirely of asphalt tiles. As usual, the front steps and sparse lawn were sprinkled with students engaged in their customary activities: chatting as they put cans from a drop box into paper bags for the Catholic Soup Kitchen, calling to one another as they threw footballs back and forth, or counting out bills from a cash box as they sat at card tables, readying themselves to sell tickets to one event or another. Why weren't these kids in class? I always wondered. They must have the last period off, I figured. And they wanted to get the jump on parents arriving to pick up their kids. Who knew? Anyone arriving might order a dozen tickets to **Bye Bye Birdie**!

Marla ran the gauntlet with me. I followed as she scampered through, donating fifty bucks to the Halloween canned-food drive and purchasing a pair of tickets to **Twelfth Night**. We pushed through the doors to the lobby. It was as unprepossessing as the building's exterior, a wide, low-ceilinged space lined with much-fingerprinted glass cases filled with CBHS hats, gloves, and sweatshirts for sale. Four metal chairs were set up at odd angles on the linoleum floor, as if students waiting for this or that permission never stayed in them for very long.

"Goldy!" cried Rose, the receptionist, who sat behind a half wall that stretched the width of the lobby. Rose, who had to be in her late fifties, had a mop of silvery gray curls, a thin, pretty face, and enormous brown eyes that were magnified by oversize silver-framed glasses. She rushed out into the lobby to greet us. Clad in a gray sweater with matching pants, Rose had the figure of a twenty-year-old. At night, she'd told me, she taught aerobics at her church. Whenever I saw her, I felt tired.

"Rose," I began, after introducing Marla, "we'd like to see Charlie Baker's paintings, if you don't mind—"

"Oh, I'm already prepared for you." She held up a formidable bunch of keys. "Just follow me."

We dashed along behind her, following her trail of faint floral cologne that was somehow at odds with the atmosphere of office paper, floor wax, and metal lockers that stretched down echoing hallways. We walked past numerous large prints depicting saints in one or another act of goodness, and at length came to an oversize double wooden door.

Rose proceeded to unlock one of the wide doors. Then, with practiced dexterity, she switched keys to open what looked like a cage door, the kind you see in front of a bank vault.

"I was so sad when we had to do this," Rose explained as the cage door shuddered and creaked open. "But the school was broken into once, and my cash box was stolen. It only had a hundred dollars in it. Just think if the thieves had gotten one of these!" She reached in to flip on an overhead panel of fluorescent lights, which buzzed and then flickered to life. Rose shook her head before leading us into the gallery.

About two dozen paintings by Charlie Baker hung on yellow-painted cement-block walls. They were all pictures of food—that is, of the dishes he'd loved to prepare. Charlie had laughingly told me that he was a "recovering chef," one who had turned to cooking for friends and painting—for himself, for fun—after a distant aunt died and unexpectedly bequeathed him "a packet," as he jokingly put it. After quitting his job—he'd been one of the early chefs at the Roundhouse, in its heyday—Charlie had gleefully retired. But he hadn't stopped working. Instead, he treated friends and neighbors—yours truly included, since we baked cookies and pies together each year for the St. Luke's bazaar—to his exquisite, lovingly prepared dishes.

And here some of them were, in paintings that stood out against the bland yellow walls: Braised Chicken Breasts with Fresh Tomatoes and Scallions, All-American Apple Pie, Chocolate-Dipped Dried Fruits, even the Asparagus Quiche Julian had mentioned. Charlie had reveled in painting pictures of the dishes he prepared, and he always rendered the ingredients underneath in perfect calligraphic letters. Those of us who had been lucky enough to eat at his house were able to **ooh** and **aah** over the artwork, once we'd **oohed** and **aahed** over the dinner.

I think Charlie would have been content just to keep cooking and painting for himself and his pals forever. But then Father Biesbrouck, a former rector at St. Luke's, had urged him to try selling his paintings at the bazaar. Somehow, a reporter for a national magazine had ended up at our yearly event, and she'd been so taken with Charlie's art that she'd written a long piece about them, including photographs. She'd entitled the article "Hidden Food Treasures in the West." And the rest, as they say, is history.

Or was. Charlie became prolific and expensive. Oddly, the rector who'd recommended that he sell his art had had a nervous breakdown—cause unknown—and had committed suicide. This past January, Charlie had been diagnosed with the pancreatic cancer that should have been his death knell, if he hadn't suffered a fatal fall in March. Late at night, he'd lost his balance and slipped, the police had hypothesized, so that he'd tumbled down the long, curved staircase at his house. He'd broken his neck. With no signs of foul play and no suicide note, law enforcement had concluded that Charlie's death had been an accident.

Reportedly, he'd left his estate, plus a huge inventory of paintings that were meant to be sold, to benefit two causes: the Christian Brothers High School, where he'd been raised, and St. Luke's Episcopal Church, with the proviso that the funds be used to build a clergy retreat house in Aspen Meadow. Charlie had told me that he wanted clergy to be able to rest and pull themselves together when they were feeling low, instead of taking Father Biesbrouck's suicidal route.

"Look at this one," Marla said, startling me. It was entitled **Chocolate Pie with Pecan Crust**. Charlie's thick brushstrokes and lovingly rendered rich tones of brown and gold made the crust look realistically crunchy and the pie filling beckoningly thick and creamy. "Makes me hungry just looking at it," Marla said, her tone morose.

"You see anything you want to make?" Rose's voice rose querulously in the hushed space. "The booklets with his recipes are over here. I just thought you might want to look at these before you made your decision."

I blinked once, twice. Okay, so I hadn't had more than two hours of sleep since . . . well, when? Wednesday night? And now it was Friday afternoon. But still, I couldn't help but reflect that my dear, sweet, young neighbor was lying in the Furman County Morgue, and I was here looking at artworks and talking about recipes, trying to figure out if Charlie could have messed up ingredients for any other dish. It was all too much.

"Maybe we should buy that recipe leaflet from you now," I said to Rose, my voice cracking. "I need to pick up Arch and Gus. Thanks for showing us the paintings," I added belatedly.

"I understand," Rose said in a soft voice, and for a moment, I wondered if she had heard about Dusty, too.

Leaflet in hand, I followed Marla back out to her Mercedes. En route, she purchased another fifty dollars' worth of grocery coupons; the kids could use them "however they wanted," Marla said, for their canned-food drive. I shook my head, but my friend muttered that it made her feel good and was cheaper than therapy.

Once Marla had started the engine and eased behind a line of vans and station wagons filled with waiting parents, she asked, "Couldn't we just have gone to the door where the students come out and waited for Gus and Arch? If there was a big crowd of students, we could just call out to them."

I actually laughed. "Not if you value maintaining any shred of your relationship with Arch. Or Gus either, for that matter. You want to embarrass them to death by **calling out to them**? Forget it. We can just hold on until they notice us. Trust me."

It didn't take as long as she thought it would, for

Arch's antennae worked pretty well in the pickup department, even if it was Marla's car and not my trusty van. Gus, who had started chatting with a group of girls, quickly slung his book bag over his shoulder and followed his half brother out to the Mercedes. Belatedly, I remembered Gus's junior-varsity practice. Would we have to wait for him?

"No practice today," Gus announced, as if reading my mind. He tossed his book bag on the floor and scooted into the backseat beside Arch. "Coach is on a business trip. Thanks for getting us. Hi, Marla."

"Yo, kid. You, too, Arch."

"Marla," Arch said patiently, "don't try to talk jive. It doesn't work, okay?"

Marla sighed and hit the pedal. Soon we were on our way back up the interstate. How was I going to gauge if Arch was upset about Dusty? He hadn't ever known her very well, which, at this juncture, I took to be a good thing.

I turned around and faced the boys. Gus, ever energetic, had brought with him the clean smell of boy sweat and notebooks. As he rustled around in his book bag, Arch, quiet and always worried, sat very still and frowned at me for paying undue attention to him.

"What is it, Mom?"

"Just checking on you, that's all."

Gus stopped rummaging around in his books and flopped back on the seat. He raised his eyebrows at Arch, as in **What's she talking about?**

"Our neighbor, Dusty Routt, died this morning," Arch said quickly. To me, he said, "Does Tom know anything yet?"

"No. Sorry, hon."

"Does that mean we can't sell magazine subscriptions tonight?" Gus asked. "I mean, are the neighbors going to be all upset? We've got a deadline on this drive. Maybe we could go to another neighborhood. Marla, could you drive us?"

Marla opened her eyes wide at me, as in **How did I get dragged into this?** But she said, "I suppose so."

Thick pillows of gray cloud had moved in while we were waiting for the boys. As we ascended the steepest part of the interstate, snow began to fall. First there were just a few flakes, rushing toward Marla's windshield at a slant. When we crested the peak of the interstate and entered the wide downward curve to Aspen Meadow, the fall of tiny flakes suddenly thickened. On either side of us, cars began to slow; wipers started sweeping away new layers of flakes.

"I guess this means we won't be able to sell subscriptions," Arch said, with the relief audible in his voice.

"Oh, it's okay to sell stuff when it's snowing," Gus replied, his voice as confident as ever. "I used to do it all the time in Utah. Especially if you don't wear a hat and you have, like, icicles frozen in your hair. Then people buy all kinds of stuff, 'cuz they feel sorry for you."

Arch snorted. "I hate people feeling sorry for me. I've had it my whole life, and it sucks."

Gus said, "Trust me, Arch. It's like power. People feel sorry for you, you can get whatever you want."

I wasn't sure that was true. But with the memory of Dusty's inert body so fresh in my mind, I was reluctant to venture an opinion. In our cooking lessons, I'd come to feel heartily sorry for Dusty, with her lack of money and her high ambitions. Now I'd heard the sad story of her bad luck and mistreatment at the hands of a drama teacher. And then, just when she'd gotten a good job and was moving up in the world, someone had strangled her.

Yes, I felt very sorry for Dusty. I also felt painfully sympathetic toward her mother, Sally.

As Marla pressed the accelerator and urged the Mercedes back up the mountain, I bit the inside of my cheek. Gus could talk all he wanted about sympathy generating power. But it seemed to me that neither Dusty nor Sally had, or had ever had, any power at all.

Chapter 8

When Marla swung into the driveway of Aspen Meadow Imports, a tall mechanic with long, droopy cheeks and a gray ponytail came out waving a rag.

"Wait," he called to us. When he was beside the Mercedes, he said, "You can't leave that food truck here. That van. What does it say? Goldilocks' Catering. We've had trouble with a bear coming down every night and foraging in our garbage."

Under her breath, Marla said, "One bear's food is another bear's trash. But still, can mountain bears read?"

I hated it when people made fun of my Germanic maiden name, but I was prepared to ignore my best friend. To the mechanic, I said, "I'm moving it. I was just helping out a friend."

The mechanic's cheeks drooped even farther. "Okay, lady. Those bears can smell food. I wouldn't want to be responsible if one of 'em broke into your vehicle."

"I'm moving it!"

Marla laughed, then promised she would call if

she heard anything. I thanked her for the ride and bustled Gus and Arch into the van.

At the boys' request, I left them off three blocks from our house. They swore they'd be home by half past five, because they'd be **famished,** Gus said, his smile huge. As usual, Gus was upbeat at the prospect of being a fund-raising vendor of magazines. Arch, on the other hand, was morose, as he hated selling more than having his teeth pulled without anesthetic. But I couldn't even try to cheer him up the way I usually did. In point of fact, I didn't feel as if I had any cheer left.

I pulled my van into the driveway rather than parking it on the street. If by some miracle the plow came through that night, I didn't want to get walled in by a hardpacked, man-made snowdrift. I also didn't want to risk leaving my van on the curb again. When I stepped out into the three-inch-deep icy carpet of snow, I shrieked with surprise. But that didn't stop me from traipsing up and locking the van doors with the remote. I pressed the button twice, so that the security system beeped. This time, I wanted to be **sure** the van was locked.

Completely chilled, I raced through the fall of flakes to the front of the house. Once I'd slammed the door, I leaned on it and shuddered. I let my coat slip to the floor, limped to the living room, and flopped onto the couch. Tom was rattling around in the kitchen, for which I was thankful. Apparently, he hadn't heard me come in.

But our animals had. Scout the cat and Jake the bloodhound rushed to greet me. Well, I shouldn't say that Scout rushed, because that cat never went quickly to anything, even food. But he did stride into the living room and, sensing I might need comfort, dropped his back on top of my shoes and rolled over, all in one smooth movement. **You can pat me if it will make you feel better**. I did, while Jake slobbered kisses on my cheeks. The large hound also began to whine between large liquid tonguings. Don't tell **me** animals can't sense moods.

"There you are," said Tom as he whisked into the living room carrying a silver tray sporting two glasses of sherry, homemade crackers, and a wedge of sharp English cheddar, his favorite. "It's a bit early for a cocktail." His tone was cheery, his handsome face the picture of confidence. "Then again, I thought you might need one."

"What I need most of all is to talk to you."

"One thing at a time, wife."

I smiled my thanks and left to change and wash my hands. By the time I'd pulled on sweats and returned to the living room, Tom had built a cozy fire and set the silver tray on his antique cherrywood butler's tray, which he'd judiciously placed in front of my old sofa when he'd moved into the house.

The scene was typically Tom-and-Goldy. On the one hand, there was Tom's lovingly purchased, laboriously polished cherry furniture. He said taking care of his pieces helped reduce stress from the job. And then there was my old sofa. Once I'd kicked out the Jerk, I'd wanted to remove as many memories of his presence as possible, and I'd had every piece in the living room reupholstered in the cheapest fabric available. It was a sunny orange that I'd determinedly told myself was going to match my new circumstances. Unfortunately, the orange had turned somewhat dingy, and I kept thinking I was going to have everything redone one of these days. But so far, that day had not materialized.

And then there was the sherry, aged and golden, bought by Tom. He'd poured it into antique cut-crystal glasses that had belonged to my grandmother. These, too, felt like Tom's, since he'd salvaged them from a basement cardboard box that I'd hidden behind our Christmas decorations. Talk about erasing memories: I hadn't even remembered packing up the crystal and putting it out of sight some years before. In any event, the glasses were what remained of my breakables, as I'd come to think of them, after John Richard had smashed every dish of our Minton bone china, in one of his numerous fits of rage. Thinking about the Jerk didn't do much for my mood. Squinting at

Tom's tray, I stood at the edge of the living room, immobile.

"Miss G.! I can tell you're not doing so hot. Come and sit by me. Talk to me. I know what you need." Tom's eyes were steadily trained on my face. "You need to eat, drink, talk, and go to bed. How many hours has it been since you had some real sleep? Too many. **Way** too many."

"The last thing I want to do is go to bed," I heard my voice say. "I want to be with you, and with Arch . . . and I'll eat and drink and—" What was that last part? Oh yes, talk. There was that.

"All right," Tom said gently, patting the couch. "Maybe you won't be merry. But at least sit down until you can start cooking and **doing** again."

"Okay, okay."

I moved with a kind of stiff uneasiness onto the couch. I tried not to think. After a minute, I took the glass Tom proffered, and sipped. The sherry tasted like liquid fire. But it helped. So did the crunchy, surprisingly flaky homemade crackers. I took a second bite and looked at Tom. Sharp cheddar cheese? Tangy English mustard? Imported cayenne pepper? I couldn't get my mind even to work on that superficial level: food, work, prepping, catering. I blinked at the fire, and realized this was the first time I'd been sitting still and relaxing in the past twenty-something hours. Even so, all my muscles felt bunched up, tense with despair and confusion.

I felt the glass slip between my fingers. In a voice that seemed to be coming from across the room, I said, "What the hell is going on?"

Tom snagged my glass and put it on the table. "You're tired, wife. You're drained. Maybe you should just go to bed." But instead of ordering me upstairs, he pulled me close and rubbed the small of my back. After a few moments of this, the tautness began to melt.

"I'm afraid to . . . to think."

"I know, I know," Tom murmured. "Why do you suppose I polish furniture? Just take it easy for a few minutes and don't try to use your brain."

But I couldn't. I pulled away from him. "Tell me what's going on at the department," I demanded. "What have they learned?"

Tom ducked his chin. His sea-green eyes assessed me. Then he pulled his mouth into a straight line. "Let's go into the kitchen and work. We can talk there."

Mechanically, I followed Tom to our cooking space. He'd thawed a tenderloin of beef, and I helped him tie it into a perfect roll. Tom had become obsessed with beef lately, and had added to my mail order—the best way to get prime, I'd learned, if not the cheapest—on more than one occasion. In fact, I was serving tenderloins at Donald Ellis's birthday party . . . oh Lord, I didn't want to think about that.

Tom used one of my new sharp-as-the-dickens Japanese knives to insert slivers of garlic all along the surface of the beef. Then he rubbed the roll with oil, sprinkled it with dried rosemary and thyme, packed it with a gravelly layer of ground black peppercorns, and sprinkled it with our French sea salt. And suddenly, with that small detail, I felt my mind drifting back here, to our family, to our life together. Salt. Salt. What had my son said about it, when Tom had waxed lyrical on the taste value of the new crystals?

"Yo, Tom! NaCl is NaCl," Arch had observed, shaking his head.

"Oh, ye of little faith," Tom had intoned, before serving us steaks sprinkled with the little nuggets of flavor. I'd thought it was wonderful; Arch had remarked that it was "still just salt."

Remembering this now, I began to cry. No sobbing, mind you, just a wholly unexpected spill of tears. Oh, what was the matter with me?

Dusty, Dusty. She had been part of a family, too, the Routts, a loving family whose loss I could not begin to contemplate. My mind brought up the image of her pronated wrist, my seemingly endless attempts to breathe life into her limp body.

I'd seen dead people before, of course. But Dusty had been so young, and so loved . . .

Tom had not seen me start crying, as he was busy inserting a thermometer into the meat. When he placed the pan into the oven next to half a dozen baking potatoes, I ordered myself to get my act together.

Without much forethought, I marched determinedly to the walk-in refrigerator, wrenched open the door, and stared into the cool darkness. What would we have with this particular tenderloin?

Why, béarnaise sauce, I thought, and reached for a small tub of Tom's meticulously clarified butter and a bunch of fresh tarragon. **Charlie Baker made a great béarnaise, that's what he would have served,** I thought instinctively. **Be quiet,** I told my mind. **Concentrate**.

I melted the butter, separated the eggs, and pulverized a handful of tarragon leaves in my herb grinder. Once I'd beaten and warmed the egg yolks and swished in some tarragon vinegar, I whisked in drops of melted butter. The concentration required for these tasks finally began to soften the agonizing tension in my brain. Beside me, Tom was assembling a salade composée of Wagnerian proportions: steamed fresh grean beans, asparagus, and peas, arranged on a lush bed of arugula leaves.

"What have they looked at, Tom?" I asked. My

gaze never left the sauce. "The cops, I mean? The detectives. What have they found?"

Tom continued carefully to lay out rows of green beans. "Well, they haven't found much yet, except that it looks as if she was slapped in the face, got her head bashed into a painting, and then she was strangled to death. The questions they'll ask, investigating? First, was this a robbery gone bad? Was Dusty supposed to be there, or was she an unexpected complication?"

"It didn't look like a robbery. I mean, I didn't see any signs of a break-in."

"There wasn't a forced entry. So it didn't look like a robbery **to you**. But with so much information on computers and disks these days, who knows? Maybe the office had valuables, too."

"You mean, the kind you'd keep in a safe?"

Tom shook his head. "No. The kind you put on display. Gold clocks. Sculptures by famous—"

"Wait. There were expensive paintings on the walls. You know, by Charlie Baker. Fifty thou each, why wouldn't somebody steal those?"

Tom shrugged. "Kind of hard to shove those into a getaway bag, although you could. That partner, Richard Chenault? He's helping them with an inventory. So is the office manager. Louise Upton." I scowled, but Tom grinned. "I haven't talked to her, but Boyd did. She told him to call her 'ma'am.'"

He went on: "Then again, maybe it wasn't a robbery. Say Dusty knew something, had discovered something, had asked questions she shouldn't have, was making a pest out of herself . . . any of a number of things. So somebody says he wants to meet her before she helps you with the bread. Your unlocked van is on the street, so first he turns the lights and radio on, draining the battery so you'll be late. It doesn't take long to kill someone."

"So, the department is constructing scenarios about what could have happened? Developing suspects from that?"

"Not yet. They have to ask lots of other questions first. Who were her enemies? Did she owe anybody money? Was she doing any **dangerous** work? Did anyone resent her for **any** reason? If so, who resented her, and why?" Tom sighed. "But as I say, the very first thing they have to figure out is if she walked in on a burglary, or if someone was waiting for her. Right, no forced entry, so somebody might have had a key. On the other hand, the security at that office was not that tight. Somebody could have come in, posing as a client or delivery person or whatever, and then never went out. He or she waited until everybody left, and then started to rob the place. Dusty could have surprised this person, and he might have killed her to avoid apprehension."

"Or maybe someone was waiting for her and then wanted to make it look like a burglary."

"That, too." Tom's tone was rueful. After a moment, he said, "We did find out one thing concerning her work. From Richard Chenault, her uncle."

"I'm listening."

"He said that Dusty spent quite a bit of time working with Charlie Baker, once he found out he had pancreatic cancer. Charlie wanted to tidy up his correspondence, his bank accounts, his legal affairs. He and Dusty got along well, and he liked having her there to help him out."

"I know she knew Charlie, but I guess I didn't know she was actually working closely with him. How long had this been going on?"

"Since the beginning of this year."

"Have the cops found any connection between Charlie Baker and Dusty that could have spelled trouble for her?"

"Not yet. But they're looking into it."

We worked in silence for a while. I set the heavenly scented béarnaise sauce over barely simmering water and hoped Arch and Gus would arrive home soon. The October evenings were already rushing toward early darkness, and with someone who might have sabotaged my van out there, I felt uneasy.

"Look," I said, "I keep going back to my van. If I hadn't been late to the H&J office, then what? Would I have been strangled, too? Or could I have saved her?"

"I already talked to Arch about the van this morning. He is absolutely sure, completely positive, that he turned off the radio, because he'd come to the end of a Dave Matthews song. Then he remembers picking up his book bag, opening the passenger door, and slamming it shut. He remembers the slamming because he said he was in such a bad mood. Plus, he recalls staring at the car for a minute, making sure he had everything he needed for his homework."

"Right. And I suppose he's absolutely positive he locked it, too."

"No, that he's not sure of. In fact, he thinks he didn't, because his hands were full with his book bag and books." Tom stopped laying down hard-boiled egg halves and waited until I met his gaze. "He's sure he **didn't** leave the radio and lights on. He's sure he **didn't** remember to lock the van."

"So you do think somebody tampered with my car. Or my son has a conveniently slippery memory."

"The former. My theory is, someone was watching you, knew your schedule. Knew when you left for the firm to go make the bread for the

Friday-morning meeting." He finished the salad and covered it with plastic wrap. "I told the investigators to send our guys out to canvass our neighbors, check if anyone saw somebody, anybody, messing with your car. We need to know if a neighbor saw someone scouting you out. I also told our guys to look at any folks who might have seen an odd, as in out of the ordinary, vehicle over by H&J that late at night."

Someone scouting you out. I tried to rid myself of the memory of Vic Zaruski and his long, furious face, of his boatlike white convertible, and of the many times it had been parked in the Routts' driveway. In the Routts' driveway or **on the street**. He wouldn't have messed up my car, would he? He wouldn't have strangled a girl he cared about, or had once cared about, would he?

"Goldy?" Tom queried. "Think. Look back at that scene you came upon in the office. Something missing? Something out of place?"

I sighed. I'd already told the investigators down at the department that I couldn't tell if the place had been robbed, that I'd been concentrating on Dusty . . . and then I remembered I hadn't yet told Tom about the bracelet. Where was my mind?

"Tom," I began, "I need to talk to you about a piece of jewelry that Dusty was wearing last week." Tom raised his eyebrows and cocked his chin, as in **Go on.** I told him all I'd shared with Britt and how I'd been unsure whether Dusty had been wearing the opal and diamond piece around her wrist when I'd found her.

"You don't know where she got it?" Tom asked.

I shook my head. "She promised to wear it last night, and to tell me about it."

"And you can't remember whether she had it on when you found her."

"Nope. It's as if the memory is just out of reach."

He told me to sit down, then pulled up a chair for himself. Then he took my hand and told me to shut my eyes. This I did.

"Now picture the office after you tripped and got up," he said softly, "and describe every aspect of it to me."

I did this, too. At one point Tom told me to imagine that I was seeing Dusty, and gently rolling her over.

"Was the bracelet there?" he asked.

In my mind's eye, I looked at Dusty's wrists. They were empty. I said, "No. There's no bracelet, no watch, nothing."

"Now open your eyes and talk to me."

I hesitated. "Do you think Sally Routt would tell us if she'd seen Dusty wearing an expensive bracelet?"

"She might tell **you.** I doubt very seriously she'd tell me, or any cop, for that matter, given her attitude toward law enforcement." Tom stared out the window, where new snow clung to every pine needle, every branch of aspen leaves. "The last few weeks or days," he said finally. "How did Dusty seem? Didn't I hear Sally Routt talking to you about that?"

"Sally said Dusty had been secretive."

"And was she? I mean, apart from dodging the bracelet question?"

I stopped to think. "She did seem like . . . like someone with a secret."

"Or secrets," Tom said, his voice low.

Gus and Arch were not due back for a while, so I slipped back over to the Routts' house. Sally was still crying incessantly. I said I had something important to ask her, and she quieted for a moment. Had she seen Dusty wearing a bracelet? I asked. Opals interwoven with diamonds? I drew a quick sketch on a piece of paper offered by Sally's father, who tapped his way to the kitchen and opened a drawer to pull out a single sheaf. For a blind man, he could get around remarkably well, but he undoubtedly had every inch of the house memorized. Sally blinked at my crude drawing. She said she'd never seen anything like it, on Dusty or anywhere else. When she described the bracelet to her father, asking if he had felt anything on Dusty's forearm when she hugged him, he simply shook his head.

"Dusty didn't tell us everything," Sally told me, handing the paper back. "And as I told you before, she'd been keeping something to herself, or so it seemed to me, lately. Of course, I was always worried when it came to our relationship. You know, I'm a single mom who's made a bunch of mistakes. She knows I didn't want another repeat of the Ogden mess."

"Um, did the cops take everything from her room? Jewelry box, everything?"

"Yes," Sally said, with a sharp intake of breath. "She had a jewelry box, but they showed it to me, and there was just an old silver charm bracelet in there. I told them they could take it, but they didn't. They did turn her mattress upside down, since that's the main place people hide things, apparently. They looked in our freezer, too. **Second** place people hide things. Nothing there either."

"Yeah. Well. If there's anything you think of, Sally, anything she might have said to you, anything she might have been keeping that seemed strange to you, would you please tell me? It would help."

Sally bit her bottom lip so hard I thought it would bleed. But she merely nodded before she began weeping again. I told her I could see myself out.

Back at the house, I told Tom I'd come away empty. Did this mean the killer had stolen the bracelet? I asked.

"Not necessarily," he replied.

"Maybe it was in her purse," I said numbly. "Did the cops find her purse?"

"Yeah, they did. I think they would have told me if they'd found a real expensive piece of jewelry in there." I must have looked despondent because then Tom said, "Why don't you give me your Picasso there, and I'll fax it down to the department with a note? They alert all the pawnshops, in case something turns up. A twenty-thousand-dollar bracelet ought to raise a few eyebrows on East Colfax, in any event."

"Aren't there pawnshops anywhere else in Denver?"

"Just a figure of speech, Miss G." He finished his note to the department and punched in the fax numbers. "It's always a good idea to cover all your bases."

I was wondering if that was a figure of speech, too—did it mean you had to have a guy on each base defending it, or did it mean you had to cover the bases if it started raining—probably not that one, I reasoned—when the boys returned. It was already five forty-five. Gus clutched such a large handful of twenties and checks that when he slapped them tri-

umphantly on the kitchen table, a third of them
drifted to the floor. Behind him, Arch, cautious as
ever, had folded his much smaller take into a careful
package that he placed on the counter, along with
the magazine order form. Gus's blond-brown hair,
several shades lighter than Arch's toast-colored
locks, framed his face, halolike, as he grinned, ebul-
lient. The two of them resembled the faces of
Janus: Arch ever worried and scowling, and Gus optimistic and brimming with confidence.

"Arch, where do you put your stuff?" Gus demanded as he unzipped his down jacket and
dropped **it** to the floor. "Oops." Gus, his appealing face shiny with melted snow, gave me a wide
smile and scooped up the coat.

"I'll show you," Arch said, frowning. He hung
his and Gus's jackets on the hooks in the kitchen,
then turned to give me a serious look. "We invited
somebody to dinner."

"What?"

Immediately defensive, Arch retorted, "It's what
you would have done! We found her crying in her
house. It's Wink Calhoun, Dusty's friend. You
know, the one who adopted Latte? Anyway, she's
coming, and she's bringing Latte. Hope that's okay.
They'll both be here in about five minutes—"

"I've already invited Wink, but not Latte—" I
began.

"C'mon, Mrs. Schulz," Gus pleaded, his cheerful, red-cheeked face upturned to mine. "That's a really cool dog, and we don't have one at my grandparents' place. Anyway, he took right to me! We both said it would be okay if she brought him."

"Call me Aunt G.," I told him, and he broke into a huge smile.

"Okay, Aunt G.," which came out sounding like **Angie,** "we had to do it. Wink was Dusty's best friend. Plus, she lives in a garage or something."

"I know, I know, I've already asked—"

"Actually, Wink lives in a guesthouse," Arch corrected, in a tone that made me cringe, since it echoed my own. "It's a garage that somebody turned into a guesthouse on Pine Way. Nobody was at the big house, so we backtracked to the driveway and followed the sound of the crying. And get this, she's only a receptionist, and she bought three subscriptions."

Tom asked, "Is that how she described herself, 'only a receptionist'?"

"Yeah," the boys chorused.

"She's the receptionist at Hanrahan & Jule," I informed the boys as the doorbell rang. Then I said, "You boys need to go find Scout the cat and put him in the cage we use to take him to the vet. If he attacks Latte again—"

But the boys were already scrambling away, calling exuberantly for the cat.

When I opened the door, Wink Calhoun, tall, pretty, and pink-eyed, hesitated before stepping across the threshold. Her flat, oblong face always seemed just a bit too large for her body, and a pronounced underbite prevented her from being beautiful. But she had a ready smile and a retro look, complete with finger-waved light brown hair that gave her an undeniable charm. She wore a navy blazer over a white oxford-cloth shirt and a long blackwatch-plaid kilt that complemented her slender, shapely figure. She also wore tassel loafers, which I noted were soaking wet.

Her lack of movement at the door frustrated Latte the basset hound, however. He let out several loud barks and bolted into the house, tearing the leash out of Wink's hands.

"I'm so sorry!" Wink began as the boys tumbled out of the kitchen to welcome the dog. Wink called to Latte to calm down. Not only did the basset hound ignore her, he started barking wildly as he raced around in a circle from the front hall, through the living room, then the dining room, then into the kitchen, back through the hall and the living room . . . until he hit the dining room again. Scout the cat, who had been hiding in the basement, took that opportunity to streak up the stairs, where the boys squealed and pounced on him. Jake the blood-hound, who had been sitting in his usual spot out on the deck, was clawing madly on the back door to be let in, all while howling at the top of his lungs to be allowed to be part of the fun. Latte, who seemed to be encouraged by the chaos, continued to make a mad circular dash through the rooms on the main floor, until Tom scooped him up in his arms.

"I'm telling you, Miss G.," Tom called over Latte's hollering, "apprehending criminals is nothing to this!"

"This is so cool!" Arch said, smiling gleefully, when he and Gus returned to the kitchen.

"Here, let me have him," Gus was insisting to Tom. Tom allowed a squirming Latte to be taken by Gus. Latte, sensing the weakness of the transfer, wiggled madly and leaped out of Gus's arms, only to begin his crazed circuit once more. Tom caught him again in the kitchen, and quickly transferred the dog outside.

"I made it!" Wink said. "You wanted me to come over, and the boys said—"

"Tom's fixing a roast. Come on in."

I shut the door behind her and opened my arms. She walked into my hug and began to shake with sobs.

"I'm so sorry, oh, dear Wink, I'm so sorry," I repeated over and over.

Tom peeked out the kitchen door. The boys' voices behind him were querulous. Where's Mom? Why won't you let the dogs in? Why doesn't Wink come into the kitchen? But when Tom caught my eye and saw the embrace, he backed silently into the kitchen and quieted the boys.

At length, Wink stopped crying. She took a tissue out of her blazer pocket, cleaned up her face, and regarded me.

"Let's talk in the living room," I said gently. "How about a glass of sherry?"

Wink swallowed and didn't move. "Sorry about falling apart. Dusty was my best friend in the firm. This happens to other people. It doesn't happen to people you know."

"The cops are working on it," I reassured her. "It's a good sheriff's department. And later on, you and I can talk about what they were all up to."

Wink pressed her lips together firmly. "I don't think the cops are going to find out what happened to her."

"What do you mean?"

"You don't know these people the way I do."

Chapter 9

"So tell me about them," I said.

"I wasn't trying to scare you. I really do want to find out what happened to Dusty," she said. Her mouth turned down. "I just don't want to hear any of the gory details, you know?"

"Don't worry."

"And I can't divulge any, you know, of the confidential business stuff, although I really don't care at this point."

"The cops talked to you, right?"

She looked over at the fire. "Yeah."

"You told them everything pertinent, I hope?" When she nodded, I said, "Let's go sit down."

I led her into the living room, where I poured two glasses of sherry. I knew I probably shouldn't have more booze, especially after I'd had only a few hours' worth of sleep the previous night, and part of that slumber had taken place in a moving car. But I'd hardly touched the glass Tom had given me, and I wanted Wink to feel better. Plus, I wanted to loosen up her tongue, even to facts she might not think were pertinent.

"What do the cops know so far, about Dusty's death?" she asked, once she'd thanked me for her glass of amber liquid.

Immediately wary, I said, "Not much." The coroner and the rest of law enforcement usually kept secret the cause and manner of death, in the hope that a killer might unwittingly give away some detail that had not been released to the public. I wished Tom would join us, but I could hear him out in the kitchen. He'd closed both doors, had let both hounds back in, and was now listening to Arch and Gus alternate in telling stories about the people who'd bought magazine subscriptions. Without thinking, I checked Wink's wrist. I was ashamed to be looking, even unconsciously, for Dusty's bracelet. But crooks, Tom was always telling me, were notoriously stupid. Wink's shirt had long sleeves, and I couldn't see anything. Still, I told myself I was being ridiculous. Wink had been Dusty's best friend.

I said, "What did you mean when you said I didn't know these people the way you do? Do you think someone will hurt you if you tell the cops something? Or even if you tell me?"

"I'm just spooked." She took a sip of sherry and looked around the living room, apparently as confused as most visitors by the combination of cheap orange upholstered furniture and clearly valuable antique wood pieces. "Somebody has good taste," she said, but without sounding bitchy.

"Tom's a collector."

"How's Sally doing, do you know?"

"She's doing terribly, Wink. And if it will make you feel better about telling me about the folks in the firm, she's asked me to investigate Dusty's death. On my own, that is, without law enforcement." I sipped my sherry and decided just to wait. It didn't take long.

"I do have something to tell you," she said, glancing up at me. "Something I didn't tell the authorities, because they didn't ask me a direct question about it, you know?" She shook her head. "Listen to me, I sound just like **them.**" She thrust out her small chin, as if steeling herself. "I wanted to tell you over the phone, but I wanted to think about it first. Then King Richard came over, wanting me to do some typing, if you can imagine." She took a long slug of sherry. "Louise Upton needs money. She was married once, if you can believe it." Wink shook her head, as if forestalling my question. "She just tells people to call her 'Miss Upton.' There's no law against that, I think. Anyway, her ex-husband doesn't work, and he sued her for alimony. He came into the office one time, screaming and yelling that Louise was late with that month's check. He was such a brute, I almost felt sorry for Louise. After he left, Claggs told me about the alimony situation."

"And so you think this has something to do with Dusty?"

Tears erupted from Wink's eyes. "Oh God. I **told** Dusty. I mean, we were close, you know? And last week she was complaining about what a bitch Louise was, always wanting to have everything just so. She'd started calling her Miss Uptight, which I thought was hilarious. She said between Miss Uptight and King Richard, it was a wonder we got any work done at all. So I just told her about Louise having an ex, and how she had to pay him alimony. I shouldn't have, but since I didn't **technically** break my vow of confidentiality to Louise—I mean, I didn't tell any of the **guys** at H&J— I thought it was okay. Listen to me. I'm starting to sound like one of **them** again."

"Do you think Dusty threw it back in her face? Maybe one time when she was angry for being corrected?"

"Well, that's what I'm afraid of." Wink rubbed her forehead. "It was a disaster waiting to happen, since Dusty and Louise didn't get along."

"What did you get out of promising not to tell

the guys about the alimony? Did Louise offer you anything?"

She looked down at her hands. "No," she muttered, her voice barely above a whisper. "I guess she sort of wanted to be friends. Maybe not, though."

"Do you know if Dusty didn't get along with anyone else? Or if she had any romantic liaisons?"

Wink, still staring at her hands, shook her head forcefully. "Didn't get along? I don't know. Romantic liaison? I don't think so." She paused to think. "Okay, Claggs had just won a lot of money in a poker game in Central City. I heard them laughing about it. Dusty and Alonzo, I mean. But Claggs is married to Ookie. Happily married, I think."

"So Claggs is a gambler?"

Wink shrugged. "I think he does it for fun. You know, to relieve stress. Until ski season starts, anyway."

"Any idea how much money he'd won? Or how he'd spent it?"

"Not a clue. But there is something I've always wondered about. I mean, Ookie teaches squash at the Aspen Meadow Country Club, and most of the other lawyers work out there, too. So why does Claggs work out at the Butterfield Rec? Why did he work out with Dusty, I mean?"

"Because Dusty couldn't afford to join the country club?" I offered.

Wink's tone turned stubborn. "I just think she would have told me if she was romantically involved with him."

I thought, **Would she have told you, if it was meant to be a secret**? "So except for working out together, you had no inkling as to whether she was seeing Claggs outside of work?"

"I'm telling you, she really didn't talk to me about **Claggs**!"

"Do you know if she was seeing **anybody**?" I pressed.

Wink wrinkled her face. "If you're looking for romantic-type information, Dusty had been going out with Vic Zaruski. They'd just had a bad breakup. The end."

I pressed my lips together. "I didn't get much of a feeling for the atmosphere at Hanrahan & Jule," I said, my tone innocent.

"You didn't, really?" She took a deep breath. "The whole place feels as if it's in a constant state of power struggle."

"Between whom?"

"Between the partners over whose cases are more important. Between the associates over who has the most work. Between the lawyers and the paralegals, when we had two of them, over whom the paralegals should be working for. And that leads to stress. You couldn't complain, because . . . well, just because."

When she didn't offer any more, I asked, "Was Dusty in this power struggle? And did it turn deadly?"

"I **don't know**. And that's what I told the cops, honest."

There was another long silence, finally broken by Tom calling us to dinner. As she was about to follow me through the kitchen door, Wink stopped. I turned back to make sure she was okay. That little chin of hers was wobbling again, and her hands were clenched. All her pale brown hair's tiny waves seemed to tremble at once. She dashed wetness out of her eyes, then cleared her throat and moved into the warm, inviting space, where the rich scent of roasting beef filled the air like a cushion.

"Hi again, Wink," Arch said, his voice grave. "I'm glad you came. My mom's a really good cook."

"Hey!" Tom interjected, his voice playful. "Who's cooking this dinner, anyway? By the way, Wink, I'm Tom."

Wink nodded to Tom, then smiled at the boys and me. "Thanks, Arch, I already know how good a cook your mom is. She brings . . . brought us breakfast at the firm, and everybody was always fighting over the food." Her cheeks colored.

"Sorry about what happened," Gus chimed in. "Arch said the dead girl was your friend."

"She was." Wink swallowed and struggled for control.

"That **sucks**," Gus said.

"Welcome anyway, Wink." Tom moved forward and yanked out a chair. "Come sit down."

This Wink did. Tom pulled the tenderloin out of the oven to let it rest, then began to assemble the baked potatoes, steamed broccoli, and cheese sauce that he knew Arch enjoyed having with friends. I nipped back out to the living room and picked up Wink's sherry glass—I'd managed to get through our conversation with only a couple of small sips—and brought it back out to the kitchen. I checked the thermometer that Tom had left inserted in the meat. I was happy to see that the beef juices had settled, and the temp indicated a perfect medium rare. In addition to the cheddar-cheese sauce, Tom had managed to reheat the béarnaise I'd made, without curdling it.

"You didn't think I could do two sauces at once, did you?" he asked mildly, when I raised my eyebrows at the pair of gravy boats with their perfectly smooth, golden loads. "Why don't you sit down, Miss G.?"

So I did. To my great astonishment, I was famished. And then I remembered that I hadn't actually had breakfast. Come to think of it, I hadn't had much of a lunch, either. (A salad didn't count as a meal, I always told myself.)

Tom had shaken up a mild balsamic vinaigrette and now he sprinkled judicious amounts over his salade composée. Arch, Gus, and even Wink poured rivers of creamy cheddar sauce over their potatoes and broccoli, while Tom and I opted for salad. The tenderloin was done to perfection: pink and tender on the inside, with a crunchy, delicious roasted exterior bearing crisp herbs. With some reheated soft rolls that we all slathered with butter, it was a feast. Hunger makes the best sauce, I'd learned when I was nine. No kidding.

And perhaps wine makes the best smoother-over of distraught emotions, I thought after a while. Wink had twisted her rail-thin body into what looked like an impossible yoga position to watch Tom open a bottle of Burgundy, a Côte de Nuits. Our dinner wasn't exactly a cause for any kind of celebration, but the meal and the wine made us feel better. Cared for, even. Which was what Tom was good at, I reminded myself.

"They keep hundred-dollar-a-bottle Côte de Nuits Burgundy in a locked cabinet at the firm," Wink observed. "But it's just for meetings between the partners and the clients. Not for the receptionist and paralegals, I mean." She looked at

Tom with sudden interest. "Would the cops have gone through all the locked cabinets?"

Tom's eyes were hooded. "I'm sure they're over there going through everything, trust me."

I took a big forkful of salad, curious myself to know what they might have found inside there, since I, too, knew of the locked cabinet. But like the receptionist and paralegals, the caterer wasn't allowed to fiddle with the heart-of-maple cabinets, either. Still, Tom was right: searching for Dusty's killer, the cops would have demanded entry to every locked drawer and cabinet in the place. There was no question that our sheriff's department was good at crime-scene mechanics, largely, I think, because they feared having Tom bawl them out if they screwed up.

The Burgundy was delicious. I'm not one of those folks who can say a wine has complex chocolate and citrus notes along with undertones of blackberry, but I **can** say, "Omigod, this stuff is fantastic!" Tom beamed.

The wine also seemed to have a calming effect on Wink. Arch and Gus, oblivious to our pleasured imbibing, were going over to Gus's grandparents' condo to spend the night, and they continued to chat and burble and interrupt each other about the video games they were going to play and the movies they were going to watch.

Every now and then they asked Wink, but not us, if she had seen this or that movie. Most of the time she had, and the boys invariably found this cool. Meanwhile, the redness began to dissipate from Wink's eyes, and I thought I detected the tension melting from her face.

At length, Wink drained her wineglass. Smiling, she said, "Hey, Gus! I read in the St. Luke's bulletin that you were going to be baptized."

"Yup," said Gus, his standard affirmative.

"By Sutherland?" she asked.

"Yup."

"Well, you know," Wink continued with a sly smile, "he always quizzes the confirmands ahead of time. Takes them into a Sunday-school room and asks them about the sacraments and how God structured things so we could be saved. You know your stuff?"

Gus was looking at her with alarm. "How'm I supposed to know how God structured things?" he cried, his eyes wide. "I don't even know how the **government** structures things! This **really** sucks."

"Aw, don't worry, Gus," Arch said authoritatively. "It's not that bad. It's sort of like Dungeons and Dragons. You have to learn how any particular world works before you can move around in it. You ever play D&D?"

Gus's forehead wrinkled. "I learned some witchcraft in the commune."

"Let's not go there," I said quickly.

"But . . . you're still coming to my christening, aren't you, Arch?" Gus asked, suddenly worried. "Maybe you could give me some answers, you know, like on what he's going to ask before I have to take this quiz."

"I've sort of fallen away from the church," Arch admitted.

"Man," Gus retorted. "I thought this was important to you; that's why I'm doing it!"

"Right, right, I know," Arch said. "It is important to me, I promise. I'm coming to your thing, even if I haven't been going to church for a while." He gave Gus a reassuring smile. "It'll be okay."

The way you've been driving lately, I thought, **you might want to start praying**. But I kept mum. Meanwhile, Tom picked up the Burgundy and poured Wink and yours truly a second glass. No question about it: I **was** going to sleep tonight.

"You didn't drive over here, did you?" Tom asked.

"I'll be fine," Wink insisted.

The boys sang out, "Uh-oh," then scampered off to watch television until Gus's grandparents arrived.

"We could drive you home," I offered. "Or you could stay here," I added as an afterthought. If we didn't know the people at H&J the way Wink did, maybe she would feel better not being alone tonight. "We could make up the couch in the living room, or you could stay in Arch's room, since he's going over to—"

"We'll think of something," Tom interrupted, shooting me a warning glance: **Best not to distract someone whom you want to get going telling you her story.** If your informant—or helpful person, as Tom sometimes called them—starts worrying about who's outside, or where they're going to have lunch, or if their car is parked legally, then the flow of data is going to come to a sudden halt.

Of course, I didn't know whether we should be interrogating Wink or not. But I let go of it. If she needed to spill her guts about her relationship with Dusty, or goings-on among what Sally Routt called the "vermin" at H&J, then fine. Still . . .

My train of thought was derailed by the phone ringing. Eight o'clock on a Friday night? Must be a client.

"I checked with my husband," Nora Ellis said without identifying herself, "and he wants to proceed with the party."

"Fine, fine," I replied, trying to make a smooth transition. "You're talking about Mr. Ellis wanting to go ahead with his birthday celebration. I understand."

"He said it would be what Dusty wanted us to do."

"He thinks it's what **Dusty** would want you to do?"

"Goldy," she said, her voice suddenly kind. "Forgive me. I'm just nervous about this going well. I want Donald to love it. Okay? I'll see you tomorrow morning at ten. And I've gotten you some help, as I promised. I hired Louise Upton to oversee things in the kitchen."

"That is so unnecessary," I said. I made **my** tone gentle, too, to keep from screaming. But she had already hung up. To Tom and Wink, I said, "Nora Ellis is going to proceed, as she called it, with her party for her husband. Apparently, Donald Ellis thinks it's what Dusty would have wanted them to do. And Nora hired Louise Upton to oversee things in the kitchen."

Wink snorted. "Poor you. And Dusty wasn't even **invited** to their party. None of the staff is ever included in their reindeer games. Plus, Miss Uptight will just make your life miserable."

"That doesn't surprise me," I said in a low voice. I couldn't imagine Louise Upton shedding her armor to be helpful in the kitchen. Would she carry her own sword? **For heaven's sake,** I told

myself, **shut up and stop being such a bitch.**
Somebody had loved Louise once, a husband, now
an ex-husband, who was milking her for alimony.
If that was what made her difficult, then I could
suddenly understand her a lot better.

"I know you had to talk to the cops, too," Wink
said, her eyes on me, her tone half questioning.

"Yeah, I did. How'd it go for you?"

Wink rubbed her forehead with both hands.
"Not too bad. Some of the same stuff you were
asking me in the living room. Who didn't get
along with Dusty? What was she working on?
Man, it got boring. Then they'd ask me the same
question in a sort of different way, like I'd trip
myself up in a lie, or something."

Tom's grin was good-natured. "Well, how do
you think we'll catch folks who aren't telling the
truth?"

Wink straightened in her chair. "Dusty was
working on a few things. She'd been working since
January for Charlie Baker, trying to help him get
his affairs in order. She was spending her office
time on a big oil-and-gas-lease mess, part of a
ridiculously complicated estate that won't be settled before I'm forty."

"Don't knock turning forty," I said lightheart-
edly. "It may seem far off now, but someday . . ."

Wink managed to smile. "Anyway, the lease

thing was with Donald Ellis, who isn't a partner. Can you imagine trying to find anything, much less oil-and-gas leases, in Donald Ellis's office? But he's a hard worker, I'll give him that. Anyway, then in March, Charlie Baker died, and Richard, who **is** a partner, was handling the estate. So all of a sudden Dusty wasn't helping Donald anymore at all, she was working full-time for King Richard, trying to get everything in Charlie's big estate in order."

"So did the cops make anything out of all that?" I asked.

"I don't know. You'd have to ask Georgina, the one paralegal we have left."

"You had more paralegals before?"

"Yeah," Wink said. "Two others. But they were hired away by another firm last year. They haven't been replaced yet. Marilou, the legal secretary, has been interviewing replacements for the secretary Richard fired. The guys have been bringing in extra paralegals, too, when they're really snowed under. They get a **lot** done."

"Do you mean the paralegals?" I asked, confused.

"Of course I do! You should see how hard those extras worked, when they were with H&J. Plus, Dusty was like a slave to the guys. Marilou and Georgina are, too, when they're not in Hawaii taking notes at meetings that the attorneys are supposed to go to. Let me tell you what I've learned from working in the law firm. Here's what paralegals can't do: They can't give legal-costs estimates to the client. They can't share in the firm's profits. And they can't talk in court. But they do all the other work, trust me. Show me a group of male lawyers who don't have most of their work done by female paralegals, and I'll show you a graveyard."

"Now there's a happy thought," Tom said cheerfully. "So if Dusty was getting so much work done for the firm, why would someone kill her? Did she have enemies in the firm? Or not?"

Wink shook her head sadly. "She and Alonzo were close. They worked out together. Really, the problem was, except for the occasional flare-up with Louise Upton, Dusty got along with everyone."

"Why was that a problem?" I asked.

Wink leaned forward. "Because you don't mix with the other levels of the fief in a fiefdom. You don't try to get along with everyone, because it's only going to make you miserable. And most of all, you don't get ambitious."

"How was she ambitious, specifically?" I asked.

"She answered questions the lawyers should have," she said. "She was possessive about her relationship with Charlie Baker. If you're not even a paralegal yet, you **don't** make yourself the guardian of one of the firm's biggest clients." I raised an eyebrow at Tom. Now he, too, wanted to know if Dusty's legendary determination and get-up-and-go-ness were what had gotten her killed.

The phone rang. Not another client. Not at this hour. Besides the Ellis party, the only upcoming events I had were the reception after Gus's christening on Sunday and the post-ribbon-cutting celebration for the Mountain Pastoral Center on Monday night. The menus were set; the checks had been written; the food had been ordered. The caller ID gave no hint. I made a quick apology to Tom and Wink and pressed the talk button.

"Goldilocks' Cate—"

"Goldy? This is Miss Upton."

Oh, boy. Past eight o'clock on a Friday night? No, it was more likely that the formidable office manager wanted to give me some new instructions. **We'll need you to bring breakfast in on Monday to a new location . . . Oh, and by the way, no mention of the unfortunate event of Thursday night . . .**

"Miss Uh—" I began again.

"Mr. Claggett and Mr. Ellis and I will be over in a little bit."

"Be over in a little bit?" I squawked, glancing

around the kitchen with its mass of dirty dishes and sauce-coated pans. "Can't we just talk on the pho—"

Louise Upton cleared her throat. "We will be over in a little **bit**."

"**What** little bit? I've got—"

"About twenty minutes."

She hung up before asking me if I was mourning the death of my young neighbor, if I would be home, if I had people here, if I had work to do, if her visit was in any way inconvenient . . . all of which were true. But did she care? She did not. At least she was acting in character. I told Tom and Wink that Miss Uptight, plus Alonzo Claggett and Donald Ellis, would be arriving momentarily, and could they help me wash, or at least hide, all these dishes?

The last, the very **last** person I wanted to see that evening was Louise Upton. She would want to know every single detail of my discovery of Dusty, so that her mind could begin working on a spin that exonerated the firm. For Miss Upton loved the firm, she glorified it, she obsessed about it. She had told me once, "I am married to this firm."

I'd avoided saying, "Poor you." And now there was this ex-husband saga to deal with . . . should I tell Tom about that before Miss Uptight arrived?

Still, my promise to Sally Routt loomed in my mind. **I will try,** I'd promised, **to find out what happened to Dusty.** If anyone knew what negative tales could be told about H&J, it was Louise Upton. But that old legalism about a wife not testifying against her husband pertained to the nth degree here. Louise Upton would rather be stripped naked on Main Street than spill her guts about the firm.

And what about Alonzo Claggett, the gambler, and Donald Ellis, the oil-and-gas guy? Alonzo had been embarrassed by not knowing something that Dusty had known, and I was willing to bet the same thing had happened to Donald. Maybe one of **them** had had it in for her.

"Man, what are you thinking about, Goldy?" Wink demanded. "You look as if you just bit into an onion."

"A minute ago, I was thinking about Miss Uptight standing naked in the middle of Main Street."

"I'd rather bite into an onion," Wink acknowledged. She finished drying the gravy boat and put it on a shelf. "I need to rock on home. Thanks for dinner. And I'm fine, I've only had two glasses of wine, total."

"Nope," Tom said. "I'll drive you and then walk back here. You only live two blocks away."

Tom eyed the kitchen, which was clean. "You okay with this, Miss G.? If I go right now, I'll probably be back by the time they arrive."

"Sure, of course."

Wink handed Tom her keys and told him her car was the black Jetta. Tears welled in her eyes as she turned back to me.

"Please don't tell anybody what I told you. About Miss Upton. It could get me into trouble."

"I'm not going to get you into trouble," I said gently. "But you should tell Tom what you told me. About Louise's ex-husband, the alimony, and her needing money. It might help the police, in some way that you can't imagine at the moment." I added, "And you can call me about anything else you might think of."

Wink slipped into her blazer and worked on gathering up Latte, who, after all the commotion, had fallen asleep on our couch. She heaved the slumbering hound up into her arms, where he sagged like a sack of blocks. Panting, Wink started down the hall. Almost as an afterthought, she said, "It's unlikely I'll think of anything else."

Chapter 10

Tom was back within half an hour, with no Louise Upton, Alonzo Claggett, or Donald Ellis in sight. Tom reported that Wink had told him about Louise's ex-husband and her need for money. He was going to hurry and call the department about it, just in case Louise hadn't been forthcoming about her background. But he needn't have hurried, as it was another hour before the doorbell rang.

I desensitized our security system and opened the door for Donald Ellis, Alonzo Claggett, and Louise Upton. Twenty minutes had become ninety. Let's see, if I'd been billing them in six-minute increments, then I'd have made, oh . . . well, I needed a calculator.

"Goldy," said Donald Ellis, his thin voice low. "Thank you for seeing us."

"No problem," I replied.

"Yeah, thanks!" said Alonzo Claggett, who sounded a bit too cheery, it seemed to me, for someone who had just lost a friend at his workplace.

"Your house is very hard to find," Louise snarled, as if their tardiness were my fault.

I assumed my most hospitable voice. "Please come in. Here's a mat for your boots." I pointed behind them. "And there's the coatrack."

Donald murmured their appreciation while Louise tsked, stamped, and complained about the parking on our street. Claggs, perhaps to counteract Louise's brusqueness, commented on what a nice house we had. He noticed the cherry sideboard and buffet in our living room, both of which had been brought by Tom from his cabin. He and Tom fell into an easy conversation about Chippendale while Donald helped Louise remove her outer garments.

"How come you know so much about antiques?" Tom asked Alonzo.

"Oh, my family had lots of them in their Roland Park house. They gave Ookie and me a whole lot of them, but we sold them when the going got rough in Vail." He rolled forward on his toes and winked at me. "Didn't endear me to my folks, needless to say."

"I'll bet. Want to come in?"

But they did not, apparently, want to come into the living room and be treated as real guests. This put me on my guard. Why were the three of them here? Whose idea had it been to come to Tom's

204 DIANE MOTT DAVIDSON

and my house so late at night the day after one of their staff had been killed?

"We're not going to stay long," Claggs gushed. "We promise. We just wanted to see if you were okay. Ookie sends her regards, by the way." He dug into his dark brown slacks and brought out an envelope. "She says my clients—the Fieldings?— loved the breakfast you fixed for us so much, they went on and on to her about it."

"Well, you did their will, Mr. Claggett," I murmured, embarrassed to have Tom, Louise, and Donald Ellis witnessing this effusive praise. "I just did the quiche and fruit—"

"No, no," he interrupted me. "It was the whole package. Quiche, fruit, and will. That's what they told Ookie! Anyway, in appreciation, Ookie wanted you to have a guest pass and a coupon for six free squash lessons."

To me, "free squash lessons" implied someone teaching me to make zucchini bread, but never mind. I took the envelope and thanked him.

Louise whispered to Donald, "That is really so very unnecessary," her voice loud enough so that I would hear it. Donald reddened to the roots of his red hair, and recoiled as if stung. I thought for at least the hundredth time how much Donald Ellis reminded me of my son. Arch was fifteen and a half now, but Donald's invariably vulnerable expression recalled Arch's at an earlier age—say, eleven. Back then, Arch had been particularly susceptible to the taunts of bullies and braggarts. Even the untoward remark of a teacher could cause him to blush scarlet, as Donald was doing now.

Still, there was one thing I had learned about Donald Ellis: for all of his weak, defenseless appearance, clients loved him. He always ushered them into the conference room, as his office was too much of a wreck for even one person. These meetings were special for the client, as Donald would invariably book me to do a special lunch for them, usually a cold roast-beef salad with shaved Parmesan or chilled grilled salmon topped with caviar. After I'd cleared the dishes away, Donald would pull out a single yellow legal pad. This he would cover with his tiny scrawl as the client outlined what he or she wanted.

And then a week later there would be a will to be signed. The client would reappear, beaming and grateful, satisfied that his wishes after death had been set down. In the three-plus months I'd been at H&J, I'd seen it too many times to doubt it. Clients wanted Donald because he seemed so, well, sensitive. "Especially for a lawyer!" I would hear them whisper sometimes. And in the end, they felt they had helped him as much as he had helped them. And apparently, they liked that feeling.

While Donald was only a bit taller than I was, which would put him at about five feet three, Claggs was taller, better looking, more authoritative, and goodness knew, much more aggressive. Must have been all that advanced-run skiing, I'd figured once. Still, where Donald was quiet, Claggs was effusive, good-humored, always joking. When he was expecting an especially bellicose client, he'd regale the guys at the attorneys' breakfast about the client being furious because he'd been beaten in the "race to the house." The race to the house, I'd learned, was the way estate lawyers referred to heirs or wannabe heirs dashing to the residence of the recently deceased, to plunder whatever wasn't locked away or nailed down. There was also "the icy hand from the grave," another reference to clients, usually the ultrawealthy ones, who wanted to structure their wills in such a detailed manner that not a single heir would be getting a penny without jumping through a dizzying number of hoops.

"Well, everybody," Tom said, to break the standing-in-the-hall stalemate, "if you don't want to come into the living room, let's all go out to the kitchen and have some cake and coffee; how about it?"

Claggs followed Tom with alacrity. Louise lifted her chin and plowed in my direction. I found myself scrambling out of her way, a soldier jumping out of the path of a Sherman tank. At the door to our cooking area, she whirled, almost knocking over Donald Ellis. Now I had the full benefit of her glare. "Although we have to say, we would like to know what you were up to, coming into the law firm at ten o'clock at night to make bread!"

"I was doing my usual prep for the Friday-morning meeting," I replied evenly. "If you don't believe me, ask Richard."

But she was long gone, the kitchen door swinging behind her. Donald Ellis lagged behind. Finally he said, "I . . . we just wanted to make sure you were all right." His nearly colorless blue eyes implored me.

I almost burst out laughing. Was **this** the real reason the three of them were gracing me with a late-night visit? **Tell us you're all right. Tell us you're not going to sue us for the trauma you experienced tripping over a corpse in our office.**

"I'm fine, thanks. Or as well as can be expected."

Tom, sensitive to my absence, pulled open the kitchen door. His handsome, imperturbable face took us in. Donald nodded at Tom, his face again scarlet from . . . what? Embarrassment? Who knew?

Tom said, "Something going on out here?"

"We're fine," I said.

In the kitchen, Claggs was remarking on the "fantastic" job that Tom had done putting in the oak floor and installing the marble countertops. He moved his hands lovingly down the front of one of the cabinets. Had Tom done all this custom work with cherrywood, too? he wanted to know. Tom replied that he had. Louise had enthroned herself on one of our kitchen chairs and was listening with interest to all that Claggs was pointing out. Was I being paranoid, or did I imagine that Louise felt the kitchen was a bit too grand for the caterer who prepared the attorneys' breakfasts? I put the idea out of my mind.

Tom fixed the drinks: bourbon on the rocks for Claggs, scotch and water for Donald. Louise, who was rummaging around in her capacious purse, said she would like nothing, thank you. It was not a sincere expression of gratitude, but again, I told myself to let it go. Once Louise had retrieved her PDA, she began tapping the stylus on the screen. After a moment, she looked up at me in triumph. "I have no Friday-morning meeting for Mr. Chenault recorded here!"

"It was his **regular** meeting with clients! Are you saying I was **breaking into** the firm to leave some yeast and flour late Thursday night?" I said, with more heat than I intended. "Should we call Richard Chenault at home and check with him?"

"Miss Upton," Tom said gently, "why don't you give Goldy a break." It was not a question.

I punched buttons on my business computer, which occupied the far end of our kitchen countertop. My calendar for the third week in October flashed into view, and I pointed to Friday, October 20. "Miss Upton, would you like to have a look at this?" I tapped my own screen for emphasis. "'Thursday night, ten o'clock, arrive law firm, make dough. Friday five A.M. Bake bread for Chenault breakfast meeting.'"

Louise Upton stood, stepped to the counter, and peered at my computer screen. I could see her eyes focus downward not on Thursday or Friday, but on tomorrow morning, Saturday. **Ten A.M., arrive Ellis house for birthday party prep. One P.M., birthday party.**

"Well!" she said, staring at the computer.

She continued to read my screen, glancing from side to side at every single event I had listed as she pursed her lips and shook her head. I swallowed: was she looking to prove somehow that I truly was not supposed to be at H&J the previous night? Or was she just being nosy? Suddenly, I was immobilized. Miss Upton had the ability to get me fired, of that I was quite positive. And yet surely this was not appropriate . . .

With a conspicuous cough, Tom slid his big, athletic frame between my screen and Miss Upton. Caught off balance, the office manager teetered on her thick heels and groaned out a loud "Oof!" as she backed into Donald Ellis. Donald, short and slender and not known for his athleticism, listed backward until he collided with our kitchen table, which sent his scotch and water spewing through the air.

A set of chair and human dominoes tumbled loudly onto our oak floor. The chairs clattered away. Miss Upton, her legs flailing, struggled to right herself: a giant sea turtle squashing a worm, which was Donald Ellis. His thin, pale face had turned more purple than cooked beets.

Claggs knocked over his own drink as he fell to his knees and began pulling on Donald.

I bent down, grasped Miss Upton's carrotlike fingers and fleshy forearm, and tried to pull her up. Unfortunately, she was much stronger than I was, and her prone position plus the laws of physics gave her an advantage. I felt myself being pulled downward and squawked, "Tom! Help!"

With his usual efficiency of movement, Tom took two long steps around to Donald Ellis, reached in under his shoulders, and yanked him out from under Miss Upton. Unfortunately, when Donald's torso was about halfway free, Miss Upton lifted her monumental head and bonked it back down, directly onto Donald Ellis's scrotum.

Donald let out a high screech. With a massive effort, Claggs and Tom managed to heave Donald out from under Louise.

"Okay, big fella." Tom spoke reassuringly to Donald Ellis, Esquire, Champion of Hardworking Husbands Seeking to Cut Inheritances from Willfully Spending Wives and Profligate Progeny, as he dragged the unfortunate lawyer toward our back door. "You're going to be **just** fine in a minute." Before I could think of what to do, Tom shifted Donald's weight onto his strong right shoulder. Meanwhile, Claggs had opened our back door. In one smooth movement, Tom yanked Donald through the door. Claggs followed them onto the deck.

From the floor, Louise Upton wailed, "Could somebody please help me?"

Between Miss Upton's ham-hock forearm and what I could remember of Archimedes' lever principle, it only took a few moments of thrashing about to get the two of us vertical again. She was pale and disconcerted; I was more exhausted than if I'd landed a marlin. And not nearly as happy.

Still, I thought the best tack was to be conciliatory. I said, "I'm terribly, terribly sorry, Miss Upton. How about if we go out to the living room and sit down?"

"Two of my lawyers are outside. I think I should wait for them."

Excuse me? Two of **your** lawyers? But I let this pass, walked to the back door, and peeked out to the deck. Tom was standing protectively over Donald Ellis, who was sitting, his back hunched, his body shuddering, on a deck chair. Claggs was standing with his hands in his pockets, surveying the backyard. I could hear his voice through the glass. He was telling Tom how wonderful he could tell the landscaping was, even with the snow. Had Tom put all the plants in himself? Claggs wanted to know. I motioned to Tom for them to come inside, which they did, Donald leading with a slow, tentative gait, Claggs and Tom following.

This visit, whatever it was about, wasn't going very well.

After a few minutes, the five of us were sitting, albeit awkwardly, at our kitchen table. Donald, recovering some of his manliness, had sat up straight and asked for a second scotch. Claggs said he would pass on another bourbon, thanks. I mopped up the two spilled drinks while Tom poured Donald a second hefty dose of Johnnie Walker Black. He splashed a few drops of water on top, plinked in a couple of ice cubes, and placed it in front of Donald Ellis, who took a large gulp. Donald's face had taken on an even more pallid cast than usual, and he couldn't seem to stop blinking.

Arch poked his head into the kitchen. "Everything okay down here? We heard a lot of crashing and banging and were worried."

Miss Upton whirled in her chair and gave Arch a daggerlike look. She cried, "Young man! We're having a meeting in here, as you can see. Now, if your presence is required, we will summon—"

Arch disappeared.

To Louise Upton, I said evenly, "If you ever, and I do mean **ever,** want me to cater at Hanrahan & Jule again, you will not, I repeat, **not,** ever speak to my son again in that manner."

Louise Upton, immediately defensive, said, "I don't know what you're talking about."

"Oh-kay," Tom said, getting up. "Know what? This so-called meeting is over. Next time any one of the three of you wishes to speak to my wife, we'll set up a meeting at the sheriff's department. In an interrogation room."

"I'm sure that isn't necessary," Donald Ellis whispered. He took another long slug of his drink. "Louise, do you mind?" He gave her a meaningful look, and she sat back in her chair, silenced. Man, I wish **I** could do that. "Louise and Claggs and I," Donald continued, his voice now firm and authoritative, "just wanted to see how

Goldy was doing. We were worried. About her. Please, we're sorry to have intruded here . . . and to have caused a, uh, disturbance." He turned his liquid eyes on me. "I would like you to accept our most sincere condolences. We know Dusty was your friend and neighbor. That's the only reason we're here. On behalf of the firm," he added.

"We'd also like to know what Dusty was doing there at that hour—" Miss Upton began again, her tone unrepentant.

"Dusty was at the firm to help me with the cooking for the Friday meeting," I said, my voice steely, "as I have already told both you and the cops."

Louise opened her mouth to speak again, but she was silenced by another stern look from Donald Ellis.

"If you have any idea of what might have happened, or why," Donald said, his tone again soft, "we would sincerely like to know. We do feel terrible about Dusty. Poor dear girl."

"We do," Claggs echoed.

Tom sat back down. "Don't worry, Mr. Ellis. Mr. Claggett. Miss Upton. The sheriff's department is working on the case. We don't need any lawyers just yet."

"Well!" interjected Louise Upton. "Did she commit . . . I mean, did she fall down and . . . or what exactly did happen?"

Tom smiled and said, "Miss Upton, what exactly was the nature of your relationship with Miss Routt?"

"Well, I, uh . . . we should probably be going," Louise stammered. "But wait, Mr. Ellis hasn't finished his drink."

Donald Ellis lifted his drink to his lips and drained it. "I'm done," he said to no one in particular.

Claggs said, "Thanks so much for having us, Goldy. This is a great house, really. Glad you're doing okay—"

Louise stood abruptly and started down the hall.

We were interrupted from finishing our farewells by a loud honking, a fearsome crash, and yells erupting from the street. Louise Upton, who was not quite at the front door, started screaming. Tom bolted for the front door and strode down our sidewalk. I followed, pushing past Louise Upton and Donald Ellis, both of whom were gaping at what appeared to be a hit-and-run pedestrian accident. Walking fast, Tom had already arrived beside the pedestrian, who was sitting on the snowy street beside the curb. He appeared somewhat dazed, and it was my guess he'd narrowly avoided being run over.

Tom helped the pedestrian to his feet. The man was tall, and wore a dark ski hat and coat. He leaned over the grille of a nearby pickup, coughing. I wished I knew what had happened or how badly hurt the guy might be. I looked up and down the street. A couple of inches of snow covered everything: the cars, the lawns, the houses, the pavement. Otherwise, there was no movement at all.

Blinking against the cold, I moved awkwardly toward Tom, who was now talking to the moaning man. Maybe Tom would want me to summon an ambulance or get the department car up here. But when Tom gave me a sideways glance, he held up his hand, indicating I should not come closer. I hugged my sides and waited.

The color of the pickup the pedestrian had landed on, or jumped for, was obscured by snow. On the pavement just beside the pickup sat a large, oddly shaped metal box. It looked as if the man had been holding the box when he'd been avoiding whatever vehicle had been coming down the street. So had the box skittered out of the man's hands when he'd slammed into the truck's hood? Maybe his load had been so heavy that he'd slipped on the ice, lunged forward, and lost his balance. But there had been that honking, the yelling.

Wait. The box on the ground was a computer.

Or had been. I sure hoped whoever owned it had backed up his data.

Murmuring among themselves, Louise, Donald, and Claggs clomped quickly through the snow and down the street toward the spot where Donald had parked his black BMW. They seemed to be concerned about whether Donald's car had been hit. Convinced the Beemer was okay, Claggs helped Louise into the backseat, then got in beside her.

Donald Ellis paused and looked back at us. Since he was standing right under a streetlight, I could see his sheaf of red hair hanging like a broom over his forehead. There was pain in his face, and perhaps some question as to what had happened. Something in the tilt of his head made me think he wanted to come back and help. But then he averted his eyes, climbed into his car, and drove away.

Chapter 11

"It's Vic," Tom said as he crunched through the snow to my side. "He's insisting on bringing that thing in himself." Behind him, Vic had ducked down to pick up the computer. "He was bringing it over when the driver of one of those supersized SUVs almost hit him. Vic's sure the driver saw him, too. But that's all he can remember."

"What?"

"Look, you're freezing out here. Let me get Vic inside, then we'll talk. Okay?"

I nodded and started back up the sidewalk. Then I turned. "Tom? I already have a computer. Why was he bringing me one?"

"It's Dusty's!" Vic's voice as he lugged the computer to the curb was somewhere between a cough and a gasp. "Her mom didn't want the cops to have it. She wanted **you** to have it."

"Is that so?" Tom asked mildly as he helped Vic up onto the curb.

"Yeah." Vic's long legs were having trouble getting a purchase on the sidewalk. "She's not thinking too great. I'm sure she didn't mean you, Mr.— Officer Schulz. Oh God, I probably just screwed everything up." When Tom stood him upright on the sidewalk, Vic put the computer down, leaned his head back, and took a deep breath. His exhalation came out as a cloud.

"Look, I'm okay," he said, his voice still wobbly. "Let me bring in this computer the way I promised Mrs. Routt."

After much shuffling and grunting, and a slip in the snow that almost spilled computer guts all over our yard, Vic manhandled the computer onto our dining-room table. He stretched his back, then wiped his hands on the seat of his jeans before running them through his curly hair. "I'm just trying to help Mrs. Routt, you know?"

A honk from outside interrupted us. It was the Vikarioses, pulling up in their Cadillac to pick up Gus and Arch. I called upstairs for the boys, who came tumbling down carrying backpacks and duffel bags.

"Thanks for dinner, Aunt G.!" Gus sang out. "Did you bring that D&D stuff, Arch?"

"Yeah, I've got it," my son replied. To me he said, "Man, who was that mean lady?"

"Somebody I work for."

Arch rolled his eyes in disgust. "And I thought school was bad." We agreed I would call him the next afternoon. He wanted another driving lesson, he announced gaily. I held my tongue instead of saying how great that sounded (not). He told me he'd wait for my call. Before I could say I didn't know when I would be done with Donald Ellis's birthday party, he and Gus were gone.

Tom and Vic had passed me on their way into the kitchen. I followed them. Hot chocolate was in order, no doubt about it. Vic had brought over Dusty's computer? I might have been tired before, but now I was wide-awake.

"Here's the deal," Vic said, once he had shed his cap, jacket, and boots, sipped some cocoa, and stopped shivering. "You know Mrs. Routt is not a big fan of the Furman County Sheriff's Department."

Tom nodded. "Are you trying to tell me this is evidence she withheld from the detectives?"

"She wants Goldy to have it." Vic's tone had turned stubborn.

"Goldy can see it," Tom replied evenly. "But tomorrow morning, I'm taking it down to the department. And I'll try to convince our guys not to arrest Mrs. Routt for withholding evidence in a homicide investigation."

Vic's face turned pale under his freckles. He

seemed to be struggling with a response when the phone rang. I checked my watch: almost eleven. This was turning into a very long evening.

"Is Vic there?" Sally Routt asked, her voice breathless. "He never came back, and one of the neighbors just called and said somebody was hurt in the street." She snuffled, then started to sob. "I can't, I can't . . . take any more."

"Vic is fine, Sally," I reassured her. "We're just going to let him rest for a minute. Then he'll be on his way back over."

"I'm just jittery about everything; sorry." She stopped and took a deep breath, as if trying to keep her composure. "Colin can't seem to stop crying, and I'm trying to get him back to sleep. It feels as if everything is falling apart."

"Do you want to come stay with us? It would be fine, Arch is going over to his half brother's—"

"I just would like you to send Vic back over. I know I didn't want to see him earlier, but now he's being awfully nice and helpful . . ."

"Right. I'll send him back."

When I told Vic that Sally needed him, he shook his head and stood up. "Yeah, I stayed too long." Vic's dark eyes caught mine. "Mrs. Schulz, you look awfully tired."

I nodded grimly. I did feel numb from exhaustion, not only because it was getting really late, but because thinking about Donald Ellis's party was draining what little late-night energy I had managed to summon after the visit from Claggs et al. In point of fact, I wanted this particular day to end as soon as possible. Still, though, what had Vic said? **I'm just trying to help Mrs. Routt, you know?** No, I didn't know. Why, all of a sudden, was Vic Zaruski trying to help Sally Routt? Were they particularly close? Or was Vic trying to stay close to the investigation for other reasons? And furthermore: as long as I was being suspicious, had Vic really almost been run down by an SUV? Or had he staged a near accident to make himself sympathetic? Hmm.

"Just a sec, Vic," I said. "Where'd Dusty get the computer? Do you know?"

"St. Luke's parish office. The church was getting a whole new system, so they gave that old thing to Dusty." His face became serious again. "Anyway, Mrs. Routt thought it might be useful to **you** in looking into Dusty's death."

"I'm not an alternative to the cops, Vic. Remember what Tom said? He's taking it down to the department. In any event, even if I could get something out of that bashed-up machine, which is a pretty big if, I'd be guilty of concealing evidence and obstruction of justice and God only knows what else, maybe material witness after the fact."

"You can give the cops information that might lead to an arrest, Sally says," Vic continued. "She just doesn't want embarrassing stuff about Dusty appearing in the paper, you know. In case she was, you know—"

"Having an affair with a client of H&J? Selling drugs? Swapping sexual favors for expensive jewelry?"

Vic shrugged. "Whatever. Look, I gotta go."

"Tom," I said after I'd closed the door, "do you trust Vic?"

He cocked his head and gave me his patented half smile. "I don't trust anybody until we've got a strong case against a suspect in custody."

"Right. Well, in the meantime, would you be willing to have a look at Dusty's computer?"

"In the morning, Miss G. It'll keep. Meanwhile, you look exhausted."

I peered into the antique gilded mirror that Tom had hung in our front hall. The light shining through the crystal drops of our small overhead chandelier—another antique find of Tom's—cast a prism across the front hall. My dark-circled eyes, pallid face, and head of flattened blond curls did not look too good.

"Exhausted, nothing. I look like hell." I glanced

back at the kitchen. "You go on up. I'll be with you in five minutes."

"I need to take care of the animals first. Miss G., do not try to mess with that computer tonight. If you do, I'm going to carry you up to bed myself."

"Yeah, yeah, tough guy," I muttered as Tom moved quickly into the pet-care area adjoining the kitchen, where he was greeted by Jake and Scout. Instead of following him, I veered into the dining room. Fatigue or no fatigue, I was consumed with curiosity regarding Dusty's computer.

I frowned at the big plastic-encased box with its small moss-colored screen. The thing was not just a dinosaur, it was a **Tyrannosaurus rex** that had fallen off a cliff. I didn't recognize the brand, but that didn't mean anything. Like most kids of his generation, Arch was the technological wizard of the household. And he was away, spending the night with his half brother. Since the next day was Saturday, he wouldn't be home before Tom carted the thing off to the department. **Dammit**.

The plastic housing was dented and the screen scratched where Vic had slammed into the car on our curb. **Probably won't even boot,** I thought as I plugged in the cord. To my surprise, when I pressed what I thought was the on button, the box started humming. But the screen remained dark. I checked the wires for a loose connection and tapped every button I could think of that might bring the thing to life, with no result.

Of course, I was desperate to know what Dusty had recorded, if anything. Perhaps she'd fingered someone she hadn't been getting along with, even said how scared of him she was. Yeah, right. Maybe her hopes and dreams were recorded in a separate file. There might even be love letters. I imagined myself reading the inner workings of Dusty's mind. A knot of grief formed in my chest and I rubbed my face. From the entry to the dining room, Tom cleared his throat. He held out his hand. I grasped it and followed him up to bed.

I woke during the night, not because of any noise, but because of the sudden silence. A monumental stillness blanketed our house and neighborhood. **More snow,** I thought. I'd been too preoccupied with disaster to check the forecast. Worse, I had an event to cater that day, a party that I'd be driving to in a van with only marginally safe radial tires. Then I remembered Dusty, and scolded myself for being upset about something as insignificant as the status of my wheels.

A sob erupted from somewhere in my gut. It took me more by surprise than it did Tom. Tom, immediately alert, pulled me in so that my back was warmed by his chest.

"It's going to be okay, Miss G.," he murmured. "You're going to be all right. Everything will work out."

I cried until I was too tired to cry anymore. Then I allowed Tom's warmth to circle me like a mantle. Like the house, I fell into a deep hush.

When my alarm went off at five, everything outside was still quite dark. I slipped out of bed and tiptoed to a window. About four inches of new snow nestled against the ledge. **Not as bad as it could have been,** I thought as my eyes inevitably sought out the little Habitat house where the Routts lived. A streetlight nearby barely illuminated the place, which was shrouded in darkness. Sally would be getting up this morning without her daughter there, without her daughter ever coming back. My mind jumped to the thought of the funeral. When would it take place? Too shocked with reality, no one had spoken of it the day before. I hadn't a clue when the coroner's office would release Dusty's body. It was the weekend, so things could be backed up . . .

Liquid concrete seemed to be pouring into my chest again, so I turned away and sat on the navy, burgundy, and cream Oriental runner Tom had placed in our bedroom for me to do my yoga every morning.

"You should not face the world if you are unable to give to the world," André, my catering mentor, had been wont to say. No question about it, I did not feel able to face the world this morning, much less give it a thing. But I needed to go forward. I closed my eyes and prayed for Dusty and her family. Then I crossed my legs and surveyed my narrow piece of carpet. A few minutes later, I began with the cleansing breath and started to move, slowly, slowly through my asanas. Whenever thoughts raided my head, I put them aside with another cleansing breath. It helped.

Something else that would help was a major dose of caffeine, I told myself as I took a quick shower and zipped myself into a clean catering outfit of black pants and white shirt. The house felt cold as I stole down the stairs, and I tried to recall if Tom or I had remembered to turn on the heat. If either one of us had, and the heat wasn't working, that meant there'd been a power outage because of the snow. If we'd lost power, then the espresso machine would be out of commission, and if I couldn't have a four-shot latte before finishing up the prep for the Ellis party, I was going to have to find a tractor to drive into the house of the power company's CEO.

And here I'd been thinking that prayer and yoga had rendered me serene. Well, there were limits.

But the power was on. In less than two minutes I'd turned on the heat in the main-floor rooms and was sitting on one of our new kitchen stools, sipping a quadruple-shot latte made with whipping cream. I slurped down some more coffee and stared at the screen of the kitchen computer. For Donald Ellis's birthday party, I'd already made the empanadas, guacamole, and stuffed Portobello mushrooms. Now I just had to pull together salad ingredients, crush herbs to sprinkle over the beef tenderloin, and prep the ingredients for the Parmesan mashed-potato mounds. The steamed broccoli, snap peas, and pattypan squash, along with their cherry-tomato garnish, could be prepped at the Ellises' house, and the frozen homemade sourdough rolls just needed to be thawed. And there was the Old Reliable birthday cake, which Julian had wrapped and put in the walk-in, and I only needed to frost and decorate the thing.

The other eight H&J lawyers were still in Maui, ostensibly pursuing their continuing-education courses; Georgina, the firm's paralegal, and Marilou, the legal secretary, were taking their notes for them. And Georgina and Marilou wouldn't have been invited to Donald's party, in any event. So the folks from the firm would be Richard Chenault and K.D., his soon-to-be ex-wife, whom Donald had asked Nora to invite, since, Nora had said, she was "such a wonderful person." Claggs and his wife, Ookie, would also be in attendance, Nora had told me, although she warned me that "Ookie always gets plastered at these things, so watch the wine." Oh yeah, right, between roasting the tenderloins and heating the potato puffs, I would just dash out and check on the levels of Chardonnay and Pinot Noir. But I had said nothing as Nora had breezed on with the list of guests. Along with Nora and Donald and Nora's father, Bishop Sutherland, there would be three other neighbor couples, "two attorneys and their wives, and a couple, the Odes, who are clients of Donald's." I had catered to a few of these folks, but knew none of them well . . . except for Michael Radford, the divorce lawyer whom Marla had hired when she'd wanted to protect her wealth from the Jerk. Michael Radford had been good at that.

Now, because that only made thirteen, Nora had asked if I knew of a single female around town who would be appropriate. I'd immediately supplied Marla's name. Nora had barely been able to conceal a wrinkle of disgust—she knew Marla from St. Luke's—before she drew her pretty, impish face into a smile and said that would be fine.

Luckily, Marla, the self-proclaimed scourge of the country-club set, could usually be counted upon to keep one or another conversational group laughing. Or crying. But she'd liven up the party, no question. When I'd brightly told Nora this, she'd muttered, "I'll bet."

I removed the tenderloins from the refrigerator. Since the beef required just a short time to roast, I'd be cooking them at the Ellises' house. I washed my hands, took out a batch of frozen homemade sourdough rolls, and started in on the potatoes. Julian had placed himself in charge of the vegetables and salad. I glanced at the clock: incredibly, it was six already. Julian had promised to be here by seven with his supplies, and he was unfailingly punctual.

While the potatoes were boiling, I pulled the sheet cake out of the freezer and placed it on the kitchen table. Nora had directed me to decorate it with something "lawyerly," whatever that meant. But after staring at the large rectangle for a while and trying to think what she meant, I realized I should make the whole thing look like a legal pad. A frosted yellow rectangle covered with thin blue frosted lines shouldn't be so difficult, I thought, as I softened unsalted butter and pulled out confectioners' sugar, cream, and vanilla. Then on one of the lines I'd carefully write "No Law Against

Having a Happy Birthday, Donald!" Honestly, the stuff caterers are called upon to do.

While the beaters were mixing the ingredients into a creamy mélange, I hunted up my cake-decorating tools, professional food colors, and a plastic ruler. I could only find an old one of Arch's, so I washed it three times in the hottest water I could stand, since I didn't want any bits of dried school glue or old chewing gum sticking to Bishop Sutherland's, or anyone else's, teeth. Frosting the cake itself took concentration, but it was fun, sort of like an elementary-school art project. Once it was done, I snapped a hard plastic sheet-cake cover over my creation. It wouldn't do to get my masterpiece smashed by an errant raw tenderloin. I whacked the walk-in door fully open and carefully placed the sheet cake on a shelf.

Julian was almost due to arrive, so I drained the potatoes and started gathering the serving platters and utensils we would need. Nora's maid was setting the table and cleaning up; Nora herself had ordered Chardonnay to go with the appetizers as well as the Pinot Noir that I had suggested be served with the beef. We would arrive at ten to set up, finish the cooking, and serve, and everything should go like clockwork.

I stared at the steaming potatoes and tried to think, but couldn't. I fixed myself another latte and sat down at the kitchen table. Why had Dusty told me she wanted to learn to cook so she could snag a rich dude? Had she had someone in mind? Did the bracelet that I wasn't supposed to see mean she'd **found** that wealthy guy? I had no idea, and my memory of Dusty seemed to mock me. Every time she'd mastered a new dish, she'd thrown back her head and laughed with such innocence that I'd found myself smiling. Now I wondered why this had amused me.

Buck up, I ordered myself. But what if Sally called today asking if I'd figured anything out? Dusty's computer, which might or might not yield up any secrets, was worthless until someone was able to fix it, and even that was doubtful. **Please find out what happened to my baby,** Sally had begged me. I banged my cup down on the saucer so hard that both of them broke.

I cursed and cleaned up the mess. Then I buttered my muffin tins, mashed the potatoes and mixed in cream, seasonings, and Parmesan, and carefully scooped out smooth balls of this mixture and dropped them into individual muffin cups. So now I was done until Julian showed up. I fixed myself a plain espresso—well, those last four shots had been mixed with cream, so they hardly counted, did they?—poured it into a plastic cup, and scooted back up to my computer screen. I would open a file on Dusty and put in everything I knew so far. I'd pose a few questions, too.

Sipping the dark stuff, I typed up the names and positions of every single person who'd been working at the law firm as of Thursday night, excluding the lawyers, paralegal, and legal secretary in Hawaii: **Richard Chenault. Donald Ellis. Louise Upton. Wink Calhoun. Alonzo Claggett.** Had Dusty had problems with any of them that neither Wink nor I knew about? Wink had said Dusty had been working on some complicated oil-and-gas leases for Donald Ellis. But then, after Charlie Baker died, dealing with his estate had taken precedence. This work had been bumped up the totem pole because Richard was handling it, and Richard was, as Louise Upton never tired of reminding us, the boss. I wondered if Wink knew the details of either of those chunks of work.

What about clients? I knew some of them from when they facetiously requested my advice, and was occasionally introduced when I brought in drinks and comestibles. Who would know more about the clients with whom Dusty had contact? If anyone would, it would be Wink. I reminded myself to put a call in to her a bit later in the morning.

What else? Well, there was Vic Zaruski. He and Dusty had just broken up, but could he have given her the bracelet when they were going together? I was pretty sure Vic's salary at Art, Music, and Copies could not be much above minimum wage. I also knew vaguely that Vic was trying to make it as a musician. But I doubted any of his gigs would have generated enough cash for him to purchase anything as elaborate as that bracelet.

Could Donald Ellis have given Dusty the bracelet? He was a nerd who was married, and his wife was worth a mint. He sure didn't seem like the cheating type, but maybe he fooled around anyway. Could Richard have given the bracelet to Dusty, as a gift for her work at the firm? If so, why would it have been such a big secret?

And then there was Alonzo Claggett. He was much better looking than either Donald or Richard, and if he gambled and his wife drank, maybe he was looking for an understanding young paralegal-in-training to comfort him. And if Dusty's beau had been Alonzo, Donald, or a married client, then that would explain why she'd felt the need to keep things secret. Or maybe she had worried about the wrath of Louise Upton, if Louise had thought totems on the pole had become involved? Then again, had Dusty been concerned about Vic getting jealous? Who knew?

What about one of the lawyers who was in Hawaii? Was any one of them partial to Dusty?

Who would know? Maybe a more appropriate question would be, Who would tell me?

This wasn't much to go on, I reflected as I slid from my seat. But it was a start. Would Alonzo, Donald, or Richard be willing to talk to me about Dusty at the party? Working at the firm, I'd learned lawyers loved to gossip more than high-school girls. Maybe they'd let me in on some inside scoop.

I glanced over at the potato puffs, which seemed to be calling me. Well, I had made plenty. I melted some butter in a small sauté pan and fried a fourth of one until it was golden brown. My mouth watered as I placed the potato puff on a plate. With the first bite, I almost swooned. The crispy exterior housed a hot, thick, cheesy interior. Talk about comfort food. Why didn't folks have mashed potatoes for breakfast?

The phone rang. It stopped ringing before I'd finished my last bite, which irritated me no end. I certainly hoped it wasn't Julian, informing us his Range Rover was stuck in a snowdrift.

Tom shuffled into the kitchen in his robe, a mangy gray thing that I was dying to steal and throw away when he wasn't looking.

"That was the coroner's office. Cause of death was lack of oxygen. Manner of death was strangulation. She fought with her attacker, but didn't get any skin under her nails, unfortunately. The coroner's investigating some other things, and we should know more later in the day. Looks like Dusty broke glass in one of the picture frames, or was slammed into it. Anyway, that was indeed the cause of the gash in her forehead, and all the blood."

"Have they figured out the time of death, anything like that?"

"Whoa, Goldy, we're lucky to have that much. They'll establish a window for time of death when they do the full autopsy. He said they're not too stacked up there."

I looked out the window at the snow and tried **not** to think of corpses accumulated in piles.

"Did they find anything at the crime scene? Like that opal and diamond bracelet I was telling you about?"

"Nope. No bracelet. No sign of forced entry either. What's the security like there, anyway?"

"Old-fashioned," I replied. "Keys. Everybody had a set."

Tom looked around the kitchen. "Well, they want me to go in and help them out. I'm going to have to take the computer."

"Tom, please. I don't want to get Sally Routt into trouble."

"Gotta do my job, Miss G. And I don't think you'd fancy being charged as a material witness."

Oh, so **that** was what I was facing. I put two cups under the spouts of the espresso machine, pressed buttons, and tried to think.

"Okay, look," I ventured. "The computer won't boot. Could you see if you can fix it? If you can, I'll print out everything that's in it and look it over. I'll see if Dusty said anything about a new boyfriend, or enemies, or rich clients, or even folks at the law firm. If I recognize any of the people she's talking about, I can tell you. Meanwhile, if it won't boot, you can take it and I'll tell Sally she needs to trust law enforcement more."

Tom raised his eyebrows. "I'll give it an hour. The team won't be assembled down at the department until nine."

"Get it to work, and I'll make your sausage-and-potato casserole for dinner tonight."

Tom chuckled. "You make that casserole, I'll get somebody here **now** to fix that machine."

Tom moved into the dining room and began puttering with the old computer. As he grunted and complained under his breath, I assembled boxes to take over to the Ellis place. Julian called and said a Volvo had crashed into a BMW at the bottom of Marla's driveway, and he couldn't get out. Apparently, a tow truck was on the way. He also offered an unprintable curse on folks who didn't know how to drive in snow. He promised to be at the house by eight. I told him it was no problem, I was running ahead of schedule.

Five minutes later, Tom hollered, "Yeah, baby!" in the excited tone he used to celebrate a Bronco touchdown. I hurried into the dining room; the computer screen was lit with a screen saver that was a picture of little Colin Routt. "One of the wires was loose," he offered. I told him I'd checked all the connections. Tom shrugged, then double-clicked and brought up a list of documents.

"Okay, Goldy. I'm going to connect my printer to this thing so you can get all the stuff you want. It's better than my messing with your printer, then having to hook it back up to the kitchen computer. Okay?"

"Great. I'll get everything printed out before you leave, trust me."

Tom reached out and pulled me in for a warm hug. "Aren't you glad you have a husband who can fix things?"

I kissed his handsome face on both cheeks, then looked into his green eyes the color of the ocean. "I'm glad I have you. I don't care about the fix-it part."

"Yeah, right." He released me and ambled off to the basement, where he kept his computer, files, and printer.

It only took about another ten minutes before Tom's printer was connected and merrily spitting out reams of paper from the Routts' files. There was a lot of material. Recipes. Addresses. Bills. What looked like drafts of papers and briefs Dusty had written for her first semester of paralegal training courses. There was a file marked "Journal," but I didn't take the time to read any of it, as I was in a hurry to finish. The journal itself was forty-odd pages long, single spaced.

"Done," I said to Tom as he reentered the living room, freshly showered and looking snazzy in jeans, turtleneck, and a chocolate-brown wool sweater I'd given him. He glanced at the stack of pages: about four hundred. He cocked one of his sandy-colored eyebrows at me. **When are you going to have time to read all that?** Then he disconnected the computer and heaved it onto the kitchen table. He pulled on his boots, overcoat, and cable-knit brown wool cap, another gift from me. When he was dressed for the outdoors, he pulled me in for a long kiss that reminded me again why I was glad this particular man was my husband, fix-it genius or no.

"I'll call you," he said after he let go of me.

"Wait a sec. When you're down at the department, could you ask the detectives if they picked up on anything in the romantic department for

Dusty? I mean, if she was having a fling with someone who gave her that bracelet, would the lawyers or staff be duty bound to tell your guys?"

"Oh, absolutely. I'll ask."

A moment later he was pushing out our back door holding the computer. "You're going to have your cell?"

"I'm putting it in my pocket right now."

Which was what I did. No sooner had he backed carefully out of our driveway than Julian pulled into it. The Rover engine growled as Julian made short work of the snow. On the way in, he put down his bags to pat Scout and Jake. Then he picked up his loads and stamped across the deck to the back door.

"Dammit to hell and back that folks from Florida feel they have to make a trek to the farthest grocery store available to get milk when it snows!" were his first words once he'd come into the kitchen.

"And good morning to you, too, Goldy," I said.

"Yeah, yeah." He placed the bags on the counter and gave me his patented furious look, although I knew him well enough by now to tell it was bogus. "From now on," he announced, his dark hair quivering, "I'm going to start filling a really big thermos with espresso and sugar before I go **anywhere**. Either that, or have a battery-operated coffee machine put in that car, I swear."

"Great idea. Have some caffeine, then let's finish up the food for this lunch."

Julian fixed himself a quadruple espresso, which he doused with his usual numerous heaping teaspoons of sugar. I tried not to look, like on those nature channels where you really **don't** want to see the alligator eat the flamingo. But it was too late.

"As long as you were running ahead of schedule and I wasn't going to be here on time, I stopped at Aspen Meadow Café to pick up some pastries and run them over to Meg Blatchford," he said. When Julian smiled, his entire face lit. "The oldest Episcopalian in Aspen Meadow was out in the snow, no less, practicing pitching her softball into that bucket in her yard. But there was something else."

"Something else?"

Julian chugged his espresso and set his cup in the sink. "There wasn't anything physically wrong with her. You know her, she's so healthy she should be the cover girl for the AARP magazine. What I mean is that she was agitated. She said she'd like to talk to you. Said it couldn't wait until tomorrow's christening."

I looked ruefully at the stack of pages I'd printed out from Dusty's computer. A snowstorm, Julian delayed, and now the ordinarily docile Meg Blatchford needing to see me ASAP. When was I going to get to read what Dusty had put in her computer? What if Sally called demanding to know what progress I'd made?

Julian, sensing my distress, washed his hands, then began retrieving the vegetables he'd brought and running them under cold water. Over the gush from the faucet, he said, "We could make it to Meg's, you know. If we left here at nine instead of nine-thirty. I can finish the prep while you pack the van. No, wait. I had a look at your tires the other day, and you don't want to take the van in this snow. Let's take the Rover."

"Your Rover's not approved as a food-service vehicle."

"Yeah? There isn't going to **be** any food service if we get stuck in a ditch."

"Look . . . Julian?"

"Oh, boy. Here it comes."

"I have some stuff I'm desperate to start reading before we go. Any chance you could do all the prep and pack us up?"

"Absolutely." He grinned widely. "I'll go **really** fast."

I fixed myself another espresso with cream and carried it into the dining room. **One of these days, I told myself, I've got to start drinking decaf.**

I figured I'd begin with the journal. Dusty didn't say at the beginning, "In the event of my death, please destroy," but I still felt as if I was invading someone's privacy. I told myself I was doing this for Sally. I also prayed that I'd find something helpful to the sheriff's department investigation.

At least she had dated the entries, which I began to skim. She'd been working for the law firm since just before the beginning of the year, which was when she'd started the second semester of her second year of paralegal night classes. Almost right away, Richard had given her all kinds of work to do, including helping the artist Charlie Baker, who'd just been diagnosed with pancreatic cancer, get his papers in order. But Dusty had enjoyed the work. She hated trying to find anything in Donald Ellis's office, loved working out with Alonzo Claggett, but never thought she'd be as fit as his wife, Ookie. She also dodged Louise Upton at every opportunity.

The next few pages were devoted to talking about how she never had enough money to buy the things she wanted. She listed the things she wanted: **To learn about the law, everything about it.** And after that, she'd like a Porsche SUV, a place of her own, a trip to Mexico . . . On the sixth page, a despondent note crept in.

March 22: Charlie Baker died last night. Fell down his stairs, somebody said. It's weird, especially after what I was called in to do the night before that. Oh, I'm so sad I can hardly

write in here. How long had I been working with him, getting his stuff in order? Three months. At least he thanked me by giving me the you-know-what. Now when I look at it, I'll always think of him. The cops asked me if Charlie was sad. You know, depressed. If you had pancreatic cancer, I asked them, wouldn't YOU be depressed? They looked at me like I was nuts. I **WISH I WAS ALLOWED TO TALK ABOUT THE OTHER THING.**

The "you-know-what"? **At least he thanked me by giving me** . . . what? A bracelet? A painting? And what was the "other thing"? Was that what she'd **been called in to do**? Dusty was sure of what she was talking about. But it seemed to me she'd been worried someone else might be reading this. Because if someone did read it, which was, in fact, what I was doing, he or she would have to guess as to the nature of the "you-know-what" and "the other thing."

I skimmed about ten pages, in which she talked at length about how much she disliked Miss Upton, whom she did indeed call "Miss Uptight."

On March 27, she wrote, "Now that I know Miss Uptight is strapped for cash, I don't have to be so scared of her anymore. It takes her power away. I wonder if she'll know I know. Maybe I should act as if she still frightens me."

She talked about the oil-and-gas work with Donald Ellis, which had to be "the most boring thing on earth. And here I thought studying the law and learning about it would be fun. Those great big long drawers stuffed with his maps are the most confusing things in that entire wreck of an office. Where is the map of the southern Wyoming gas deposits, he wants to know? Who has ANY IDEA? Not me." She said she couldn't find the missing papers and maps in Donald's office unless she had a year and a staff of six, all professional organizers. Which she didn't.

Richard she referred to as "King Richard," "the Chief," and "my screaming uncle." She resented taking time from the "oil and gas mess" to tend to Charlie's estate, which "just makes me feel sad."

April 1: So now it's my job to go over to Charlie's and clean out the refrigerator, take the fish out of his aquarium, and dispose of his plants. It's snowing outside! I can't put two dozen houseplants that Charlie sprayed and watered and doted on into a trash bag and leave them to freeze out on the curb! Sometimes I think the Chief has no feelings. Correction: I know he has no feelings.

April 30: I go over there and I pick up the mail every day. I get the bank statements, the bills. Not the most entertaining work in the

world. But at least I stop in to see Meg, and that's fun.

In June, she began to mention wanting to learn to cook.

June 15: I am so bummed! I wanted to take cooking lessons at Aspen Meadow Café, but they say their kitchen is too small. I'm in love. But I'm afraid this is another Mr. O. Still, how am I going to make great meals for my new Mr. O. if I don't know how to cook? Oh God, I'm so in love with him. I've never been in love like this before. One day I was normal, you know, just me. Then I was a new person. I'm just going to call him New O.

New Mr. O.? New O.? Who was that?

I quickly read the rest of the pages. There was talk of work, talk of seeing "New O.," talk of being in love. Her last entry read: "Now I can compare them."

Compare what?

"Julian," I called. "Do you know all the guys Dusty was involved with?"

"I think so," his voice echoed from the kitchen. "There was Dick—Dick Shenley, from Elk Park Prep, although I never thought they were that serious, even though they went together until Dusty got involved with Mr. Ogden. Then there was Mr. Ogden, of course, that drama teacher I told you about. You know, I think she loved Mr. Ogden.

The mistake she made was that she thought Mr. Ogden would leave his wife, but he didn't. And of course she made a **huge** mistake to let him get her pregnant."

I stared at the sheet in front of me. "Anyone else with a last name beginning with **O**? Or a first name beginning with **O**, like, say . . . Otto?"

Julian stopped packing up our boxes for the party and came into the dining room. "Nope. There was only one Otto in our class, and he was gay." He thought for a minute. "I don't know any guys our age in town with a first or last name beginning with **O**." He pulled out his cell. "Let me phone a friend who went to Elk Park Prep."

Meanwhile, I put a call in to Wink Calhoun, who so far, hadn't seemed to know very much about her best friend. After I identified myself, I asked, "Do you know of a Mr. O. whom Dusty might have been involved with?"

"Mr. O.? Um . . . no. Wait. Donald Ellis has a client named Rock Ode, if you can believe it. He's gorgeous, very flirtatious, but also recently married. Dusty and I called him Rock 'n Roll."

"Do you think Rock 'n Roll and Dusty might have had something going besides flirting and working?"

"Goldy. Rock 'n Roll's just married a **model**."

As if that answered everything, I thought, smiling. I'd catered for a fashion photographer a while back, and the models had been the least scintillating conversationalists I'd ever met. "Look," I said, beginning to feel anxious about the upcoming party, "could you just think about it? When will I see you again?"

"I'm coming to Gus's christening. If I think of anything, I promise to tell you."

I gnawed at the inside of my cheek. "How about if we do it both ways. If **I** think of anything, I'll call you, too."

"Whatever you want."

I thanked her and nipped back into the kitchen to work on the boxes. Julian, still on his cell, wrote me a note saying he'd called two friends who hadn't gone to Elk Park Prep, but instead had graduated from Aspen Meadow High School. No **O.** His tone at the moment was compassionate. He scribbled, "Now I'm on with Sally Routt."

"Just a couple of quick questions," he murmured. "No, no, we're just trying to clarify one thing." Hearing this, I grabbed his note to me and wrote, "Ask her if she knows whether Charlie Baker gave Dusty something, and if so, what?" He posed the question, furrowed his brow, and waited. Then he thanked her for her help and came back out to the kitchen.

"There were four guys with first or last names beginning with **O** in the last three years at Elk Park Prep," he announced. "One was the Otto I told you about. The other three were O'Meara, O'Laughlin, and Orck. O'Meara died in a car accident last year. O'Laughlin's in the army serving in Germany. His wife and two-year-old twins are with him. And she didn't know what happened to Orck, but she thinks he moved to California."

I closed the flaps on the box with the cake. "Maybe this O-guy is someone she met in paralegal school."

"That's why I called Sally Routt. She's never heard of anyone with a first or last name beginning with **O**. It took her a few minutes, but she went to check the photograph of Dusty's first-year night class at Mile-High Paralegal Institute. No **O**s in there. Sally says Dusty met **Vic** at paralegal school. He dropped out because it was too boring, he said. So he's trying to make it again as a musician. Also, Sally doesn't know of a single thing that Charlie Baker gave to Dusty."

So there'd been no one at Elk Park Prep or Aspen Meadow High School with a first or last name beginning with **O**. There was no one at Dusty's paralegal school or at Hanrahan & Jule with last names beginning with **O**. There was only a flirtatious, wealthy, married H&J **client** named Rock Ode, which sounded like the title of a compact disc. Great.

But oh my, Dusty was dying to cook for this person. She was in love. Her life had started over, she was a changed woman! If Dusty had acquired a new boyfriend, especially one who was hungry for gourmet meals, and rich enough to afford an expensive jeweled bracelet, wouldn't she have told somebody?

Maybe she was planning on telling me, and then she was killed.

Which left me with a question: **Who in the world was this New O.?**

Chapter 12

I gathered the papers together quickly, as Julian and I needed to hustle if we were going to have time to visit with Meg Blatchford. Since we were going in the Rover, and that was an SUV, another SUV thought flitted across my mind: What if I was wrong to suspect Vic had concocted the story of almost being mowed down by an SUV? After all, there had been that honking horn, and Vic did seem genuinely shaken up, and worried that the computer had been damaged. What if the person who'd killed Dusty had been watching the Routts' house last night and had seen Vic coming out with the computer? Thinking the machine might contain incriminating information, had this watcher tried to run over Vic and his load so as to destroy any electronically stored data?

I dismissed this idea as paranoid. Then again, some folks say paranoids, like pessimists, are realists.

I pressed my fingers to my temples to forestall a headache. If such a theory was even marginally true, could that errant driver now think **we** had the computer? Had he seen Tom go out with it? I reminded myself to turn on the security system before Julian and I left. Then I clipped together the printed-out papers from Dusty's computer and shoved them under the skirt of our living-room couch. Once we were out on the street, I'd see if any of the parked vehicles looked unfamiliar.

Julian had transported all but two of our boxes out to his Rover. I put on my parka and boots, and with a last heave-ho, Julian and I picked up our big cartons and pushed through the back door.

Outside, I was momentarily blinded by sunshine reflecting off the snow. Blinking, I reshifted my box and tried to bring the deck into focus, because I most decidedly did **not** want to catapult down the steps and send fifteen pounds of cake, frosting, plates, and candles skittering across our backyard. Each piece of our deck furniture, I saw, bore a thick white cap. I'd forgotten all about my poor geraniums; they were probably done for. Oh, well. I had bigger problems. Much bigger.

I put my box down on the picnic table and pressed the buttons to set the security system. Any intrusion would summon the security company, Tom, and Tom's .38.

Turning toward the garage, I shifted my box again and glanced overhead. Caterers always worry about the weather: Will there be trouble getting to the event? Will people arrive late and screw up the food-serving schedule? If the driveway is slippery with snow, will either Julian or I slip and break an ankle while retrieving the boxes from the Rover? I prayed that the Ellises would have an empty bay in their garage that we could use.

Shiny white clouds sporting gray underbellies raced across the sky from west to east. As soon as a nimbus obscured the sun, the light quickly went from bright to dark. It didn't look as if more precipitation was imminent. Still, we'd received enough snow that mud could be a problem. All around our backyard, pine and aspen trees were heavily laden with the white stuff. Explosive thumps signaled loads of snow sliding off branches and landing on the ground. In many ways, it was a typical autumn day in the high country. "Season of mists and mellow fruitfulness"? As Arch would say, I don't **think** so.

Julian and I stomped through the snow toward the Rover, which he had turned on to warm up. When I stopped to rest—I was still suffering from a sleep deficit the size of the national debt—I could hear brave song from the few remaining birds. Well, I consoled myself, at least it wasn't winter yet. Not technically, anyway.

When Julian eased the Rover to the end of our

driveway, I looked up and down the street. Unfortunately, every single vehicle bore a thick hat of snow, making the cars unrecognizable. But nothing looked suspicious, and I couldn't imagine that any wannabe hit-and-run driver would have spent the entire nineteen-degree night parked by our curb, waiting for something to happen. At least, I hoped not.

The roads were treacherous, with a thick mixture of ice and slush plastering the pavement. As we headed up Main Street toward the lake, I was glad we were in the Rover. Furman County's gargantuan plows had swept the snow into a mountain range of mire bordering the sidewalk through town. Shop owners, eager to entice customers driven inside by the storm, were out brushing new white hats off their jack-o'-lanterns, giant black felt spiders, and witches.

Two of the merchants had thrown in the towel on Halloween. Instead, they'd hastily festooned their storefronts with garlands of twinkling red and green lights and signs announcing the numbers of days and weeks left until Christmas, a holiday Dusty Routt would not see. I sighed. But then the SUV in front of us skidded sideways on the uphill approach to the lake. Julian, who had allowed plenty of room for such an eventuality, gently pressed the brakes.

I was tempted to holler at the SUV driver. Apparently he hadn't heard, or didn't care to know, what longtime Coloradans knew well: four-wheel drive helps you go in **snow,** but it does not help you go, much less stop, on **ice.**

Julian slowed to a crawl, which caused a line of impatient drivers—all from out of town, I was willing to bet—to form behind us. After we circled the lake, the road finally widened and a bevy of drivers tooted triumphantly as they zoomed past. I gritted my teeth. An obese, bearded, particularly infuriated fellow driving a Volvo flipped us the bird as he whizzed past, too closely, on the left. Since we were still going uphill, Julian stared grimly ahead and kept his snail's pace. And then, twenty yards in front of us—oops!—the Volvo went into a wild skid across the left-hand lanes and collided with—oops!—a state patrol car hidden in the pines. The boom and crunch of crashing metal and breaking glass made the Rover shake.

"Oh my God," said Julian, as he slowed the Rover even more. "That guy in the Volvo is so unbelievably screwed."

"Julian!" I admonished him. "Are the two of them okay?"

He stared out his window. "Sure. The state patrolman just got out of his wrecked prowler, and he is **not** a happy camper. And look at that—the fat bearded guy is waddling toward him and yelling, 'cuz he's mad the cop was in his way. Oh, man, I am **so** glad I'm not out there."

"Me, too." And then I thought of Arch, fifteen and a half and clutching his freshly minted learner's permit. How would he have done piloting a vehicle in this mess? I immediately felt nauseous, and banished the thought. I was supposed to call him a bit later, so we could coordinate another driving lesson. I glanced at my watch and reminded myself that in teenage-boy time, half past nine in the morning was early yet. My cell was safely tucked in my pocket, as I'd promised Tom, and working out our mom–son instruction could wait until Julian and I had finished setting up at the Ellises'.

Once we were through town, Julian headed toward Flicker Ridge, where both Meg Blatchford and the Ellises lived. Flicker Ridge, an ultraposh area developed in the last decade, was also where Charlie Baker had purchased a house, once the prices for his paintings had skyrocketed. I wondered if his many-windowed mansion, perched at the top of the ridge, had been put up for sale yet. How long did it take to settle an estate, anyway? I had no idea.

Julian moved cautiously around a plow in the

right lane. I pressed my lips together. Catering in a firm specializing in estate law, you'd have thought I'd have picked up lots of legal knowledge odd-ments, such as the period of time it took to settle the estate of a single man. But in fact, I hadn't picked up a whole lot. Folks had their wills and revocable and irrevocable trusts, plus writs and motions and suits, and they scurried around, yelling at one another, ushering in clients, or hid-ing out in their offices and calling me on my cell to bring them coffee, preferably made without any of Richard's booze mixed in. Which, of course, I was happy to do.

The one thing that I had learned, though, I thought as Julian eased the Rover around another collision, was the meaning of the word **tort**. A **tort** was any type of wrong. Fraud. Embezzle-ment. Theft. Something a wealthy client could get sued for. And what every attorney I knew moaned and groaned about was attempts at **tort reform,** meaning caps being put on the amount of money the good little guy could take from the rich bad guy. With tort reform, they all shrieked, they would all be out of business. Torts kept many a lawyer alive, but they made everyone hysterical.

I'd take the other kind of **torte** any day.

Julian's voice startled me out of my reverie. "Look at how gorgeous everything looks!"

With his left hand, he was pointing at the wide field and dense evergreen forest rising on our left. The snowy meadow sparkled in the sunshine. Up in the woods bordering the flatland, every tree's branches bore a sculpted cargo of ice. Multiplied thousands of times, the profusion of whitened branches was indeed breathtaking. At the base of the hill, several stands of tall, gray-barked aspens stood out in sharp relief. Their snow shed, the branches were still trimmed with thick bouquets of yellow leaves the color of a school bus.

"You know what they say about Aspen Meadow, don't you?" Julian asked. "You take half your pay in scenery."

I smiled in spite of myself. There had been much protest from town environmentalists over the building of Flicker Ridge, which was coming up on our right. The exasperated developer, now-deceased Brian Harrington, had given three thousand acres of meadow and wooded hills—largely unbuildable, cynics had pointed out—to Furman County Open Space. Brian's critics had shut up, Brian had taken a huge tax write-off, and Aspen Meadow now had miles of hiking trails that enticed tourists all through the summer months. During the fall, winter, and spring, the Harrington Hills, as Brian had insisted they be called, attracted only the most dedicated of snowshoe

enthusiasts. With each new snowfall, the hills became more impenetrable—and more stunning.

A moment later we turned through the stone
entryway to Flicker Ridge. Because the home-
owners here had contracted with their own snow-
removal folks, the roads were better plowed than
the ones in town. Julian gave the Rover some gas.
On either side of us, enormous, villalike houses,
gray and beige and pink, rose like ghosts above
rolling expansive yards, now patchwork fields of
green and white. There were no kids, no sleds, no
snowball fights. It was eerie.

After a mile, Julian maneuvered the Rover
around a left turn and gunned the engine toward
the peak of the ridge. On a treed spread across
from Charlie Baker's many-windowed McMan-
sion, Meg Blatchford lived in the one log residence
Brian Harrington had been unable to get torn
down. I could just imagine Brian going head-to-
head with Meg Blatchford. Brian might have been
able to handle troublesome eco-activists, but he
was no match for seventy-nine-year-old Meg.

Meg's half-mile-long driveway had been
plowed, I was thankful to see, but the fact that it
was shaded meant much of it was still icy. After
some skidding, Julian decided to park halfway up.
We could hoof it the rest of the way.

The house, which was a cabin that had been

added onto on both sides by Meg's father, was set in a thick stand of lodgepole pines, those towering, slender evergreens whose trunks, tourists were always amazed to hear, had been used for the actual **poles** for the **lodges;** hence the name. In a cleared area, Meg had set up her softball pitching-practice area. She had built a mound at one end, where she kept a covered basket of softballs. At the other edge was a wooden wall with a painted **O**. She had told me one time that once she had a spot to practice every day, her pitch became more deadly than ever. I was very willing to believe her.

Meg, appropriately wearing a thick gray jacket with the hood up, came out to greet us.

"Oh, look!" she exclaimed. "Julian! Goldy! You came. Oh, dear Julian, look at you, the second visit in one day. Can you come in for a quick cup of tea?"

I nodded, and we stamped the snow off our boots. I was **so** glad we weren't going to have to stand outside while she did more pitching practice. Meg Blatchford, tall and athletic, with a head of white curls and a spring in her step, played on several women's senior softball teams, and she was the star pitcher on each one. She was the most inspiring older person I'd ever met. Her wrinkled face was always tan—dermatologists be damned—because one of her teams traveled year-round, to places like Phoenix, Tucson, and Fort Lauderdale. Her brown eyes sparkled with life, and her broad-shouldered, slender frame moved more quickly than mine ever had. Far from doting on her, members of our church community were often proclaiming Meg's latest doings: **Meg's team just took the tristate trophy. Meg won most valuable senior softball player in the state. Meg Blatchford just snagged the Denver-area Senior Female Athlete of the year! (And we're just betting she could take out the winner of the Junior Female Athlete of the year and kick her butt!)**

Julian and I followed Meg's straight-backed, nimble step up the wide redstone steps that led to the old cabin part of her residence.

This central section had been decorated by Meg's mother, Eugenia Blatchford. The living room's beamed ceiling was low, which made the large room feel snug. One whole wall was made up of a massive hearth that Eugenia had painstakingly composed of layer after layer of smooth river rocks. The other walls were hung with a dozen-plus sets of elk and deer racks. Between all those horns, Eugenia had placed black-and-white photos of Blatchford ancestors posing in late-nineteenth- and early-twentieth-century Aspen Meadow, when it was first a trading post, then a lumber town. I was also surprised to see two Charlie Baker paintings, one on either side of the room. I didn't remember that Meg had had any.

While Julian and Meg commented on how the snow had snarled traffic in Aspen Meadow, I nipped over to look at the painting to the right of the fireplace. It was titled **Venison Stew**. The central image was a lone deer standing in a snowy pine forest. With his usual thickly applied brushstrokes, Charlie had just caught the filtered sunlight illuminating the tawny browns, deep greens, and pearly ground. Underneath the image was Charlie's list of stew ingredients, inscribed in gold calligraphic letters, and, typically, without directions. As in the other paintings I'd seen, the perimeter of the painting was filled with fanciful decorations. Here the images looked like little rectangular blocks embellished with squiggles. With my nose almost on the painting, I squinted and finally made out tiny sticks of butter, animated with thin legs and arms and smiley faces, marching in a merry band around the deer and the stew ingredients.

Meg settled herself in a chair near the hearth. Her two couches and four chairs were all constructed of rough-hewn logs. Each one sported horsehair cushions and was piled with Native American woven blankets in shades of rust, sand,

and gray. The decorator of the H&J reception area might have thought she was evoking the Old West, but this was the real deal. I picked out a chair near Meg and sat down.

"Goldy and I have a party to do in a little while," Julian said from the doorway. "Why don't you let me get the tea so you all can have time to talk?" Before we could respond, Julian trod quickly across a Hopi rug of the same weave and earth tones as the room's blankets and cushions. "Don't worry," he said as he disappeared around a corner. "I'll find what I need."

I felt suddenly awkward, sitting in this Old West living room with a woman whom I admired but did not know very well. Meg, usually so forthright, smoothed imaginary wrinkles out of her jeans and stared at the ashes in the fireplace. "I don't know where to start, and I know you can't stay long." Her voice trembled. "I talked to Sally Routt this morning, and I feel so disconnected . . ." She pulled a tissue from where she'd tucked it into her waistband, and began to weep quietly.

"I understand," I said softly. I felt my own throat close. Maybe coming over to this house had not been a good idea.

Meg dabbed her eyes and nose. "Sally said you were trying to help figure out what happened to her daughter. She said you'd promised to keep the police and press out of it."

"That's not exactly—" I began, but stopped. "Look, Meg. I am trying to help Sally. Why don't you start by telling me why you wanted to see me."

"Well." Meg cleared her throat and gave me the benefit of her clear brown eyes. "You remember my neighbor Charlie Baker."

I nodded. "We were friends. We used to cook together sometimes."

"He was a wonderful, eccentric old coot." She smiled, remembering, then frowned. "You know how much Charlie adored our congregation, and the feeling was mutual. He always insisted on making all the pancakes for the Shrove Tuesday supper. He relished running the luncheon café at the church during the Episcopal Church Women's home tour."

I tried to keep the impatience out of my voice. "We did the baked goods for the bazaar together."

"You remember how upset he was when Father Biesbrouck died."

"I do."

"But never mind," she said brusquely. "That hurt us all. When Charlie found out he was sick, he had a lot to do, you know, legally. H&J was his firm, and they sent Dusty over to work with him, to get his affairs in order. She . . . she came every day. What a dear girl. She would help Charlie, then she would always come over here to say hello, bring me some warm whole wheat bread or something else that Charlie had made for me. Even though he was sick, he still baked. Dusty said he claimed it made him feel as if he could live forever." She stopped talking for a moment. "Poor Charlie. He wanted to have one last show, in March."

"I know," I interjected. "I did the food for it—"

She waved this away. "People came from all over, they bought Charlie's paintings. He sat in a chair and soaked it all in. But when I drove him home, he was in a foul mood, poor thing. There'd been an accident outside the gallery, and that slowed us down . . . but he hardly seemed to notice it. When I left him off, he asked me if I knew of any private investigators."

"A private investigator? To find out what?"

Julian appeared, carrying tea things. After he'd set down the tray, he said, "Do you all want me to leave?"

"No, no," Meg said, her voice distressed. "It's all right." Julian poured the tea and gave me a wide-eyed look, as in **What's going on?** I shook my head quickly, then took the proffered cup, which Julian announced was Darjeeling. Meg barely nodded when Julian put her cup down on a small table made of intricately twisted branches.

Meg fixed me with that gaze of hers. "I told him to try H&J. He said he had other business to do there."

"What kind of business?" I asked.

"I don't know, he didn't say." She frowned, lost in her reminiscence. "I guess he meant his will, but that's just conjecture."

"Uh," Julian interjected, "I don't want to be rude here, but Goldy and I need to think about getting over to the Ellises' house."

Meg stood up. "All right, then," she announced. "I didn't ask you to come here because of Charlie. I wanted to see you because of Dusty." She glared at the tea things, as if they were somehow getting in the way of her story. "Could you bring your tea into my workout room? I'll show you . . . what has me disconcerted."

Julian and I glanced at each other, then picked up separate mugs. Julian doused his with sugar, and then we dutifully followed Meg down a narrow hallway and into a small log room that had bookshelves on three sides and a wall of wavy-glassed casement windows overlooking the ridge. Incongruously, a treadmill and two weight machines were placed in front of the shelves and windows.

"Used to be my father's office," Meg said by way of explanation. She moved over to the treadmill, which had been placed next to the bank of windows on the far side of the room. "I walk here, and run a bit, too. Do my exercises, push-ups and working with weights. Looking out the window keeps me from getting bored."

I peeked out the window, which had a view through the pines . . . to Charlie Baker's house. In profile, the house looked like the glass prow of a ship, set at anchor overlooking Flicker Ridge. From the window, one also had a good view of the iron fence around Charlie's house, and the gate to his driveway.

"That lot was empty for many years," Meg told us. "When Charlie became successful, he asked me if I would mind if he bought the land from the Flicker Ridge developers. I told him if I was going to have a neighbor, it was better to have him than a member of the nouveaux riches. That's a category that you can put your friends the Ellises in, by the way."

"They're not my friends," I corrected her. "They're my clients."

"Touché," said Meg. "So Charlie built that monstrosity of a house. Talk about people living in glass houses. Well. When I walked on my treadmill, I would see cars, trucks, repair people, anyone coming and going from that house. I knew Dusty's Civic by heart. Whenever I saw it, it would make me happy, because I knew she was helping Charlie, and that she'd be coming over soon with fresh, warm bread." Meg smiled faintly at the memory.

"So," I prompted her, "you saw something having to do with Dusty?"

Meg lifted her chin. "Dusty told me, after Charlie died, that the law firm had put her in charge of picking up his mail on her lunch hour. She said that was part of settling an estate." She shook her head. "I suppose I was wrong to expect her to keep coming over. I mean, Charlie wasn't there anymore, so there was no bread to bring. And a young girl's lunch hour is only sixty minutes, after all. But . . . well, it just used to comfort me to see her car in Charlie's driveway every day. All of a sudden, after Charlie died, she began to pull into his garage and put down the door. I don't mean to sound like an old woman, because after all, I **am** an old woman. But I'd be over here on my treadmill, thinking, The days are getting longer, why doesn't she park outside? And why does it take her entire lunch hour to pick up the mail? She was like clockwork, though, after Charlie died. Drive through Charlie's gate at ten after noon, go straight into the garage—I suppose she had a remote control for that—close the garage door. Then the garage door would open at ten to one, and out would come the Civic. Don't you think that's odd? Does it take an hour to pick up someone's mail?"

"Maybe she had other things to do for the law firm," I offered. "Inventory Charlie's stuff, that kind of thing."

"Right," said Meg, nodding. "That's what I thought, because I asked a friend on one of my softball teams. Lots to do, check out bank account statements, find assets, and so on. But then . . ." She stopped talking.

"Then?" asked Julian, his voice betraying a hint of impatience.

"Then Tuesday **night** of this week, Dusty's Civic was there. She came through the gate at about a quarter to five. Didn't park in the garage. Ran up the steps of Charlie's house and came out less than five minutes later. She was carrying a tube."

"A tube like a tube of toothpaste?" Julian again.

"No, no, no," corrected Meg. "A tube like the kind you send through the mail."

Right, I thought, a tube like the kind you send through the mail. Or like the kind you use for a rolled-up painting.

Dusty was doing the inventory. I may not have

learned much of what they did at H&J, but I certainly remembered the lawyers' joke about the "race to the house." That was why you had locks changed right after someone died. Dusty had told me she had received the new locks to Charlie's house from Richard himself, who was Charlie's executor. She'd also told me that **no one** was allowed to take anything out of Charlie's house until the estate was settled, and that wasn't going to happen until she had completed the inventory, which was extensive.

Would she have dared to take a painting? Why? If she had stolen a work of Charlie's, how could she possibly have thought she would get away with it? I felt more confused than ever.

And what was this with the closed garage doors on her lunch hour?

"Wait," I said, thinking of the "New O." from Dusty's journal. "Do you have any idea what was going on in Dusty's life at the time? Like maybe she had a boyfriend or something?"

Meg's face wrinkled in disgust. "She never discussed her social life with me, Goldy."

"Okay." Now I felt embarrassed, and covered it by taking another sip of tea. "Let's go back to the tube. Did she say Charlie had given her something?" I pressed. "That he had left her something? A painting, maybe?"

"No," Meg said. "And I have no idea what Dusty was doing over there on her lunch hour every day. Working on the inventory? Then why not stay longer? And working on what?" Meg paused. "I never found out any of those things because two days after Dusty came out with the tube, you found her in the law firm. Dead."

Chapter 13

So: Two days before Dusty was killed, she had carried a tube—maybe the kind used to store paintings—out of Charlie Baker's house. She'd been in love with a boyfriend nobody, not even her mother, seemed to know anything about. What else? Let's see: When the weather had been blizzardlike, Dusty had parked her Honda in front of Charlie Baker's house, and walked inside to do his legal work. Once Charlie had passed away, Dusty had received new keys to Charlie's house, been assigned to inventory Charlie's estate, and do other odd jobs such as pick up his mail every day. But by the time she'd been assigned to do all that, the weather had turned **pleasant**. Nevertheless, she'd driven her Civic into Charlie's garage when she arrived . . . and closed the door behind her.

Goodness me, I thought grimly as Julian piloted the Rover back down to the main road that ran through Flicker Ridge, all this info was not helping to clear up anything. I sighed. Dusty Routt had been dead for over twenty-four hours, and all I'd picked up was information that seemed, at best, disconnected. Worse, I'd made no progress trying to figure out what had been going on in her life that had prompted someone to kill her.

I didn't even want to contemplate the inevitable meeting with Sally Routt.

Once Julian was on Flicker Ridge Road, he headed the Rover toward the western edge of the development. Donald and Nora Ellis lived by Flicker Ridge's border, on a dead end that over-looked hundreds of acres of pine forest, all part of Furman County Open Space. It was prime real es-tate that kids could have run and played in, but the Ellises had no children. If anything, they were a typical example of the housing reversal that had become part of the demography of Aspen Meadow, and perhaps the rest of the country. To wit: the fewer kids and the more money you had, the bigger house and yard you demanded. On our lower-middle-class street, the lots were tiny and the houses small. Yet after school every day, kids spilled out of the driveways and onto the side-walks to kick soccer balls, throw baseballs, and toss Frisbees to their dogs. When a blizzard moved through and school was canceled, the kiddos would grab their big toboggans and slide merrily down our road, yelling "Yahoo!" all the way, until they made a sharp right turn into the last driveway before Main Street.

Then again, Nora and Donald Ellis weren't entirely without family, as Bishop Sutherland, Nora's father, had been living with them for almost ten months. What I had picked up from Nora was **not** an isn't-this-fun-Dad's-come-to-stay-with-us attitude. When I'd booked the party, Nora had tossed her blond hair and announced, "Yes, my father will be at Donald's party, because he will still be living with us. That's why I had to invite Marla, so we'd be an even number at the table. God! The sooner my father's out of here—" She'd stopped. Then she'd laughed, as if it were all a joke. "Maybe he'll hook up with Marla, get married, and have all kinds of money to spend on medical treatment for that damn arrhythmia! Not to mention unlimited funds for clothing, cars, trips, and anything his big old diseased heart desires."

Well, I definitely didn't want somebody with medical problems to hook up with my best friend, who'd already had a heart attack, thank you very much. On impulse, I put in a cell call to Wink Calhoun. Luckily, she was at home.

"Wink," I asked casually after I'd identified myself, "do you know anything about Bishop Uriah Sutherland? I'm just wondering, because he's my closest friend's sort-of date for the party today, and I don't know anything about him, apart from the fact that he's been helping out at our parish for a while."

Wink was uncharacteristically silent for a few minutes, and as Julian drove past the For Sale sign outside Richard and K. D. Chenault's big stucco house, I thought we'd been disconnected. "Wink? You there?"

"Yeah," she said tentatively. "I know a little bit about him. You mean Donald's father-in-law, right?"

"That's right," I said, immediately on guard myself. She'd been forthcoming before. Why was she hesitant now? "Something wrong?"

"No. Well, not exactly. Bishop Uriah just gives me the creeps when he comes sprinting over to the office from their house, supposedly to say hi to Donald. And he's always all covered with sweat, like he's been in a race. Sometimes I'm afraid he's going to collapse on our floor, and I'm going to have to do CPR."

"You're saying he **runs** over to H&J?" I'd seen Uriah running, too, along the Upper Cottonwood before the snow had moved in. But I'd learned in Med Wives 101 that folks with arrhythmia were supposed to **walk**. Walk **slowly**. Maybe it had been too many years since I'd been a med wife to know the latest thinking in the cardio department.

"Yeah," Wink went on. "I thought one time that he was trying to get there before anyone else arrived. Once? I caught him going through our trash in back of the law firm. He said he'd lost something."

"How could Uriah Sutherland have lost something in the firm's garbage?"

"I don't know. Plus, when he comes in? Even though he says he's there to see Donald, I just always get the feeling that that's **not** what he's there for. I mean, it just feels weird. He likes to poke around, ask questions. He's nice and all, but just . . ." She left the sentence unfinished.

"What kind of questions does he ask when he pokes around? Does he have legal problems?"

"If he did have legal problems, Goldy, he sure wasn't going to tell me, the lowly receptionist. But the questions he **has** asked me are all stupid stuff, like, 'How long does it take to get a will through probate, anyway?' That kind of thing. Dusty and I would always tell him just to ask his son-in-law. We didn't know whether he ever did. So Dusty and I used to wonder if Donald charged him." She laughed.

"But, Wink," I protested as Julian gave me a questioning look, "if the bishop has legal problems in addition to his medical issues, why doesn't he pay for advice someplace else? He must be able to afford it. I mean, he doesn't have rent to worry about, and he should be eligible for payments from the church's pension fund."

Wink sighed hugely, then seemed to think for a moment. "I don't think the bishop necessarily has a lot of money. At our staff Christmas party last year, Donald Ellis got a little drunk and complained about his father-in-law. He said Bishop Sutherland had champagne tastes, but Kool-Aid income. Want to hear the dirty details?"

"I specialize in dirty details," I replied, then put my hand over the receiver and asked Julian to pull over. He groaned, but acquiesced.

According to Wink, who'd gotten her info from the half-inebriated Donald, Bishop Uriah Sutherland had not endeared himself to his daughter any more than he had to his ex-wife, Nora's mother, Renata. According to Wink via Donald, Renata Sutherland, a transplanted-to-Denver Connecticut socialite, had been smart—or wily, or cruel, depending on your point of view—enough to construct an elaborate prenuptial agreement before tying the knot with Uriah, who was then a priest at Renata's Denver parish. This agreement had put all of Renata's considerable dough into an unbreakable trust for any **offspring** she and Uriah might have, but not for Uriah.

Renata and Uriah's bitter divorce, when Nora

was fifteen, had left Uriah virtually destitute. He'd been forced to live on his very modest priest's salary, in a house the parish provided. Even worse, Uriah's daughter, Nora, had blamed her father for the divorce, and had gladly moved to Connecticut with her mother. Nora had made her yearly trips to Denver to visit her father only under duress, until she was twenty. Then she'd suddenly turned enthusiastic about coming to the Mile-High City, but not because of her dad. No: she'd wanted to escape her mother's obsession with matching her up with the sons of her friends . . . and she'd begun a secret romance with Donald Ellis, then a deeply indebted student at the University of Denver Law School.

According to Donald, Uriah's parish still loved him, even if his wife didn't. And Uriah had endeared himself to someone else. When Uriah had been making rounds at a Denver hospital, he'd met a much-younger Charlie Baker, then suffering from shingles. A nominal Catholic since his orphan days, Charlie had been deeply grateful for Uriah's kindness and daily visits. Charlie, then a chef at a Denver restaurant, had become an Episcopalian. When Aspen Meadow Country Club had needed someone to run their renovated kitchen, Charlie had been hired. He'd moved to our little burg, joined St. Luke's, and done his painting on the weekends.

Uriah Sutherland's ex-wife, meanwhile, had died, leaving an **über**-size packet to Nora. Nora had promptly married the fellow she loved, Donald Ellis. When Donald had graduated from law school and been offered a job at H&J, Nora and Donald had set up camp—a luxurious, mansion-size camp—in Aspen Meadow. Donald had been at H&J almost five full years, and was waiting to find out if he'd made partner. Nora definitely had enough wealthy contacts that she could bring big business to H&J, Donald had told Wink, which could label him a "rainmaker," thus enhancing his prospects in the partner department.

In the meantime, Uriah Sutherland had been chosen as bishop of the Diocese of Southern Utah. But after only a couple of years, he began experiencing arrythmia. He had taken early retirement at the first of the year . . . and had promptly announced he was coming to live with his daughter, Nora, and her husband in Aspen Meadow.

"I didn't get the feeling Nora and Donald had invited Uriah to stay, and I **certainly** didn't pick up on any good feelings for the bishop." Wink hesitated. "Is that the kind of information you were looking for?" she asked, clearly relishing her role as gossip provider.

"I don't know what I'm looking for," I said ruefully. "But I still think it's interesting that Bishop Sutherland keeps poking around at H&J. Did he have any connection to Dusty? Did they get along? What about Charlie Baker? Was Uriah mentioned in Charlie's will?"

"I have no idea. You could ask Alonzo, though. He and Dusty worked out every day, and I know they were close." This last was delivered in a way that again sounded off-key. I decided to press my luck, even if it sounded a tad nosy.

"Wink? You and Dusty were friends. According to a couple of people I've talked to, Dusty and **Alonzo** were friends. But you and Alonzo **aren't** friends. Am I getting this straight?"

She sighed. "I'm not quite cool enough, or pretty enough, for Alonzo. Nor do I quite measure up to being noticed by his squash-playing bitch of a wife, Ookie."

"Ookie's a bitch?" I asked innocently. "Was she a bitch to Dusty?"

"**I** don't know. All I know is that when Nora Ellis invited me to play squash over at the club's courts? Ookie came up to me and said, 'Excuse me! These courts are for members only.'"

"What did you say?"

"Nothing! I was too surprised. Then Nora sauntered up and said, 'Now, now, girlfriend. You know as well as I do that these courts are for members and their guests." Wink tsked. "I think that Nora and Ookie are friendly to each other on the surface, but underneath they're a couple of sumo wrestlers. **Skinny** sumo wrestlers."

Now there's an image, I thought. Still, all this stuff about Uriah poking around at H&J, literally and figuratively, was pretty interesting. I wondered if I'd get a chance to poke around at the **Ellises'** house, maybe to see why Uriah was so interested in trash. Pretty risky, even for me.

Julian and I had to get a move on, but Wink had offered a lot of information, data that might prove useful at some point. "Just one more question," I said. Beside me, Julian exhaled. "Where'd you get the name Wink?"

"From my father. It was a nickname. Just think, I could've gone through grade school with kids yelling, 'Catch the ball, Mildred!'"

"That's not **so** bad."

"Maybe to you it isn't." She signed off.

As Julian began driving again, I tapped the dashboard and tried to think. Bishop Uriah Sutherland had had heart problems, I did know that. But he'd recovered sufficiently by the time he'd been in Aspen Meadow a short while to start helping out at St. Luke's. When our rector, Father Pete, had had a heart attack—was there something about being a clergyman that induced cardiovascular illness?—Bishop Uriah had smoothly and kindly stepped in and taken over liturgical, pastoral, and administrative duties. The St. Luke's budget had been stretched paying two salaries, it was true, but nobody wanted to deny a recovering Father Pete **his** income. I'd asked myself—but nobody else—why we had to pay Uriah Sutherland, too, since he lived at his daughter and son-in-law's palatial estate in Flicker Ridge. But my wondering had seemed smug and self-righteous even to me. If Uriah had been an arrhythmia-prone caterer who'd suddenly had to go back to work, I wouldn't have wanted to deny **him** pay, would I?

And now I knew what he spent money on: stuff that folks with champagne tastes always spent money on: fashionable clothes, fancy cars, extravagant vacations, jewelry . . . wait a second.

Was it even possible that Bishop Uriah had been "New O." in Dusty's diary? Had he given her the bracelet? He was old enough to be, well, almost her grandfather. But she'd already had a fling with an older man, Mr. Ogden. Was it possible?

Well, I suppose anything was possible. It just didn't seem probable. It also was very odd that Uriah had been poking around at H&J. What had he wanted to find, or find out? Something in general or something in particular? And if he had champagne tastes, why not indulge them by getting a downtown Denver lawyer to answer his queries?

I pursed my lips, recalling what Wink had said about Bishop Uriah being an old friend of Charlie Baker's. The bishop and I had chatted briefly at Charlie Baker's last show in March, the night before Charlie died. That night, Uriah seemed much less of his usual charming self. In fact, he appeared downright upset, swallowing and looking from picture to picture, as if paintings of cookies and brownies were more indecipherable than quantum theory. I thought of the bishop's arrhythmia, and of Charlie's incurable cancer. Maybe Uriah was contemplating his friend's coming death. When I asked if he was all right, he assured me he was fine.

Charlie Baker, his moon face shining, his body weak from failed chemotherapy, laid his hand on mine and patted it.

"Don't worry, Uriah's just a worrywart," Charlie said in his soft voice that always sounded as if he had a slight lisp.

"What's he worrying about?" I asked.

"Me, probably," Charlie replied, his voice low and cheerless. "I'm going to die soon, and Uriah knows it. But he's a clergyman, and he's not allowed to show his distress the way other people are."

"Oh, Charlie, please forgive me for being so insensitive," I protested, feeling like a heel. "Now, what can I bring you? Some of my ginger snaps? Or how about some chips and dip, the recipe for which is none other than our favorite food artist's?"

His gaze had been forlorn. "Oh, Goldy, I wish you'd let me leave you a painting in my will."

"Charlie, would you quit being so morbid? I've already told you, I can't afford the insurance. But you're sweet."

I'd wanted desperately to get Charlie's mind off of dying, but I'd been unsuccessful.

And then, without warning, Charlie was gone, and I was awash with the grief one feels when a dear friend dies suddenly, and you're left with all the things you didn't say. **You're such a great friend, Charlie. This is the best dip I've ever tasted. The next time we cook together, we'll make your chicken piccata . . .**

Don't, I reprimanded myself, as Julian slowed the Rover. Charlie had been more than a friend, he'd been a culinary comrade-in-arms. I swallowed and told myself to snap out of it. Caterer's rule for parties: **Let the mood fit the food.** It was time to **act** festive, even if I didn't feel it.

"What are you thinking about?" Julian asked. "You don't look so hot."

"I'm fine, thanks. I'm just concentrating," I reassured him as he turned onto Woods' End, the cul-de-sac where the Ellises' manse was located. I certainly did not want to depress Julian by talking about Charlie. Then we'd **both** be down, and that was not what we needed before doing a big—and, if Nora Ellis was generous with gratuities, potentially quite profitable—party.

The Ellises' enormous stucco residence sat on the top of a gentle slope that received enough southern exposure for the sun to have melted most of the snow on their front yard. Between the remaining patches of white, the grass was lushly green, even in October. The perfectly trimmed aspens, plethora of fruit trees, and long serpentine rock wall topped with stunning shrubs all screamed **Professional Landscaping Service**. The house itself, which was at least twice the size of the Chenaults' mansion, boasted numerous jutting spaces capped with red tile roofs. There was a massive, three-story entrance. The whole place looked as if six Taco Bells had been used as building blocks: four on the bottom, two on top.

"We should have brought burritos," Julian mused as the Rover crunched over some residual melting ice on the long driveway. When he'd pulled the Rover halfway up the driveway, he craned his neck back to check out the underside of one of the tile roofs. "I didn't know lawyers made this much money. Isn't Donald Ellis just an associate at H&J? Not a partner, right?"

"Not yet," I replied. "But Nora's the one with the dough, as she told me at least fifteen times when she was booking this event. She inherited twenty million from her mother. And if we do a great job today, maybe some of that **dinero** will come our way. Are you up for it?"

Julian gave me a high five and pushed open his door. We were still a ways from the arched entrance to the kitchen, which boasted a new carved sign over the lintel: "Welcome to Our Cucina!" it screamed. Cute, very cute. I wondered if Donald Ellis had received it as an early birthday present.

A shout from the end of the driveway interrupted my musings.

"Hey, you two!" came Marla's voice. "Wait up, okay? I've got something to tell you!"

"Hey, Marla!" Julian and I called back in unison. I was happy to see her, but puzzled. It was not quite ten. The party was not set to start until one. Was Marla's news so compelling that she couldn't even wait an extra couple of hours?

"Anyway, I thought you might want some company," she called, in answer to our unspoken question. "Maybe some help, too!" she added. Carefully carrying a stringed shopping bag, she

was stomping up the driveway in a politically in-
correct mink coat and even less correct mink-
trimmed black Italian leather boots. I could only
imagine what kind of Halloween-colored outfit
she would be wearing. Whatever clothes she wore,
they were sure to be made of silk, fur, or something else highly destructible, and there was no
way I was letting her near the butter, wines, lemon
vinaigrette, or any other of the food necessary for
today's lunch prep. Still, Marla's aid was usually of
the emotional variety, anyway.

"Hello?" said an accented voice from the ha-
cienda doorway. It was a heavy, older woman with
short gray hair and an easy smile. Judging by her
black uniform with its white apron, she was the
maid. I hadn't met her the last time I was here.
She introduced herself as Lorraine, and said she
worked for Mrs. Ellis. She was here to help, she
told me. And Miss Upton would be here shortly.
Miss Upton would be helping, too.

"Oh, marvelous!" I replied, trying to sound enthusiastic instead of sarcastic.

"One thing, though," Lorraine said, indicating
the Rover. "Won't your work be easier if you pull
your SUV into the garage, close to the kitchen?
Then you could open the back?"

"Sure, that would be great. Thanks." As Julian
traipsed through the ice back to the Rover, I no-

ticed that one of the Ellises' BMWs was parked out on Woods' End. Had that been intentional, too? So that people driving up could see how rich the Ellises were? Somehow, I thought so.

Julian moved the Rover into the end spot of the four-car garage. We shouldered our first loads. Marla, chatting merrily about how snow seemed to melt faster in some parts of town than others, trailed along behind us. I gritted my teeth and told myself to be upbeat.

The kitchen, which I had scoped out on my earlier visit, was a huge, high-ceilinged, light-filled space that featured a rosy, wide-paneled oak floor, expanses of black-and-silver granite, two bay windows, and long lines of gleaming cherrywood cabinets. The Ellises, or Nora anyway, had spared no expense on two top-of-the-line ovens and a six-burner stovetop. I heaved my first box on the granite-topped center island that was the size of a small barge. I also wondered for the umpteenth time why people who had money for big kitchens almost never actually **cooked** in them.

"Gosh," Marla trilled as she followed me inside, "I feel as if I'm in a naked centerfold for **House & Garden**!" She placed her enormous gift bag on the island and shrugged her mink coat into Lorraine's waiting hands. Sure enough, Marla's Halloween-appropriate attire was a pale orange silk dress trimmed in horizontal strips of black silk fringe. It looked great on her, complementing her brown-blond hair and twinkling, diamond-crusted barrettes. But it would look **awful** splashed with vinaigrette before the party even began.

To Lorraine, Marla said, "Thanks a million. Could you please show me where you're going to put it? Just in case I want to beat a fast exit."

"A fast exit?" cried Louise Upton, whom I hadn't even heard come in. Under a tentlike white apron, she wore a beige turtleneck and a dark gray skirt. Her black shoes were the wide tie-up variety with sensible low heels. "Why would you be making an exit, Mrs. Korman? And since you're one of the guests, why are you here so early?"

"Trying to help," Marla replied under her breath, surreptitiously rolling her eyes at me.

"That's quite a dress," said Louise. Marla obliged by twirling in the black-fringed dress. Louise made her voice caustic. "So for Halloween, you're going as a jellyfish?"

"You work for H&J, right?" Marla replied evenly. "Doing something? Do you really think your employers would be happy about you interrogating their guests? Why don't you see if you can be useful somewhere else?"

"Uh!" cried Julian, as he heaved two boxes through the doorway and dumped them on the island. Sensing the tension in the kitchen, he looked from Marla to Louise Upton and exclaimed, "Wow! That's such a pretty dress, Aunt Marla." He nodded at Louise Upton. "You look nice, too, ma'am."

Louise said, "Thank you, young man."

"His name is Julian Teller," I offered. "He's my assistant, Miss Upton, and—"

"Yes, this is Louise Upton," Marla informed Julian, "and she doesn't have to wait until Halloween to be a **witch**!"

Why is this happening to me? I thought. But I was spared an all-out catfight by the appearance of Donald Ellis. He slid into the kitchen wearing a gray sweatsuit and high-top sneakers, his hair damp either from exertion or a recent shower.

"Happy birthday, Mr. Ellis!" I called.

"Would you please start setting up the buffet?" Louise Upton demanded of me. To Donald Ellis, she said sweetly, "Mr. Ellis, your wife had to go out to pick up a few things she forgot. She said she'll be home before the party. Don't worry, I'm taking care of things here in the kitchen."

"G-g-goodness," Donald Ellis stammered, sweeping his bright red bangs off his forehead. "Well, that's great."

"Maybe you want a sip of this wine I brought you, Donald," Marla offered, pulling a bottle from her gift bag. "You could have a happy birthday now, quickly, before this witch starts swooping through this great big house, cackling and—"

The slicing look that Louise Upton gave Marla could have bisected a pumpkin.

"Oops!" Marla chuckled. "Guess I shouldn't have been such a bitch. Hey! That rhymes! Bitch! Witch!"

But her words were lost as Donald Ellis slithered out of the kitchen, with Louise Upton fast on his heels.

"Are we having fun yet?" Julian asked.

We managed to get started on the prep. Julian busied himself unwrapping the potato puffs. I pressed cloves of fresh garlic and kneaded them into unsalted butter along with dried herbs. When the concoction was thoroughly mixed, I placed it into the refrigerator until it was time to coat the tenderloins.

"You told me to keep my ears open for things about Dusty," Marla said, when she returned from a sneaky trip into the living room, where she'd managed to pour herself a rather hefty brandy snifter full of what looked like sherry. I certainly hoped it was sherry, because if it was brandy, we were all going to be in trouble even sooner than I'd thought possible. And also . . . had I asked her to keep her ears open for news about Dusty, or did Marla just

imagine I'd asked her? After taking a long sip of the golden liquid, she said, "And I did. Keep my ears open, that is. Now, though, I've been witness to an actual **event**. But you won't ask me what it is."

"I'm asking," I said eagerly, as I began to wash the vegetables.

"Vic Zaruski took a diamond ring back to Aspen Meadow Jewelers when it opened today. I know, because I was there, too, looking for some earrings with orange in them. Did you know there are no precious gems that are orange?" She took another slug of liquor. "Anyway, Vic talked in a real low tone, which made me edge closer to the conversation, of course. Vic said that the ring had never been worn, and he wanted to return it. **'Please,'** he said, 'cuz he didn't have much money. Our town jeweler, who, remember, is not the most tactful person in the universe, said, 'So things didn't work out, eh?' And Vic, who needed the money from the ring, let's remember, threw that little velvet-covered box **through the window** of Aspen Meadow Jewelers. Do you know how hard it is to break plate glass? Oh, well, I guess **you** do, Goldy. In any event, even if a diamond is the hardest substance on earth, it was still inside that little box, so it couldn't have helped—"

I turned away from the vegetables. "Was anyone hurt?"

"Nah. There was glass everywhere, and the jeweler yelling, 'You're going to have to pay for that, buddy! And I don't take back used jewelry!' Vic was outside searching in the debris for his little box, which I guess he eventually found, 'cuz then he took off."

"Oh, man, he's playing the piano for the birthday party today," I said mournfully, thinking now we had one more person not in a party mood. I felt guilty, too, because I'd precipitated the wave of glass-breaking that was now taking place in our little town. "Do you know who the ring was for?" I asked. "Dusty?"

Marla took another long pull on her drink, then smacked her lips. "Well, you know what I always say: 'One can only presume.' But yes, I'd say it was for Dusty."

"Doggone," I said, the vegetables momentarily forgotten. Luckily, Julian picked up where I'd left off.

But wait. Since Vic was playing the piano today, why couldn't I ask him myself about the ring? How deeply had he been disappointed by his breakup with Dusty? And did he happen to catch the license plate of the SUV that supposedly tried to mow him down when he was carrying Dusty's computer?

"And there's more." Marla's husky voice indicated something of a sexual nature was about to be divulged. "Donald Ellis? Our birthday boy?" she whispered. "According to one of my friends who called after I asked for info at Creekside Spa, Donald had an affair with Wink Calhoun last year."

I turned to her. "You're kidding. Donald and Wink?"

Marla drew herself up. "I am not kidding, or at least my friend isn't. She's not the most reliable person in town, but she does pick up a lot of scuttlebutt."

"I can't believe it," I said, thinking of Donald Ellis's short stature, unappealing red hair, completely nonathletic build, and poor-me demeanor. "Did Nora know? Is she the jealous type?"

Marla shook her head and downed more of her drink. "Neither, according to my friend. Nora was and is clueless. Rich, but clueless."

"I just hope she's rich and **generous,**" Julian said.

"Maybe that's why Wink wasn't invited to the party today," I commented. "Nora didn't want to see her."

"Wink is **staff,** Goldy," Marla said, before draining her snifter. "She wouldn't have been invited anyway."

Julian, intent on the vegetables, said, "You never know."

And indeed, you never do know, because when I tried to call Wink back on my cell, there wasn't any answer. Swallowing hard, I left what I hoped was a benign-sounding message. I really needed to talk to her, and could she please meet me in the St. Luke's kitchen the next morning, at half past eight? The christening ceremony didn't begin until ten, but I needed to be there early because of the food. **And because I want to see the expression on your face when I ask why you conveniently left out a big chunk of H&J gossip,** I thought, but of course didn't say.

As I energetically juiced the lemons for the vinaigrette, I was kicking myself for not wondering why Wink had had so much time to visit with a supposedly inebriated Donald at the H&J Christmas party. Was it possible Donald had actually told Wink that whole long story about Uriah . . . as pillow talk? Was it possible she'd said Uriah was always poking around at H&J because the bishop had once caught them in flagrante delicto?

I twisted the last lemon down hard on the juicer. Of course, Wink's sex life, and what she might have done with Donald, was none of my beeswax. But I had to pose another, more troubling question: Was there any chance meek, mild Donald was "New O.," and that Dusty had supplanted Wink, thus making Wink murderously jealous? If so, how in the world was I going to ask Wink such a thing?

I groaned. Dusty and Uriah. Dusty and Alonzo. Dusty and Donald. And then there was the client, Rock Ode, whom I was set to meet today. These were definitely too many possibilities to contemplate.

I resolved to turn my attention back to the party, even though this was becoming difficult. But then Marla announced she was going next door to visit a friend from the country club. Louise Upton was nowhere to be seen or heard. So Julian and I finally had a chance to finish the setup, uninterrupted. Better yet, we eventually mustered up pretty good moods.

At half past eleven, tall, blond Nora Ellis, looking juicy in raspberry-sherbet-colored Juicy Couture sweats, came into the kitchen looking harried. She dropped off four bottles of wine and called for Louise Upton, who made a silent appearance by the island. Nora said she was dashing up for a shower and could Louise please greet the guests? Louise responded in the affirmative, then disappeared again. If I'd been Louise, I wouldn't have wanted to risk another encounter with Marla either. I decided not to tell Louise that Marla had gone next door.

At half past twelve, Vic Zaruski, looking solemn, knocked on the kitchen door. He wore an impeccable white shirt and perfectly creased black pants. In his right hand, he was clutching what looked like sheet music.

"Um, is this where I'm supposed to be?" he asked, smiling nervously. "I'm playing the piano for the party."

"You're in the right place," I assured him. "Have you had anything to eat?"

He eyed the tenderloins and potato puffs, and shook his head. "I haven't been hungry since, since . . . you know." He lowered his voice and avoided my eyes. "Were you able to get any information off of Dusty's computer?"

"Not yet," I lied. "It was pretty banged up after being dropped in the street. Listen," I said as if it had just occurred to me, "did you make a police report about that attempted hit-and-run?"

He gave me a startled glance and blushed to the roots of his mop of curly hair the color of straw. "No, I just thought . . . I didn't think it was that big a deal."

"I don't suppose you had a chance to catch even a part of the license plate."

He shook his head ruefully. "I didn't even see the make of the vehicle. Or whether it was, you know, black or dark green or, uh, navy blue."

"Right," I said. I kept my voice sympathetic. His answer felt a bit too rehearsed. Had the police spent much time with him after I found Dusty? Did they consider him a suspect? Julian was out in the dining room arranging the serving utensils for the buffet, so I said quickly, "I heard you had a troublesome incident at Aspen Meadow Jewelers."

Vic opened his brown eyes wide. His cheeks were still flaming. "Well, I guess I need to go set up my sheet music." He quickstepped out of the kitchen.

I didn't get a chance to ask him any more questions before the party, nor did I feel comfortable snooping anywhere in the house. I still had to unwrap the chilled cake, a job that had to be done at the last possible moment. It was a good thing it was my final task, because once I was done, two of the three neighbor couples appeared at the back door bearing gifts. I supposed the main entrance was so imposing, nobody wanted to use it. I ushered them into Louise's waiting hands in the living room, then hustled back into the kitchen.

As Julian and I were passing around the first platter of appetizers, Vic began playing "Sgt. Pepper's Lonely Hearts' Club Band." Out the front window—one of them, anyway—I could see that Richard and K. D. Chenault were arriving in separate black BMWs. A nanosecond later, Alonzo and Ookie Claggett pulled up in **their** black Beemer, which they parked behind Nora's, which was **also** black. What, did these people all go shopping for cars together? If so, did they get a discount?

I moved into the living room with a platter of stuffed Portobello mushrooms. Richard Chenault, wearing a silvery gray turtleneck and charcoal slacks, caught my eye and nodded. He looked ragged. When K.D. saw our exchanged glance, she sidled up to me and nabbed a mushroom. Her chestnut hair was swept over to one side, and she wore a loosely cut black silk top and black pants. She looked ravishing, and I thought Richard Chenault was an idiot. Or maybe they were both idiots. K.D. whispered that she'd try to come into the kitchen to visit soon.

Unlike the Chenaults' subdued appearance in the living room, Claggs and Ookie made a grand entrance, shouting their hellos so loudly all the guests could hear. Ookie, her shiny brown hair pulled up into a windblown coif, looked lovely in a slim black dress hemmed with a blue ruffle. Her noisy greetings to friends had caused heads to turn . . . and they stayed turned. I watched her for a moment as she seemed to pounce on one guest after another, like a bee buzzing impatiently from one blossom to the next.

To my great astonishment, she eventually sashayed forward, took a mushroom, and then called to Richard, "Hey, partner guy! How does it feel to have one of your associates living in a place that's twice as big as yours?"

Richard Chenault merely pursed his lips and looked away. Had Ookie's javelin hit its mark, or was the Chief just feeling so low about his niece's death that he didn't care what Ookie did?

Without missing a beat, Vic shifted into "Yesterday."

Returning to the kitchen, I replaced the empty mushroom platter with a large glass platter that held smaller glass dishes, plus room for rows of empanadas and a glass bowl of guacamole. With a pile of napkins held snugly in my left hand, I began a lap of the enormous living room. Nora Ellis appeared, looking radiant. She had changed into a calf-length chocolate-colored corduroy jumper and matching long-sleeved turtleneck. She'd swept her blond hair up into a twist, and she wore more gold jewelry than a rap singer.

She smiled broadly until her glance fell on Ookie, whose strident voice was hard to miss.

Nora's expression became grim until she noticed I was right next to her, watching. Then she smiled.

"Empanada, Nora?"

"No, thanks. But they look wonderful."

I was hurt, since she'd claimed to love them back at our tasting. I was about to move on when Bishop Sutherland, wearing a purple shirt and clerical collar, walked into the center of the living room. He put one arm around Nora and the other around Donald.

"My dear daughter and son-in-law have made every day in my life feel like a birthday!" he cried. Everyone clapped as Uriah hugged first Nora, then Donald, who appeared mortified, like Goofy when Mickey squeezes all the air out of him. Julian caught my eye and surreptitiously pointed to a large, elaborately framed needlepoint sign hanging on the wall behind me. It read: "Have You Hugged Your Lawyer Today?"

Once Uriah had released his son-in-law, I moved up to Donald and Nora and offered them empanadas, even though Nora had already refused them. Donald gave me a look that indicated what he really wanted was a shot of Demerol.

"Birthdays are rough," I whispered conspiratorially.

His smile was resigned. "Yes, but consider the alternative."

Nora's expression hardened. "Goldy, don't you want to make the rounds of all the guests?"

Instead of saying, "I was just getting to that," I nodded deferentially and moved off with my tray. Nora had been exceptionally nice to me so far, and I didn't want to ruin our chance of a supersize gratuity.

Alonzo Claggett, who looked dashing in khaki pants and a long-sleeved light blue shirt that complemented his Italianate features, olive skin, and dark curls, was talking to Marla. They were discussing tax-avoiding trusts. Bishop Sutherland was standing with them, his head leaned in to their conversation. Vic was playing "I Want to Hold Your Hand."

Marla said, "I thought the IRS wouldn't go for that unless the trust was irrevocable."

"Why don't you come over to my office sometime?" quipped Alonzo.

"Why don't you come over to my house and see my etchings?"

"We could meet at my place in the Bahamas," Alonzo countered.

"How about Trancas?" Marla asked. "It's more upscale."

"There's always Lichtenstein."

"But would the trip be deductible?"

At this juncture, Marla reached for my proffered tray. Bishop Sutherland drank from his glass. When Marla dipped her two empanadas into the guacamole, Alonzo winked at me. Of all the folks at H&J, Alonzo was the one person who didn't seem broken up over losing Dusty. He'd acted upset at first, but then had bounced back with vigor. What was **that** about?

After Marla had finished chewing, she sucked in her cheeks and glanced in the direction of Donald Ellis, who was standing by the massive hearth. "The birthday boy looks as if he's at a funeral."

Alonzo followed Marla's gaze. "He's always like that."

"Should I have **him** draw up my trust?" Marla asked playfully. "Would it cost less to have one associate do it than to have another associate do me? Oh, dear, did I just say that?" She opened her eyes wide and stuffed another guacamole-slathered empanada into her mouth.

Alonzo flashed his pearly whites. "I would love to do you, Marla. Come to think of it, Donald's more of a generalist, while I specialize in trusts. I'd make it worth what you pay me."

Marla finished her appetizer and assumed a disappointed tone. "You mean I'm going to have to pay?"

Only Bishop Sutherland laughed.

Alonzo and Marla moved off to greet some friends from Aspen Meadow Country Club, and I was left with Bishop Sutherland. Since caterers are fine-tuned to noticing when their guests' moods have fallen off, I was suddenly aware that the bishop's facial expression had turned bleak.

"Bishop Sutherland?" I inquired. "Are you okay?"

He pressed his lips together and shook his head of white hair. "Not really. Birthday parties always make me feel low, the way some people say they can't stand Christmas. It reminds them, or us, I should say, of folks who aren't around anymore."

I nodded sympathetically. "You seemed so happy hugging your daughter and son-in-law."

"I'm a good actor," he replied, then was quiet for a few uncomfortable moments, during which I didn't know if I should leave or stay.

"Well," I said finally, "are you missing somebody in particular?"

His shoulders slumped. "Yes, Mrs. Schulz, I'm missing somebody in particular. Today was Charlie Baker's birthday. My poor dear friend. I miss him. When he had shingles on his birthday, one of the nurses made him a cake, and we had a party in the hospital. It was one of the best celebrations I've ever attended, because everyone who was there—patients, nurses, even a doctor—was there because he or she **wanted** to be there. We sang and laughed and ate cake and ice cream . . ." He sighed. "Oh Lord. I miss my friend."

"I'm sorry."

He gave me a half smile. "Thanks. Most people don't care about clergy . . . they want clergy to care for them. Sometimes I just . . . get real lonely all of a sudden."

"You don't have to stay here, you know," I said in a low voice.

"Yes, I do. But thanks for being nice." And before I could say anything else, the bishop had moved off to visit with some people who were standing near the kitchen.

At this juncture, since neither Marla nor Alonzo seemed to want more empanadas, I moved off in the direction of the Ellises' neighbors, who were standing near Donald beside the massive hearth.

"I'd love to have something from your plate," came a sexy male voice from behind me. I turned, startled. "Please."

I was facing a belt and a pair of white slacks. I looked up, up, up at a man as tall as any guy playing for the NBA. This fellow was at least six foot ten, with ink-black hair parted boyishly on the side. He wore a black shirt that matched his hair, but the effect would have been more appealing if the shirt had not had the first five buttons undone, revealing a dark, hairy chest. The guy had bright blue eyes and was drop-dead gorgeous, although it was a little hard to see his face without a telescope. And what if I trained the telescope on his chest? It would look like a rain forest. So I turned to the tall fellow's right, where an ultraslender young woman stood. Like her tall companion, she was also quite beautiful.

The woman said, "I am Natasha Oat." Oat? Oh, wait. **Ode.** So these were the famously beautiful Odes. One of the tidbits I'd learned working for the fashion photographer was that Natasha's thick Russian accent, as much as her looks, gave away the fact that she was a model. The United States, I had observed on my former gig, imports a lot of beauty from the former Soviet Union. No doubt, modeling pays more here than it does, or ever did, over there. Natasha nodded upward. "And zis eess my husban', Rock. He eess clien' of Donal'."

"I'm Goldy Schulz." I lifted the platter of empanadas. To my great horror, Rock dipped two of his long **fingers** into the guacamole, then transported the load of green stuff up to his mouth, far, far away. Honestly. In the catering biz, something always happens to lower your already subterranean view of the human species.

"Rock' eess also model," Natasha rushed in to say, as if this explained everything.

"Goldy Schulz," Rock boomed from above, "did Nora give you the key to her wine cellar?"

"Uh, no."

"Well, go ask Donald for it. Tell him I said it was okay. Then bring us a bottle of '49 Châteauneuf-du-Pape. A thirty-fifth birthday is a time to celebrate!"

"Well!" I replied, swallowing. Could this really be the "New O." of Dusty's journal? Somehow, I doubted it very much.

"Are you going to get that key, or not?" demanded Rock.

"Let me just go, uh, uh . . ." I turned too quickly, and the bowl of ruined guacamole hemorrhaged down the front of Bishop Uriah Sutherland's purple shirt.

"Oh my God!" I cried, then reddened, remembering that this was a **clergy** shirt I'd just wrecked. "Oh God, I'm sorry!" I plunged on. **Shut up,** I ordered myself, and used the napkins from my opposite hand to dab at Uriah's chest.

But Bishop Sutherland was laughing, thank . . . well, heaven. He'd managed to snag the bowl before it had fallen to the floor, although **all** the rest of the green stuff was now plastered on his shirt-front like green clay. And now that wet clay was slithering downward. The bishop replaced the glass bowl on my tray and took the napkins from my hand. As he deftly wiped huge globs of guacamole off his shirt, I wondered what I was going to say to him besides sorry, sorry, so sorry, I'll bet this doesn't help your emotional issues with birthdays.

K. D. Chenault saved me by walking up to us. "Oh, dear, Goldy, looks like somebody goofed!" She smiled hugely. "Why don't you offer me your last empanada there, and introduce me to this fellow whose shirt just got wrecked?"

From my tray, I handed her a small glass plate and one of my remaining napkins. She took both carefully with her left hand so she could have her right free for shaking Uriah Sutherland's right hand, the one not holding the green-smeared napkins.

"K.D.," I began, but then became confused, probably by everything that was going so badly. Maybe I'd go lock **myself** in that wine cellar. "Excuse me! **Doctor Chenault**, I should say. This is Bishop Sutherland." I cleared my throat, trying to regain my composure. "Bishop **Uriah** Sutherland. I would have thought the two of you would have met by now."

"Glad to meet you, Katy!" Bishop Sutherland said, his tone friendly. "I actually haven't met—"

But that was as far as he got, because K.D. gasped and dropped the glass plate I'd just given her. She covered her mouth with one hand and her cheek with the other. Bishop Uriah beamed, as if he often had such a volcanic effect on women. But K.D. was wide-eyed, gaping at Uriah Sutherland as if he were a ghost.

The whole room moved at once, with people coming to see what was going on. K.D. was leaning against a wall, blinking. Julian had immediately set aside his tray and moved to help her. I shooed people away from the broken glass. Nora Ellis did not look happy. Ookie Claggett rolled her eyes and began to whisper to the people next to her.

Vic Zaruski, apparently accustomed to the sound of shattering glass, smoothly moved into an upbeat version of "Breaking Up Is Hard to Do."

Chapter 14

"Eighty-six on the glass plate," Julian commented, once he'd retrieved some wet paper towels from the kitchen. Nora had walked carefully across the living room and shepherded K.D. down a long hall to a bathroom. Now Julian crouched next to me on the floor, picking up shards. The bishop had sidled off to change his shirt, and the rest of the crowd had gathered around the piano.

"I'm fine," Julian and I heard K.D. protesting to Nora. "I just—I just remembered a file I need to check at the hospital."

"Yes, yes, of course, K.D.," Nora replied, "but just splash some cold water on your face anyway. Please."

"Oh, Nora, for God's sake—" But then we heard a door close. I beat a fast retreat into the kitchen for more mopping supplies.

When Nora's heels came clickety-clacking back, Julian and I were almost through cleaning up the stray shards from the broken dish. The place where K.D. had dropped the plate was a hallway paved with slate. Stone, I had learned all too well at other catered affairs, will break anything that's dropped on it. When Julian heard Nora approaching, he scooped up the last bit of glass he'd found and mumbled that he would check on the lunch.

Nora stooped down beside me. "What did you say to her?"

"Nothing," I protested. "I introduced her to your father, and then she—then she seemed to see something across the room, and dropped the plate. Is she all right?" I asked.

"Of course she's all right. This is just one of K.D.'s typical drama-queen stunts. I told her **Richard** was going to be here, and that's probably when she decided to pull something like this. I didn't want to invite her anyway; Donald did," she said under her breath. She glared at me, keeping a sweet smile on her face in case the guests, who were singing "Smoke Gets in Your Eyes" around the piano, were watching. "Did my father say anything to upset her?"

"No, nothing." I continued to wipe up glass and wished she would go away. I'd known K.D. a lot longer than Nora had. K.D. definitely was **not** a drama queen.

"What did my father say, exactly?"

"He said, 'Nice to meet you, Katy.' That's it."

"As if I didn't have enough trouble with my father covered in guacamole," she began, but then stopped short.

Hmm, I thought as I swept up the final bits of glass with a wet paper towel. Anyway, I had picked up a few interesting tidbits I hadn't learned in my four months at the law firm. Donald Ellis, who was as far from a stud as anyone could imagine, had supposedly been putting the wood to Wink Calhoun the previous year. Dusty and Alonzo Claggett had been **close friends**. Ookie was a bitch, as I'd pretty much deduced. Today I'd learned she was also a **loud** bitch. Plus, Nora thought Dr. K. D. Chenault was a drama queen. Nora also was profoundly embarrassed by her father, although I'd been the one to spill the guac.

And I would never, ever cater for some people named Ode.

"Julian," I said when I returned to the kitchen, "I need to get cracking on the salad service. Could you start the tenderloin and vegetables?"

He nodded and hustled across the kitchen.

What had made K.D. gasp like that? I wondered as I turned my attention to the salad. Then again, my awful ex-husband had made me squawk all the time, sad to say. I moved my concentration to the salad.

I'd already placed the plates in the refrigerator

to chill. I shaved ultrathin slivers of Parmesan and set them aside. Then all that was left was the lettuce and the croutons.

Homemade croutons are the best way to make yourself a beloved caterer, even if you do have to fuss over them at the last minute. I measured out cubes of homemade French bread, then melted a stick of butter in a wide frying pan I'd brought. When the butter had just begun to sizzle, I dropped in the croutons and began stirring. The bread cubes soak up an unbelievable amount of butter. But that's what makes them taste so great. I preheated the oven and went back to my stirring. A heavenly scent bathed the kitchen . . . just the thing to get appetites juiced, I'd found. When the croutons were golden brown and crispy, I put them into the warming oven.

Next I ran cold water over the cleaned heads of romaine, carefully separated the dark green leaves, and patted the best ones dry with clean towels I'd brought. People often comment on how delicious salads made by a caterer are, and it's because our ilk rely, once again, on several tricks. The cold salad plates are one. Another is picking out the youngest, best-looking heads of organic lettuce. After rinsing the cleaned heads under running water, we wrap the separated, cleaned, patted-dry leaves in cloth towels, then put the whole kit and kaboodle in a plastic bag and place it in the refrigerator. The cloth wicks away any remaining moisture, and the resultant leaves retain an almost magical crunchiness.

This done, I preheated the oven for the Parmesan Potato Puffs while Julian finished trimming the broccoli and snap peas for the veggie dish. Here again, many people at catered functions **want** to be able to look at the food and say, "I could do that. Why bother to hire a caterer?" And since that is the very **last** thing a caterer wants a guest to think, we gussy up even the plainest of green vegetables with **something**. Preferably with several lovely somethings.

In this case, Julian was using fresh cherry tomatoes from Tom's hanging-upside-down plants in our basement, and tiny pattypan squash that he'd brought from Boulder the previous day. Barely steamed along with the broccoli and snap peas, the juicy, bright red tomatoes and crunchy yellow squash would look lovely against the deep green broccoli and snap peas. Tossed with salt, pepper, and just a hint of finely grated lemon zest, then topped with melted unsalted butter and tossed again, it was the kind of vegetable dish that guests look at and taste longingly and say, "I would never go to all this trouble." Which is precisely what the folks in our biz **want** them to say.

I put the prepared tenderloin in to roast along-side the potato puffs. When we were checking to make sure everything was moving along, K.D. slipped into the kitchen.

"K.D.!" I cried, but she put her finger to her lips. I whispered, "What happened? You look like you saw a ghost."

"I sort of did. Maybe. Anyway, I was just rattled." She bit her bottom lip. "May I call you later? I'm hoping we can talk."

"You can't tell me what it's about?"

"I'll speak to you after I get something at the hospital."

"**What** at the hospital?"

"A name. Then I have a shift." She was already making for the kitchen door. "Maybe we could talk tomorrow morning, before the christening."

I didn't have time to say that that was when I was supposed to see Wink, because no sooner had she left than Nora opened one of the other doors to the kitchen. "We're ready to start." She looked at both of us. "Richard's got a little something planned, and he wants everybody, even you two, out there to witness it."

"Okeydoke!" Julian replied cheerfully.

"Does either of you know if K.D. will be returning?" she asked, her voice high and querulous.

"Uh, no, she won't," I said. "She suddenly remembered something she had to do down at the hospital."

Nora sighed. "And she told **you** this, but not me?"

"I guess so," I said, putting on a meek tone.

Nora scanned my face for signs of sarcasm. Seeing none, she shook back her curtain of blond hair and went on, "Would you all like Louise Upton out here to help you? She's been pouring the wine, but if you need her, she could come back." Nora pressed her hands with their long tapered fingers together and began wringing them. "I just wanted this celebration to be a success—"

I stopped placing the broccoli in the steaming basket and gave her a reassuring look. "Oh, it's going to be a great party. Trust me. Everyone seems to be having a super time. I mean, everyone **is** having a great time. Really. Several guests have already commented on it, and Julian and I see all kinds of parties. This is fantastic. A-plus."

A tiny smile crept onto Nora's lips. "Do you really think so? Several guests have commented?" When Julian and I nodded vigorously, she said, "Well, then, I suppose everybody should see what Richard has planned. I already know what it is; it took him forever to get it set up." She eyed the island. "Are you ready to go with the salads?"

"Give us one minute."

"All right," she said, her mood suddenly charitable. "Come out to the living room as soon as the salads are on the table." Then she disappeared.

"Several guests have commented?" Julian remarked. "Who, exactly?"

I checked the meat thermometer. "Nobody. I was just trying to reassure her."

I pulled the crisp, buttery croutons from the second oven while Julian laid out the chilled plates. Then I nabbed the bag of lettuce and handed Julian the cheese. We began to circle the island. I placed chilled romaine leaves on each plate; Julian sprinkled on the Parmesan slivers as well as judicious amounts of chopped chives— never scallions, as this was another thing the do-the-catering-yourself crowd kept their eyes out for. We'd top the salads with the warm croutons after we'd sprinkled on the dressing.

We placed the salads around the table. I noticed Nora had whisked away K.D.'s plate and place card and rearranged the dishes so that nothing was amiss. So then what had Nora been upset about? Then again, what were catering clients ever upset about? I put most of their tantrums down to preparty nerves.

When Julian and I were done, I nodded to Nora, who raised an eyebrow at Richard, who in turn moved over to the wall beside the hearth. From there, Richard gave a signal to Vic Zaruski, who began playing "Autumn Leaves." At the same moment, Richard tugged on a nylon string I hadn't noticed before. From overhead, hundreds, thousands of yellow and red leaves came cascading down, sort of like balloons at a political convention. The guests squealed with delight . . . all except for Donald, who had looked up too soon. Now he was carefully trying to remove a batch of sycamore leaves from his mouth. But apparently they had become stuck deep in his throat. Involuntarily he hawked, then spit.

Unfortunately, this sputtering occurred just as Vic ended the first verse of "Autumn Leaves." As a result, the coughing-up was much louder and more emphatic than Donald had anticipated, and the guests watched in fascination as Donald disgorged a bouquet of half-chewed leaves glued together with saliva onto one of Nora's white sofas. I watched in horror. First the guac, now this? What was next?

Richard clapped Donald on the back. He hollered, "Take it easy, little guy. Just keep spitting till you get it all out. My soon-to-be ex-wife was the only doctor here, and I don't know the Heimlich maneuver."

Nora clenched her teeth, but managed to pull herself together. She trilled, "The birthday lunch has begun! Please take your seats, folks!"

And so they did. While Richard continued to whack Donald between the shoulder blades, Julian managed to snag a couple of maple leaves that had drifted onto several plates of romaine. Was maple poisonous? I hoped not. Eventually they both found their way to the table.

Following Nora's directions, I had lit the candles at the table, even though it was the middle of the day. But she was right; this did make things look more festive, and luckily none of the leaves had caught fire. Vic had moved into playing some easy-listening versions of Beatles songs that were, I was surprised to admit, good dining music. Julian moved around the table filling wine and water glasses. Good thing most folks lived nearby and could walk home. While the guests were working on their salads, I removed the tenderloins from the oven so that they could rest. Louise Upton said she had to leave for a doctor's appointment. I thanked her sincerely for her help, and since I didn't know whether Nora had given her anything extra, I handed her two twenties from my purse. She could barely conceal her astonishment.

"Why, thank you, Goldy. I don't really need this. I work for H&J."

"Today you did double duty for Goldilocks' Catering, and you deserve the gratuity."

When I returned to the dining room to collect

the salad plates, the guests were discussing Dusty Routt.

"Do you think one or more thieves might have murdered her?" asked Michael Radford, the divorce attorney.

"I wonder if she could have been helping the thieves," Ookie Claggett said. I wanted to drop a plate of vegetables in her lap, but refrained.

Richard Chenault shook his head. "That's my niece you're talking about." He sighed. "She worked hard, but she wasn't always able to keep up. So I guess it's possible she fell in with the wrong crowd, but I hate to think that might have been true. I just hate to think it."

"She didn't fall behind when she was working for me," Donald piped up. "Richard? She labored endlessly for me over a very complicated case—"

Michael Radford went on: "I don't know. I just think paralegal work is too demanding for a twenty-year-old who hasn't been to college."

I was picking up Donald Ellis's plate and was thus close by him and able to hear his whispered "Baloney."

"Donald, come on," Richard put in. "She really **couldn't** manage your oil-and-gas-lease bequeathal, plus do all the work for Charlie Baker, which turned into work for Charlie's estate."

"Richard, Charlie Baker was **ecstatic** with the

work Dusty was doing for him," Donald said, his tone defensive. "He told me so himself."

There was a silence: an associate had corrected a partner, and that partner, I well knew, had what they call in the psych biz "ego issues." I paused, a dirty salad plate in each hand.

"Now, Donald," Bishop Uriah Sutherland said mildly, "careful. Remember the old saying in the church: 'He who is too big for his breeches may soon lose his shirt.'"

"Did Jesus say that?" Marla asked, her face wrinkled questioningly. "I never actually saw that anywhere in Scripture. Bishop, maybe you could remind me of the exact—"

"Actually," Nora Ellis piped up, "Louise told me that **she** suspected Dusty of **stealing** from the firm."

"Stealing?" Donald said, dumbfounded. "Stealing what—pencils? Legal pads?" I wondered at his courage at contradicting both his boss **and** his wife.

"You had a lot of valuable stuff in there, Donald," Nora went on. "Richard put in quite a few lovely things, didn't you, Richard? They're yours, right? And not the firm's?"

Richard Chenault beamed. "Yes, they're mine." Then his face soured. "They're lovely things that I may end up selling, if K.D. and her ravenous lawyer have their way."

Nora sighed. Marla snatched a glance at me and rolled her eyes.

Back in the kitchen, I was filling the steamed vegetable platter when my cell phone buzzed. Omigosh, I had forgotten to call Arch.

"Mom," Arch began. "You promised I'd be able to have a driving lesson today. Did you forget?"

"We'll do it, we'll do it," I promised. And then I remembered that we had Julian's Range Rover. "Oh no, hon, maybe not. We're just here in Julian's Rover, and it might not work—"

"Should we just do it another time?"

My shoulders slumped in defeat and guilt, a stance I took quite often as a mother, matter of fact.

"What does he want?" Julian whispered.

"To have a driving lesson in your Rover," I replied. "I forgot I'd promised him."

Julian shrugged. "So let him. Tell him to have the Vikarioses drop him off over here. Or they could walk, I guess." Then he lofted the tray containing the tenderloins, potato puffs, and vegetables. Out in the dining room, the guests were still talking, and Nora hadn't appeared to tell us to hurry up with the next course.

"All right, hon, listen. The clients are just starting the lunch, and then we have cake. Mrs. Ellis has a maid helping who's going to do the cleanup. Julian says you can drive his Rover—"

"Wow! Is he sure? When do you want us?"

"Look," I said, "why don't you and Gus **walk** over here"—this would take almost an hour—"and by the time you get here, Julian and I will be able to go. Or at least, we should be."

"Really?"

"We'll be **ready**."

And surprisingly, we were. The guests all loved the beef, so much so that they downed it and the accompaniments in record time. Vic Zaruski played a rousing rendition of "Happy Birthday" as we presented Donald with his cake, complete with tall candles. He still didn't look entirely happy. But he did brighten up during the opening of the presents. Richard gave him a couple of expensive silk ties. The neighbors gave him history books, to which he was apparently partial. And Marla gave him four bottles of wine that I knew had cost her two hundred bucks a pop.

"Oh, Marla, thank you," Donald said, with the first truly appreciative tone he'd had all day.

"Well," Nora announced, "I have two things for you. First is a trip to a place where they make that wine, the Burgundy region of France."

"Oh, honey, you shouldn't have," Donald Ellis said, and leaned over to give his wife a kiss on each cheek.

"And your final gift," said Nora, "is behind the needlepoint I gave you last year."

Donald wrinkled his brow while his wife carefully removed the lawyer-hugging needlepoint. Behind it was a framed picture by Charlie Baker. It was entitled **Journey Cake**.

It really was gorgeous, and vintage Charlie Baker, which tugged at my heart. While Nora explained to Donald how valuable the painting was, part of the **Cake Series II** that Charlie had been doing when he died, I read Charlie's list of ingredients. Flour, cinnamon and other spices, sugar, butter, cider. But I stared at the painting. Something was **still** wrong with this recipe; I just didn't know what. I happened to glance over at Richard, who was smiling more widely than Donald.

Alonzo Claggett commented, "That must have set you back a few pretty pennies, Nora."

Nora ignored him and put her hand on my forearm. "Don't you like it, Goldy?" She seemed eager for approval, even if it was from the caterer. Richard was murmuring praise of the painting.

"It's fabulous, Nora," I said. "Happy birthday, Donald. You're a lucky man."

Donald Ellis gave me another Demerol-deprived look. I smiled sympathetically and bustled back out to the kitchen, where I could quietly begin to round up our supplies and almost be done with this job.

Arch and Gus arrived just before two, their faces flushed from walking. Arch's countenance was its usual pessimistic self, as if he didn't believe I was actually going to let him drive. Gus was bubbly, as usual.

"This house is so cool! And you worked here? Did you fix tacos? Just kidding," he burbled on, in typical Gus fashion.

Julian tousled Arch's hair, a show of affection my son still permitted, but only from Julian. "Big Arch! Going to drive us home, eh? And in the Rover, too?"

"I'm going to go study your dashboard," Arch announced, his voice serious. "So I can know where all the controls are."

Julian and I used the last of our time packing up the steamer and other utensils I'd brought. Nora Ellis actually came out to help us.

"Hi there!" Gus greeted her. "I'm Gus Vikarios. Were you Goldy's boss today?" When Nora replied that she was, Gus piped up, "How did she and Julian do? Did you have a nice party?"

"Yes, it was very nice," Nora said, pushing her blond hair out of her face.

"Are you going to give them a good tip?" Gus asked brazenly.

"Gus!" I cried, although I was wondering the same thing myself.

We immediately followed Nora back in for our last box so she could be spared an answer. As we were leaving, she said, "Could you take the trash out, please? Lorraine has so much to do."

With a quickly mumbled "Of course," I started toward the enormous black plastic sack she was pointing to. And then, out of the blue— the unconscious, or wherever these things come from—I remembered Wink's comment about Uriah Sutherland: **He likes to poke around, ask questions** and **I caught him going through our trash**. My question was this: Why? Furthermore: Hadn't he seemed a bit too attentive to Alonzo and Marla's discussion of trusts? And hadn't that also been Dusty's area of expertise? Also, how about that bracelet? Had Uriah's champagne tastes—in women, say, or jewelry— made him look for a receipt for something he'd given to a young lover—say, Dusty? Or what if you flipped things upside down? Maybe doesn't-like-birthdays Uriah Sutherland had poked a little too hard in the wrong place, been discovered, and been forced to destroy the evidence—that is, Dusty.

"Let me get it," Julian said, his voice edgy. Without looking at Nora, he handed me the box, which was, I was quite sure, about twenty pounds lighter than the trash bag.

"And oh!" Nora said, as if she'd just remembered it. "Your gratuity!" She reached into her purse and pulled out four twenty-dollar bills, which she tucked into one of my hands that was holding the box. With a smile and a wave, she walked back into the living room.

"What's that, about a thirty percent tip?" Julian asked. "Fantastic!"

"Yes," I said quietly. "It's great. But listen, I want you to put that trash in your Rover. And put any other trash in there that's outside in their cans."

"What?" Julian cried.

"Just do it. With hired help taking out the garbage on a regular basis, they'll never miss it."

Once we were all settled in the not-smelling-too-great Rover, Julian said, "I'm going to back out, and then you can take it the rest of the way, okay?"

"Sure," said Arch, who sounded none too sure.

Unfortunately, Julian was unable to make even a five-point turn to get us going forward. "You want to back down the driveway, Arch? The house is on a dead end. You'll be fine."

"I'm not so sure," I began, but received a furious look from Arch.

Julian and Arch exchanged seats. Arch, unaware the car was on, turned the key in the ignition. The engine shrieked.

"Happens to everybody," Julian said from the backseat.

Stay calm, I told myself, **very calm.** I closed my eyes and did a yoga breathing exercise while Julian quietly told Arch that he'd have to take the Rover straight back, then gradually turn to the left, so he could make it into the street.

"Wait!" Julian said sharply. "Somebody's coming."

It was Donald Ellis. He was a little out of breath.

"I wanted to thank you all for doing such a great job," he said. "I had a fabulous birthday. Here." He pressed a hundred-dollar bill into my hand.

"Mr. Ellis, your wife has already tipped us, and that is far too much—" I began. But he was already gone.

"Can we go now?" Arch asked. His voice was so nervous I wasn't sure he really wanted to drive, but there was no way I was going to embarrass him in front of his half brother and Julian.

I looked in the rearview mirror on the passenger side. "Sure. Give it a little gas."

Arch began to inch down the driveway, tapping

the brakes every two seconds in the way of new drivers, giving all of us in the car whiplash.

I frowned at the mirror, and realized we were up so high in the Rover that I couldn't see exactly where the driveway was. Since the very last thing I wanted was to whack into Nora Ellis's carefully planted fruit trees, I opened my door a smidgeon.

"Okay," I said encouragingly, my heart light from having received two big tips. "Give it just a teensy bit more gas."

Which is what Arch did. In fact, he gave the Rover a rather large bit of gas, with the big SUV still in reverse. This sent it catapulting into the Ellises' serpentine wall, which tore off the open passenger-side door.

Chapter 15

I raised Tom on his cell. He had been investigating another case nearby, and could be at the Ellises' house within fifteen minutes. He told us he would call a tow truck, because he knew a guy who would respond right away. I thanked him profusely.

"And see what Julian's schedule is like," Tom added. "If he can stay with us until the department cleans up this murder, so much the better."

"You mean, because it'll take forever to get the door replaced? Or do you think our family is in danger?"

"Neither," Tom replied calmly. "But we've got a lead on who tried to hit Vic out in our street, and I just want as many folks in the house as possible, to watch each other's backs. Plus, if you're going back to do any cooking for that law firm, I don't want you alone."

I exhaled, thanked him again, and signed off. Then I checked out the serpentine wall. That thing must have been made of concrete, because it was completely unharmed. Thank the Lord for small favors.

As if he'd heard Tom discussing him, Vic Zaruski came ambling down the driveway. His smile was wide. "Mr. Ellis just gave me a hundred-dollar tip! Man, I want to come back here! They've got a Steinway that nobody plays. What the—" He was staring at the Rover door, which was lying halfway across the driveway, where it had landed. Then he looked up at our foursome: Julian, Arch, Gus, and yours truly. Vic's grin returned. "Somebody is screwed!"

Arch and Gus were still young enough that any untoward use of profanity could send them into paroxysms of laughter.

"Vic, please. Not in front of the kiddies."

"You should sue Rover," Vic said, his voice suddenly serious. "A door shouldn't come off like that, you know?"

"Well," Julian commented, "help is on the way. And I don't think Rover would pay for someone backing into a wall."

"Julian," I began for at least the fourteenth time, "I am so so so sorry—"

"No, it was my fault," Arch said. He'd been alternately apologetic and upset since we'd all hollered for him to **"Stop!"** This in turn had sent me backward, then rocketing forehead-first into the dashboard. I fingered the spot gently; the bruise was already swelling. I wanted to think about something, anything, besides Arch driving. Or not driving, as the case might be.

"It was **my** fault, Arch," I said with a finality that I hoped would close the argument.

Gus said, "This is just like what my grandfather is always saying." Gus lowered his voice. " 'Take responsibility, Gus. That's what no one does these days. Take responsibility!' "

"I'm going to run inside," Julian said. "You need to get some ice on that forehead, Goldy." The very **last** thing I wanted was to bother the El-lises, and have them come out here. But Julian was already racing up the driveway. I prayed that he would meet Lorraine, who would help him out.

"Vic," I said lightly. "Your playing was great. I love those old sixties songs. You did a marvelous job."

He blushed to the roots of his tightly curled straw-colored hair. "Why, thanks." Then his face turned glum. He shook his head.

"What's the matter?" I asked.

"Oh, I used to hope that, you know . . ." He looked into the street, as if thinking about what he used to hope.

Gus and Arch had moved into Woods' End, where they were throwing a Frisbee that had popped free from Julian's storage area behind their seat. So with just Vic and me in the driveway, I wondered if he'd talk to me a bit about Dusty. About why he threw a diamond ring through the window of Aspen Meadow Jewelers. About what he had hoped.

"No," I said, my voice low. "I don't know."

To my great surprise, as well as Vic's, I imagine, tears spilled out of his eyes. He muttered another profanity and wiped his eyes with his sleeve. I pulled a tissue out of my pants pocket and handed it to him. Julian still hadn't returned, and the boys were yelling and racing back and forth as they tossed the Frisbee.

I said, "Vic, is there something you want to say to me?"

"Yeah," he mumbled. He searched in his pockets and brought out a crumpled pack of cigarettes. "Mind if I smoke? Think the Ellises will mind?"

"I'm sure it'll be okay," I said, although I was sure of no such thing. Still, some folks' tongues were loosened up by booze; maybe nicotine could do the same thing.

The match flared; Vic took a deep drag and looked at me. "You probably heard Dusty and I broke up."

"Yes, I did."

He looked toward the trees that edged the far border of Woods' End. "Well, that's what I told the cops, you know, when they took me down to the department. We broke up, end of story. 'So what were you doing in that copy place at that hour of night?' 'Yo! I work there,' I told them." Vic shook his head. "I just thought you would have heard about when I was in interrogation, because you're married to a cop. I figured, you know, they talk."

"Well, that's not the case with Tom. Sometimes I hear things, sometimes he discusses cases with me, but I know to keep my mouth shut."

Vic took another drag on his cigarette. I guessed Julian and Lorraine were waiting for the ice maker to fill. At length, Vic said, "I hoped Dusty and I would be able to tour together. She wasn't a great singer, but she was a pretty good one. And she loved the music, man. She just **dug** it." Another drag on the cigarette. "But she didn't dig me. In the end, she didn't dig me."

"Look, Vic, I'm sorry. Is there something you want to tell me that you haven't told the police?"

Vic dropped the half-smoked cigarette and twisted it under the toe of his black boot. "I hit her. Oh God; now there, I've said it. It was only once." He began to cry again. "I'm so sorry, and you with your history and all, that the whole town knows."

Very softly, I asked, "Did you tell the cops you hit her?"

He put his head in his hands. "No. I couldn't."

"Where did you hit her, Vic? Where on her body, I mean. Where and when?"

He blew out air. "I slapped her face. It was that night, around seven. She came over to Art, Music, and Copies to return a ring I'd given her. I was so—" He couldn't finish the thought.

I said, "Did you trash her car? Because if they find the hammer or whatever it was at your place—"

"No, no, I didn't trash her car. I even wanted to apologize to her. But I was just so mad. I was just so **damn** mad."

Angry **and** mad, perhaps. But I was still treading gingerly. "Was there someone else?" I asked. "Someone else in her life, and that's why she broke up with you?"

"I asked her. She said no. I wasn't sure I believed her. She yelled at me, and I yelled at her, and then I—" He closed his eyes at the memory.

"The pathologist will find the mark you made on her face," I said solemnly. "Sometimes slaps even match certain people's hands—"

"What am I supposed to do?" he asked. His eyes flared. "Call the sheriff's department and say, 'Uh-oh, I forgot to tell you that I hit my girlfriend, I mean, my ex-girlfriend'?"

"That is precisely what you need to do," I said as Julian came sauntering back down the driveway, using both hands to hold a cloth towel bulging with ice. Just then, Tom's trustworthy car came into sight, with trustworthy Tom behind the wheel. The boys snagged the Frisbee and raced toward us. "Let me say something to you, Vic," I said, trying to keep the urgency out of my voice. "You need to tell the cops just what you told me. Because you're right, they're going to find out. Sooner or later. And if they discover you haven't been forthright with them, things are going to get very bad for you."

Tom pulled his car into the Ellises' driveway within a foot of the hapless Rover door. "Hey, everybody!" he sang as he jumped out. He looked over his shoulder at Vic's Sebring, which was parked on the dead end. Tom hooked a thumb over his shoulder. "Now **that's** a convertible." He shook his head at the doorless Rover and pointed at it. "That is not how you want to get air inside a car." When he saw my expression, his joviality disappeared. "C'mere, Miss G. You look like the Jerk just walked back into your life."

"Not quite," I whispered, and glanced at Vic. He gave a barely perceptible nod. "Vic has something to tell you, Tom. He's going to do it now."

So all our plans changed. Tom, as might be expected, was immediately somber. He wanted to take Vic down to the department right away to make a statement. Vic agreed.

When we were discussing how we were going to do the vehicles, Julian, who could sense something was up without being told what it was, said, "I could wait here for the tow truck, ask the guy to take you all home, then come back for me after he drops off the Rover."

"No, thanks, but no," I protested, unwilling to calculate how long it would take to have the tow-truck driver chauffeur us hither and yon, even if he was willing to do it. The next day was the christening reception, and like it or not, Julian and I needed to do the prep.

Vic pulled his keys out of his pocket. "Take the Sebring." When I gave him a dubious look, he said, "It's okay. I trust you." He gave a humorless laugh. "Just park it on the street by the Routts' place and I'll get it later."

How did I feel about taking a suspect's car back home? Guilty? Worried? Actually, I was too tired to have any feelings. We lived less than half an hour away, and Tom would be back soon. Even he seemed to think it would be okay, so I acquiesced. He also murmured that he would call Brewster Motley if it looked as if Vic was going to be charged and needed a criminal defense attorney.

Within five minutes, the boys were again shrieking with laughter, this time at the prospect of yours truly driving them in a convertible with the top down, all the way home! Imagining the windy drive back to our house, I thought I'd be lucky not to get the flu.

As Tom was departing with Vic, the tow truck pulled up, thank God. It was only a matter of minutes before the driver and Julian managed to hook the truck up to the Rover. I gave the driver my credit-card number while Julian tossed the errant door into the back of his car.

He slapped his hands together and gave me a wide smile. "I never liked that door anyway."

You gotta love the kid, I thought as I hustled Arch and Gus into the rear seat of the convertible. And so I drove us all home, with the boys hollering, "This is so cool! This is so cool!" the entire way.

Once Julian and I were back in our kitchen, I had two things to do: start on the prep for the christening reception, and call the Routts. Make that three things: I needed to start on the dinner dish I'd promised Tom. The sausage-and-potato casserole was a hearty entrée that Tom had adapted from Julia Child, and he loved to dig into it when the weather turned cold. With the thermometer hovering right at thirty-two degrees, that was precisely what it was, despite my son and his half brother's glee at being driven home in an open-air vehicle.

"When the temperatures drop, I don't even drive with my windows down," Julian said, once he'd donned an apron. "I feel as if my ears are frozen to the sides of my face."

"I may never talk again," I said, feeling my chilled lips. "Some people might not see that as a bad thing."

Julian merely shook his head. I told him what I'd planned for the christening reception: Prosciutto Bites, Charlie's Asparagus Quiche recipe from the booklet we'd bought at CBHS, Homemade Breads, and Fresh Fruit Salad. Aspen Meadow Bakery was doing an enormous sheet cake, so I didn't need to bake another Old Reliable. Julian started tapping my computer keys. The printer began spitting out recipes and prep sheets, and the two of us gathered ingredients from the walk-in.

"You might want to make an extra quiche, a

small one," I warned Julian as he was grating cheese. "The dinner Tom wants is a meat lover's extravaganza." Julian mumbled something unintelligible about heart disease, but said it was no problem. "Can you manage in here," I asked, "if I go see the Routts?"

"Of course," he said. "But if I'm going to be spending more than just one night here, at some point I need to go get my clothes."

I told him that Tom would like him to stay with us for a while, at least until Dusty's murder was solved, but only if he could swing it with the bistro where he was working. Julian promised he'd be able to switch some shifts. But he still needed clothes, he reminded me, or a car to go get them in. We agreed to go to Boulder the next afternoon, Sunday, after the service.

I rummaged around in the freezer until I found an oblong dish full of spaghetti and meatballs that I had made for one of the fund-raisers at Christian Brothers High School. I wrote out directions for heating it. Before starting for the Routts' house, I asked Julian to come out onto the front porch and watch me. This he did, and I also looked both ways, because I sure didn't want somebody to mow down my casserole and me.

Sally answered the door after I'd knocked several times. Her hair looked even more straggly and unkempt than when I'd seen her the day before, and the odor emanating from the house was foul. Maybe she was embarrassed to have me come in, and that was why she'd been reluctant to see who was on her front stoop.

"Do you have anything to tell me?" she asked. Her expressionless gaze skimmed the street. "Why is Vic's car parked in front of your house? Is he over visiting you? Will he be back to see us? I feel so bad about not letting him in the other morning . . . and he's been so helpful and kind. Is he coming over here?"

"Uh, no," I stammered. I was not going to tell Sally the reason for Vic's sudden trek down to the sheriff's department, as that would upset her even more. "He's with Tom. He'll be back soon." When she didn't say anything, I went on: "Could you let me in? I need to put this casserole in your refrigerator . . . and ask you a few questions."

"The police have asked us enough questions to last us a lifetime," she said, but she pulled the door open and I followed her to the kitchen.

The cause of the odor was immediately apparent, as the smell was much stronger by the sink. No one had taken out the trash.

The trash! I'd forgotten all about the mess in the back of Julian's Rover. I checked my watch: just after five. I knew Aspen Meadow Imports, where the Rover had been towed, closed soon. I would just have to get it the next day. No wait, that was Sunday. By the time I got it Monday, Julian's vehicle would be permanently infused with the smell of garbage.

Well: to the task at hand. I didn't ask for Sally's permission to remove the trash; I just did it. It had probably been Dusty's job. I toted the bulging plastic bag out to the garbage container, thankful that no bears had been reported in our neighborhood. When I came back inside, Colin's disconsolate crying filled the house. I guessed that he'd just awakened from his nap. But this was only a guess, because Sally remained glued to the couch.

"Let me go get him," I offered. And so I washed my hands and went to fetch the little guy, since Sally still wasn't moving. Colin, his face mottled from weeping, needed a change. It had been well over a decade since I'd changed a diaper, and when I started I realized Colin needed a bath. Poor kid.

"All right, buster, let's go," I said to him in as commanding a tone as I could muster.

Fifteen minutes later, I brought Colin, bathed, changed, and clothed in clean garments, into the small living room. Sally had not stirred. After I put Colin down, I came and sat beside her.

"You know, Sally, maybe we should get a counselor to come here to the house. I can call one, if you'd like. You need help."

"What I need," she said in a monotone, "is to find out what happened to my daughter."

"Okay, okay," I said as I pulled my cell from my pocket. "But may I get somebody here to help you?"

"Do whatever you want."

I walked into the kitchen and put in a call to Furman County Social Services, steeling myself for the usual bureaucratic runaround. To my astonishment, I was only transferred once, and the office said they would send a grief counselor up that evening. I also put in a call to St. Luke's. Thank goodness some foresighted soul had thought to put in confidential voice mail for Father Pete. He'd just been over here the previous day, but hopefully he could manage another visit. I added that if he was aware of anyone in the Episcopal Church Women who knew the Routts, and would be willing to stop in once a day to do some cleaning and cooking, that would be great.

"Have you eaten today, Sally?" I asked when I came back out to the living room. No to that, too. Which probably meant that Colin was hungry, as well. Where was Sally's father? Perhaps he napped in the afternoon. But a happy cry from Colin and a rush of hurried baby steps indicated that John

Routt had made his appearance from the other side of the small house. For that I was thankful.

Ten minutes later I had heated up slices of ham left by a parishioner, a pan of macaroni and cheese—the ultimate comfort food—and placed these next to small dishes of chilled applesauce. It was the kind of not-quite-balanced meal we used to get in the school cafeteria when I was a kid, but I figured it would do. For Sally and her father, I set up the metal TV tables that had been part of the sparse furnishing the parish had done for the house. Colin slipped easily into his yellow chair-within-a-table, even called out gleefully when he saw the applesauce. I cut his ham and macaroni into bite-size pieces and served them. To my great surprise and satisfaction, they all, even Sally, ate hungrily.

I didn't want to make them uncomfortable while they were enjoying their food, so I washed the two pots I'd dirtied, then cleaned out the refrigerator. I took out two of the church's offerings as well as my casserole-cum-directions, and put all three into the Routts' small freezer. By the time they were finished eating, I had the counters cleaned and the little dishwasher—but at least they had one, and built in, too—almost loaded. I put in their dishes and silverware, and figured it was time to talk.

With Colin settled in on the far side of the living room to watch **Sesame Street** on the portable TV, Sally, with some color in her cheeks and looking far less desolate, moved the two living-room chairs over by the spread-covered couch, so she and her father and I could visit.

"I haven't found out much," I warned them. "Just rumors at this point, that kind of thing."

"Was there anything in the computer?" Sally asked.

"Sort of," I said. "I know Julian called you to ask about this, and you said you hadn't heard of it, but are you sure that Dusty didn't have a friend-who-was-a-boy with the first or last name beginning with **O**?"

"Positive," Sally said. "She had been going out with Vic Zaruski, but that had ended, I'm pretty sure."

"Was he nice to her?" I asked. "I mean, did she ever complain that he was not nice to her?"

Sally shrugged. "She didn't say one way or the other. Why?"

Before I could talk about the face slap, John Routt piped up: "I believe there was more affection on his side than there was on hers."

"Did she tell you that?" I asked.

"No," he said. "But when you're blind you pick up a lot of nuances and attitudes from speech."

I steeled myself for my next question. "Okay, there's an attorney with whom Dusty was friends. They worked out together. Did she ever mention doing exercises or weights with someone, someone whom she might have cared for romantically?"

"She never mentioned anyone," said Sally. "Who is this person?"

The less said about any specific attorney, the better, I figured. I didn't want Sally going on an ill-conceived vigilante mission. "Just a guy," I said, my tone light. "This next part is important. Did Dusty talk to you about working for Charlie Baker?"

"Oh yes, Charlie Baker," Sally said. "She really did like him. He died, but I guess it wasn't wholly unexpected."

"No," I said. "Anyway, she mentions a gift from Charlie. Then another time, just a couple of days before she was killed, one of Charlie Baker's neighbors saw her carrying something out of his house, in a tube. A long tube, the kind someone might use to store paintings. Do you know anything about this?"

Sally shook her head, clearly frustrated that there was so much about her child she hadn't known. But wait. The last entry in Dusty's journal had said: "Now I can compare them." I'd thought she meant boyfriends, but maybe she meant something else. I ran this by Sally.

"Compare what?" Sally asked, hooking her straggly hair behind her ear. "The only thing Dusty cared about was **learning the law**. I think her dream was to become a lawyer someday. But you can't carry law books in a tube. And anyway, if she had taken anything, the police would have found it when they searched our house."

"All right," I said wearily. "I guess I'll have to go down to Mile-High Paralegal Institute to see if she had a locker—"

"Wait," said John Routt. "She might have left them with me."

"Dad?" asked Sally Routt, clearly astonished.

"Let's go into my room." He stood and began tap-tapping his way down a short hall.

I remembered this room: it had been designed as a porch with a separate entrance. And it could have been used as a porch, if it hadn't been assigned to Sally's father, who'd come here after his wife died. The windows were the jalousie type, now tightly shut against the chill. The futon with its striped pillows was still there, as were the mismatched chairs and the small table with the saxophone on top. On summer evenings, John would open the windows and play the saxophone, and we lucky neighborhood folks could imagine we were outside a New York jazz club. In one corner was a space heater, its orange wires glowing brightly. I didn't see anything that could fit into a tube.

"Are you facing the interior wall of the house?" John asked. "That's where Dusty hung two things. She told me to take care of them, no matter what."

I turned around. And there, suspended from hooks, were two paintings by Charlie Baker.

I stared at them. One was titled **Trustworthy Chocolate Cake**. It was an old recipe for an extraordinarily fudgy cake that I knew well. Like the Journey Cake recipe, it contained no eggs, and yet somehow, this recipe looked correct. Was I missing something? My sleep-deprived mind refused to provide an answer.

The other painting was for something Charlie called Plum Kuchen. In the fall, when those small, tart Italian plums are plentiful, I frequently made plum kuchen myself. I stared at the recipe. Here, as with the Journey Cake recipe, reading the ingredient list made me uneasy. Something just didn't look right. I peered at the lower right-hand side of each painting, and there was Charlie Baker's signature.

"Does this help?" John Routt asked into the air.

"It might," I said, not wanting to discourage him.

"Our Dusty wouldn't have stolen anything."

"I know that. Do you mind if I use my cell phone?"

He replied that he didn't, and he would leave me to conduct my call in private.

"I just finished practicing," Meg Blatchford said, after I identified myself. She was panting.

"Meg, do you know if Charlie ever left an ingredient out of his recipes?"

Why should I have been surprised when she said, "Oh yes, always. Didn't you know that?"

"No. Tell me."

I could hear Meg clattering ice cubes into a glass. "Wait a sec," she said, still gasping a bit. "All that pitching works up a thirst." After a moment, she said, "You know, Charlie's financial success came somewhat late in life for him. Because of that, he became anxious about his work. He . . . was always afraid of . . . imitators."

"Imitators?"

"Yes, he was terrified that a guest or intruder would sneak into his studio while he was in another part of that big house, sleeping, or cooking, or whatever. He worried constantly that this unwelcome someone would steal the painting or paintings, before they went to the gallery. He told me once that he was even anxious about someone coming in and taking photos of his works in progress, so they could do an imitation or forgery."

Meg stopped to sip water. "But in case someone got the not-so-bright idea to try to sell forged or stolen works before Charlie set them up at the gallery that represented him, he did a little joke. A little joke that made him feel more secure."

"What kind of little joke?"

"Well. When he hand-lettered the recipe under the painting, he would always leave out the very last ingredient. However! He always put it in the margin, to remind himself of what it was. When he got to the gallery to help set up his paintings, he would always go around and hand-letter the very last ingredient of each recipe. You remember my stew painting? Did you see the merry little sticks of butter running all around in the margin?"

"Sure," I said, still puzzled.

"Well, if you look carefully at the very last ingredient that's hand-lettered in there, it's a stick of butter, that you put in for enrichment of the stew. Charlie was very old-fashioned in the area of cholesterol."

I stared hard at the margin of **Trustworthy Chocolate Cake**. It was filled with cheerful little cups of water, prancing around the edge of the painting. And the last ingredient on the hand-lettered recipe was "1 cup water."

What was missing from Charlie's recipe for Plum Kuchen? All I had to do was look in the margin, right? And there were spoonfuls of sugar, cavorting happily all around the edge of the painting. Of course. You made the butter-rich batter, spread it into a springform pan, laid on the plums, and finally, sprinkled them with a couple of tablespoons of sugar before the lovely concoction went into the oven.

And what had been missing from the Journey Cake recipe? I asked myself. Baking soda, I realized just as quickly. Baking soda, baking soda, baking soda. Without eggs, you definitely need an acid **and a base** to make the cake rise. Julian and I had had the acid, which was the cider, but not the base, soda. My inner ear provided Arch saying "Duh, Mom."

I thanked Meg, signed off, and again looked at the paintings. **Trustworthy Chocolate Cake** was a complete painting. **Plum Kuchen** was not complete. And the Journey Cake recipe, the one on the painting Nora had given her husband, had not been complete. "Now I can compare them," Dusty had said in her journal. Indeed.

I punched in our home numbers, praying that Tom had returned from the sheriff's department. When he answered, my shoulders slumped in relief.

"Tom," I said breathlessly. "How did Vic do?"

"Okay, I suppose. Our guys took his statement and released him. We don't have enough evidence to charge him. Yet."

I swallowed. "Well, listen. I need you to drive over to the Routts' house."

"Wait," my husband said. "I just saw Vic off, and now you want me to get in my car and drive across the street?"

"Yes," I said, "I don't want anyone to see what I'm taking out of this house and bringing to our house. I . . . I think whoever killed Dusty may be having her house watched somehow. Or our house watched. That would explain why Vic was almost hit bringing the computer over."

"I still haven't told you about my line on that, by the way."

"Tom! This isn't like my bringing a casserole across the street, okay? Would you please just drive over?"

"I could get some cops to park at both ends of the street. Create a roadblock down on Main."

"Are you going to make fun of me, or are you going to come help me smuggle some key evidence out of the Routts' house?"

"Key evidence that you're touching, no doubt."

"In four seconds, I am walking out of this house."

Tom said, "I can't believe I'm doing this."

Chapter 16

I took the paintings down from the wall. They weren't suspended from hooks, as I'd thought, but were attached with plastic clothes hangers. Once I had them both down, I started rolling them up, carefully, very, very carefully. But it was difficult, because something was making the paintings bulky . . .

On the backs of each of the paintings was a form, with several typed sheets attached. I probably shouldn't have, but I delicately lifted the tape holding the papers in place.

The form began: "In the matter of the estate of." And then someone had typed "Charles Baker." I skimmed down to the title of the form itself: "Inventory." Hmm.

While I was waiting for Tom, I scanned the rest of the first page, which contained a summary of "Schedule A (Real Estate)," "Schedule B (Stocks and Bonds)," and so on through "Schedule F (Miscellaneous Property)." One portion of the form was highlighted in yellow: "Decedent's estates: Assets shall be listed and the fair market value given as of the date of the decedent's death. The inventory shall be sent to interested persons who request it or the original inventory may be filed with the court . . .'"

I frowned at the form taped to the back of the other painting, the one I now knew had an incomplete recipe. The form appeared to be the same as the first, with the same area highlighted. A four-page printout had been stapled to both forms. My eyes crossed trying to read the single-spaced typing. "Chairs, Sculptures, Crystal, China . . ." I just couldn't do this with any kind of understanding right now. Which was a good thing, because that was when Tom's sedan crunched over the gravel and ice in the Routts' driveway.

To his credit, Tom did not grumble or complain when I crept out the back door of the Routts' house carrying a large trash bag filled with my loot. I got into Tom's sedan and began the arduous one-second trip across the street.

"Whatcha got there?" he asked, once we were inside.

"Charlie Baker paintings. Two of them. From Dusty's journal, I think he gave her one of them, as a thank-you for the work she had done for him. I'm afraid the second one is unfinished."

"Unfinished?"

"Yes, Charlie's friend Meg said he never wrote down the last ingredient of his recipe until the very end, when the paintings were going to be sold at the gallery, or given to someone like Dusty. Some of the paintings that are floating around now have an ingredient missing. And get this— there are some inventory forms that the department will want to go over. Dusty had taped them to the backs of the paintings, so she was trying to keep them from **somebody**."

Tom cocked an eyebrow. "Inventory forms taped to the backs of the paintings?"

"Don't worry! I'm not going to keep them. I'll leave figuring them out to the geniuses down at the department. But listen, I suspect that Nora Ellis bought an unfinished Charlie Baker painting, thinking it was a completed one. So I hope your guys can go talk to her—"

Tom held up his hand. "You're going to have to explain all of this to me, and then maybe I can send a detective to go talk to the Ellises. Okay?"

"Sure. Now tell me your news."

"We have a line on a guy, but not the guy himself, who tried to mow down Vic. You know how crooks are always the worst rats?" When I nodded, he went on: "Seems a guy we'd had a forgery warrant out on got himself arrested. First thing he tries to do is deal. Seems he has a friend named Jason Gurdley—" I shook my head. "Hey, his mother named him, not me. Anyway, Jason bragged about being paid a thousand bucks just to run over anyone bringing any stuff out of the Routts' house."

"**What?**"

"Apparently, someone was afraid of what Dusty had."

"This is where you tell me that you found Jason, and he gave up the name of whoever paid him to try the rundown."

Tom smiled at me. "Hey, you can't have everything. Jason Gurdley has skipped to parts unknown. We've left messages all over saying we need to talk to him pursuant to a murder investigation, but that might cause him to stay hidden, wherever he is. Still, now we know someone was behind the attempt to kill Dusty's computer."

"And Vic."

"Yeah; him, too." His eyes gleamed. "Our guys did arrest someone else, though."

"When were you going to tell me this?"

"Well, you had me chauffeuring you around with your paintings—"

"Who, dammit?"

"Somebody tried to pawn that opal-and-diamond bracelet in Denver, just this afternoon. The pawnshop owner had gotten our fax of your drawing and called the department. The detectives drove down and showed him photographs of Vic and everyone who worked at the law firm. He picked out the person who attempted to pawn the bracelet. So our guys got the fastest search warrant on earth, and found something **extremely** interesting in the Dumpster outside the apartment of our would-be bracelet seller." Tom paused for effect. "Try a sledgehammer covered with some dark red car paint and glass fragments."

"Oh Lord."

"Our guys just picked up Louise Upton."

"**What?** Maybe the bracelet was Louise's, and she loaned it to Dusty—"

"Or maybe Dusty gave Louise a sledgehammer in exchange for the bracelet. Do you think?"

"But what motive would Louise have to **kill** Dusty?"

"Goldy, I don't know. She saw the bracelet and thought she could pawn it for needed cash. She struggled with Dusty and ended up strangling her. I'm telling you, that woman, Louise Upton, is as hard as granite. She didn't even protest when they arrested her. She just said she wanted an attorney. Look, I'm going to call the guys at the department, have them come get this evidence."

"Just wait a sec, okay? Tell me why you think Louise would have used a sledgehammer on Dusty's car."

Tom held the phone loose in his hand. He said patiently, "Crime of passion? Say a guy is going to kill his ex-girlfriend and trash her car, too. We find slashed tires, broken windshields, garbage dumped all over a lawn? We know somebody's been hurt real bad. Hurt in the **heart**. Problem is, this behavior is well known, 'cuz stories about it are in the paper all the time. Now, a perp wants to make it **look** as if he's killed out of passion, instead of just trying to shut somebody up, say? He'll get out the hammer and go after his victim's **stuff**."

I still was doubtful. Louise Upton under arrest for Dusty's murder? Okay, Louise was desperate for money. Had she stolen something besides the bracelet—say, a painting or two—and been discovered by Dusty? But if Dusty had discovered Louise was involved in nefarious doings, Louise wouldn't have been stupid enough to kill Dusty and leave her corpse inside the office of the firm she said she was married to, would she?

Then again, my brain yelled back at me, **Louise might have left Dusty's body if she'd killed Dusty in a burst of panic.** So it **was** possible.

"Tom," I said tentatively while he was dialing, "may I just look through Dusty's things for a couple of minutes?"

Tom's shoulders slumped. "All right, go get

some of those surgical gloves your favorite health inspector says you have to use when you handle poultry."

I responded with alacrity, which was one of Arch's vocab words that I particularly liked. It meant that you got your butt in gear with enthusiasm **and** speed.

Five minutes later, I was wearing a pair of my surgical gloves and sifting through the papers attached to the inventory forms. It was becoming increasingly difficult to see what exactly **about** the law it was that Dusty found attractive. I didn't understand why the forms couldn't merely state: "Attach a list of the dead guy's stuff." But in the last analysis, I guessed that wouldn't work.

After a few moments, I finally got the bright idea to compare the two lists, page by page, side by side. After straining my eyes for what felt like an eon—Julian even came out of the kitchen to see what was going on—I saw the discrepancy. Or thought I did. On one page listing miscellaneous assets, someone—Dusty?—had typed "45 paintings." On the page that matched it from the other inventory, the same listing indicated "9 paintings."

So, could I make the deduction that there were thirty-six Charlie Baker paintings out there, all missing one ingredient, that someone had stolen and was trying to sell? I thought so. And Nora Ellis, who had plenty of money but no cooking ability, wouldn't have known a recipe for Journey Cake from one for beef stew, right?

But where had she gotten the painting? From Richard, who supposedly had been in charge of getting new keys and locks made for Charlie Baker's house? From Louise, or from Wink, either of whom might have been actually ordered to get those new keys and locks made? From Vic, ever hard up for money and, until recently, Dusty's boyfriend? He could have borrowed the keys from Dusty, stolen the paintings, and returned them without her knowing, couldn't he? But would Vic be able to change the inventory sheets? That would indicate someone in the law firm. What about Alonzo Claggett, who was Dusty's workout buddy . . . might **he** have snagged and copied the keys? I had no idea.

I told Tom my theory, but lack of a clear suspect, when he got off the phone.

"You think somebody killed Dusty because he, or she, wanted to steal some paintings?"

"Yeah, maybe. And then that person—maybe Louise, okay—started selling the paintings to people with lots of dough who want a genuine Charlie Baker."

Tom considered this for a moment. "How's Julian doing on your cooking tomorrow?"

"I can check. Why?"

"Be a good idea if you typed up everything you've figured out about the paintings. We can give it to the guys when they come up."

Alacrity was getting to be my middle name. I hopped up and headed for the computer in the kitchen. There, Julian had finished the Asparagus Quiches, which were rising in the oven and giving off an enticing scent. Now he was peeling apples.

Apples? "What are you making?" I asked. "We don't have anything on the menu tomorrow that includes apples."

Julian peered down at the prep sheets. "Prosciutto Bites—prep is done, but they have to be finished at the last minute. Asparagus Quiches—done. Fruit Salad—ditto with the last-minute thing. So . . . there I was looking around in your walk-in, and what do I find but a bunch of apples? Time for an apple pie. Or a couple of apple pies, so I can take one over to the Routts if they aren't too burned out on apples after your Apple Betty. I'm going to use Charlie's recipe for All-American Apple Pie. What do you think?"

"Who can say no to apple pie?" I smiled and said, "I think you're great." Then I stared at the computer screen and skipped over to the file I'd opened regarding the investigation. It didn't take long to write up my analysis, or theory, really, about the paintings that Dusty had cleverly hidden by putting them in her blind grandfather's room. The cops who'd searched the Routts' house wouldn't have known they were significant; how could they have? But they were. Or at least I believed they were. And the attached inventories, I added, might indicate that something was up with accounting for Charlie Baker's assets, assets that needed to be reported to the probate court. When I was done, I printed out the sheets for Tom, who thanked me and said he would wait in the living room for the department guys to show up.

Well, I hoped my ideas would be some help, I mused as I started a big pot of water boiling for the potatoes that would go into the sausage casserole. While I was peeling the potatoes, I told Julian about the most recent developments in the Dusty case. Julian shook his head and rolled out the pie dough. I dropped the potatoes into the water and then began earnestly chopping onions. After a few moments, I wiped tears away. The hard place behind my heart, the place that was still holding on to Dusty, wasn't softening.

I washed and trimmed the mushrooms, squeezed them to release their liquid, and melted a big hunk of butter in a large sauté pan. I tossed in the chopped onions and mushrooms, and soon the kitchen was filled with the delectable scent of onions and mushrooms sautéing in butter. Perhaps drawn by the sound of the sizzle in the pan, or maybe by the fragrance wafting upstairs, Arch and Gus came clomping down.

Gus pushed through the kitchen door first. "Man, what are we having?"

I had cut off the casings of the sausages and added them to the sputtering onions and mushrooms. Gus watched in fascination. I told him about the sausage casserole, and he beamed.

"Uh-oh, pie!" Arch yelled, when he saw Julian carefully spooning a mound of spice-laced apple slices into a waiting crust. "Is that for us, or is it for a job?"

Julian lifted his chin and winked at Arch. "Hey, would we make apple pies for clients, and not make one for the family?"

"Yes," Arch said, his tone accusatory.

"One's for us," Julian said. "And one's for the Routts."

There was an awkward moment when Gus and Arch looked at each other, as if trying to think of something to say. Teenagers have a hard time talking about the death of someone they know. I worried about Arch. Maybe the death of Dusty was bothering him more than he was letting on. As usual, my son was pretty hard to read.

"Let's go throw the Frisbee for Jake," Gus said finally, and the two boys raced out of the room.

"I think Arch is having a difficult time," I told Julian. "When death strikes this close, all that comes up is fear for the people he loves."

Julian nodded as he concentrated on the apples. Not so long ago, he had lost a young woman he loved in another murder; this had changed him, made him a little more serious. I suppose kids in their twenties have the same fears.

Once the pies were baked and cooling, we had a jolly dinner. Julian indulged in a small quiche made from leftovers, while the rest of us dug into the rich, juicy casserole, with its layers of potatoes, mixture of mild and hot Italian sausages, and creamy binder of eggs, half-and-half, and Gruyère cheese. I thought back to when a critic asked if I was cooking for the National Cholesterol Institute. There was actually no such thing, place, or restaurant. But if there **were,** this recipe would certainly be on their menu.

When we finished eating, Tom insisted on doing the dishes so that the boys could watch a movie and Julian and I could plan upcoming events. We didn't have another scheduled affair until Monday, when I was supposed to do breakfast for Hanrahan & Jule. I wasn't so sure how I felt about going back to the H&J offices where I'd found Dusty, but I was still under contract to the law firm, and the place would probably be cleaned and open for business by then. We decided on a frittata made with fresh chopped scallions and Tom's cherry tomatoes. That night, we'd be doing a dinner for ten big donors and a few others involved in buying the land and designing the Mountain Pastoral Center. The funding to build and operate the center would be coming from Charlie Baker's bequest, once the will finished wending its way through probate. Our catering client was the Episcopal Diocese of Colorado itself. The meal would be simple: Chicken Piccata, steamed asparagus, and wild rice. Julian frowned and asked about possible vegetarians. I said I didn't know of any who might be coming, but if he wanted to think about a possible dish, that would be great. For dessert, the events coordinator had said they just wanted "something spectacular."

Julian snorted. "Chicken and 'something spectacular.' What is this, an amusement park?"

I sighed. Every now and then, Julian was showing signs of becoming a chef. "We can invent whatever we want, to go with the vegetarian dish you've yet to come up with."

"Thanks, boss," Julian replied, with an enormous smile.

Julian went off to watch the movie with the

boys. Tom and I were left sitting in the kitchen. For some reason, I felt totally wired, and said so.

"Couldn't be those sixteen shots of espresso you had this morning, could it?" Tom asked mildly.

I gave him a sour look. "Have you told Sally and John Routt about the arrest?"

"That's not my job. But they'll be informed soon."

I blew out air. I had done so much talking to people in the past two days, made so many attempts at investigating Dusty's bizarre death, tried so hard to fulfill my promise to Sally Routt . . . and what had it come to? Nothing. Well, a bit more than nothing. The inventory for Charlie's assets had some discrepancies. And I had lots of suspects in mind for the person who could have stolen the paintings and manufactured a fake inventory.

Tom's phone beeped. When he got off, he said, "Hmm."

"That's not very enlightening."

"Louise Upton and her lawyer say she found the bracelet in her car. As far as the sledgehammer goes, she has no idea whose it is. She's never even handled a sledgehammer, she insists, and we weren't going to find her fingerprints on the thing. And get this—she and her lawyer **invited** the cops to search her house, see if any of her shoes or clothing had any glass on 'em."

"She **invited** them?"

Tom cocked his head. "She must be pretty sure of her innocence." He chuckled. "She told the cops they weren't to make a mess in her house."

At that, I actually laughed. Then the same buzzing sound in my brain, the crazed energy that I'd been feeling ever since I'd come home from the Routts' house with the paintings, took over. I zipped around the house, putting stuff away, tossing trash, and leaving each room spotless. What else could I do? Well, I could finish reading Dusty's journal. And . . .

Maybe I could prevail on K. D. Chenault to come over to the house tonight. I simply couldn't wait until the next morning to hear what she had to say, not with Louise Upton behind bars and so many questions unanswered.

I put in a call to K.D.'s separate line at the Chenault home. I know that it's time-consuming and expensive to find lovely housing, and I'd heard of more than one Aspen Meadow divorce ending up with a physical splitting of the big mansion, but goodness! I never could have lived with my soon-to-be ex under the same roof, once I had decided the marriage was over. But people were different. Maybe divorce was friendlier these days. Somehow, I doubted that.

K.D. answered on the third ring, sounding as if

I had awakened her. Feeling like a heel, I identified myself and apologized for calling at eight on a Saturday night. She said it was no problem, she just tried to sleep when she could, since late Saturday night and the wee hours of Sunday morning were prime times for ER activity, and she could be called in at any minute. I explained that I would love to hear what she had to tell me, if she was up to it. And, I would dearly like to listen to her story tonight, because the police had arrested Louise Upton for Dusty's murder.

Her predictable shock propelled her out of bed. "I don't want to talk about this over the phone. You still live right off Main Street?"

I told her that we did. She said she'd be right over.

Tom, Julian, Arch, and Gus decided to watch yet another movie, and I was left with a clean house and a bundle of energy the size of a nuclear reactor. The sheaf of unread pages from Dusty's journal still beckoned.

I scanned through April, May, June, and July, all still with references to "New O.," and how much she loved him, and how he said he felt as if he had just been born. Apparently their lovemaking was quite athletic, with her saying, "I just can't keep up with him! Does that sound dirty?"

No, I thought, **you poor girl. It just sounds as if you're in love.** But I was still left with the question: Who was this New O.? And if he loved Dusty so much, why wasn't he over at the Routts' house offering condolences? I reminded myself that with all I'd had to do at the Routts' house—bathing and changing Colin, cleaning out the refrigerator, making a meal, taking down the paintings—I'd forgotten to ask about the funeral. St. Luke's would be absorbing the expense, no doubt, but I had no idea when it was going to be. Maybe I'd see the mysterious Mr. O. then.

Even though it was after eight at night, I must have been daydreaming, because my attention suddenly snapped back. I reread an entry made this month. "October 6: Somebody is taking stuff. I don't know who. But I am going to FIND OUT."

Well, what **do** you know. I raced up the stairs and handed the page to Tom so as not to interrupt Clint Eastwood dispatching about half a dozen bad guys. Then the doorbell rang: K. D. Chenault.

She was dressed for work, in a camel-hair coat covering a sensible brown tweed skirt and white silk blouse. I knew that she, like the other docs, kept a locker down at Southwest Hospital, because the last thing anyone wanted was to bring home blood-spattered scrubs to do in the home laundry. With her chestnut hair pinned up in a twist and her expertly applied makeup, she might have been going off to work at an expensive women's clothing store or to manage an upscale bank. You never would have guessed that she was about to go attend to folks with gunshot and stab wounds, to horribly mangled car-accident victims, or to kids who had just opened a four-inch gash in their foreheads, slipping in the bathtub.

"Sorry for the cloak-and-dagger," she said, once she was settled in the kitchen and sipping a soft drink. "It's just that Richard listens in on my calls, which drives me nuts. And since this involves hospital business, I didn't want him to have anything to hang on my head at the next meeting with our attorneys. 'My wife doesn't guard the confidentiality of her patients,' that kind of thing. I wouldn't put anything past that man."

I wouldn't put anything past anyone, I thought, but said nothing. I didn't care about patients' records and wondered if this had anything to do with Dusty Routt.

K.D. licked her lips. "Actually, the patient in question is dead." When she shook her head, a few strands came loose from her French twist. "Let me begin at the beginning." She inhaled. "Last March, Flight for Life brought an elderly woman into the Southwest ER after she'd been struck by a car. She was a pedestrian up here in Aspen Meadow."

"I remember, I think. Wasn't she the lady who was run down on the street outside of Charlie Baker's last exhibit? I did the catering and she attended the event. I even saw her talking to Charlie for a while. Then we heard the sirens and found out there had been an accident."

"Yes, that sounds right. The highway patrol came to question the woman at the hospital. But she had already died, so they wanted to talk to me, to see who she was, and if she'd said anything. They said there were no witnesses to this woman being hit. And no skid marks on the pavement."

An icicle plunged down my back. I asked, "So who was she?"

"Her name was Althea Mannheim, and she was from Utah. I talked to her cousin at length later. Her only relative, living in Boulder now." K.D.'s voice turned impatient. "The thing is, when they brought Ms. Mannheim in, she was conscious, but hysterical. She was basically talking a bunch of nonsense. Or at least, I thought it was nonsense. She was absolutely covered with blood, plus we were sure she had internal injuries, and she kept saying, 'Steals. Steals. That's why I'm here.' I thought she was just suffering from shock, delirium, that kind of thing. We needed to get her stabilized, and I kept asking her to calm down while the painkiller took effect. She kept saying, 'Nobody else will tell them so I'm telling them. That bitch your eye steals.'"

" 'Bitch your eye'?"

"I thought maybe she was referring to a woman named Yoreye, as in that bitch, Yoreye. Or something like that. She kept saying, 'That's why I'm here. To tell people. That bitch your eye stole our pattern.'"

" 'Bitch your eye stole our pattern,' " I repeated. I wanted to make sure I was hearing this right.

"Then today, you introduced me to **Bishop Uriah,** from southern Utah."

"Oh my God."

"Yes. But a pattern? What pattern? I mean, how many men do you know who **sew**?"

I nodded, but not because I knew any men who did sewing. My mind was going along different lines: liturgical ones. I was also remembering what Meg had told me, that when she'd driven Charlie home from the party, he'd been agitated, and wanted to hire a private detective. And then there was what I'd just read in Dusty's journal: that someone was stealing paintings from Charlie's house. And now I was convinced that in fact someone had tampered with my van so I'd be late the night Dusty was killed. And all of this— all of it—could be related to why and how Dusty had been killed, and by whom.

On the other hand, it could have nothing at all to do with Dusty, or even Uriah Sutherland. It might simply be a coincidence that Althea Mannheim was visiting from Utah, went to Charlie's exhibit, and was killed in an accident nearby. She indeed might have been mumbling nonsense that K.D. had misinterpreted when she heard the unusual title and name, Bishop Uriah. Uriah certainly seemed an unlikely possibility for a painting thief, especially from a man who was an old and cherished friend. Richard Chenault, it had to be said, was a better possibility as someone who had access to the paintings and the inventories of Charlie's estate.

"Wait, K.D." I was thinking how to ask her if she'd seen any of Charlie Baker's paintings somewhere in that big house that she and Richard still shared. "Do you know anything about Richard's dealings with Charlie Baker?"

"Couple of things. Why?"

"Well, did you ever see any of Charlie's paintings in Richard's part of the house? Paintings that you didn't think he'd bought?"

She considered. "No. The most we ever do is have some wine together. Okay, it's not the most we've ever done. Once we had a lot of wine," she said with an embarrassed laugh. "And then one thing led to another . . ."

Aha! I thought. Maybe there was more than one reason they were still sharing a house. And I had to admit, albeit shamefully, that the Jerk had successfully seduced me a couple of times, after we were separated.

"Funny you should ask about Charlie Baker, though," K.D. said. "The next night, I mean the night **after** the show, Richard came home just looking miserable. I asked him if he wanted a glass of wine, and he said no, he wanted a glass of bourbon. He hardly ever drinks the hard stuff, Goldy. But he looked like hell, so I fixed him a drink, and I fixed one for myself." She shook her head, seeming apologetic. "Richard always talks too much when he drinks, and that night was no exception." She paused and gave me the full benefit of her hazel eyes. "He said Charlie Baker had come into the office that day and changed his will."

My mouth fell open. "Changed his will?" I echoed. So much for client confidentiality. "Changed his will how?"

"Well, I don't know, Goldy. Richard wouldn't tell me that. Why? Do you think Charlie wanting to change his will has something to do with Uriah Sutherland?"

"I'm not sure. I do know the bishop has been involved in setting up the Mountain Pastoral Center, which is being funded by Charlie's bequest. Maybe Charlie was planning to leave some of his paintings to Uriah, but then what Althea Mannheim told him changed his mind. Or maybe there's no connection between Mannheim and the bishop at all. You're not certain exactly what the dying woman was saying, K.D."

K.D. furrowed her brow and considered. "No, I'm not certain. Still, her words were so strange that they stuck with me. And then when you introduced us at the party . . . well, you saw how startled I was. I hadn't had a chance to meet Nora's father before now. I've been pretty busy this year, and then I just tried not to have much to do with anyone at the firm because, well, because of everything. And then this horrible disaster with Dusty happened . . . and oh my God, then Louise was arrested for it. And now you're bringing up Charlie Baker."

A bad thought entered my brain. Althea Mannheim, who may have known something about Uriah Sutherland, had died outside of the gallery mounting Charlie's last exhibit. Not long after that, Charlie had asked Meg about finding a private investigator . . . maybe to check on Uriah's past in southern Utah? And Charlie had also told Richard that he wanted to change his will. The next day . . . the **very** next day, Charlie had fallen to his death.

What if Charlie's death had not been an accident or suicide, what if he'd been pushed? What if everything that had happened so far was connected to Charlie, to his will, or to the stolen artwork? If so, Dusty had been in the thick of it. I figured she must have had a role in Charlie making changes to his will. She'd said as much in her journal: **Especially after what I was asked to do tonight.** Dusty was the one whom Charlie trusted . . . maybe even more than he trusted Richard. It made sense that she would have helped him get rid of a bequest to Uriah or whatever he'd wanted altered in the will. And depending on what those changes were, they might have been what led to Dusty's death.

I said, "This next part's important, K.D. What happened to the new will?"

"Well, that's what I wanted to ask Richard, with Charlie falling down the stairs so soon after Richard had told me Charlie was changing his will." She snorted. "But he'd sobered up by that time, and didn't want to talk to me about it."

"Did you tell the cops?"

"I wanted to," she said, biting the inside of her cheek, "but Richard said he could be disbarred for telling me about the new will, and then I would have to pay for his defense, plus get nothing from the divorce settlement. Oh, we had an awful fight. But in the end, he told me, 'There is no new will.'"

"I thought there **was**."

"No, Richard told me, 'There's no new will if the person making it doesn't come in to sign it, once we have it all typed up.'"

I felt as if all the air had gone out of my body at once. Could the alterations Charlie wanted to make to his will have been unimportant ones? Or had someone murdered Charlie so that the new will would never be valid? Maybe, if, could be. I kept running into dead ends. I wanted to ask K.D. more questions, but at that moment, her cell phone beeped.

"Gotta go," she told me, once she'd hung up. "They've got a kid coming in to the ER whom they suspect has shaken baby syndrome." She gave me a rueful glance. "And as if I didn't have enough problems, somebody sideswiped me on the way over here, and I'm going to have to have my damn car—"

"Whoa, whoa," I said, suddenly alert again. "Listen, K.D., the police are tracking a guy who may have tried to run down someone who's helping the Routts. And this Althea Mannheim was killed by a hit-and-run driver, remember. A wannabe killer in a car is not something you even want to be thinking about. In fact, would you vamoose out of town for a while?" I was remembering K.D.'s intense, frightened reaction to Uriah's name at the birthday party. If Nora's father was somehow involved with Charlie's or Dusty's death, or if he'd had a hand in the theft of Charlie's paintings, he might now view K.D. as a threat. Then again, someone else could wonder what K.D., as Richard's wife, knew. My paranoia might be running overtime again. Still, at this point it seemed best to be cautious about the good doctor's safety.

K.D. put on her camel-hair coat. "Well, I suppose I could use a break from Richard and his moods. Not to mention how he listens in on my calls."

"Best not even to tell him you're going." I thought of how Tom had wanted to take Vic right down to the department. "But I'll need your cell number, because I know Tom, or somebody from the department, will want to talk to you when your shift is over, before you go anywhere."

"Okay." She reached inside her purse, rummaged around for a bit, and pulled out a card. "I'm building a house in Santa Fe, with a guesthouse, too. It's too big for me, but it's my reward to myself for putting up with Richard and his antics. The guesthouse is done, and I can get on I-25 and drive straight through after I talk to whoever comes down from the sheriff's department. That card has my Santa Fe number, which Richard doesn't know, and my cell, which has caller ID."

She dug around in her purse again and brought out another card. "Almost forgot. I wrote down the name, address, and number of Althea Mannheim's cousin in Boulder. That's what I had to go to the hospital for this afternoon. Grace Mannheim, on Pine. Nice lady. Elderly, like her cousin. I know she wouldn't mind talking to you."

"You're going to get out of town as soon as you talk to the cops?" I asked her, just to be sure.

She opened our front door and peered into the darkness. "Well, I suppose. But it's already past sundown, and when you have to get out of Dodge—" She stopped again, grinning at the stricken expression I knew was on my face. "All right, all **right**. Can't you take a joke?"

Chapter 17

Once I'd had a shower, I fairly flopped on our mattress. It had been such a long day, with a party, a wrecked Rover, a lot of cooking, and ending with an enigmatic visit from K. D. Chenault. My old pal K.D., who had been sideswiped, and whom I'd urged to get out of town. I'd had wild fluctuations in energy levels all day, and I finally felt as if I'd reached the nadir.

Tom had been in the shower when K.D. had been called away for the shaken baby. When he came out, he said he was getting Julian settled in a sleeping bag between Gus and Arch, in Arch's room. From the sound of their talking down the hall, it was going to be a Long Night in Boyville. I was, as ever, thankful for Julian's presence in our family.

Once Tom had moved into bed next to me, I told him about K.D.'s visit. When I got to the point about the will change, Tom sat up, turned on the light, and reached for his trusty spiral notebook. I said, "I think Dusty referred to the will change in her journal. She said there was something she wasn't allowed to talk about. Dusty was the person Charlie trusted, so I think it's entirely possible she helped Richard draw up the new will."

Tom finished taking notes, then called the department and got patched in to one of the detectives who was working on Dusty's murder. He related the salient details, then gave the fellow K.D.'s numbers.

When he was back beside me, he reached out and pulled me in close, snuggling my breasts into his warm, still-damp chest until I giggled.

"I'm so glad you don't have to go down to the department," I said.

"Good," he said. "Then I don't have to explain to you why we have to gather a lot of information while we're in the process of a murder investigation. A lot. And unlike some caterers, we don't go barging in trying to gather evidence and arrest people—AGH!"

I'd found just the spot on his abdomen that, if I tickled it with my fingertips, would drive Tom wild.

And it didn't stop there.

Sunday morning arrived cool and sunny, with one of those deep blue skies you see in Colorado and nowhere else. Most of the snow and ice had melted, and the golden-leaved aspens quaked in a breeze off the mountains. Julian and I whipped around the kitchen, drinking espresso, checking our supplies, and readying all the foodstuffs to take to St. Luke's. To Tom I had given the unenviable job of rousting Gus and Arch from their warm beds, getting them showered, and making sure they were dressed in clean, not-needing-mending clothes. Luckily, the boys wore the same sizes, so if there was a sock or shirt missing, they could probably do some borrowing to come up with two clean outfits and matched pairs of shoes.

Tom also got the job of stuffing the guys with some breakfast, as the service was long. No promise of after-service brunch, it had been my experience, was enough to get a kid to quit complaining about being starving during church. Tom promised to meet us at the church fifteen minutes before the service. This was a good thing, as I wanted to have plenty of time to visit with Wink Calhoun, **if** she bothered to show up, as I'd requested.

Once Julian and I had set up in the church kitchen, the Episcopal Church Women arrived and began unfolding the long tables that would hold the food and beverages. While Julian was doing his perfect slicing job on the fruit, I finished the Prosciutto Bites and laid them out on cookie sheets. This particular combination of crunchy, warm croissant, piquant preserves, delectable prosciutto, and dots of cream cheese had been a great favorite at H&J. I wanted to pop one in my mouth, but resisted. I was stronger than an adolescent boy, right?

Wrong. So . . . there I was munching on one of the Bites, when Wink Calhoun, her eyes still rimmed with red, appeared in the church kitchen.

"You wanted to see me?" she asked, without preamble.

The kitchen was empty except for the two of us. Keeping my voice neutral, I said, "I need to ask you about your affair with Donald Ellis."

She lifted her chin. "I don't know what you're talking about."

"Yes, you do, Wink. Other people saw you together."

She began to cry. "I can't talk to you about it."

"I don't want to intrude unnecessarily into your personal life, but this is important. Was Dusty involved with Donald?" This made her sob even harder. "Wink, you said you wanted to help figure out what happened to Dusty, and you promised you'd answer my questions. I told you we think Dusty had a new man in her life, a relationship she was keeping secret. Could it have been Donald Ellis?"

"I don't know. I don't know. I don't know. I was involved with him, yes. But I broke it off because I felt so guilty, you know, having a fling with a married man."

"Did Nora know about your affair?"

"I don't think so. Donald hates Nora, though, did you find **that** out?"

"No. Why don't you tell me about it?"

"They have terrible fights. Once she was so mad at him, she hit him across the face. Not a slap, but a real"—here she demonstrated—**"whack."**

"How about you, do you get along with Nora?"

"She's been pretty nice to me. We've played squash a few times, since I told her I played in high school. And there was that time I told you about, when she stood up to Ookie for me at the club, but that may have been just to annoy Ookie. They're always trying to one-up each other."

Peachy, I thought. I decided to change course. "Do you know anything about Charlie Baker changing his will right before he died?"

"**What?** Who told you **that?**"

"How about paintings missing from Charlie's house?"

Wink's mouth hung open. "Who told you **that?**"

Out in the narthex, the choir was warming up.

This was my cue to remind Wink that the sheriff's department would not be happy that she had been withholding critical information from them. But she started to cry again, so instead I simply told her not to share the details of our conversation with anyone. I took off my apron and went in search of my family, not feeling as if I'd really gotten any closer to the truth.

Gus's grandparents arrived, looking nervous. But they were so enthusiastically greeted by Gus, that their agitation seemed to melt. They, in turn, embraced Arch, which made him feel wonderful, although he pretended to act embarrassed. With no grandparents living nearby, he reveled in their attention, their store-bought cupcakes, their inappropriate, but still treasured, gifts of stuffed animals, jacks, and marbles. We were all like the boys' clothing: we could fill in one another's gaps and, between us, make a big family.

During the service, I watched Bishop Uriah Sutherland closely. K.D. had given me information about him that might or might not shed light on who he really was.

Could he be the thief who took Charlie's paintings? Even worse, could he have killed or been involved in the deaths of Dusty or Charlie? I shuddered to think such a thing. It definitely didn't sound plausible. Some mumbled words from a dying woman wouldn't be enough to get a search warrant for the Ellises' house. Yet I couldn't dismiss the possibility that those same mumbled words might have been a secret about Uriah, as K.D. suspected, something very damning, and that those words might have been what Althea told Charlie Baker at his last show.

I focused my attention on the service. Gus beamed when he flipped back his hair, wet with holy water, after he'd been dunked. He looked right at me and smiled. **Dear Gus,** I thought. **I am so thankful for you.**

The highlight of the service was the moment when Meg Blatchford, whose smile was as wide as Gus's, announced to the congregation: "You may welcome the newly baptized!" And everyone clapped.

After the service, parishioners young and old chowed down enthusiastically on Asparagus Quiche, Prosciutto Bites, fruit salad, and sheet cake. It didn't take long for the little kids to realize that their plastic plates—slick with bits of asparagus, jam, and cake frosting—made really great Frisbees. Before you could say "definitely unorthodox," disks were sailing across the parish hall more thickly than flying saucers in a science-fiction movie. Bishop Sutherland's chasuble took a direct hit from a plate covered with plum jam. Luckily, several members of the Episcopal Church Women insisted on bustling forward with cold wet towels to minister to the bishop and his vestments. He laughed just as he had before, at Donald's party, with guacamole down his shirt. He seemed jovial and relaxed, and imagining him as a thief or killer began to seem foolish.

The only dark cloud to pass across the lovely morning occurred when Richard Chenault, fire coming out of his eyes and sparks coming off of his silver hair, stalked up to me in the parish hall and asked what I'd done with his wife.

"What have I done with her? Nothing!"

"She was on the phone with you. You told her to come see you—"

"Are you adding eavesdropping to your list of sins, Richard?" I asked mildly.

"She came to visit you, didn't she? Next thing I know, her answering service is saying she'll be out of town for a couple of weeks! And the hospital won't tell me where she is!" He must have realized he was sounding a bit shrill, so he forcibly got himself under control. "I just want to talk to her."

I didn't say what I thought, which was: **If you're getting a divorce, why don't you go through your attorneys?**

"Goldy," he said, "I'm sorry. I apologize for my

tone. I just . . . need to talk to her." He licked his lips, then said, "I understand from . . . from, well, I understand that you were quite close to my niece."

"Yes, she was a neighbor. And a friend." I swallowed, determined not to melt down.

"She didn't leave anything for me, did she? With you? The cops won't tell me anything, and I'm missing some important papers."

"She didn't leave anything with me," I said truthfully. "Did you talk to Sally?"

When he straightened his tie and said yes, I felt a flash of fear: What if Sally had told him about the paintings I had taken? Had I told her not to tell anyone? I couldn't remember.

"With Louise arrested—" he began. "You did hear that, didn't you?" When I nodded, he said, "With Louise under arrest, the office is once again being searched. So I don't believe we'll be needing you tomorrow morning."

The ultimate power jab. But I smiled anyway. "Thank you for telling me. I guess I'll see you and the Ellises tomorrow night. At the ribbon cutting for the Mountain Pastoral Center." He looked momentarily confused. "I'm catering the dinner afterward."

Richard turned and made a discreet motion to

Donald and Nora Ellis, as well as Alonzo and Ookie Claggett, all of whom had been hovering nearby. I smiled in spite of myself. Richard and K.D. had joined St. Luke's because they'd wanted to be married there. Nora Ellis was an Episcopalian because her father was a clergyman, and it was easy to see how Donald had taken the path of least resistance. Alonzo and Ookie, I suspected, had joined for social-climbing purposes. But before I could give voice to these theories, Richard and his retinue departed.

I mumbled, "I am not going to let this upset me, I am not going to let this upset me, I am not going to let this upset me," all the way out to the church kitchen, where I pulled out my cell phone and one of the cards K.D. had given me. I punched in the numbers for Grace Mannheim, cousin to Althea Mannheim, the hit-and-run victim whom K.D. had tried to save in the Southwest Emergency Room. Because I needed to know **if Althea Mannheim did indeed have anything to do with Bishop Uriah Sutherland.**

I thought I would get no answer, or a machine. But Grace Mannheim answered on the first ring. I identified myself and nervously announced that I was a friend of Dr. K. D. Chenault, who had treated her cousin, and would she be willing to speak with me? Today, if possible? I was coming to Boulder anyway, I offered, hoping I didn't sound rude or forward.

She immediately told me to call her Grace. She heard the chaos in the background and told me laughingly that she had already been to church. Yes, she would be glad to see me that afternoon when I was coming over anyway. She might be out for her afternoon walk, or her P.M. constitutional, as she called it, but I could wait for her on her porch.

Tom agreed to take care of the boys, who wanted to do homework together at Gus's place. Arch asked if he could drive Tom's sedan to the Vikarioses' house. I could have married Tom all over again when he immediately said, "Of course."

Once Julian and I made it over to Boulder, I dropped him off at his apartment, as promised, so that he could gather some clothes and odds and ends. I promised to pick him up in an hour, and took off to meet the departed Althea's cousin.

Grace Mannheim lived in a creamy-lilac Victorian on the north side of Pine Street in the old Mapleton area of Boulder. Bordered on either side by lovely old homes, Pine Street sweeps upward in a graceful arc to the west, where it is bordered by a particularly spectacular section of the Front Range. As per my phone instructions from Grace, I waited on the house's front porch while she was out having her afternoon constitutional.

After about ten minutes, I was almost enjoying a warm autumn breeze that was showering golden sycamore leaves onto Grace's thickly green lawn, a lawn that bore only a trace of the previous day's snow. I couldn't completely enjoy the wind and the leaves, though, because I'd had another disheartening, and ultimately puzzling, encounter with Sally Routt on my way out of the house.

As I'd been backing out of my driveway, she'd appeared at my driver's-side mirror, her face gaunt, her eyes wild. She'd asked if I'd found out anything new about her daughter. I said no, which was technically the truth. She looked questioningly at Julian, who shook his head.

"I had a very strange visit from Richard Chenault," she said, her voice lowered almost to a whisper.

I'd turned off the van engine. "Should we go inside?" I asked.

"No, no," she replied, glancing from side to side. But there were only kids outside, calling to one another as they kicked balls back and forth in the street, which was almost dry.

"You know, he's the brother of my ex, who skipped out when I was pregnant with Colin."

She lowered her voice to a whisper. "Richard gave me a check for eleven thousand dollars. He said it was the most he could give me without incurring the gift tax."

My voice wobbled when I said, "Eleven thousand bucks, huh?"

Sally hooked her hair behind her ear, then made her face into an agonizing mass of wrinkles. "He wanted to know"—her voice cracked—"if Dusty had left anything for him. I said, 'Yeah, Richard, she left her secondhand clothes, what do you think?'" Sally shook her head. "I should have been nicer, I guess." She began to weep.

I eased out of the van and embraced Sally. "Don't worry, everything is going to work out." I didn't know what else to say.

"He wanted to know," she sobbed, "if she'd left any artwork. 'Anything at all,' he said. What a prick! I said, 'Yeah, Richard, check out the Picassos on the walls of my Habitat for Humanity house. You want to buy one?' Oh, I should have been nicer, I should have been grateful. I'm such a bitch. That's what my exes always used to say, and I'm sure that's what Richard was thinking."

"No, no, no." I patted her back.

Sally had raised her fatigued eyes to me. "Should I have told him about the paintings you took out of my father's room?"

"Absolutely not. No way. Not now, not ever. Don't talk about them with anybody except the cops."

"Have you made any more progress in your investigation?" When I shook my head, she said, "Was he accusing Dusty of stealing? Is that why she was killed?"

"I don't know," I said truthfully.

"The police called and said they've arrested the woman who manages the H&J office."

"I know they have."

"Do you think this woman strangled my Dusty?"

"Actually, I'm not sure. But listen, Sally, I want to warn you about Richard, or anybody else, who comes over to your house. Would you consider staying with us for a while?"

"No! I'm not being forced out of my home, not after everything else we've been through."

"Would you please, please keep your doors and windows locked, then? And if anything strange or suspicious occurs, you need to call the sheriff's department right away."

But Sally didn't want to talk anymore. She let

out another sob and covered her mouth. Then she turned and dashed back across the street, overcome with tears.

"Dammit to hell, anyway," I said in a low voice.

"Damn **what** to hell?" a woman's voice demanded, startling me. I turned to the sidewalk, where a tall, tan, slender woman, her short white hair fluffing out all around her head, her white eyebrows raised expectantly, approached me.

"You could hear me out there?" I asked, stunned.

Her arms pumped enthusiastically as she made short shrift of her sidewalk. "I work with the deaf," she explained. "I read lips."

"You could see my **lips** from out there?"

"Just call me Superwoman." She took off a glove and grasped my hand. "Grace Mannheim. You must be Goldy." Her cheeks were pink, her eyes a very dark blue. She wore a no-nonsense gray sweatshirt and the athletic type of walking shoes I'm always telling myself to get. "How about some spiced tea?" When I said yes, thanks, the smile in her elfin face brightened even more.

"How 'bout you put some of that superlipreading powder in my tea," I said, as she held the white painted door open for me. I walked down an immaculately clean wood-floored hallway almost bare of furniture. Was Grace Mannheim poor, or did she just like the spare look? Once I was in her sunny yellow kitchen, with its high ceilings and yellow painted cabinets, I decided on the latter. She was still laughing at my superpowder comment.

"My neighbors claim I work for the CIA, my lipreading is that good." She dropped tea bags into a pair of mugs, picked up an electric kettle, and filled them with steaming water. "That's just Boulder paranoia. The garbage people moved to smaller trucks, and everyone insisted the trucks were really police vans with advanced listening devices. No matter how many times the waste folks said it was because everyone was recycling, and there wasn't as much trash as before, it did no good. But don't try to tell left-wingers the government isn't keeping track of them, or it'll destroy their reason for living." She placed the mugs on a tray that already held a plate of what looked like homemade chocolate-chip cookies.

"You shouldn't have gone to so much trouble," I said, feeling apologetic.

"Let's go back to the porch," she said, lifting the tray and indicating the front of the house with her chin.

Once we were settled on wicker rocking chairs on the porch, I thanked her again for the tea and cookies, and got to the matter at hand. "As I told you on the phone, I'm wondering if you could tell me more about your cousin Althea."

Grace Mannheim's face turned solemn. "You're not really wondering about her, are you? I mean, since you're from Aspen Meadow, I'm assuming you want to know about the accident."

I frowned. "Yes. I could read the police report, of course, but I pretty much know what that's going to say, since the accident was covered in our local paper. Hit-and-run, right?"

"Yes."

"And they never found the driver."

Grace Mannheim fiddled with her teaspoon. "No." Her voice had turned soft. "No, they didn't."

"Did she tell you why she came to visit Aspen Meadow?"

"She was going to an art show. Which I thought was odd, since my cousin did not collect art."

"Do you know **why** she was going to the art show?"

Grace sighed. "All she would tell me was that she wanted, and I'm quoting here, 'to make sure right was done.'"

I said, "She didn't give you any hint as to what that meant?"

Grace shook her head. "Althea was not the gossiping type."

"I'm not meaning to gossip," I replied, then reminded myself to keep the heat out of my voice. "A young friend of mine was killed. A neighbor. A member of the church," I added, in the event that would help my case. I could hear Tom's voice inside my head: **You have no shame.** As delicately as possible, I said, "It's possible that the person who mowed down your cousin killed my young friend."

Grace's voice turned mildly sarcastic. "Then surely the police should be coming to visit me."

Don't call me Shirley, my brain mocked, but I said only, "It's more a hunch of mine. The cops in Furman County are very shorthanded—well, not really—"

"So they've asked a young married caterer to help them with their case? What does your son say?"

"My son?" I asked, bewildered. Maybe this woman didn't work for the CIA, but who was she, Daughter of Sherlock Holmes? "You know I'm a caterer? Married? With a kid? How?"

Grace Mannheim laughed. "I'm a walker, as I told you. You called and asked if you could see me, and I said yes. But I'd already finished my P.M.

constitutional, and I just kept walking until you arrived. I came up behind your van. I know every vehicle on this street, and 'Goldilocks' Catering, Where Everything Is Just Right' is not one of them. You wear a wedding ring, and your van has two bumper stickers: 'My Son Is an Honor Student at CBHS.' That's the proud mama's sticker. The other one? 'Give Blood, Play Lacrosse!' I would venture that one is your son's. How am I doing so far?"

"You should be investigating the death of Dusty Routt, not me."

"Ah, so your neighbor was Dusty Routt, a member of **your** church? And you're an Episcopalian, too?"

"You're going to have to show me where you keep that crystal ball of yours," I said, with true admiration.

She smiled, pleased. "I play Colorado Women's Senior Softball with Meg Blatchford. I also give to Habitat for Humanity, and Meg has told me about the family, the Routts, that St. Luke's helped support through that program. I don't know them, though. I am sorry your young friend is the victim in this case."

"Sounds as if the Furman County Sheriff's Department could use your help, though."

"The Boulder Police Department could use my

help," she said, her voice taking on that withering sarcasm again.

Let's not go there, I thought, and then was thankful that my cell phone started ringing. Grace waved that I should go ahead. It was Julian.

"Are you coming to get me, boss? Or should I take the bus to Aspen Meadow? I might get there sooner."

"Sorry, sorry, I'll be there."

"So did the lady help?"

"Yeah, she's great. We're almost done."

"I'm getting old here."

"Ten minutes."

Julian groaned.

"Well, someone wants you," Grace said. "I'm afraid I haven't been very helpful."

"Actually, your cousin might have known that young man who just called. His name is Julian, and he's an Episcopalian from Utah, too. Sorry, maybe not. I know it's a big state. A **very** big state. But not with too many Episcopalians, right? Anyway, Julian was involved in the church there, in Bluff."

Grace brightened again. "Is he Navajo?"

"No, but he spent a lot of time with them when he was growing up. Much to our son's amazement, Julian can speak Navajo, too, the way the code talkers did in the Pacific during World War Two."

"Goodness me."

Neither one of us moved. Grace seemed to share my disappointment at not being able to give me more substantial information.

Finally I said, "There isn't anyone up here, or in Utah, who would know more about what your cousin was doing in Boulder, so far away from home?"

Grace's head made a quick shake. "Believe me, I wanted to know. She hadn't told me, which was frustrating, and when she was killed, I went down to southern Utah, where she lived. Of course, I had to sell her house and dispose of her effects, but I also wanted to see if there was any-one who could shed light on the purpose of her trip. There was only one woman at St. Stephen's who seemed to know something, but when I pressed her on it, she said, 'I'm not allowed to talk about it.' "

"Talk about **what**?"

"That's what's so frustrating; I don't know. There was no journal, no diary, there were no notes, nothing that Althea had left that would in-dicate why she would think she had to go to an art show to make sure right was done."

I pulled a pad from my purse. "Could you give me that woman's name? It's a long shot, but my husband is a homicide investigator with Furman

County, and he might be able to get the cops down there to ask her a few questions."

"Frederica Tuller." It was the first time I'd heard any bitterness in Grace's voice.

I exhaled heavily. "You went through all your cousin's stuff." It was more a statement than a question, but I was just making sure.

Grace canted her head to one side. "She'd specified that all of her clothing be donated. I went through every pocket. She gave me her small amount of furniture. I checked every drawer. There was nothing."

Dammit to hell, indeed.

"When I got back home, her suitcase was still here. That's the one thing I didn't donate. I gave the clothes away and threw out most of the odds and ends—you know, tissues, candy."

Still feeling dispirited, I did manage to say "Most?"

Grace's smile was wan. "My cousin loved magazines. There were five of them in her suitcase, can you imagine? I told her she'd rupture a disk in her back carrying such a heavy load, and she told me she liked having reading material on trips, even if I disapproved. I told her I didn't disapprove, but I pointed out that she hardly ever traveled, and these days, you can get **Woman's Day** and **Family Circle** almost everywhere.

That's when she said I should mind my own business. But she said it in a nice way. That was the way she was. She said I could throw her reading material away as soon as she was done with it; she'd just buy more at the airport. She knows— she knew—I'm not a pack rat. Far from it, I like clear spaces." Grace sighed. "Really, though, I haven't had the heart to throw those magazines away."

My cell rang again: the caller ID said it was Julian. I threw the phone back in my purse.

Grace frowned. "Your young man is impatient. Shall I get you the magazines? You can take them home if you want. In fact, you can toss them—"

"I wouldn't dream of it," I interrupted, although I couldn't imagine how women's magazines would help the investigation. "Thank you. I'll mail them back to you, I promise."

She disappeared, and I considered calling Julian and bawling him out. But a moment later, Grace pushed through her screen door holding an old grocery bag. "Thank you for being willing to send them back. I don't think of myself as sentimental, but I guess I am."

I stood up and took the bag. Then I hugged her. It was the second time that day that I'd embraced someone who'd lost a beloved relative, and I didn't particularly like the way it made me feel.

Once I was back in my van, my cell phone began ringing again. What was **with** Julian, anyway? We had no catering events that night, we weren't going into H&J in the morning, and we would have plenty of time to prep the food for the next night's dinner when we got home. I resolved to give him a good ribbing as soon as I picked him up.

Feeling perverse, I reached into Grace Mannheim's grocery sack and pulled out her cousin's magazines. **Family Circle. Oprah. People. Woman's Day**. And **The Living Church,** the national magazine of the Episcopal Church. I held each one up and shook it, but no paper with Althea's reason for attending Charlie Baker's last show fluttered out. Feeling desperate, I looked for dog-eared pages, too, and in the first four, there were none.

The Living Church did have a dog-eared article, however, and I flipped to it and began to read.

My cell phone began its incessant ringing again. But I didn't answer it. I couldn't. I thought my heart had stopped.

Chapter 18

The article, from February of this year, was entitled "The Gift That Gives Forever." There was a picture of a wan and clearly weakened Charlie Baker, his brave smile a tiny line within his moon face. The article talked about the unusual aspects of Charlie Baker's will. Since Mr. Baker, as the magazine deferentially referred to him, had been an orphan raised by the Christian Brothers, he was bequeathing half of his total estate to the Christian Brothers High School. The other half of Mr. Baker's considerable fortune would be used to build and operate a retreat house for clergy, tentatively named the Mountain Pastoral Center. Buried at the end of the article was the following sentence, which Althea Mannheim had underlined: "Charlie Baker has named retired bishop Uriah Sutherland, formerly of the Diocese of Southern Utah, to be director of the center in perpetuity, with a salary to match his responsibilities."

I had known that Uriah was helping set up the pastoral center and had continued the work after

Charlie's death, and I had speculated that Charlie might have left his good friend something in his will. But I'd had no clue that Charlie was granting the bishop a sinecure post as part of his estate. Besides Charlie's lawyers, only Uriah and officials at the Diocese of Colorado would have been informed of the bequest. Since Charlie's will was still going through probate, Uriah could not yet officially take up his duties as director of the center, but it wasn't unusual for the diocese to issue a press release to record a gift that was coming. It makes the donor—the testamentary, if you want to get technical—happy to be celebrated for his munificence during his lifetime.

I didn't read **The Living Church**—I didn't have time—and apparently no one in Marla's gossip network did either, as we'd picked up no word of Uriah's windfall. Certainly, his position-to-be had not been publicized in Aspen Meadow. But in Utah, Althea Mannheim had seen the article about it, and had promptly traveled to Colorado and met with Charlie Baker. Which meant that she had indeed been talking about the bishop when she was dying in the Emergency Room. Suddenly the vague possibility of connections had become a live circuit.

So the question became, What specifically had Althea known about Uriah and imparted to Charlie? If Uriah had stolen something, as Althea seemed to claim, what was she accusing him of stealing? K.D. had thought Althea had muttered "a pattern." **Hmm.**

As Grace had pointed out, I was an Episcopalian, too, and a long-time one, at that. Plus, I was married to a cop. So I had all kinds of knowledge about the church and its liturgies, and unfortunately, I knew all too well about the valuable ecclesiastical stuff that could be filched. One time, Tom had prosecuted thieves who'd stolen a gold cross from St. Luke's. After that, Father Biesbrouck had been forced to lock up the church building at night. Another time, a shady husband of a member of the Altar Guild had purloined a jewel-encrusted chalice, and tried to pawn it.

But there was another item of potential value that someone could steal. I doubted that Bishop Uriah, aka Bitch Yoreye, had pocketed a **pattern.** I conjectured—and maybe it was a leap, but not that much of one—that he'd pilfered a **paten,** the dish that holds the Communion wafers at the Eucharist.

If the bishop had stolen a paten, and if this had successfully been kept secret, could the bishop have stolen paintings, too?

Although I was trying to wean myself off of cell-phone usage while I was driving, I did put in a call to Tom. If it was possible that Bishop Uriah stole something, and delivering the news had had deadly consequences for Althea Mannheim, then it was time to get law enforcement to bring in Frederica Tuller, ASAP. Perhaps she could be scared into breaking whatever confidentiality she'd felt bound to keep, by hearing about what it meant to be a **material witness after the fact**.

When I'd given Tom an abbreviated version of my visit with Grace Mannheim and the article in **The Living Church,** he said he would get right on the phone with law enforcement in Utah. Meanwhile, he said, he was fixing Mexican food for us for dinner. And oh yes, the events planner with the Diocese of Colorado had called, and could we please prepare a separate vegetarian entrée for tomorrow night? Two of the attorneys did not eat meat.

"Not at meals, anyway," I muttered, but Tom only laughed. I said we should be home in an hour.

"Finally!" Julian cried when he hopped in the car. "I've been wanting to tell you something. Whole Foods is having a special on organically raised chicken, and I thought you might want to pick some up for tomorrow night."

"We could do that, but you'll be delighted to know you were right. We do indeed need to come up with a vegetarian main dish for a couple of lawyers. And pick up some high-quality whipping cream, would you? We need a multilayered, show-stopping dessert. A dark torte."

Like Tom, Julian laughed. But at Whole Foods, I gave him free rein to choose ingredients to make whatever main dish he thought would suit the dinner. Then he got serious. And he appeared flattered.

A little over an hour later, we were all back in our kitchen, bustling around with our various projects. Arch and Gus were spending the night over at the Vikarioses' house. All weekend homework had been done, they'd assured Tom, and Gus's grandparents would take them to school the next morning. I certainly hoped the two boys would not get tired of each other, but Tom assured me that they had quite a few years to catch up on being brothers, and they were going to be just fine.

Julian announced he was going to come up with an Artichoke and Brie Pie for the next night. Once he'd decided on that, he concentrated on slicing Brie and lightly steaming artichokes. He filled a deep pie dish with the egg-laced mélange, placed it in the oven, then hunted around our cupboards for some dried fruits. Once he'd found some glacé apricots, he began melting dark bittersweet chocolate and unsalted butter over the stove and said he would have some Chocolate Lovers' Dipped Fruits ready to go with, as he disdainfully put it, "your showstopper."

Yeesh!

For my part, I needed a dark torte, one that did **not** include chocolate, so the flavors from Julian's dessert wouldn't clash with my own. I found some eggs in the walk-in, then worked on pulverizing zwieback biscuits and pecans, locating the most deeply flavored cinnamon money could buy, as well as measuring out ground cloves that were so fragrant they made me want to swoon.

Tom was putting the finishing touches on a sauce made of fresh tomatoes, chilies, and onions that he intended to pour over a dish of fat cheese enchiladas that he had already made for us for dinner. About halfway through mixing up the torte, I had some trouble stirring all the ingredients into the batter I'd concocted. So I asked Tom for help.

"I'm making a dark torte, husband. Could you help?"

"A tort like a wrong, or a torte like a cake?"

"What do **you** think?" I asked.

"Miss G., with you there's no telling."

Honestly, that man. The three of us were having so much fun working together in the kitchen, I began to ponder the age-old question posed by the same folks who came up with the chicken-and-egg conundrum: Which is more fun, cooking or eating?

Well. As soon as I sank my teeth into Tom's juicy, fat, sizzling enchiladas, with their filling of three luscious melted cheeses spurting out beneath his savory topping of chilies, onions, and tomatoes from our own plants, I knew the answer to **that** one. And it wasn't that cooking was more fun.

"You haven't asked how I did with Utah law enforcement," Tom said, when we'd all **oohed** and **aahed** over his enchiladas.

"I wouldn't have thought you'd have heard back this quickly!" I exclaimed.

"Oho, Frederica Tuller sang like the proverbial Arizona cardinal."

"She's in Utah," Julian reminded him.

"Yeah, but I couldn't think of a good—"

"Tom!"

"Take it easy, Miss G. All right. To escape possible prosecution for obstruction of justice, Frederica Tuller told us the whole story. The reason Althea Mannheim probably was reluctant to tell her cousin Grace why she was visiting is that it was something belonging to their mutual grandparents that had been stolen. An antique gold chalice and paten, used for Communion services on Holy Days there at St. Stephen's Cathedral. But they were found at Bishop Sutherland's residence. When he was apprehended, he said the chalice and paten had been given to **him,** not to the cathedral. Which of course was baloney, since they'd been used at the cathedral since long before he'd gotten there."

"Oh, for heaven's sake."

"Well," Tom interjected, "for the **church's** sake, everything got covered up. Because once Bishop Sutherland was caught, he worked out a deal with the Diocese of Southern Utah. A confidential deal, with the only people participating being the bishop-elect, the chancellor, who's their lawyer, I guess—"

"That's right," I said.

"And Bishop Sutherland."

"How did they ever apprehend him?" I asked.

"That's where our friend Althea Mannheim comes in. You see, she's on the Altar Guild. And even though Bishop Sutherland had counted on getting away with this, he hadn't counted on Althea Mannheim discovering the loss . . . and breaking into his house and searching it until she found them!"

"I've heard of taking the law into your own hands," I said.

"This is the Wild West," Julian said. "What did they do to Althea?"

"You ever try to arrest an elderly woman who's just uncovered, via breaking and entering, a three-million-dollar heist?" Tom asked mildly. "Piece of advice: don't."

"Three million dollars?" I repeated, incredulous.

"Black-market value of antique gold chalice and paten," Tom said ruefully.

Julian asked, "Did the church get their stuff back?"

"Yes," said Tom. "And Uriah Sutherland claimed he had heart problems. That's how he got out of Utah with his reputation more or less intact."

"Less and less," I said, "the more I know. Do you think Uriah Sutherland ran down Althea Mannheim?"

"We don't know," Tom said. "But we're working on that, too."

The next morning, it snowed. Gus and Arch called to say how ticked off they were that CBHS was still having classes. But as Gus's grandfather drove oh-so-slowly down to Denver, the radio announced that CBHS had been closed after all. Arch called us, gleeful, from the road.

The plumbing contractor who'd been working on the lines at the Roundhouse called to say he had good news and bad news. The good news was that the plumbing lines were done and that the Round-house was good to go for our dinner tonight. The bad news was that his subcontractors had tracked in "quite a bit" of mud over the past couple of weeks. If we were going to go ahead with the dinner in the Roundhouse that night, we might want to come in and do some cleaning.

I said, "You can't win."

Tom announced that they'd called from the department asking him to come in early, but he could stave them off for a few hours to help with the cleaning. I told him to go on, deal with Louise Upton. I'd rather clean.

Julian cheerfully offered to help me with the scrubbing. Marla, who had had a sore throat—all that gossiping, Julian teased her—since the party Saturday afternoon, had missed the christening and was therefore "starved," as she put it, for news. She would go to the grocery store and buy ammonia, buckets, and brushes, she promised, and might even help us do the work, she promised further, if we would fill her in on what she'd missed over the past—well, let's see—day.

We said we'd take all the help we could get.

The actual mess at the Roundhouse would have been colossally depressing if I had not had Julian and Marla to help clean up. Marla, dressed in sequined orange jeans and silk T-shirt with matching headband, proved true to her word and immediately began wiping down the tables in the Roundhouse's hexagonal dining room. Julian had claimed the kitchen, with at least half an inch of dried mud covering most of the wood floor, as his special province to get into working order.

"You two will want to visit anyway," he said by way of dismissal. "And I've heard all the latest gossip from Goldy already."

So I told Marla everything as we worked for six hours cleaning the Roundhouse. I told her about the paintings and inventories Dusty had hidden in her blind grandfather's room, the arrest of Louise Upton ("I never trusted her" was Marla's comment), my visits with K. D. Chenault and Grace Mannheim, and Bishop Uriah Sutherland's stealing of valuable antiques. And then there was Charlie Baker's changed will, the contents of which I doubted Richard Chenault would give up without a fight over a client's right to confidentiality. Oh, confidentiality! Is it ever enforced?

"And it may not matter to Richard," I commented bitterly, "since Charlie's dead."

"Charlie is indeed dead," Marla replied. "But Uriah or no Uriah, once Charlie's will is done slogging its way through probate, this Mountain Pastoral Center will get built, and Charlie will live through an institution that will do good things for clergy. Needed things." She looked around the dining room as she stretched her back. "Listen, girlfriend, I'm officially wiped out. I'm supposed to be going to this ribbon cutting, and coming back here for the dinner, since I'm one of the ones who put up additional money so that the center could be started before Charlie's estate was settled."

"Oho," I said, "so that's how they got the construction going so early."

"It is indeed," said Marla. "But Meg Blatchford will be coming, too, to both the ribbon cutting and the dinner. So the evening won't be totally without the possibility of fun. Meg," she added, "was a great believer in Charlie and his work, too."

"I know," I said quietly.

Marla said she was too sweaty to give me a hug, but would give me a huge one once she returned for the dinner.

Julian had wrought a miracle in the kitchen, every surface of which sparkled. This was a good thing, as it was already four o'clock. At five, the guests were having champagne—paid for by an anonymous donor, the events coordinator had assured me when she dropped off the ice cream—up by the construction site. I chuckled and shook my head. Marla had probably heard the diocese wasn't planning to serve booze at the ribbon cutting and had immediately rectified that situation.

At twenty to five, when I had almost worked my way through the necessary pounding of the chicken breasts, my cell rang. **Aspen Meadow Imports?** I was sure it was a wrong number, but I answered it anyway.

"This is Gary over at A-M Imports," came an insistent, hoarse male voice. "You the lady tore the door off the Rover?"

"Um, well, sort of."

"Well, is you or isn't you?" More impatient this time.

"I am! I am! Have you found a replacement door already?"

"No, but what I **do** got is a bear coming down every night, getting into our garbage! Had to put it inside, lock the doors, you unnerstand?"

"Yes, but I've got a dinner—"

"Just listen, will ya? You got garbage in this damn Rover! And it stinks! Bear comes down every night, starts pawing at the garage door, he can't get in, so last night he broke one of the garage windows—"

"Okay, okay," I said, feverishly imagining the guests at the ribbon cutting swilling their champagne and commenting to one another about how hungry they were getting. "Tell me what you need."

"What I need? What I **need** is for you to come get your trash, lady! We're on Highway 203, near the innerstate. Close at five. You don't come get this garbage, I'm rolling the Rover into the street."

"No, don't do that—"

But he was gone.

"Julian," I said desperately, "we've got a problem." I explained to him about the garbage situation, and how it was my fault.

He stopped working on the wild rice. "Oh my, I forgot all about that trash."

"So did I. It was back when I first suspected Bishop Uriah was up to something. He was listening too intently to some of the conversations at the party, and I just thought . . . oh, never mind. It was a long shot. But if I don't go get the garbage, Ghastly Grammar Gary is going to roll the Rover into the street—"

"You want me to go get the trash bags?" asked Julian, eyeing his watch. "Or are you asking if you should . . . wait. You go. I've been working in a restaurant, I can get these dishes out in a hurry. I know what I'm doing, Goldy. You'll be back by the time we serve."

Unfortunately, I wasn't. Because the snow we'd had the previous evening had turned to ice with the setting of the sun, it took my catering van with its nearly bald tires almost forty minutes to get to

Gary's, well past closing time. Gary, who'd stayed late, was none too happy. But then he saw my van with its logo, and he hit me with a barrage of questions about the best way to cook brats. Unfortunately, I couldn't ignore this interrogation because Gary still had the Rover locked inside his garage with its bear-broken window. I didn't ask him why he hadn't moved the car out into the street as he'd threatened, because at that point I was ready to roll Gary out into the highway myself.

"Just cook the brats in beer!" I cried, exasperated. This, like "Drink me," was the magic word that opened the door, and Gary explained that that was **exactly** how he'd told his wife to cook 'em, but she wouldn't listen.

"I wonder why," I muttered under my breath, as I grabbed the Ellises' garbage bag, heaved it over my shoulder, and raced to the van. Gary was still calling questions to me, this time about whether you should put mashed potatoes into taco filling. But I ignored him.

Back at the Roundhouse, Uriah was addressing the group of assembled big donors. Judging from the glazed looks in the guests' eyes, if they had the chance to do it all over, they would give their money to the library.

"Gosh, boss," Julian reprimanded me. "What the hell! Did you have to pay him for that trash?"

"Pretty much," I said, without elaboration.

Julian, as usual, had managed magnificently. Everyone, he reported, had flipped for the Chicken Piccata, with its tart, creamy sauce of lemon, white wine, and butter. The Artichoke-Brie Pie had gone over well with the vegetarians. Even the wild rice and green beans had been hits.

"Thank you so very, very much," I kept repeating. "What's happening?"

"They've had their torte and chocolate-dipped fruits. Richard Chenault introduced his dear friend Nora Ellis, or at least that's what he called her. Nora Ellis introduced her father, Uriah, Charlie's dear friend, and so forth."

I eyed the stacks of plates. "Can we start on the dishes?"

"Nope. Donald Ellis squirted back here a few minutes ago and said his father-in-law had asked for quiet while he's talking."

I sighed. Marla slipped into the kitchen, holding her throat in a gagging motion.

"Tell me how I can give this guy the hook," she said to me.

"I don't know," I said. I was frustrated, too. We had a ton of dishwashing still to do, and it was getting late. "Create a disturbance. Oh, wait. Raise your hand, and ask about the provisions of Charlie's will. Then ask if he knew if

Charlie had planned to change parts of his will."

"All right," said Marla.

"I'm kidding! I'm kidding!" I called after her, but she was gone.

Well, she did it. And the question provided such an excruciatingly awkward moment, followed by several more awkward moments, that Richard Chenault ended up jumping from his seat and thanking everyone for coming. He said they'd be getting a formal notification when Charlie's will was settled, and more work could be done on the site, blah, blah, blah.

Meg Blatchford, her hands loaded with a stack of plates, followed Marla into the kitchen. "You've got guts, Marla," Meg said admiringly. "I'll give you that. Do you think you'd ever like to play senior softball?"

"No, no," Marla replied, but she giggled at the thought.

"You better go dump that garbage," Julian said to me, as he began loading dishes into the Round-house dishwasher.

"What garbage?" Meg asked, puzzled. "Won't the bears get it if you dump spoiled food at night—"

I didn't stay to hear the rest, because I couldn't go through the same story twice in one day.

I lugged the bag over to the sidewalk. Inside the Roundhouse, I could make out Meg and Marla, alternating telling Julian stories about how things used to be in Aspen Meadow, how we used to have Aspen Meadow Taxi, one guy with one old car that used to be a hearse, how we used to have a bona fide art-film theater, and it was a regular theater, not a multiplex . . .

I stared at the Ellises' trash and thought about my earlier assessment of going through it being a long shot. What was I looking for? Communications from Utah about Uriah's illicit past? Evidence of stolen paintings or legal skullduggery? A copy of Charlie's altered will, unsigned, that Donald might have tossed away? Or maybe a receipt for an opal-and-diamond bracelet . . .

I really wasn't convinced I wanted to go through somebody's sure-to-be-spoiled trash. But I tore open the sack anyway . . . and was rewarded with a stinking spill of coffee grounds.

Okay, I thought as I removed wads of wet, crumpled-up paper. I had resolved to look for some of Bishop Uriah's correspondence, or notes, or something. Or maybe I was looking for something else. I just didn't know what.

Had Nora known that somebody was selling her a stolen painting? I wondered as I began to smooth out the first wad of papers. Had she suspected?

Maybe there was a bill of sale in here? And why did the Ellises have to crumple all their paper trash into teensy-weensy balls that were impossible to open? I'd have to go back and check my psych books, see if that was a sign of anal— Wait a minute.

I was looking at a very wrinkled piece of yellow legal-pad paper that had been completely covered with what looked like shading, done with the side of a pencil tip, not with the point. Whoever had done the shading had revealed writing on a note that had been done on top of it. Well, for goodness' sake. I didn't know people did this anymore. Kids, yes. Grown-ups, no.

I was tired. My body hurt and I knew I didn't smell very good. But now I was consumed with curiosity. Meg, Marla, and Julian were still merrily conversing inside the Roundhouse as they clattered clean dishes back into the cupboards. Meg was doing most of the talking, it seemed to me, but that was okay. Marla isn't a particularly good listener unless she's really concentrating, but maybe that was precisely what she was doing. Julian, on the other hand, is a very good listener and can make anyone feel treasured.

I needed better light. I eased under one of the outside security lamps I'd had installed, and suddenly the writing was as clear as if it had been written in white ink.

I swallowed, and all my senses were suddenly alert. The date was October 18, the day before Dusty had been killed.

Michael,

You know I'm a generalist and don't really handle this kind of thing. I need to talk to you in a professional capacity and don't want to risk e-mail or telephone. I am seeking a divorce—

But that was as far as I got in Donald Ellis's note to divorce attorney Michael Radford. Because suddenly I couldn't breathe. I gasped. There was a thin rope around my neck, and it was pulled tight. I tried to cough but couldn't. I simply could not bring any air at all into my lungs. Black spots appeared before my eyes.

"Our trash goes out on Monday," Nora Ellis whispered in my ear. "Imagine my surprise when we hardly had any, especially since we'd just had a party over the weekend. Now walk."

No, I was not going to walk. I thrust my hands back, trying to get some purchase on her. I clawed, shoved backward, and tried to slam her with my head. Then I fell to my knees, refusing to budge.

But I had underestimated Nora and her strong, squash-playing body. She yanked on the rope and deftly moved in front of me, pulling my body away from the Roundhouse with its security lights . . . and into the shadows. I coughed and choked and tried to get my fingers under the rope, to no avail. Instead, Nora was tugging me into the darkness, toward the lake. The lake, that was already beginning to freeze. If I wasn't dead by the time I got there, she could push me in and I'd die of hypothermia.

I couldn't get my legs to move. I was stumbling forward, unable to see, unable to breathe, across the uneven ground between us and the lake.

You know I'm a generalist.

You know, I think she loved Mr. Ogden.

You know . . .

How was she keeping that rope so tight? I wondered even as I felt my consciousness bleeding away. She must have had some kind of knot on it. She was holding the rope with both hands and pulling hard. Was there any way I could get her to lighten up on her grip? My mind groped for answers, but my ability to think was fading, fading . . .

Julian had said, **She thought Mr. Ogden would leave his wife, but he didn't . . .**

Dusty had written in her journal, "I'm afraid this is another Mr. O."

Wait, I thought when we reached where the

ground sloped down toward the lake. **If I push mightily toward one side, that could create slack in the rope. Then I could try to slip away, call for help . . .**

I stopped stumbling and leaped sideways. The rope went slack for a nanosecond. I managed to take a gasping breath, that was all, not make a cry for someone, anyone, to come to my aid . . .

You know I think she loved Mr. Ogden . . .

"Goldy?" a faraway voice called. Was it my mother, calling to me, beckoning me to the grave? "Goldy?"

And then there was a sudden loosening of the rope, and a thud. Nora cried out and broke away from me. There was another thwacking noise, and Nora shrieked and ran toward the lake. Hacking and coughing as my lungs remembered how to work, I looked in the direction of the Round-house. I saw a bird, a ball, a rock, what was it? And why was it sailing toward me?

Actually, it was headed for Nora, who was almost to the path that circled the lake. But the third toss of a baseball-size rock from star senior-softball pitcher Meg Blatchford landed just where the first two had been aimed: on the head of Nora Ellis. She collapsed to the ground and didn't move.

Julian called the police.

Chapter 19

Why did she do it? For one of the oldest reasons: jealousy. And Nora Ellis wasn't just **envious** of Dusty, although she certainly was that. She despised what Dusty could do to her, to Nora.

Dusty had been fifteen years younger than Donald; she'd been wonderfully pretty and optimistic; she'd hero-worshiped him, even though he was an associate with no money of his own. Still, Dusty had adored Donald, and he, in turn, reveled in her infatuation. Donald wanted to change his whole life, to have more of Dusty's love. And Nora couldn't stand for that.

Because Nora had also been jealous of her place in the community. She didn't want to **divorce** Donald because she wanted to be **married** to him, to be an attorney's wife, even one for whom she'd have to bring business, to ensure he made partner. And of course, there was that twenty million. She had loved Donald so much, she had insisted her inheritance be made marital property. Later, Nora told the police what I already knew: that she'd made it jointly theirs to show Donald how much she loved him. The downside to that was if Donald divorced her, which he certainly was prepared to do, he'd be taking half of that dough with him.

Which, in Nora's mind, was all the more reason to be rid of Dusty.

But why did she have to run down defenseless Althea Mannheim? I kept wondering. Nora has now hired a criminal defense attorney, who has told her to keep her mouth shut, so I don't know the answer. But I can imagine. Because Uriah Sutherland had seen Althea at Charlie Baker's last show at the gallery. Uriah had watched Althea **talk** with a suddenly anxious Charlie Baker. And he'd been able to guess that the conversation involved Uriah's stealing Althea's family's paten and chalice.

Now Uriah has told the police that **of course** he informed Nora of why Althea was at the gallery. Uriah said he'd guessed why Althea was so urgently talking to Charlie. In fact, Uriah had told Nora all this right there at the reception. He didn't know Nora was going to run Althea over, he told the police, how could he?

So: at that same reception, when Uriah told Nora what Charlie Baker was just now learning, Nora saw Althea Mannheim as potentially spoiling **her** life. Because if Althea had succeeded in telling

Charlie Baker about Uriah's stealing, then she might tell the world. Then forget the Mountain Pastoral Center: **nobody** would hire Uriah. Nora would be taking care of her insufferable, thieving father for the rest of her days. The way she saw it, she **had** to get rid of Althea.

And she had to get rid of Charlie Baker, too. Because once Charlie Baker learned the truth about Uriah, he would inevitably change his will, which was precisely what he had tried to do. And if he changed his will, everyone would learn **why** he'd changed his will. Once again, Nora would be stuck with Uriah and be socially embarrassed in the community. So she paid Charlie Baker a visit. Everyone in town knew Nora had scads of money. Had she pretended to be interested in buying a couple of his paintings, to get him up to his studio? It would have been easy to push the frail, cancer-ridden Charlie down the stairs, a fall that would be sure to kill him.

Two other people had known that Charlie Baker was changing his will: Dusty Routt and Richard Chenault. Richard did admit to the police that Charlie had a new will drawn up that he'd never had the chance to sign and validate. He said he hadn't tied Charlie's desire for a new will to his death the next night. It had been none of his business, he told the cops. What he didn't tell law enforcement was that Charlie's sudden death gave Richard the idea to lift some of the paintings in Charlie's house and create a fraudulent inventory to cover his theft.

For that is what he did. The dual inventories that Dusty kept, plus her journal, helped to prove that. "I am going to FIND OUT," she'd written. And where had Richard hidden the paintings? Why, in Donald Ellis's mess of an office, that's where. People who work on oil and gas leases have to have those large, long, map-size drawers, the same ones Dusty had complained about in her journal.

Imagine Donald's surprise, the morning after his wife was arrested, when he opened a drawer to check a map of the Wyoming gas fields Dusty had grumbled about not being able to find. Instead, almost three dozen unfinished paintings of Wedding Cake, Sponge Cake, and Cherry Coffeecake all spilled out. Unlike Louise Upton, when Donald Ellis discovered stolen goods, he reported them to the police. And right away, too. He didn't even touch the paintings, he just left them on top of the mountain range of paper already decorating his floor.

Investigators took fingerprints from the paintings, and some matched those of Richard Chenault. With that evidence plus the dual inventories, the cops had plenty of evidence to arrest Richard Chenault for felony theft. He'd also sold stolen property: Nora Ellis was only too happy to finger Richard for stiffing her for forty thou, which was what he'd charged her for the unfinished Charlie Baker painting of Journey Cake. Betraying a client's trust, felony theft from an estate, and selling stolen property: very dark torts, indeed.

But why had Richard stolen from dear, deceased Charlie Baker? Well, Richard was jealous, too. Jealous of all the things—cars, houses, vacations, women—his associate Donald had been able to have. Donald even had a wealthy, stay-at-home wife, which Richard had not had. No, Richard had been married to K.D., a successful professional woman who couldn't abide his infidelity. I treasured K.D., whose care for a dying woman had led to the exposure of Uriah's thievery and the motive behind the killing of Charlie Baker.

I'd always suspected the cops didn't have their man, or woman, as the case was, when they arrested Louise Upton. As it turned out, Dusty **had** been wearing the bracelet the night she died. It had been an early birthday present, Donald Ellis told the cops later, because opals were the birthstone for October. Donald had given Dusty the bracelet because he really did want to marry her, and he'd wanted **her** to know the level of his commitment. Maybe the bracelet, Donald's divorce, and their desire to marry had been what Dusty had wanted to tell me that last, fateful night. But never mind all that, the cops said, because the important thing was that Nora had ripped the bracelet off Dusty's wrist, once she was dead.

I felt sorry for Wink Calhoun, because after Nora was apprehended, Wink's conscience went into overtime. In one of their oh-so-friendly squash games, Nora had asked Wink if anyone in the firm was in dire financial straits. Wink had confided that Louise Upton needed money, and how. This was the data Nora had been seeking. Unfortunately, Wink then had taken the enormous guilt leap that this knowledge had helped Nora conceive her plan to kill Dusty, and blame Louise in her place. But I told Wink no. No: it had been Donald's desire to get out of his marriage that had made Nora kill Wink's dear friend.

So: Nora had been aware that Louise Upton was strapped for money. This was why Nora had hired Louise to "help" with the party at her house. Once Louise was inside the house, Nora had easily dropped the opal-and-diamond bracelet through a slightly open window into Louise's car. Louise, thinking a wealthy guest had lost the obviously valuable piece of jewelry, had tried to pawn the thing that very day. Also, when Nora was supposedly out running a few errands, and Louise was safe at the Ellises' house setting up for the party, Nora had zipped over to Louise's townhouse complex and left the sledgehammer she'd used on Dusty's Civic in Louise's Dumpster.

But Louise wouldn't, couldn't, have killed Dusty. She might have been envious of the young, perky paralegal-to-be, but she was too protective of H&J to have its image sullied with a murder. Meanwhile, she's planning on suing the cops for false arrest.

Perhaps most inscrutable in all this was Donald Ellis. Who was he? He'd had affairs with both Wink and then Dusty, young women who had adored him. And maybe that was what he had been jealous for: adoration. Dusty had had no material goods, and had worshiped Donald because he represented what she was passionate about: the law, or maybe just being attached to a rich lawyer. He loved her, he said. That's why they'd made love every lunch hour, with him hidden inside Dusty's car as she drove it into Charlie Baker's garage.

I wondered. Dusty, judging from her journal, had only **wanted** to learn about the law, and to be in love. Donald, on the other hand, had wanted a new **wife**. And his note to his neighbor, divorce lawyer Michael Radford, had sealed Dusty's fate.

Nora Ellis had known about Dusty the way she had known about Wink; she'd just looked the other way. But then she'd sketched over a pad to find a note Donald had written to a premier divorce attorney. Facing a divorce and losing half of her inheritance—well, Nora just couldn't have **that**.

And now, ironically, Donald was getting just what he wanted. First, freedom from Richard and his envy and criticism. And he was getting, finally, freedom from Nora, whom he was divorcing, against whom he was testifying, and whose money he now had to spend. But he wasn't getting **just** what he wanted. He hadn't gotten Dusty.

The cops never did find Jason Gurdley, the fellow who tried to mow down Vic. Vic is doing better now, and we have him over to dinner sometimes. At least, he's doing a lot better than when he almost was killed holding Dusty's computer. In any event, I was certain that Nora had hired Gurdley to watch the Routts' and later our house. When Vic came out of the Routts' house with a computer, Gurdley had decided to play it better safe than sorry, and attempted to destroy the computer.

Gurdley also could have tried to sideswipe K.D.'s car, since Nora might have worried that K.D. knew something about Uriah, based on her reaction to meeting him at the birthday party. K.D. returned from her hideout in Santa Fe, shocked to learn that what she'd suspected about the bishop had turned out to be true—and that her own husband was also a thief. On the bright side, she no longer has to fight with Richard over the divorce, and seems ready finally to get on with her life. She moved out of the house in Flicker Ridge and into a gorgeous townhouse right near Southwest Hospital.

As for Nora Ellis . . . she was indeed that very wealthy lady who'd wanted, as Julian had characterized her, "the best-quality stuff, but only at a steep discount." Facing grand larceny charges, Richard Chenault is now working on a plea bargain that begins with him sharing information. The first thing he told Detective Britt was that Nora Ellis had wanted to buy a Charlie Baker painting for Donald's birthday present. Nora had asked Richard if he could "help her out," as she put it. Since Richard had stolen a number of Charlie's paintings, he'd sold Nora the one for Journey Cake at a huge discount. Nora, gleeful, hadn't questioned the price, nor had she questioned the recipe, which had been one of the ways that this whole puzzle concerning Dusty's murder had unraveled.

Well. As things stand now, Nora Ellis is going to be tried for three murders: those of Althea Mannheim, Charlie Baker, and Dusty Routt. In Colorado, she faces the death penalty.

· · ·

The funeral for Dusty Routt was a somber, stunning affair, with Father Pete presiding. Several of Dusty's former classmates at both Elk Park Prep and the Mile-High Paralegal Institute gave testimonials describing their fun-loving, hardworking friend. Sally was able to pull herself out of her funk to attend; Marla had bought her a new black dress to wear, and arranged for a hairdresser to visit the Routt home prior to the service. The church was filled to overflowing, and Sally, who'd felt stigmatized for so long as a "welfare person," appeared both gratified and overwhelmed. Julian and I provided the postliturgy refreshments, and as is often the case with these things, the food seemed to set the mourners off on a renewed path to life.

Meg Blatchford came, and spoke movingly about what Dusty had provided for all of us: a view of zest, ambition, kindness. We all thanked her afterward. I also told her that she was my new hero, since she'd saved me from being strangled by Nora Ellis. Meg said, "Aw, it was nothing." I said, "Yeah, right, Sandy Koufax," which was a compliment with a historical context she could appreciate. She beamed, and invited our whole family to visit her at her Scottsdale home. She's already packed up her place in Aspen Meadow and headed to Arizona with Grace Mannheim. After all, the winter season for senior softball is about to get under way.

Julian is doing well. After Dusty's funeral, he went back to Boulder, where he's begun working again at the bistro. I talked to him yesterday. He said, "Life is so much less eventful here than it is in Aspen Meadow. I may have to come over to that nice, quiet mountain town, just so I can inject some excitement into my life."

To which Tom said, "Nice and quiet we're not. But come anyway."

Tom is better than ever. He's back down at the department, working a big forgery case. When I asked him to tell me about it, he refused.

I'm not working at H&J anymore. For my part, I'm a little jealous, too: but only for peace and quiet. We'll see if I actually get it. But in the meantime, our extended family has grown to include Sally, John, and Colin Routt at big biweekly dinners. Tonight Gus is spending the night with Arch, and the two of them have vowed to teach Colin how to throw a Frisbee. For dessert, we're having the carrot cake that was meant to be Dusty's birthday cake, and will toast her memory. Tom, bless his heart, had thought to wrap it up and freeze it. My dear husband is also making us gnocchi in veal sauce.

I can't wait.

Acknowledgments

The author would like to acknowledge the help of the following people: Jim Davidson; Jeff, Rosa, Ryan, and Nicholas Davidson; J. Z. Davidson; Joey Davidson; Sandra Dijkstra, my phenomenal agent; Carolyn Marino, my brilliant editor; Jennifer Civiletto and the entire stupendous team at Morrow/HarperCollins; Kathy Saideman, for her insightful reading of the manuscript; Susan Stewart, fine artist, Littleton, Colorado; Ann Bunn, collage artist, Evergreen, Colorado; Dee Minault, partner, Cumberland Art Conservation, Nashville, Tennessee; Lisa Shannon Davidson, paralegal, Chicago; Roz Lynn Dorf, freelance paralegal, Boulder; the following helpful folks from Holme, Roberts & Owen in Denver: Wendy Tellier Casaday, paralegal, Frank Erisman, Esquire, and Judson Detrick, Esquire; Stephanie Kane, Esquire, Denver; Brian Streelman, Esquire, Golden, Colorado; Diane Barrett, Esquire, chancellor of the Episcopal Diocese of Colorado; Ken Iwamasa, M.A., associate professor of art, University of

Colorado; Shirley Carnahan, Ph.D., senior instructor in the humanities, University of Colorado; Patrick N. Allitt, Ph.D., professor of history, Emory University; the following writer friends, who supplied ongoing support: Jasmine Cresswell, Julie Kaewert, and Leslie O'Kane; the Reverend Jean Treece; John William Schenk and Kirsten Schenk, caterers extraordinaire; and as always, my unparalleled source on police procedure, Sergeant Richard Millsapps, Jefferson County Sheriff's Department, Golden, Colorado.

Recipes in Dark Tort

1. Dark Torte
2. Chicky Bread
3. Prosciutto Bites
4. Tom's Savory Sausage Casserole
5. Asparagus Quiche
6. Chicken Piccata Supreme
7. All-American Deep-Dish Apple Pie
8. Strong-Arm Cookies
9. Chocolate Lovers' Dipped Fruits
10. Blue Cheesecake
11. Journey Cake with Hard Sauce

Dark Torte

6 large eggs, separated
1 cup granulated sugar, divided
1½ cups ground zwieback crumbs (1 six-
ounce box)
1 teaspoon baking powder
½ teaspoon ground cinnamon
½ teaspoon ground cloves
(high altitude: 1 tablespoon cake flour)
⅛ teaspoon salt
⅛ teaspoon cream of tartar
1 cup finely chopped pecans
Sherry Syrup (recipe below)
Whipped Cream Topping (recipe below)

Preheat the oven to 375°F. Butter two 9-inch cake
pans. Butter two cooling racks.

In a large bowl, beat the egg yolks until they are
light and lemon-colored. Remove 2 tablespoons of
sugar from the cup of sugar and set aside. Gradually beat the rest of the sugar (1 cup minus 2 tablespoons) into the egg yolks. In another large bowl,
combine the crumbs, baking powder, cinnamon,
and cloves (and flour if cooking at high altitude),

stirring to combine well. Stir this mixture into the egg-yolk mixture (batter will be very stiff). Set aside.

In a large bowl, using a wire whip or whip attachment, beat the egg whites until they are foamy. Add the salt and cream of tartar, and continue beating until stiff. Gradually beat in the remaining 2 tablespoons of sugar.

Fold 1/3 of the egg-white mixture into the egg-yolk mixture. Fold in half of the nuts. Fold in another 1/3 of the egg-white mixture; then fold in the last of the nuts. Fold in the final 1/3 of the egg-white mixture until there are no traces of white in the batter. Spread the batter evenly into the prepared pans.

Bake in the center of the oven for 15 to 25 minutes, until the layers have browned slightly, toothpicks inserted in the center come out clean, and the layers have begun to shrink from the sides of the pans.

Cool the layers for 5 minutes in their pans. Place a large piece of aluminum foil underneath the buttered racks and fold it up all the way around so as to catch the syrup. Turn the layers out onto the separate buttered cake racks. Allow the layers to cool while you make the Sherry Syrup.

Using a skewer or ice pick, evenly poke holes all over the tops of the layers. (Take care not to poke the holes all the way through the cake. The holes should go down about 3⁄4 of the way through the layers.) Carefully and slowly pour the hot Sherry Syrup evenly over the layers, until it is all gone.

When the layers are cool, make the Whipped Cream Topping. Discard the foil and carefully turn the first layer onto a cake plate. Spread a thick layer of Whipped Cream Topping over this layer. Then top with the second layer. Spread the rest of the topping on the top and sides of the torte.

The torte may be served immediately or it may be chilled. Leftovers must be kept in the refrigerator.

MAKES 12 SERVINGS

Sherry Syrup

2 cups granulated sugar
2 cups spring water
1⁄2 cup dry sherry

Combine the sugar and water in a wide, heavy-bottomed sauté pan. Bring to a boil over medium-high heat, and allow the mixture to boil until it reaches the soft-ball stage (234° to 240°F). (Use a candy thermometer to ensure the proper stage has been reached.)

Remove the pan from the heat. Using a wooden spoon, carefully and slowly swirl in the sherry. When the mixture is well combined, pour over the torte layers.

Whipped Cream Topping

- 1 tablespoon springwater
- 1 teaspoon vanilla extract
- 1 teaspoon unflavored gelatin powder
- 2 cups (1 pint) heavy whipping cream, well chilled
- 2 tablespoons confectioners' sugar

Pour the water and vanilla into a small saucepan. Sprinkle the gelatin powder over the surface of the liquid, and allow the gelatin to soften for 2 minutes. Turn the heat on under the pan to medium low. Swirling the mixture frequently, cook the mixture until the gelatin is completely dissolved. Keep the heat on very low to maintain the **liquid** gelatin mixture.

Pour the cream into a large mixer bowl. Using a

wire whip or a whip attachment, beat the cream until it forms soft peaks. Beat in the sugar and whip until stiff peaks form.

With the beater running, pour the liquid gelatin mixture into the cream until completely combined. Turn off the beater, scrape the blades, and immediately spread the whipped cream topping between the layers and on top of the torte.

Chicky Bread

1⅔ cups chickpeas (garbanzo beans)
(contents of one 15-ounce can)

½ cup plus 1 tablespoon molasses, divided

¼ cup lukewarm springwater

1 tablespoon active dry yeast

1 tablespoon bread-dough enhancer
(recommended brand: Lora Brody's,
available at Williams-Sonoma)

2 cups bread flour, or all-purpose flour

1 cup whole wheat flour

2 teaspoons salt

⅓ cup rolled oats

⅔ cup springwater

¼ cup nonfat dry milk

¼ cup safflower oil

1 large egg, beaten

Drain the chickpeas, rinse them, and pat them dry. Pour them into a blender along with ½ cup of the molasses. Blend until the mixture is smooth (no chickpeas visible). Measure out 1 cup of this mixture; discard remainder.

Mix 1 tablespoon molasses into the ¼ cup lukewarm springwater and sprinkle the yeast on top. Let this sit for 3 to 5 minutes, until the yeast is completely moistened. Stir the yeast into the water and place in a warm spot for 10 minutes, allowing the yeast to proof.

Mix the bread-dough enhancer into the bread (or all-purpose) flour and whole wheat flour. Place these ingredients into a bread machine, followed by the reserved cup of chickpea mixture, the salt, oats, 2/3 cup springwater, nonfat dry milk, safflower oil, and egg. Pour the yeast in on top. Program for white bread (approximately 3 hours and 10 minutes) and press start.

After the first few minutes of mixing, lift the lid of the machine and check that the dough is neither too sticky and wet nor so dry that it cannot incorporate all the ingredients. If the mixture looks too wet, add up to 2 more tablespoons of bread flour. If the mixture looks dry, add up to 2 tablespoons of springwater. Use a large spatula, if necessary, to gently coax all the ingredients together as the blade continues to mix the ingredients. (Do not touch the blade.) What you are aiming for here is a smooth, supple dough that holds together and that the blade of the machine can knead easily. Once a smooth, supple dough is obtained, close the lid of the bread machine and let the bread-making process continue.

Once the bread is done, remove it from the machine and allow it to cool on a rack before slicing.

MAKES ONE LARGE LOAF

Prosciutto Bites

4 medium-size butter croissants (see note)
¾ cup best-quality plum preserves, strained,
    with plums reserved
6 slices prosciutto
½ cup goat cheese (or cream cheese)

Preheat the oven to 375°F.

Carefully slice the croissants lengthwise. Place the 8 croissant halves on an ungreased cookie sheet.

Spread each croissant half with 4 teaspoons of the strained preserves, spreading just to the edge.

Slice the reserved plums into fourths. Evenly divide them between the croissant halves, placing the plum slices at regular intervals on top of the preserves.

Trim the fat from the prosciutto slices. Place the prosciutto slices over the preserves and plums. Trim any overhang and place on top of the pre-serves. (Each croissant half will need about ¾ slice of prosciutto.)

Chop and crumble the goat cheese (or cream

cheese) into ½ teaspoon portions. Evenly dot the prosciutto with the cheese.

Bake for about 10 minutes, or until the cheese is just beginning to brown. Remove from the oven and allow to cool for at least 5 minutes. Using tongs, carefully place each croissant half onto a cutting board. Using a sharp serrated knife, cut each croissant half into four "bites." (Alternatively, you may serve each croissant half as an appetizer, or two croissant halves for breakfast or a light lunch.)

MAKES 32 SMALL SERVINGS ("BITES")

Note: Croissants now come in three sizes: large, medium, and small, or "cocktail." This recipe is tailored for the medium-size croissants. However, if you can only get large or cocktail-size croissants, merely adjust the proportions as necessary, making sure that the preserves are thinly spread to the edge of each croissant half, that the preserve layer is completely covered with a single thin layer of prosciutto, and that each prosciutto layer is well dotted with cheese.

Tom's Savory Sausage Casserole

1 pound new potatoes
8 ounces mushrooms, minced
2 tablespoons unsalted butter
1¼ cups minced onions
2 tablespoons finely chopped parsley
1 pound Italian sausage, hot or mild, casings
  removed
3 large eggs
1½ cups half-and-half
1 cup grated Gruyère cheese

Preheat the oven to 350°F. Butter a 9- by 13-inch pan.

Bring a large quantity of water to boil and cook the new potatoes until they are just done, about 10 to 15 minutes. Strain the potatoes and set them aside to cool before slicing.

Using a clean cloth dishtowel that may be stained, squeeze the mushrooms by small handfuls to remove all excess liquid. When all the mushrooms have been rendered almost dry, set them aside.

Using a wide sauté pan, melt the butter over low heat. Still keeping the heat low, cook the mushrooms and onions until the onions are translucent. Remove the mushrooms and onions from the pan and put them into a heatproof bowl. Stir in the chopped parsley and set aside. Using the same pan, raise the heat to medium low and cook the sausage until it is brown. Turn off the heat and set aside.

Slice the cooled potatoes into 1/2-inch slices. Place them in the bottom of the prepared pan. Distribute the mushroom mixture over the potatoes. Evenly distribute the sausage over the mushroom layer. Set aside.

In the large bowl of an electric mixer, beat the eggs with the half-and-half over low speed until the mixture is smooth, about 3 to 5 minutes. Pour this mixture over the ingredients in the baking dish. Sprinkle the cheese on top.

Bake for 35 to 45 minutes, until the top is golden brown and the egg mixture has set in the middle. Serve immediately.

MAKES 6 SERVINGS

Asparagus Quiche

8 ounces asparagus, washed, trimmed of all
   hard, tough stalks, and cut into 1½-inch
   lengths
4 large eggs
¼ cup whipping cream
1 teaspoon Dijon mustard
½ teaspoon salt
⅛ teaspoon cayenne pepper (or more, if
   desired)
¼ teaspoon paprika
1 cup small-curd cottage cheese
1 cup grated Gruyère cheese
¼ cup grated imported Parmesan cheese

Preheat the oven to 350°F. Butter a 9-inch pie
plate.

Using a small sauté pan that has a cover, heat
about half a cup of water just to boiling. Pour in
the sliced asparagus, cover, and turn off the heat.
Allow the asparagus to steam, with the heat
turned off, while you prepare the other ingredients.

In the large bowl of an electric mixer, beat the

eggs on medium speed until they are very well blended. Blend in the cream, mustard, salt, pepper, and paprika until well combined. Using a heavy wooden spoon, stir in the cheeses, stirring until well combined.

Drain the asparagus (it should still be bright green, with a tender, slightly crunchy texture). Put it into the bottom of the prepared dish. Pour the egg mixture over the asparagus, and place the quiche into the oven.

Bake for about 35 to 40 minutes, or until the quiche has puffed and browned, and is set in the center. Allow to cool 5 minutes before slicing.

Note: Since this is a crustless quiche, it should be served with rolls or other bread.

MAKES 8 SERVINGS

Chicken Piccata
Supreme

4 boneless, skinless chicken breast halves,
   pounded thin between pieces of plastic
   wrap
½ cup all-purpose flour (you will not use all
   of this—it is for dusting the chicken)
½ teaspoon salt
¼ teaspoon freshly ground black pepper
3 tablespoons olive oil, divided
2 teaspoons freshly pressed garlic
½ cup scallions, finely chopped
1 tablespoon freshly squeezed lime juice
¼ cup dry white wine
6 tablespoons (¾ stick) unsalted butter

Dredge the pounded chicken breasts in a mixture
of the flour, salt, and pepper. Set aside.

Heat 1 tablespoon of the oil in a large sauté pan
over medium-high heat. When the oil shimmers,
put in two of the chicken breasts and sauté for
about 1½ minutes per side, until the outside is

nicely browned but the interior of the chicken is still very slightly pink. Remove the pieces to a plate and repeat with the other two chicken breasts. Set aside.

Turn the heat under the sauté pan to low and add the last tablespoon of oil and the garlic. Cook the garlic very gently for several minutes, until it is very soft and cooked through. **Do not burn the garlic**.

Add the scallions, juice, white wine, and butter to the pan. Bring the heat up to medium, stirring constantly. Once the butter is melted, continue to cook and stir for a minute or a bit longer, until the sauce has reduced slightly. Keeping the heat up, return the chicken to the pan, and cook and stir until the chicken has **just** cooked through (check by cutting into one piece), about 2 or 3 more minutes.

Place the chicken on a heated serving platter. Pour the sauce over the chicken and serve immediately.

MAKES 4 SERVINGS

All-American Deep-Dish Apple Pie

CRUST:

1¾ cups plus 2 tablespoons all-purpose flour
2 teaspoons confectioners' sugar
½ teaspoon salt
12 tablespoons (1½ sticks) chilled unsalted
    butter, cut into 1-tablespoon pieces and
    chilled
3 tablespoons chilled lard or vegetable
    shortening, cut into 1-tablespoon pieces
    and chilled
¼ cup plus 1 to 2 tablespoons ice water
1 egg, lightly beaten

In a large bowl (or in the bowl of a food processor fitted with the metal blade), whisk together the flour, sugar, and salt for 10 seconds.

Drop the first 4 tablespoons of chilled butter on top of the flour mixture, and cut in with two sharp knives (or pulse in the food processor) **just** until the mixture looks like tiny crumbs. (In the food processor, this will take less than a minute.) Repeat with the rest of the butter and the lard (or vegetable shortening), keeping the unused portion of each fat well chilled until it is time to cut it into the flour. The mixture will look like large crumbs when you finish adding all the butter and lard.

Sprinkle the water over the top of the mixture, and either mix with a spoon or pulse until the mixture **just** begins to hold together in clumps. If the mixture is too dry to hold together in clumps, add the additional water until it does. Place the mixture into a 2-gallon zipped plastic bag. Pressing very lightly through the plastic, quickly gather the mixture into a rough circle in the center of the bag. Refrigerate the bag of dough until it is thoroughly chilled.

When you are ready to make the pie, preheat the oven to 400°F. Have a rimmed cookie sheet ready to place underneath the pie.

Remove the bag of dough from the refrigerator. Unzip the bag, then quickly roll out the dough (still inside the bag) to a circle approximately 10 inches in diameter. Using scissors, cut the plastic all the way around the bag and gently lift one side of the plastic. Place the bag, dough side down, into a 9-inch deep-dish pie plate. Gently remove the remaining piece of plastic so that the dough falls into the plate. Trim and flute the edge of the crust. Gently line the crust with parchment paper and weigh down the crust with rice, beans, or pie weights.

Bake for 10 minutes. Remove from the oven, take out the parchment and weights, and brush the bottom and sides of the crust with the beaten egg (you will not use all of the egg). Return the crust to the oven to bake for 10 minutes more. If the fluted edge begins to brown too quickly, it can be covered with pieces of foil until the crust is baked. Remove the crust from the oven and allow it to cool slightly while you prepare the filling and topping.

FILLING:

1¼ teaspoons cinnamon
¾ cup sugar
8 cups peeled, cored, and sliced Granny
    Smith apples

In a small bowl, combine the cinnamon and sugar. Place the apple slices in a large bowl. Sprinkle the apples with the cinnamon-sugar mixture and set aside while you prepare the topping.

TOPPING:

1¼ cups all-purpose flour
½ cup sugar
9 tablespoons chilled unsalted butter, cut into
  1-tablespoon pieces

In a large bowl (or in the bowl of a food processor fitted with the metal blade), whisk together the flour and sugar for 10 seconds. Drop the pieces of butter on top of the flour mixture and cut in with two sharp knives (or pulse in the food processor) just until the mixture resembles large crumbs. Do not overblend.

Place the apple mixture in the cooked crust. Evenly spread the topping over the apples, and be sure to put the pie onto the rimmed cookie sheet before it bakes.

Bake for 40 to 45 minutes, or until the topping is browned and the apples are cooked. Place the pie on a cooling rack for at least 2 hours so the pie can "set up." Serve with best-quality vanilla or cinnamon ice cream.

MAKES 8 LARGE SERVINGS

Strong-Arm Cookies

12 tablespoons (1½ sticks) unsalted butter at
  room temperature
¼ cup solid vegetable shortening
2 cups dark brown sugar, firmly packed
2 large eggs
½ cup buttermilk
3¼ cups all-purpose flour
1 teaspoon baking soda
1 teaspoon salt
2 cups pecan halves, toasted and cooled
2 cups dried cherries
2 cups extra-large chocolate chips
  ("chocolate chunks")

In the large bowl of an electric mixer, beat the
butter and shortening on medium speed until well
blended, about 2 minutes. Add the sugar and beat
until the sugar is thoroughly creamed into the butter mixture, about 5 minutes. Thoroughly beat in
the eggs, then stir in the buttermilk. Set aside.

Sift together the flour, baking soda, and salt.
Gently stir into the butter mixture until you can
see no more flour. Stir in the nuts, cherries, and

chips. Chill the batter, tightly covered with plastic wrap, for at least an hour and up to overnight.

Preheat the oven to 375°F. Line a cookie sheet with a silicone nonstick sheet (Silpat).

Using a 1⁄2-tablespoon scoop, measure out a dozen evenly spaced cookies. Using the heel of your hand, gently push on each cookie to flatten slightly. Bake for 8 to 11 minutes, or until you can touch them lightly and leave almost no imprint.

Allow the cookies to cool one minute on the cookie sheets before using a metal spatula to remove them to racks to cool completely.

Store the cookies at room temperature in an airtight container.

MAKES 8 DOZEN COOKIES

Chocolate Lovers' Dipped Fruits

8 ounces chopped best-quality bittersweet
chocolate (not unsweetened; recommended
brand: Godiva Dark)
1 tablespoon unsalted butter
11–12 ounces of dried fruit (apricots,
peaches, pears, etc.)

In the top of a double boiler, melt the chocolate and butter, stirring frequently. Line a cookie sheet with waxed paper. When the chocolate and butter are thoroughly melted and blended, turn down the heat under the double boiler. Holding a piece of fruit between your thumb and forefinger, gently dip one end into the hot chocolate. Immediately raise the fruit, shake it gently to loosen any stray drops, then place it on the waxed paper to cool completely. Repeat with the rest of the fruit.

Note: In summer, dip large, long-stemmed fresh strawberries. At holiday time, dip glacé apricots for a very special gift.

Blue Cheesecake

1 tablespoon unsalted butter

1 shallot, finely chopped (about ¼ cup)

24 ounces cream cheese, at room temperature

6 large eggs, at room temperature

6 ounces blue cheese (preferably Danish),
   crumbled and chopped

¾ cup whipping cream

1 small scallion, finely chopped (about 1½
   tablespoons)

Preheat the oven to 325°F. Butter a 10-inch springform pan. Place an 11- by 16-inch disposable aluminum roasting pan onto a rimmed cookie sheet.

Melt the butter over low heat and cook the shallot, stirring occasionally, until it is limp, about 5 to 7 minutes. Set aside to cool.

In the large bowl of an electric mixer, beat the cream cheese on medium speed until it is very smooth. Add the eggs and beat until they are well blended into the cream cheese, about 3 to 5 minutes. Add the blue cheese and cream, and beat over low speed until the mixture is well blended (it will be lumpy).

Using a large wooden spoon, force the mixture through a wire strainer to remove the lumps. (This takes a strong arm and some time, usually about 7 to 10 minutes.) Blend the shallot and scallion into the smooth mixture.

Pour the mixture into the prepared springform pan. Place the springform pan inside the roasting pan, and carefully fill the roasting pan with very hot water until the water comes halfway up the outside of the springform pan. Gripping the sides of the cookie sheet, carefully place the roasting pan with the springform pan inside it into the oven. Immediately close the oven door.

Bake for about 45 minutes, or until the cheesecake has puffed, the top is golden brown, and the center is set. Remove from the oven and set the springform pan on a cooling rack. Run a knife around the inside rim of the springform pan's collar to loosen any of the cheesecake that may have stuck. Carefully remove the collar.

Cool for about 10 minutes, if you are serving the cheesecake hot. (It will sink slightly as it cools.) The cheesecake may also be served at room temperature or chilled. Cover and refrigerate any leftovers.

MAKES 8 LARGE SERVINGS

Note: This is a savory dish appropriate for brunch or lunch. It is wonderful served with a tossed salad of either greens or fruit, along with French bread. Also, in case children protest about the idea of a "blue cheesecake," you can assure them that the finished cake is not even remotely blue in color.

Journey Cake with Hard Sauce

12 tablespoons (1½ sticks) unsalted butter at
    room temperature
1½ cups sugar
4 cups all-purpose flour (high altitude: add
    ¼ cup flour)
1 teaspoon baking soda
1 teaspoon cinnamon
1 teaspoon cloves
1¾ cups apple cider

Preheat the oven to 350°F. Butter a 9- by 13-inch pan.

In the large bowl of an electric mixer, beat the butter on medium speed until fluffy, about 3 to 5 minutes. Gradually add sugar, beating until well combined. Set aside.

Sift together the flour, soda, and spices. Using a large wooden spoon, add the dry ingredients alternately with the cider, stirring well after each addition, and beginning and ending with dry ingredients.

Pour the batter into the prepared pan. Bake for 35 to 45 minutes, or until a toothpick inserted into the center of the cake comes out clean.

Serve with Hard Sauce (recipe follows).

MAKES 12 SERVINGS

Hard Sauce

1 cup (2 sticks) unsalted butter
1 pound sifted confectioners' sugar
1 to 2 tablespoons rum

In the large bowl of an electric mixer, beat the butter on medium speed until it is very fluffy, at least 7 minutes. Gradually add half the confectioners' sugar, beating well after each addition. Beat in the rum, then beat in the rest of the confectioners' sugar.

Refrigerate any unused sauce.